T0190934

GANGSTERS DON'T DIE

A NOVEL

TOD GOLDBERG

COUNTERPOINT / CALIFORNIA

First Counterpoint edition: 2023
First paperback edition: 2024

The Library of Congress has cataloged the hardcover edition as follows:
Names: Goldberg, Tod, author.
Title: Gangsters don't die : a novel / Tod Goldberg.
Description: Berkeley : Counterpoint, 2023.
Identifiers: LCCN 2023018984 | ISBN 9781640093041 (hardcover) | ISBN
    9781640093058 (ebook)
Subjects: LCGFT: Thrillers (Fiction). | Novels.
Classification: LCC PS3557.O35836 G37 2023 | DDC 813/.54—dc23/eng/20230427
LC record available at https://lccn.loc.gov/2023018984

Paperback ISBN: 978-1-64009-661-5

Cover design by Brian Lemus
Cover photographs of brass knuckles © Shutterstock/Chris Hockey, road ©
Shutterstock / Ersler Dmitry
Book design by Laura Berry

COUNTERPOINT
Los Angeles and San Francisco, CA
www.counterpointpress.com

Printed in the United States of America

10 9 8 7 6 5 4 3 2 1

For Wendy, who told me to swing for the fences

Do not appease your friend at the height of his anger; do not comfort him while his dead still lies before him; do not ask him about his vow the moment he makes it; and do not endeavor to see him at the time of his degradation.

—THE TALMUD

GANGSTERS DON'T DIE

PROLOGUE

IF DARK BILLY CUPERTINE HAD TO KILL A GUY, HE PREFERRED TO DO IT UP close, with his bare hands. He didn't want to get used to it, was the thing, and if you were popping motherfuckers in the back of the head, maybe you could pretend it wasn't real, that the bullet did the work, like how all these young guys from the neighborhood talked about greasing motherfuckers in Vietnam. Just a thing they did every day. Push a button and boom. You kill a guy with your hands, you punch his teeth into his throat, you beat his eyeballs into the back of his head, you break his windpipe and watch him choke on his own blood? Man, that's yours.

"This would go faster if you grabbed a shovel," Germaio Moretti said. The two of them were in a vacant lot, surrounded by a corona of semi-built homes that would eventually become three-bedroom houses, Germaio chest deep in a grave meant for a guy named Lyle Dover, who owned a car dealership in Batavia.

Mosquitos the size of fists buzzed around them. Near dawn and still in the nineties.

Billy said, "You kill a guy, you dig his grave. That's the rules."

"Since when?"

"Since now," Billy said. Germaio didn't really answer to Billy Cupertine, since he was Cousin Ronnie's personal muscle, but Cupertines were Cupertines, and so Billy had rank. Cupertine blood ran The Family since 1896, back when it was just a crew robbing steam trains. "Plus, I'm going on vacation in the morning. I can't be showing up covered in fucking dirt."

"I'm lodging a complaint with the boss," Germaio said, not even half joking. "You know my back is shit."

Billy shook out a cigarette, lit it up, looked back across the Des Plaines River. He could see in the distance the thirty-foot-tall lights ringing Joliet Prison. His old man did three years there. Ronnie's pop, Dandy Tommy, did eighteen months. Germaio did a five-year bid, but somehow Billy had avoided spending any time there, apart from visiting his father. Longest he'd ever been locked up was a couple months off and on in juvie, then maybe three months in county, but nothing since having a kid. Because if he got arrested for the shit he did now, he'd be staring at life sentences. He told Ronnie he needed to be more careful, couldn't be doing this hands-on bullshit, that he could oversee, but he wasn't gonna be on the dirty end of this business.

Which he was largely able to do . . .

. . . save for shit like this right here.

Ronnie had inherited Dandy Tommy's used-car dealerships and was now turning them out, expanding into Detroit, thinking about maybe getting into new cars, too, hooking up with Ford, the real money in ripping people off legitimately, jacking up repair costs on Mustangs, recommending custom paint jobs on Granadas. Which meant Billy periodically had to do jobs that he found distasteful, and frankly beneath his rank, but which needed to be handled with a bit more sensitivity.

Ronnie wanted to own Lyle Dover's Chrysler dealership, but Dover wasn't inclined to sell, no matter how much Ronnie offered, no matter how many veiled threats were made. Dover was one of those old-school Chicago guys who thought he was tough because he watched the Bears and knew how to stay warm in the winter, could maybe handle himself in a bar fight because he knew no one was going to pull out a gun, had enough money that he was always threatening to sue people, but nothing really life-or-death. Just Business and Family and Jesus on Sundays when there wasn't Football.

So Lyle Dover rolled into the Lamplighter, maybe not knowing it was a Family-affiliated bar, but probably not giving a fuck, because on top of everything else he was sixty-five years old, and as a general rule no one really fucked with old guys. Twenty minutes later Billy got the call to grab up Germaio and see if he could talk some sense into Dover, and if not, bring the dog fucker to Ronnie. Which would have all been fine except Dover got mouthy in the backseat of Billy's Buick, talking about how he knew Germaio's mother, how they went to school together, how he was going to sue her, take her house, put her on the street, which got Germaio to pistol-whipping the cocksucker, and next thing, the fucker had a stroke or a heart attack and by the time they realized it, he was limp as a dick and dark blue.

And he *still* hadn't sold his dealership.

Seemed like a dumb thing to die for, and an even dumber thing to go to prison for, Billy not inclined to spend his last days on earth staring out at this very subdivision over a fucking car dealership. The subdivision, called River View Estates, was being built to coincide with an expected expansion of the prison, Joliet the kind of town that applauded increased crime numbers elsewhere in the state, because more motherfuckers in prison meant more jobs. More jobs, more houses. More houses, more cars. More cars, more traffic cops. More traffic cops, more people in county jail. More people in county jail, a bigger county jail would be needed, which meant more jobs for union carpenters and millwrights, all of whom kicked up to The Family, the whole thing a self-perpetuating cycle.

"When is sunrise?" Germaio asked.

Billy looked at his watch. It was close to four a.m. He told Arlene to be ready to go by ten. "Another ninety minutes," Billy said. He kneeled down, gave the grave a good once-over. "That motherfucker in the trunk isn't a dwarf either, so get some length on this."

"He'll bend," Germaio said. He was soaking in his own sweat.

"Into thirds?" Billy said. Germaio was about a hundred pounds overweight, so behind his back everyone called him either Fats or Tits, but to his face, they kept quiet owing to the fact that Germaio Moretti was a fucking lunatic, the kind of guy who kicked women and pulled out snitches' tongues and pissed on hookers just for fun, or at least that was the legend. Billy didn't think Germaio did much of anything these days but pant out of his mouth, given how fat his neck was, air wheezing out of him even when he was perfectly still. Billy tried to imagine strangling him, tried to figure out how he'd get his hands around Germaio's throat, but couldn't work out the geometry, nor could he accurately calculate the amount of force needed for the job. "Another foot deep, too."

"For fuck's sake," Germaio said, but he got back to digging.

After another five minutes, Billy took a final drag from his cigarette, squeezed it out between his thumb and forefinger, stuck the butt in his pocket, took out his car keys, jingled them so Germaio would turn around. "I'm gonna back the car up," Billy said. "Keep digging."

"Eat a dick," Germaio wheezed out. Or at least that's what Billy thought he heard. It was hard to make out much of anything since Germaio was almost six feet underground and the only part of him above the dirt was the back of his fat fucking head.

The level of disrespect was higher than usual, but Billy recognized they were in a heightened situation, that Germaio was dealing with the complexities of a situation beyond his limited intellectual capabilities.

Not that it really mattered.

Dark Billy Cupertine was about five hours from getting out.

For the last year, he'd pinched where he could: skimmed fourteen grand from a heroin deal with the Windsor clan up north; collected on a fifty-G debt from a mark named Victor Noe, crushed his throat using only one hand, Victor so coke sick he probably did him a favor, drove his body all the way out to Devil's Kitchen Lake, way off Route 57, dumped him out, told everyone the motherfucker had skipped then took his damn house, too; shook down some old folks in Little Ukraine, basic shit, thug shit, but whatever. He had a number in mind and after last week, he finally made it: $300K in cash, plus five guns, enough ammo to outlast most cops, stuffed in the trunk of his convertible DeVille in the garage at home, built into a contraption underneath the spare tire. He wouldn't be able to get to the guns fast, so he had one in the dash, too. If the cops pulled him over, they'd need to pile through his wife Arlene's suitcases and his son Sal's toys, dump everything out on the side of the road to find anything incriminating.

No one was going to do that, not to someone with the last name Cupertine.

No. They'd just shoot him in the face. So if someone pulled him over, well, it wouldn't get to that point. Dark Billy Cupertine was a dead man already; killing a cop on the way to his new life wouldn't matter in the long run.

But . . . well, it would be a *complication*, and Billy was in a place where complications would not do, like being party to senseless murder on his last day out, which is why when he got into the front seat of his '68 Buick Riviera, given to him right off the lot from one of Ronnie's dealerships, he rolled slowly back to the lip of the grave, made sure Germaio was right where he left him, and then slammed the gas pedal to the floor and chopped the motherfucker's head off.

BILLY DIDN'T GET BACK TO HIS HOUSE UNTIL ALMOST SEVEN. AFTER HE located Germaio's head—it had landed where the living room would eventually be—he dumped it into the hole, followed by Lyle Dover's body, then refilled the grave. By the end of the week, the grave would be covered by a foundation pour and then, eventually, an attached garage. Everyone getting attached garages these days, no one willing to walk ten feet out into the cold if they didn't have to.

He drove up 355, stopped behind a shopping center being built out in Bolingbrook, threw his shoes and jacket in a dumpster, then set it on fire, watched it for a couple minutes, made sure everything burned, headed back to his place in Alta Vista Terrace, slid into bed as Arlene was winking awake. "Give me twenty minutes," he told her, even wound his alarm clock, but she let him sleep until nine.

He pulled himself from bed, took a shower, got the last of the dirt and blood from under his nails, packed the rest of his vacation-wear, then had a thought. He opened the top drawer of his dresser, reached behind the socks he'd left behind, found what he was looking for: brass knuckles. They were fifty years old. Maybe seventy-five. Belonged to his grandfather, Anthony Cupertine, then handed down to Billy's father, Black Jack Cupertine, and then Billy took them out of Black Jack's pocket before they put him in the ground.

Going on eleven years ago now.

A heart attack on a golf course in Tampa.

No one found Black Jack for two days; the poor fucker had collapsed in a sand trap, then sat there dead during a tropical squall. Meanwhile half of Chicago descended on Florida looking for him, everyone thinking he'd been abducted, was about to be ransomed a tooth at a time, only to have him found by a groundskeeper.

Black Jack decided to hit eighteen on his own, no bodyguards, died in fucking plaid pants.

The *indignity*.

Cupertine men had been beating the shit out of people in Chicago for a very long time, and here was Black Jack Cupertine taking his dirt nap with a golf club in his hand, a load of death shit in his pants, bugs already eating his face when he was finally located. That transferred power to Black Jack's brother, Dandy Tommy, and then onto his son, Ronnie, which turned Billy Cupertine into The Spare.

Maybe if Billy had been a different kind of guy, none of this would have mattered. He could have earned a living, had a nice family, been content. But the problem with being The Spare was that there was always someone thinking about making a move, and the first move would always be to take Billy out, no use killing Ronnie if there was someone else waiting in the wings, Billy also aware that the only people who called him Dark Billy were members of his own crew.

Motherfuckers in Miami and Detroit and Memphis? They called him The Spare, big fucking jokers, each.

Fact was, though? It was true. That knowledge fucked with Dark Billy Cupertine.

Billy slid the knuckles on, made a fist. They felt smooth. Comfortable. His son Sal wasn't gonna grow up to be a pussy, but Billy would be damned if he'd be out breaking legs for a living, either. He was too smart for that. Ten years old and already reading books, getting into his grandmother's stash of Harold Robbins, but had to act dumb around his friends, idiots like Germaio's son Monte down the block, who couldn't tie his shoes until he was seven, had to get his stomach pumped after swallowing a handful of nickels. Sal could probably run the whole Family's finances right now, figure out decent investments, get everyone clean and legit. Maybe make a lawyer or a doctor or banker, help people.

What had Billy ever done? Created a network for pushing heroin. Killed maybe ten guys on his own. Twelve now. Could be more. He didn't dwell on it, because what was the use? Heroin killed more, that was sure. Made his cousin Ronnie and before that, Dandy Tommy, rich. Yeah, he'd done fine, too. Apart from living with the fear that every single day someone was going to get the drop on him. Not that the fear bothered him—it kept him sharp—rather it was the idea that it would somehow infect his wife, his kid. He'd picked this life. He'd decided to look over his shoulder in every room he entered. But having a kid changed him. Made The Spare shit more acute. Because if Billy was The Spare, what was Sal? Every day that he came home with some motherfucker's blood on his hands and he saw his son playing with his Army men, it was like getting stabbed with a dull knife.

Billy's experience, you could live with a stab wound. But then eventually, infection would get you. Eaten up from the inside.

"Are you about ready, honey?"

Billy turned around and saw Arlene standing in the doorway. She had on a sundress, her shoulders bare, a little sweater in her right hand.

"One sec," Billy said. He slipped the brass knuckles into his pocket. Once they got where they were going, he'd bury them along with every other trace of their old life. Three hundred thousand dollars wasn't a fortune. But it was enough to put some real estate between him and the rest of The Family, the plan being to get to Arizona by the end of the week. He'd decided on Sedona after watching an old Jimmy Stewart movie called *Broken Arrow* one night on WTTW. Jimmy Stewart played an ex-solider named Jeffords sent to talk Cochise into peace. He spends most of the movie staring out at the landscape and trying to figure out how to keep the U.S. military and a piss-angry Geronimo—who would have made a good capo—from wrecking a fragile détente. Hotheads on both sides would get them all killed, Cochise and Jeffords knew, so everything was a fucking negotiation, good men caught up in the mire just out of association, the red rocks watching all of it, not going anywhere, proof enough that history could outlast the foolishness of men. Billy thought Jimmy Stewart was a bit of a bitch in most cases, but he liked *Broken Arrow*, liked the message, liked how Jeffords ended up living with Cochise until he died, how the Indians in the movie weren't portrayed as animals, just people who had a code.

"Sal is already in the car," Arlene said. She was under the impression that the three of them were driving out to Lake Geneva for a week. Get out of the broiling city. They had a favorite spot they liked to go to this time every year. Shuffleboard and mint drinks and magazines and dime-store thrillers.

First they'd drive south, all the way to Texas. Eighteen hours. He had a guy in Austin with fresh identification for them. Billy would take care of him, get rid of his body, no witnesses, and then they'd keep moving, get to Flagstaff, another fifteen hours, put the family up in a hotel for a few days, then prospect out to Sedona, find a house.

"Sorry," Billy said. "I didn't expect to be out all night. One thing led to another."

Arlene waved him off. She knew who he was. "You're here now," she said. "And I get you to myself for the next week."

He stepped across the bedroom and kissed her lightly. She tasted like cigarettes, but not in a bad way. "The car all packed?"

"Only thing missing is you," she said.

He'd tell her once they were on the highway. Maybe she'd fight him at first—she had a sister, her mother was still alive, she had friends, a life—but the reality was that Arlene would do what Billy said. Because she didn't want to wash blood off his clothes. Not anymore.

"We gotta make one stop," Billy said.

FOR THE LAST FOUR YEARS, DARK BILLY CUPERTINE AND HIS COUSIN, AND DE facto boss, Ronnie Cupertine, had a standing date on the top floor of the IBM building being constructed on the corner of Wabash and State. At first that just meant going up a couple rickety floors to where Family-connected contractors were pouring concrete, but now it meant making a trip up fifty-two stories of anodized black aluminum to the last bit of open construction. The building was set to open by fall and already the city was hailing it as an architectural wonder, a monolith of power and money, like Wall Street had been cut and pasted right in the middle of the broad shoulders of Chicago, the city never content to just be Chicago, always needing to compare itself to New York. A perpetual small-dick problem was how Billy thought of it, but it infected how The Family did business, too, constantly worried that some Gambino fuck was going to show up and muscle them out of their territory. His father and grandfather had built The Family into its own thing, beholden to no one, but Ronnie, he had different ideas.

He was connecting to LA and to Memphis, had some Florida shit going on, plus their continued interests in Las Vegas, maybe even some offshore shit in the future, Ronnie always going on about how if The Family was going to survive Nixon, half of their muscle in a fucking jungle in Vietnam, the other half in prison, it had to treat its business like McDonald's, put up shop wherever there wasn't somebody else.

It was some shit he'd read in a book somewhere. So Ronnie had The Family going into small towns and blowing up mom-and-pop shops, digging graves in Omaha to get into the meat business, which was really just a way to get access to big rigs for moving product across state lines, greasing small-town cops to look the other way on gambling setups around college football season, which was how they were getting into the extortion game with wealthy farmers, Billy thinking it was all too much, that McDonald's got fries and burgers right, which is why they didn't fuck with hot dogs.

All this other stuff? It was hot dog business. It was how they were going to get caught, Billy thought. Or how Ronnie was, anyway.

"What an eyesore," Arlene said when they pulled up beside the construction entrance to 333 Wabash. Workers milled around a roach coach, sipping coffee, eating sweet rolls, bullshitting. It was just after ten thirty in the morning, but due to the heat, workers had been pounding nails since five a.m. Billy had the top down on their convertible and Arlene had her head craned back to see the top of the building.

"Yeah," Billy said. In his view, the IBM building looked like a big, black thumb.

"Why does Ronnie like to meet here?"

"Only place he knows where no one is listening," Billy said.

Arlene sighed. "He thinks Eliot Ness is waiting on top of the Sears Tower with a stenographer?"

"The Sears Tower is 110 stories," Sal said from the backseat.

"That right?" Billy said. He looked at him in the rearview mirror, Sal busy with a coloring book. The Sears Tower had just opened a few months earlier, but already Sal was obsessed with it.

"That's eight stories taller than the Empire State Building," Sal said. "And fifty-eight stories taller than this will be."

Arlene gave Sal a book called *Great Skyscrapers!* for Christmas and every night since he read the damn thing before falling asleep. The only thing Sal didn't know was who was buried under every building. Maybe he'd become an architect? The guy who designed the IBM building had died before they even started putting rebar down and yet this fucking thumb would be here another, what? Hundred years? Two hundred? How long did skyscrapers last these days? Wouldn't that be something. A Cupertine who came to Chicago and built something that lasted for a hundred years and no one got killed because of it.

"Maybe one day we'll go to the Empire State Building," Billy said. "Would you like that?"

Sal shrugged. "I guess so."

Billy reached across Arlene and into the glove box, came out with an envelope filled with cash. It was payday, Ronnie getting his cut from the H business. Twenty-five grand that went straight into his pocket, just for being Ronnie Cupertine.

"Don't be long," Arlene said.

"I won't," he said.

"Tell Ronnie that I'll give Suzette a call when we get back," she said. Suzette was Ronnie's wife. For now, anyway. She couldn't get pregnant, so Ronnie was already looking for somewhere else to put his dick.

"Keep the car running," Billy said.

"Do you need anything else?" Arlene asked. The glove box was still open, his pistol there.

He looked into the backseat again, Sal's head down in his coloring book. Maybe this would be the last day his son ever saw Chicago. Last day as Sal Cupertine, anyway. Maybe he'd come back as an adult, with a new name, barely any memories of this time when his father was in deep with this gangster bullshit. Who would Billy be by then? He saw himself owning a bar. One of those places where you could get a decent steak and a cold beer and on weekends, a little spot out back for BBQs.

Or he'd be dead.

"No." Billy closed the glove box. "I'll be right back," he said. "Ten minutes." He gave Arlene's hand a squeeze. "Hey," Billy said, and Sal met his eyes in the rearview mirror. "Look up at the top floor. I'll wave."

RONNIE CUPERTINE WAS A COUPLE YEARS YOUNGER THAN BILLY, BUT HE WAS already going gray at the temples, which made him look surprisingly dignified, so Ronnie played it up, wore nice suits, spent some money on shoes, styled his hair, even when he was going to be at a construction site seven hundred feet off the ground. He was also starting to do things like donate money to cancer research, ever since Dandy Tommy ended up with a bum pancreas that killed him in two months.

"You got a luncheon or something today?" Billy asked when he found Ronnie on the south side of the building, done up in a blue suit, white shirt, red tie, looking like the fucking flag.

Ronnie pointed out the window, which wasn't a window yet, just a square covered in clear plastic tarp. "You ever been inside that building?" he asked.

Billy looked down at the eight-story building across the street. "The *Sun-Times*? Fuck no. Spent my entire life trying to keep my name out of that fucking thing."

"I got a meeting there today," he said, Billy thinking he sounded pretty satisfied. "I'm buying some advertising."

"You fucking crazy?"

"Full-page ad," he said. "Color. Gonna run every Sunday, starting this week. Then I'm gonna have smaller ads in Sports and Business on weekdays. Thinking I might start doing some radio, too."

"How much is that?"

Ronnie shrugged. "Way I see it," he said, "once I buy into the paper and the radio, we're partners. I think they'll see it the same way. Might be I start doing TV ads. That's the next thing, Billy. They'll have more room to talk about Nixon if they aren't talking about me."

"You mean *us*?"

"You know what I mean," Ronnie said. Billy was afraid he did.

"What would Dandy Tommy say?"

"Eh," Ronnie said. "He's dead. It's a new era, right?"

"Doing shit in the open," Billy said, "is gonna piss people off."

"Who? The Outfit? New York? Fuck them. Let them come at me," Ronnie said. "It's about *complicity*. The newspaper, they aren't gonna piss on me if I'm giving them twenty Gs a month. Cheaper than paying off the cops. Cleaner than moving H, and no one's stiff in an alley because they OD'd on Mike Royko."

"Someone wants to write about you," Billy said, "an ad isn't gonna stop them."

"We'll see," Ronnie said. "In the meantime, you're holding the first month's rent."

Billy reached into his pocket, came out with the envelope. Ronnie flipped through the bills absently, then waved over a new guy, gave him the cash. Big Kirk, they called him. He was a big white kid, but his last name was Biglione. His sister Tina was married into The Family, hooked up with some motherfuckers out in Detroit who had a bingo skim going at a bunch of retirement homes. This was Big Kirk's summer job, getting sandwiches and coffee for Ronnie, standing around, looking imposing. He was maybe eighteen. Next year at this time, Billy figured Biglione would either be dead or in college. Billy hoped, for his sake, college. He counted the money.

"Twenty-five," Big Kirk said.

Billy said to Big Kirk, "You ever count *my* money in front of me again, your mother will be on a fucking feeding tube."

Big Kirk stared blankly at Billy, like he hadn't been taught that part of algebra yet. "I'm sorry?"

"Give us a minute," Ronnie said. Big Kirk went and stood beside the elevator. "Give him a break. He'll learn."

"I'm serious, Ronnie," Billy said, not that it mattered. But he couldn't suddenly be a pussy on his last day. "Count my money? Some Detroit fuck? His balls even drop yet?" Billy looked back over his shoulder at Big Kirk. Kid had a crooked look on his face, like he didn't know if he should smile or scream. "Fucking Bigliones," he mumbled, but with his eyes, he tried to will the kid to leave, go downstairs, hop on the L, never come back. "Isn't his dad a cop?"

"How you think we got into Detroit?"

"I don't like that shit."

"He's just doing what he thinks is right." Ronnie took a few steps, motioned Billy to follow him. "You know what's going on this floor?"

"I don't know," Billy said, "a thousand typewriters?"

"IBM has a government contract," Ronnie said. "Making computers for the CIA. Up here, it's gonna be all spooks and G-men. Want the walls soundproofed. They're building an interior room back over here." Ronnie pointed to an area on the floor marked off with red Xs. Maybe twenty by twenty. "They want it to have exterior walls made of metal, covered in cement. Survive a bomb. What do you think goes in there?"

"Mr. IBM?"

Ronnie considered this. "Not a bad idea." He stopped walking once they were out of earshot from Big Kirk, looked out another plastic window. "What the fuck happened last night?" Ronnie asked quietly.

"Germaio went sideways on him." Billy shook his head at the memory. "And then the fucker stroked out. Started shaking, frothing at the mouth, and then he was toast. Maybe a minute all in."

"So if I determine that we need to dig him up," Ronnie said, "coroner isn't gonna see a broken neck or missing fingers or anything?"

"Might be absent a couple teeth," Billy said.

"That can be explained. Anything unexplainable? A fucking wrench up his ass or something?"

"No," Billy said. But they would find Germaio. By then, it wouldn't matter. Billy would be long gone. "Broken nose, maybe. But he's gonna be under a house in about three days."

Ronnie pointed out the window. There were gray clouds hovering over the lake. "Supposed to rain for the next three days," Ronnie said. "Summer storm. Gonna be eight million percent humidity for the next week. You don't watch the news?"

"I was busy last night."

"I bet."

"We buried him deep," Billy said. "It could rain for a month, wouldn't matter."

"Point is," Ronnie said, "they ain't gonna be putting foundations down in the fucking rain."

"Wasn't how I had it planned," Billy said. "But Germaio wouldn't listen."

"I had you there so nothing would go sideways," Ronnie said. He shook his head. "The guys respect you. And then you let something like this go down? It's a lot of fucking cleanup."

"I didn't *let* it happen," Billy said. "Motherfucker turned blue on us. Besides, what were you gonna do with him? Have fucking tea and sandwiches?"

"I wasn't gonna kill him," Ronnie said.

"Of course *you* weren't going to," Billy said. He glared at his cousin for a few seconds; then he felt something soften inside of him. What was this bullshit? Grew up together like brothers, the only sons of two of the baddest motherfuckers on the planet, playing catch in the street with Family soldiers watching them like Secret Service, trick-or-treating as gangsters—trench coats, guns, hats, the whole nine—the neighbors giving up all their candy at once. Fast forward and no one wore costumes anymore. He reached over and took his cousin by the arm. "I'm sorry, Ron. We fucked up. Whatever it costs, take it from my end. Germaio can't afford it."

Ronnie took a deep breath, exhaled through his mouth, nodded. "Where's Germaio now?"

"I dropped him at his girlfriend's," Billy said. Germaio also had a wife and a kid. This was a lie that wouldn't last long. "Where I picked him up."

"He'd have more money if he wasn't paying for two families,"
Ronnie said. "What time?"

"I dunno," Billy said. "Six?" Billy heard a shuffling sound, turned
and saw Big Kirk Biglione trailing behind them, ten feet away. *This
Lurch-motherfucker.* "Sure he's home by now."

"I sent a couple guys over. He wasn't home. Car still in the garage.
His dumbfuck son says he hasn't seen him."

"What's his wife say?"

"Same," Ronnie said.

"He's probably scared."

Ronnie nodded. "You know how many people saw the three of you
inside the Lamplighter?"

"No one would say anything," Billy said.

"Maybe not. But you dumbfucks left Dover's car there," Ronnie
said. "I told Germaio to bring it back with him and he just left it sitting
in the parking lot. Why would he do that?"

Shit. Germaio hadn't mentioned that. "He's not real detail
oriented."

"Yeah," Ronnie said, "but you are." He stepped closer to the window, found a tiny hole in the tarp, pushed his thumb through it, and
an arrow of breeze shot out. "Dover's wife reported him missing
this morning and there was his fucking car, right where he left it.
It's gonna cost me a lot to keep this shit quiet. More than you can
afford. Which is why I'm thinking I'll just dig him up and toss him
in the lake, let him wash up in a couple days, get someone to call it a
suicide."

"They can figure that shit out," Billy said.

"Who?"

"The coroner," Billy said. "That's how Junior Pocotillo got sent up."
Billy had gone to high school with Junior Pocotillo. A big fucking Indian kid. He'd killed some Russian mope who'd tried to jack him for
his car, problem being that Junior had stolen the car in the first place.
He'd strangled the guy and then tossed him in the river, only to have

him wash up the next morning. Doctors figured out pretty quickly that the body was already dead when it got tossed in the water. Billy didn't know how, something about the lungs, but he'd avoided dumping bodies in water ever since.

"Fine," Ronnie said. "I'll put him inside a burning car with a couple hookers. That make you happier?"

"Just leave him," Billy said. "There's a problem, I'll handle it. Free of charge."

"Oh yeah?" He cocked his head to the right. "Because isn't that your car down there?"

Billy gazed out the window. The DeVille was right where he left it. Except there was a Cadillac in front of it now. And one behind it. Another pulling up across from it.

Shit.

"Yeah. I'm out of town for the next week," Billy said. "Going to Lake Geneva."

"Oh yeah?"

"Yeah. I told you."

"Right," Ronnie said. He snapped his fingers. "I remember now. You said, 'Hey, cousin, I'm gonna run out of town with a trunk full of your money.'"

Billy reached instinctively for the gun on his hip . . . but it wasn't there. Because he was out with his wife and kid. Because he was going on vacation. Because it was in his glove box. Because he wasn't thinking he was going to shoot his cousin. Not that Ronnie was holding. He didn't carry a gun. That's why he had guys like Germaio and Biglione. He was a businessman. Why he had guys like Billy.

"What's your plan? Canada? Mexico? Maybe join those Outfit assholes at the Salton Sea? Or you getting on a boat?"

There was no use lying about anything now. Billy had been in this position before. Except he was the one asking questions. It got to this point, it was already done.

"If it's about the money," Billy said, "you can have it."

"It's not about the money," Ronnie said. "It's about family. This is our shit right here, Billy."

"Doesn't feel that way," Billy said.

"You're running because you're not busy enough? Because you're dissatisfied with your job? Because you put Germaio in the dirt?"

"Look," Billy said, carefully, "one day, it was gonna be you or me looking at a gun. I'm saving us both. One of us is gonna be dead, one of us is gonna be in prison, that's if we're lucky. I don't want either. I've got my own family now. I'm just trying to walk away."

"Looks to me like you're running away."

"Yeah, well," Billy said, "consider this my two weeks' notice."

"I needed you, Billy." Ronnie spit on the ground. "We're getting pushed out of Vegas," he said. "Fucking government is all over us. Moles in our unions, fucking snitches up and down the line. This building is finished, you think they're gonna just throw up another skyscraper tomorrow? It'll be ten, fifteen years before we get a contract like this one. But the shit I'm doing is going to set this family up for the next twenty-five years. You were gonna be a part of that, cousin. I can't trust these fucking guys like I can trust you."

"I'm not in the car business," Billy said. "And I sure as fuck ain't in the newspaper business."

"You're a small thinker," Ronnie said. "It's not about the cars. It's not about the drugs. It's about the customer. Meet their needs before they even know they want something. The Outfit, the Five Families, all those fucks? They're gonna be out of business in five years. We're mechanized; they're horses and buggies."

"Don't tell me more of this McDonald's shit, Ronnie," Billy said. He reached into his pocket, felt the brass knuckles there, slid them on. "I had to bury a guy this morning. Ronald McDonald isn't capping the Burger King." Billy heard the dinging of the elevator. He looked over his shoulder and saw that Big Kirk was now only five feet away. Three Black guys appeared at the end of the floor. Billy didn't recognize any of them, which meant they were probably Gangster Disciples. The Family had been selling them guns for years. *Shit.*

"Thought you said you needed me?"

"I do," Ronnie said. "And you want to go. So you're gonna go."

"Four guys, Ronnie?"

"Out of respect," he said.

"There one you want me to keep alive? For the story in the *Sun-Times*?"

Ronnie smiled, but he didn't look happy. "What's in your pocket? Knife?"

"Knuckles," he said.

"Big Kirk could use some scars," Ronnie said.

Billy nodded, looked back out the window. "I wasn't snitching," he said. "Wasn't planning on it, either. You should know. I was just going to retire."

"Government would find you," Ronnie said. "I'd be surprised if you made it out of town. If I knew, they knew. Next time we saw each other would have been in court."

Billy nodded again. "You gonna let me say goodbye to my kid?" he asked, thinking if he got down there, Arlene would know what was up; she'd get that gun out, give him a chance.

"Sorry," Ronnie said. "I'll take good care of him while you're gone."

"Oh, I'm coming back?"

"He won't know," Ronnie said, "until he does. And that will be that."

"This isn't the life I want for him," Billy said. "Let him just be a kid. He doesn't need to be like us. Promise me you'll give him that choice."

"I can't make that promise," Ronnie said. "I don't got a son. Maybe it would be different if I did."

"If you had a son," Billy said, "I'd already be dead."

"It'll be fast," Ronnie said.

The three Gangster Disciples were beside Big Kirk now. He guessed all three were carrying. Judging from their bugged-out eyes, they were also coked-up. He could maybe take out one of them, pop him in the temple just right, get a lick or two at least on Big Kirk, who looked like he was carrying a load of shit in his pants, but not a gun. Still, four on one without a gun only worked in Charles Bronson movies. Billy flexed his fist closed.

He had one shot at this.

One shot to save Arlene and Sal from a life of wondering. How many people from his childhood had Billy disappeared under similar circumstances, Family members who strayed and ended up in tiny bits, buried under a Jewel's being built in Springfield or dumped in the Poyter landfill or tossed in any convenient and deep pond? How many families did he lie to and say they'd been sent to Sicily for a job, or that they flipped and were now in the Witness Protection Program, or that they'd fled to Canada, even when he still had their skin under his nails? No. There would be no questioning of what happened to Billy Cupertine because the end was gonna be the same. He was already dead. Ronnie had already killed him. If Billy wanted to keep his son out of this shit, the boy would need an object lesson. Sal would need to know exactly what Ronnie Cupertine did to his old man.

Billy spun toward the tarp-covered window and smashed his brass-knuckled fist through the thick plastic, slid his arm all the way down, and then did the only thing that made sense.

He jumped.

Fifty-two floors.

Took him almost six seconds to hit bottom.

Six seconds and thirty-five years.

Two years old, there were pictures of him dressed in a baby jumper that made him look like a prisoner, five years old with one of his father's unlit cigars in the corner of his mouth, ten years old he was already running errands, standing outside when the boys came over, listening to the conversations. People started calling him Dark Billy by the time he was fifteen, not because of his skin tone, but because he was a thinker and he'd get a serious look on his face, so there was

Light Billy when he was running around doing kid stuff and Dark Billy when he was working through shit in his mind, brow furrowed. Seventeen years old he'd already killed five guys. Twenty-five he was married and brokering multimillion-dollar heroin deals, ten bodies on his sheet. Thirty and he was second in line to an empire that he'd never get and didn't want. Thirty-five he was gonna disappear and leave his kid to wonder why his father left him. Sal would look at the IBM building every day for the rest of his life trying to figure out how his father wasn't able to walk back out, how he went in and disappeared and no one knew anything. Arlene would know. Which meant maybe Arlene would be put out too, car accident or an OD or a staged robbery, shit turns around, Arlene takes a bullet. She wouldn't go quietly, no matter the situation. But he couldn't let her think he just walked out on her.

So Billy Cupertine screamed the entire way down, made sure she paid attention.

Not because he was afraid.

No, because as he fell, Dark Billy Cupertine realized he was wrong about one thing in his life. Fear hadn't kept him sharp. It had inoculated him. And so as he tumbled through the air and his past, his wife and child staring up at him, their faces coming into view now, Sal's opened mouth about to make his own scream, his last thought was that he'd fucked this all up, from beginning to end. Except for that boy. That boy who'd grow up and would never make the same mistakes. He'd know who not to trust.

ONE

WINTER 2002

LAS VEGAS, NV

IF SAL CUPERTINE HAD TO EAT ONE MORE BOWL OF SUMMERLIN HOSPITAL'S
chicken noodle soup, he was going to strangle someone.

He had a list.

He'd start with the overnight nurse who liked to hum "Yankee
Doodle" when he checked Sal's vitals at 3 a.m. those first hazy weeks,
would pinch the meat on his ribs to wake him, was not terribly gentle
with the catheter or the shit pan. That fucking guy was not made for
the medical industry. If Sal could figure out his name, well, when he
got out of this place, he would pay him a visit at home, squeeze his
head in a vise to wake him, shove a dry catheter into a sensitive hole,
Sal not particular in this daydream about which one, and then crush
his fucking windpipe.

He'd then move on to the orderly who liked to talk about patients
he wished would "just die," always qualifying it with, "I'm kidding,
I'm kidding," Sal thinking, *Yeah, joke all you want when my thumbs
are touching your brain stem through your neck.*

He'd finish off his rounds with the hospital's head chef. Maybe he
wouldn't snap that motherfucker's throat. Maybe he'd drown him in
his soup.

Yeah. How satisfying that would be.

Not that Sal was feeling particularly agile at the moment, slowly
getting dressed in his private room, which was actually pretty nice
if you liked the scenic view of dumbfucks slamming into each other
on the traffic circle across the way on North Hualapai. He'd probably
need a few more weeks before he could go on an adequate revenge

spree. He was still on Cleocin for infection, which gave him joint pain and made him feel like puking, then Norco for pain, which Sal liked too much, so he didn't take enough of it, because he couldn't have the Rain Man showing up in the middle of the night on these mother-fuckers, and then a low dose of Klonopin for whatever the fuck the doctors thought he was going through emotionally, as if they had any idea. Never mind the propofol and Flexforin still numbing the edges of Sal's brain from all the surgeries. How many times had he been cut open? Five? Six? Seven? He wasn't sure, exactly.

The first ten days, he was mostly in a drug-induced coma. Also, he wasn't sure of the difference between surgery and dental work any-more, since half of his life seemed to involve some motherfucker in scrubs shoving shit into his mouth while he drifted through some kind of half sleep, worried all the while he'd blurt out the location of Donnie the Lip's body, an Outfit soldier he killed in 1989 that still kinda bothered him, because he'd liked the guy, had known him since grade school, and Donnie had begged not to die, which in the moment was a little embarrassing but now tended to show up in Sal's brain at the worst time, Sal having buried Donnie in his own backyard, the motherfucker's wife and kids never knowing, going on twenty-five years now; all this time, they probably thought their pops ran out on them, but he was rotting where their dog shit.

Still, for the first six weeks Sal was in the hospital, fantasies like these got him through a lot of hard nights, particularly after he de-veloped a MRSA infection in his jaw and had to be quarantined for two weeks. It was the longest he'd been alone since he'd been hustled out of Chicago in a truck of frozen meat nearly four years earlier. This quarantine actually gave Sal some time to think.

Which was good. He needed to figure some shit out.

He'd built a life for himself in Las Vegas as the Rabbi David Cohen, oversaw an empire of Jews who trusted him, because it turned out the longer he pretended to be a rabbi, the better at being a rabbi he became, until the difference was meaningless. He was a rabbi as much as he was a hit man for The Family and yet, he was trapped. Sal had access to cash, weapons, and cars but couldn't leave the city limits of Las Vegas. Not again, anyway. Surveillance was everywhere.

The Strip was off-limits. Same with Fremont Street. Locals' casinos were out of the question. Palace Station like a fucking FBI outpost now, with the cop bar Pour Decisions across the street. Banks were a no-go. Sports arenas. Outlet stores. Fuck a mall. That was like trying to sneak into Tehran. The whole fucking world was covered in cameras looking for bad guys, technology putting faces together with crimes, Las Vegas about to be the absolute worst city for him to be in with his old face and the Patriot Act in full effect. Even now, looking out the window at the tree-shaded suburban streets of Summerlin, Sal counted dozens of cameras—the Noah's Bagels in the parking lot of the hospital campus was fortified like a cartel safe house—never mind all the artfully designed cell phone towers gussied up to look like palm trees and cacti, all of which were nothing more than tools of government surveillance.

All those years, Sal Cupertine had achieved the American dream. He'd gotten away with murder. Not one body. Not two. Not twenty. Maybe a hundred. Could be more. He didn't keep count. Whatever the number, Charles fucking Manson would be creeped out by him, that was the truth, because Manson hadn't even pulled a trigger, and here Sal was, a guy who'd seen brains on walls and eyes on the floor and hearts through people's backs, and just kept moving, kept living, wasn't carving swastikas into his forehead, had himself a family, a reasonably good job, his full mental faculties . . . right up until the time he got to Las Vegas and found himself incarcerated in the suburb of Summerlin doing shit that was likely putting him on a watchlist with God. And now, he had to worry about getting caught by a camera? Not a cop, not an FBI agent, not even another button man. Nope. His undoing would be a machine.

Which is why the safest place at this moment was, in fact, the hospital. His problems were outside the door, lined up like dominoes.

He had former FBI agent Matthew Drew, who'd shown up at his bedside in the ICU a few weeks ago . . . and then kept coming back . . . a problem he had not yet let his boss, Bennie Savone, know about . . .

Back in Chicago, he had some Native Mob motherfucker calling himself Peaches killing his friends and family, all while trying to take over The Family itself, which was rightfully Sal's, now that Cousin Ronnie was a fucking carrot . . .

And then he had . . . everything else. Temple Beth Israel. The funeral home. The selling of body parts. The need to avoid having U.S. Marshals kick down his door, tase him in the balls, and drag him back to prison for the murders he'd been sanctioned to do over the years, plus his freelance jobs, plus everything that had gone down in Las Vegas . . .

None of that really *worried* Sal. He wouldn't be taken alive. He'd made that determination years ago. Or, at the very least, he'd take a couple motherfuckers with him. It wouldn't be one of those pleasant Sammy the Bull photoshoots, walking down a street with his hands shackled, suit immaculate, hair blown dry. There'd be body bags and red streets. But he could turn his back on each of those things if he could just figure out where his wife, Jennifer, and his son, William, were or, at the least, get word to them. They'd disappeared from Chicago six months earlier and into Witness Protection. He'd learned that much from his new friend Agent Drew. Not that Agent Drew knew where they were, or what Jennifer had given the FBI to get them into protective custody.

At least that was Agent Drew's story. He had to believe him for now.

Could be Jennifer had given Sal up, as much as she knew. Which was probably enough.

Could be that was the right move. He couldn't fault her that choice.

Could be she decided going straight was the only way to make sure William had the life she wanted for him. The life Sal wanted for him. The life Sal never got for himself. When he looked at his life objectively, Sal saw a long, flat thread separating What Had Been Good and

What Had Been Shit, and if he tugged on it hard enough, he imagined he'd end up bringing down the IBM building, all fifty-two stories, and that still wouldn't stop him from hearing his father's screams. What if they'd just kept driving that day? How many times had he asked himself that question over the years, the wondering about a different life a kind of unhealthy infinity.

He knew now that Cousin Ronnie had ordered his father's hit. Had always sort of figured it, even if he hadn't wanted to face the knowledge directly, and then spent the next twenty-five years turning Sal into the Rain Man, made violence Sal's nature, and then used that nature against him in that hotel room in Chicago, when he killed those FBI agents and touched off this whole charade, culminating with Sal Cupertine in a hospital in Las Vegas, the cut-rate plastic surgery that had turned him into Rabbi David Cohen having gone to seed, replaced with some top-shelf shit that turned his face into . . . well, Sal Cupertine.

The Talmud said there was nothing heavier than an empty pocket, but Sal wasn't sure that was true. He was beginning to believe that the weight of his own reflection was what might eventually put him in the dirt. The government would never stop looking for him. That's what happens when you kill their agents. He understood that. He'd broken the rules. He would have to pay. Even though he'd been frozen in Las Vegas, building his empire of Jews, he now understood that it was all just playacting at safety. Something bad was always coming for him, and he had to make his move.

Sal understood that what he'd dreamed of before—bringing Jennifer and William to Las Vegas, to Temple Beth Israel—was foolish. The Talmud said that a dream not interpreted is like a letter unread, and Sal had spent much of his time in quarantine pondering just what that particular dream meant, but it was all the same in the end: this shit was worthless without the two people he loved. He didn't need fucking Freud to come along to figure that out. So that was gone. He would either get away, permanently, or give up. And that last part was not in his nature. It was like asking a shark to go easy on a seal.

Sal Cupertine would handle what he could control. How Rabbi David Cohen managed through this, that would take some work. They were the same man now, Sal had to concede, at least on the face of things.

Anyway, first thing Sal and David and anyone else who popped up inside his crowded head was going to do was go to the cafeteria and get a fucking cheeseburger.

Cheeseburgers weren't kosher, so if Sal ran into someone from Temple Beth Israel, he'd either quote some made-up portion of the Midrash or stab them in the eye with a fucking spork.

Wanting to avoid spectacularly bad outcomes, he instead put a hooded sweatshirt on over his hospital gown, threw on some sweatpants, and walked out of his room, past the nurses' station, past a crew installing new lighting and another crew painting over the institutional white walls, turning them into a pleasing butter color, like everything else in the fucking city, and waited for the elevator.

When the doors opened, Bennie Savone was standing there in a suit and tie, like he was coming back from a funeral or a court date.

"Going somewhere?" Bennie asked.

"Yeah," Sal said. "I'm getting a cheeseburger before everyone on this floor ends up in a body bag. You got a problem with it?"

Bennie stepped to one side. "Floor?" he asked.

"Wherever the cafeteria is."

Bennie hit a button and the car began to descend.

"I don't suppose it's just dumb luck you were on the elevator," Sal said.

"It is not," Bennie said.

"You ever heard of HIPAA?"

"You ever heard of omertà?"

"I have a right to some privacy," Sal said.

"No you don't," Bennie said.

"You enjoy watching them pop the piss tube out of me last week?"

"At least I'm not watching you take shits anymore," Bennie said. "Most people wipe sitting down, Rabbi."

This was how it had been for the last month. Once Bennie found out Sal had been keeping his own books while Bennie was under house arrest, their relationship changed. Sal wasn't exactly in a position to give a fuck, considering he was somewhere between twilight sleep and outright coma from Christmas through the end of January, ever since some coked-up MMA fighter sucker punched him at a bar mitzvah, causing most of Sal's face to collapse like a house of cards.

His face wasn't *like* anything, really. It was a sui generis event, as his doctor liked to say, whenever he brought his interns in to view the reconstruction, Sal feeling like an exhibit at The Cripple Zoo, motherfuckers he wouldn't trust to park his car shining lights into his mouth, peeling back his eyelids, digging into his ears, touching his hair, one guy sticking a fucking pinky in Sal's nose, moving it side to side, Sal memorizing his nametag—Dr. Brennan—and his face in hopes of one day catching this motherfucker on the street.

Sal was pretty sure Bennie hadn't bugged his hospital room. Not even he had that kind of game. But he was certain that he had a janitor or two on the payroll, maybe even a nurse with a gambling habit. For sure had eyes on him. Ears were another matter.

The doors opened onto the third floor and a fucking goon in a sweat suit got in, made his way to the back of the long elevator. Sal couldn't remember his real name—his memory had been shit of late, which was of some concern, since he had a photographic memory, but that was probably just the propofol hangover—but he'd seen him with Bennie before.

He picked up Bennie's dry cleaning and Starbucks. If he was driving Bennie to court or meetings, he always wore a Kevlar vest beneath his sweat suit or over his wifebeater, like that's just how goons dressed on Casual Friday now. Sal was pretty sure he was a cousin or something. Maybe a nephew? Bennie liked helping the younger generation get into the family business. Didn't mind putting them in harm's way, would let them break someone's arm for a debt or for touching one of his favorite girls at the Wildhorse. Sal thought his name was Avi.

"Really?" Sal said, quietly. "You bring muscle to the hospital?"

"One of us has a reputation to consider," Bennie said.

"If I wanted you dead," Sal said, "we'd be having this conversation over the Ouija board."

The doors opened and Bennie put a hand on Sal's shoulder, let the goon out first. He reconned the elevator bank and then motioned both men out.

"You ain't the only bad guy in town, Rabbi," Bennie said.

"YOU LOOK FIFTEEN YEARS YOUNGER," BENNIE SAID ONCE THEY SAT DOWN with their food. His guy was at a table by the door, about twenty feet away.

"I look like my father," Sal said. When was the last time he saw his father's face? Ten minutes before he came tumbling out of the IBM building. His eyes in the rearview mirror. The shadow of a beard on his face. The smell of Ivory soap. His father stalking into the building, looking both ways before he walked into the doors, a thing he always did, a thing Sal always did, too, always checking to see who might be coming up behind you.

The plastic surgery had brought out Sal's eyes, pulled the skin back and tightened everything up, which at first gave his face a kind of reptilian flatness, but now that he'd begun to heal, there was definition to his face again. Something like . . . character. He'd always looked like Dark Billy Cupertine, he knew that, just as his own son, William, looked like Sal Cupertine, but the re-restructuring of his face had done the one thing genetics hadn't, which was remove any of the softness of his mother's traits. He couldn't see Arlene at all in this new, old face.

His mother. Jesus. Where was she? Was she looking for him? It was like this now with Sal. He'd drop a pebble in his mind and he'd try to track the ripples.

Sal took a bite of his cheeseburger. It was like eating his own tongue. He put on some ketchup.

Nothing.

Mustard.

Nothing.

Sal eyed the salt.

"Problem, Rabbi?"

"Tasteless," he said.

A smile crawled across Bennie's face. "They didn't tell you?"

"What?"

"Your sense of taste is gonna be fucked up for a bit."

"What's a bit?"

Bennie shrugged. "I don't know," he said, "I didn't listen to that part of the tape."

Sal set the cheeseburger down. "This is funny to you."

"A little bit, yeah," Bennie said. He was picking at a Cobb salad. "Makes you feel any better, this salad is for shit."

"Since when do you eat salads?"

"Since I decided I didn't want to die of a heart attack before I had the chance to figure out how to get all my money back."

"Technically," Sal said, "it's my money. I earned it."

Bennie coughed. Then coughed again. Then coughed until his eyes started to tear. He took a sip of water. "Now you got me fucking choking to death on your bullshit." He coughed again. "Did I tell you I would provide for you? That you would get your cash? Did I tell you that?"

"You did."

"And yet you stole from me," Bennie said.

"You were in jail," Sal said. "If you got shanked in the chow line, I had to be sure I had mine. You can understand that." Sal had taken a couple hundred grand and put it in safe-deposit boxes around Las Vegas. Problem was, after 9/11, he couldn't get into them with his fake

ID. "You figure out a way to get me a real license, with this new face, and you can have your money."

"It's not even earning interest," Bennie said. "If you'd been straight with me, I got a guy who could have moved that money to Laos and earned points on it. But you gotta be a sneaky fuck." Bennie shoved another forkful of salad into his mouth. "This is not satisfying. I cannot chew this in a way that expresses my total fucking disappointment in you, Rabbi." Bennie pointed at the burger. "You gonna eat that?"

"Be my guest."

Bennie reached across the table and picked up Sal's burger, took a bite out of it. "You're missing out, truly." He let his eyes wander around the joint. There were maybe fifty people spread out across the cafeteria. Doctors, nurses, administrators. A couple paramedics. Visiting family. A few patients who were either allowed to walk around the hospital or had snuck down. The food was served buffet style, but it was Las Vegas, so there was also a guy cutting churrascaria meats. A pasta station. A full taco bar. A serve-yourself gelato corner. A salad bar bigger than the fucking Sizzler Sal used to like when he was a kid. And then a full grill serving up burgers and chicken, the smell of which wafted throughout the hospital every day about this time, hence the intense fantasies Sal had harbored. "This place is pretty nice," Bennie said. "I might start taking more meetings here. Can't imagine cops can drop a wire on this place."

"You did."

"Well," Bennie said, "I'm not constricted by such things as laws."

"I got news for you," Sal said, "some suspected Al-Qaeda twat walks in here with a broken toe, they'll have a wire in every stethoscope."

"That's legal?"

"Is now," Sal said. "So maybe don't do any business with foreign terror organizations."

Bennie seemed to consider that for longer than Sal was comfortable. "The Chinese," he said finally. "That count?"

"I'd ease up."

"Why do you know this?"

"I have a vested interest in the latest surveillance laws."

"I've got a vested interest in making money," Bennie said. "And the Chinese are moving us product."

"The Talmud says, 'Do whatever the fuck you want,' Bennie."

"You're a little feisty today, Rain Man."

"I don't like being confined," Sal said. "You might remember that from the last time it happened. When am I getting out of here?"

"I've got a couple things cooking that need some . . . seasoning . . . first." He pointed up. "That floor you're on? Temple Beth Israel made a donation to thank the hospital for making sure your care has been first class. As of tomorrow at noon, when the signage goes in, you'll be staying in the Rabbi Cy Kales Memorial Wing of Summerlin Hospital."

"Rabbi Kales isn't dead," Sal said.

"Not yet," Bennie said. "It's like how you buy a tombstone before-hand. Similar plan." Bennie picked at a french fry. "You two, a real band of brothers with your plans and ideas while I was on house arrest. Like I was never gonna get out. You really think I'd let you two go to Israel? That was a good one, Rabbi."

"You don't have to worry about that now," Sal said.

"I wasn't worried before," Bennie said. "But just a note? You work for me. You might be the head rabbi. You might be my wife's spiritual advisor. You might be the most loved man in all of Summerlin, but you're alive right now because of me. Okay? Let's be real clear about that."

Sal had seen Bennie Savone angry a hundred different times. He wasn't surprised by it. But Bennie didn't seem all that pissed off. He seemed sad. Like Sal had hurt his feelings. It wasn't like Bennie could have him whacked. Rabbi David Cohen was the head rabbi of Temple Beth Israel. It was like being known in all five boroughs, all that Donnie Brasco shit, except on the real. So Bennie might well be his boss, but Sal wasn't scared of him. Never was. But especially not now, when things were beginning to come into focus.

"Will Rabbi Kales be here for the dedication?"

"No, he's fucking cooked," Bennie said. "But we got cousins flying in from around the country. You put a Jew's name on a building, they'll roll out of their caskets just for the after-party blintzes. *Review-Journal* is sending a photographer, give us some good publicity, finally. It's why I'm all dressed up. Meeting the hospital bigwigs today to discuss how the Temple and Savone Construction Partners can be of service to each other long into the future."

"What does that mean?"

"I believe my wife mentioned it to you," he said, another dig, Bennie twisting in a little on Sal, letting him know nothing between Bennie's wife Rachel and Rabbi David Cohen was privileged anymore. A change. Noted. "We're thinking of starting an assisted living facility on the grounds. We'd need a strategic partnership to pull it off."

"You think that's a good idea?"

"Which part?"

"All of it," Sal said, "but specifically the fucking newspaper."

Bennie took another bite of the burger. Ate a handful of fries. Took a sip of coffee. Pulled one, two, three paper napkins from the caddy, wiped his face. Propped his elbows on the table. "Motherfucker," he said, just above a whisper, calmly, no malice whatsoever, "the guy who sucker punched you was a ranked fighter in the UFC. I had him killed and made it look like a suicide. Hung him in his own garage. Had his fucking kid find him. I mean, we did it up. And his friends at the Temple, the Berkowitzes? I got them relocated. Husband's in Philly. Wife and kid, they're in Vancouver. I mean, they're living good lives. Or they will for as long as they don't fuck up. I did that. For you. Even agreed to pay for their little shithead son to go to private school. So that was a bill I didn't know I had coming. But let me ask. Do you know what it cost me to keep all your names from being associated with the dead guy? Nothing in the newspaper. Nothing in the blogs. No fucking Yahoo message boards. Nothing. What do you think that cost me?"

"I didn't ask for that."

"No," Bennie said, "you did. You literally did. By putting yourself in the situation where that fucking mook even had the desire to put hands on you? You asked for that. You've become cavalier while I've been gone." He straightened up. Wiped invisible crumbs from his tie. "So now, I gotta make good around town. I gotta unfuck your mistakes. I gotta go to Harvey B. Curran and ask him for a favor. You believe that? And somehow, he gives me one, because, he says, he *respects you*. Jesus fuck. He respects *you*. Heard you got tuned up by the fighter but doesn't want *you* embarrassed, so he's not gonna put some blind item in, no matter if it's true or not, but maybe I could help him out with a new thing the paper is doing? So that means buying a fucking advertorial in the *Review-Journal*." Bennie picked up the burger again, removed the bun, took off the lettuce and the onion and then peeled the cheese off the burger, wrapped it around the onion, popped it in his mouth. Seemed satisfied. "It's a fucking shakedown, Rabbi. I'm paying for the paper to come and write a nice story about the new wing."

"What's that run?"

"Color photos, eight hundred words, that's six grand," Bennie said. "Black and white, they cut you a deal; it's only $5,700. One good fucking piece of press about the Temple and a nice smiling photo of Rabbi Kales, presuming he doesn't piss or shit himself, keep your name out of it all, and I don't gotta put anybody in the dirt. Pretty good deal, in my view. So to answer your question, is it a good idea? I dunno, Rabbi, but here we are. You got a better fucking idea?"

"And what am I supposed to be doing during all this?"

"You're gonna be getting X-rays or a colonoscopy or I don't know what," Bennie said. "I vote colonoscopy, but I guess it's not my say." He shoved the burger away. "It's fucking terrible, you should know. Your taste buds might be working fine."

"So what happened to me? In case someone asks."

"You fell," Bennie said. "That's what I told Harvey B. Curran."

"That's it?"

"Rabbi," Bennie said, "they found you at the bottom of the stairs leading up to the Performing Arts Center, but your blood and hair was on every fucking step. So yeah. You fell. Whether you were pushed or tripped, end of the story is the end of the story."

"Security saw what happened," Sal said.

"Oh, yeah," Bennie said. "Add that to the fucking bill."

"I had those guys sign nondisclosure agreements," Sal said. "They'll stay quiet." Rabbi David Cohen hired a security force made up of off-duty Las Vegas Metro cops to guard Temple Beth Israel and all the other synagogues in town months before, in case terrorists decided to start killing the Jews of Las Vegas, what with all the threats they'd been receiving, many of which David called in himself. "You didn't need to pay them."

"You wanna try enforcing an NDA on cops, you go ahead. Me, personally? I believe in money, so everyone got a fucking bonus, even the fuckers who didn't see anything. But I gotta tell you, Rabbi, hiring cops, putting them under contract, to provide you with armed protection twenty-four hours a day, now that's another level of the game that I frankly had not ever considered."

"The Torah tells us to not stand idle when our brother's blood is at stake," Sal said.

"That's the kinda sixth-century thinking I appreciate, Rabbi."

Sal lowered his voice. "What are we gonna do about my face?" Sal said.

"People see what they want to see," Bennie said. "The ladies of Temple Beth Israel will continue to love you even with this new ugly mug."

"This ugly mug was on the *Today* show," Sal said. "Al Roker and Matt Lauer had a fucking conversation about me. I'm not worried about the people who know me. They'll just think I got a bad face-lift. I'm worried about the people looking for me."

"No one is looking for you," Bennie said. "You think anyone

remembers anything before the Twin Towers went down? Please. This thing of ours doesn't mean shit to anyone anymore. No one thinks the fucking Rain Man is gonna show up at their office and kill a couple thousand of their friends. You don't matter. Grow a beard, put on some glasses, gain twenty pounds, you'll be fine. Best thing that ever happened to us was this terror bullshit. Metro doesn't even show up to 911 calls from Wildhorse anymore. They just send law enforcement volunteers over to de-escalate problems. Old men in Boy Scout uniforms. They can't even write a ticket."

"It's not just the government I'm concerned about," Sal said. "What about this Peaches guy?"

"I'm trying to get a handle on that," Bennie said. "Why would Ronnie let someone else creep into his business? I mean, even before he stroked out."

He hadn't actually stroked out, as Sal had learned from Agent Drew. He'd been beaten, almost to death. Agent Drew called it an act of God, since he certainly meant to kill him.

Still, Sal gave that some thought. "Needed the muscle, that's my guess. Cartels coming up through the farmlands out there. You think you're hiring some guys to pick your crop, but you've actually got twenty-five Sinaloa hard knocks walking your property."

"Native Mob don't have the manpower to fight those guys," Bennie said.

"Maybe not," Sal said, "but I tell you what: a bunch a fifty-year-old Italians in suits don't want that smoke, either."

"This Peaches guy," Bennie said, "what's his beef with you?"

"I think he understands," Sal said, "that I'm the rightful heir to The Family."

"The rightful heir?" Bennie burst out laughing. "You actually put those words in your mouth." Bennie nodded toward his guy Avi. "See him? Not a drop of Italian in him. It's about making money, not preserving the culture. This ain't the movies. Take that antiquated shit and put it out of your mind. No one cares about blood anymore. That's some Coppola shit. No one is putting on tuxedos and fucking my daughters against walls, I'm telling you that now."

"It's all I can figure," Sal said. "Unless he wants the money the government put on my head."

"Maybe I should claim it," Bennie said. "Get my fucking money back."

Bennie picked up another french fry, blew the salt off of it, popped it in his mouth. "Chicago is unstable; that makes the whole middle of the country unstable," he said. "I got word they're moving on the casinos and bingo halls in the desert. This Peaches motherfucker."

"How's that your problem?"

"Maybe it's not," Bennie said. "Not like they're gonna show up here and take on the MGM. But we've got a pile of Mexicans waiting for your funeral blessing. We've got too much business. And your little friend at LifeCore doesn't have any demand for track-marked Mexican corpses missing their fucking eyes and fingers, so our profit isn't as good." Bennie looked around the cafeteria again, something clicking in his head. "I wonder if they'd tell me who designed this space. Get something like this in our assisted living facility, put a little less fucking salt in everything, and we'd be able to keep people alive long enough to really bleed them out."

A cop walked into the cafeteria, grabbed a booth, dropped all his shit—notepads, pens, file folders—and headed over to the buffet, never once looking at Sal or Bennie but pausing long enough to mad-dog the goon, shaking his head as he passed. Probably because you could see the Kevlar through Avi's sweat suit. Which wasn't legal, strictly speaking.

"Where'd you find that guy?" Sal asked after a while.

"He's ex-military," Bennie said. "Israeli. Rachel's second cousin. He used to come visit in the summers, then got a little too militant for Rachel's taste. That got him into some trouble back home, so we're giving him a second chance."

"What kind of trouble?"

"He's not a big fan of Palestinians. Tended to play a little rough."

"So you think bringing him to Las Vegas as your body man is the route to moral prosperity?"

"I think," Bennie said, "we don't hold someone's worst day against them forever. Which is coincidentally how you're currently having this conversation aboveground."

"He call you Poppa?"

"He calls me Mr. Savone," Bennie said. "Real respectful. You could learn from him. Fifty confirmed kills."

"Of what, women and children?"

"I didn't get biographies."

The cop walked past with a tray of food and this time he saw Bennie, nodded at him, and Bennie nodded back, the Summerlin Hospital cafeteria apparently Switzerland. He took his seat, hunched over his meal, like he was in the pen. "You know that guy?" Sal asked.

"Never seen him before," Bennie said.

"But he nods at you and you nod back?"

"We're coworkers."

Sal shook his head. "I'll never get used to this polite bullshit."

"That reminds me." He reached into his jacket pocket, pulled out a folded piece of bright-pink paper. He flattened it on the table between them. "You know this girl?"

It was a Missing flyer for Melanie Moss. Sal had killed her on 9/11, accidentally. Kind of. He killed her intentionally, but she wasn't who he thought she was. No mistakes in the first twenty years in the game then two in a row. First the FBI agents in the Parker House and then Melanie. He'd played that morning over in his mind on a loop ever since; sometimes he'd change a detail, a movement, a look, and Melanie would get out alive. But then the next day, she'd still be dead.

"No," Sal said. "I mean, I met her once. I didn't know her."

"When?"

"I guess the day she disappeared."

"A private detective came by the funeral home, interviewed Ruben

about her. Apparently he knew her pretty well." Bennie picked something out of his teeth. "I don't like it."

"She was a funeral-home investigator," Sal said. "You want Ruben
to know her. That's his job. If he didn't know her, that would be cause
for concern."

"What happens when the detective wants to talk to you?"

"I talked to the cops when they came by initially," Sal said. He had.
In October, seven months ago. A fifteen-minute conversation at the
Temple. The whole time, thinking how he'd kill the cop—he'd stab
him through the ear, he had a good angle from the way they were
sitting at his desk, had arranged the seats for just that eventuality—
where he'd bury him, ready to do it, happy to do it . . . but then it was
over; the cop closed his notebook and was out the door. "The private
detective wants to come by, I'll tell him what I told them. Color of her
blouse and where she parked her car. That's all I remember."

"Keep saying that out loud," Bennie said, "until it sounds more
believable."

"This private detective," Sal said, "what does he think happened
to this woman?"

"Raped, murdered, left for dead in the desert," he said, "that sort of
thing. They found her car in Carson City, her purse somewhere out the
same way, so who the fuck knows. All anyone can agree about is that
she was last seen with you, the day she died. So unless you want to be
on the Channel 8 news on the one-year anniversary of her death, we
need something better than your denials, at least until she turns up."

Melanie Moss wasn't just a fuckup; she was a breaking of his own
personal code. He didn't kill women. That's just how it was. Until it
wasn't.

"Have the funeral home put up a reward," Sal said. "A big one. Get
Ruben out in front, wearing a nice suit, something new, not some shit
he pinched off a dead guy, talking about what a nice lady she was, how
he can't believe she's gone, all that."

"How much?"

"Keep in mind," Sal said, "it's not real money."

"Meaning what?"

"Meaning if the cops were gonna find her, they would have already found her," Sal said, "but also, they stumble on her now, you don't pay the cops; this is private citizens only. Fine print, you make it good for six months, a year at most. Someone kicks a jawbone while jogging in ten years, you're not on the hook."

Bennie thought on that. "Fifty? A hundred?"

"Bigger," Sal said. "It's not real."

"Quarter of a million?" Bennie said.

"Now you're thinking," Sal said. "And then I'll have the shul agree to match it, dollar for dollar, which we'll actually collect, put in an escrow account in fucking Laos, or wherever you do your business now. And you can keep my half, in light of my current banking situation, okay?"

"Well look at you," Bennie said. "You're still one shystie motherfucker, aren't you?"

"Just trying to keep us both safe."

Bennie picked up Sal's tray and his own, went over and dumped them in the garbage, got himself a fresh cup of coffee in a to-go cup, came back to the table, but didn't sit down. "It was real nice seeing you, Rabbi Cohen," he said, too loudly, even the cop pausing to give notice. "Glad you're feeling better. Can't wait to have you back at the Temple."

"Thank you, Mr. Savone," Rabbi David Cohen said. "I look forward to returning as well."

"You take your time," he said. "We'll be lighting candles for you at services this week." An odd smile spread across Bennie's face then.

"What is it, Benjamin?" Rabbi Cohen said.

"You know," Bennie said, "I've kinda missed you."

"Me," Rabbi David Cohen said, "or the other guy?"

"All the same now," Bennie said. "Though I wouldn't shave if I were you." He patted David on the shoulder, leaned into his ear. "Also? Rabbi? Don't forget. I still own you."

TWO

THE PROBLEM WITH BEING ON THE FBI'S MOST WANTED LIST, MATTHEW DREW realized, was the lack of dining options. You couldn't just go to Chili's and plop down at the bar and order some chicken fingers and a Bud Light, because invariably there was a TV behind the bar and you never knew when you might show up on it. Twice he'd been in joints where they'd run news stories about the bodies found in Portland, actually mentioned his name but no photo, which was a relief, but even then, he immediately lost his appetite and was suddenly out twenty bucks. So he started eating at odd times, often in Chinatown, which rarely ran English-language TV unless there was a ball game on, or he'd buy something he could grill from the Rancho Swap Meet across from Lorenzi Park, where he was living in an RV, or he'd grab something from the Broadacres Marketplace, a maze of Mexican-food stalls and flea market vendors off of Pecos and Las Vegas Boulevard.

But even then, he always felt eyes on him, owing primarily to the fact that he was, generously, a huge motherfucker. He'd played lacrosse at Tufts but unlike most of his teammates, who were lean and fast, Matthew stood over six foot three and tipped the scales at 225, which had made him an imposing defender. Once he joined the FBI, he wanted to look cool in a suit, be able to chase a perp down and not break a sweat, so he dropped down to 215. Now, with nothing much to do but eat and work out, he was closer to 245, but that was fine. His job these days was to be as imposing as possible, so people didn't stare too long for fear of pissing him off. Turns out, though, the key to being memorable was being a giant white boy fumbling your chopsticks in

Chinatown or mispronouncing *carnitas* at the Mexican-food market. By his first month hiding in Las Vegas, vendors started to greet him with his order already written down.

So Matthew found himself eating at places owned by organized crime figures, like a Russian place called Odessa, down the block from the Hard Rock. The prices were pretty reasonable, and the clientele was primarily Eastern European goons—who would sooner shake your dick off at the urinal than make eye contact—and Russian émigrés, looking for a taste of home. The joint was owned by some Russian mobster, which didn't mean anything in this town. The entire ethos of the city—of the state, really—was that you were about to get robbed, that the only safeguard you had against ruination was your own will-power, and even that was prone to manipulation through free alcohol, sensory deprivation, and sexual coercion. No matter where you went in Las Vegas, you were totally fucked. That these mob-owned places still operated out in the open told Matthew a simpler tale: they weren't currently wired by the feds.

Plus, at Odessa, you could get a decent plate of sautéed liver and potatoes twenty-four hours a day, which was appealing since mornings were his nights now, the world easier to navigate under a cloak of darkness, which is why Matthew was sitting at the bar, nursing a large screwdriver, and reading the *Review-Journal* at 7 a.m. on a Tuesday, staring at Melanie Moss. Her family had run a full-page ad on page 3 of the paper every Tuesday for the last two months. Matthew didn't know where she was, not for sure, but he had a good sense that Sal Cupertine had killed her. The why is what baffled him. He hadn't asked Sal about it, not yet anyway, but he vowed to find out about that shit, give that family some rest. He'd run into her ex-husband and daughter in Carson City back in December, the fuse that sent him to Las Vegas in the first place. If he could solve her murder, that would be one more way to cover his ass. And he needed as much cover as possible.

Just as he was about to leave, a bald woman sat down next to him. Matthew checked her out with a glance. She had a gun on her hip.

Another on her ankle. Wouldn't be surprised if she had brass knuckles in her purse. Matthew made her for Homeland Security, one of the humps stuck in town still looking for connections to Bin Laden, months after the 9/11 bombers left planet Earth. Like maybe no one had realized OBL was chilling at Del Webb, playing shuffleboard and fucking old Jewish ladies. Typical government shit. A year behind, interrogating strippers and cocktail waitresses in Mojave Desert black sites, as if whatever evidence gleaned here might bring back the thousands of dead. It was fruitless. Bin Laden was across the world and the United States was dry-humping strip clubs in Vegas for intel about dead pilots.

Still, the bald head was a good look for the agent, Matthew thinking maybe she'd been a marine in her previous life. It went well with the guns, anyway, if you were into that. Which he was.

"I've never been here before," the bald woman said, like she felt Matthew's eyes on her. "What's good?"

"I like the liver," Matthew said.

"No organ meats for me," she said. She scanned the menu and when the bartender came by, she ordered bacon and eggs, over easy.

"Over easy," Matthew said. "Never knew a cop to order eggs anything but over hard."

"Not a cop," she said.

"Just like the look?"

"Only so many ways to wear a gun," she said. That was the other thing about dining in openly criminal operations: They were filled with cops and law-enforcement figures. No one bothered them, everyone in the game, so fuck it, have a meal, get back out on the street and do your work. Matthew had to act like he didn't give a shit, like he belonged, and then he'd become invisible, too. Maybe no one gave a fuck in the first place. "You Metro?"

"Private security," he said.

"Local?"

"No," he said. "In town on a job."

"Oh yeah?" She tapped the ad in the newspaper. "Well, that's a crazy story. Turned up missing on 9/11, her belongings scattered across the state. No body. No sign of a struggle. Car is found half a mile from her home. A real-ass mystery." The bald woman kept staring at the ad. "She was pretty."

"Maybe she still is," Matthew said.

"My experience, women don't disappear and then turn up. What happens is someone finds their DNA."

"I lost my sister," he said, "but she turned up. Part of me wishes she hadn't." Why did he say that? What was he doing telling true stories about himself to this stranger with guns? All he did these days was tell lies. But there it was, the truth, unfettered. And this woman was right. His sister didn't disappear. She was murdered by The Family or the Native Mob, or both, working together. Still, whenever he thought of her—which was often—he didn't think of her dead. He thought of her as *out there*, somewhere, floating in the distance, just beyond his reach. She was lost to him, and everything he'd done since the day he found her in the trunk of her car had been him trying to set the world right. Vengeance wasn't enough. He wanted someone to bring order to the chaos in his mind. He wasn't the man he used to be; he knew that.

"What happened, if you don't mind me asking?"

"Met the wrong people," Matthew said.

The bald woman put her hands up. "You don't need to tell me," she said. "This Melanie Moss, though. Imagine going missing on 9/11. What are the odds?"

"Same as any other day," Matthew said. "Bad shit happens 24-7."

"True. Absolutely true." The bald woman gave Matthew a wan smile. "Nothing prepares you for this life, right?" She picked up the newspaper, read the fine print, set it back down. "Temple I belong to gave the family some money for it. See?" She pointed to the bottom of the ad.

There it was, along the bottom, barely large enough to read: "The Moss family thanks Temple Beth Israel, the National Association of Funeral Home Directors, and the City of Carson City for their generous contributions, which has made this ad possible."

The bald woman didn't look Jewish to Matthew, but then in the permanent midnight of Odessa it was hard to divine anyone's countenance. But also, did this woman not know Temple Beth Israel was a criminal operation? Maybe it didn't matter. Everything was criminal. Countrywide was running a Ponzi scheme and calling them ARM loans. Starbucks was busting unions in the United States and exploiting farm workers in Ethiopia. Nike was running Chinese sweatshops. But this bald lady would likely be surprised to know her rabbi was a mob button man.

"It was the last place she was seen alive," the woman said. "And the Talmud says a lot about collective grief, I'm learning. She wasn't Jewish, but the place she was last seen, it was our home, so we pay homage to that."

"It's a nice gesture."

"It's what the culture demands," the bald lady said. "She doesn't belong to her family anymore. She's now a symbol for all the unresolved shit everyone has in their lives. The culture demands resolution. It's why people put up those missing posters in New York after the towers came down. No one really believed their loved ones had concussions and were wandering SoHo. Collective grief makes you do crazy shit that, when looked at obliquely, seems outside what you'd rationally think yourself capable of doing."

"Like this ad," Matthew said. Like trying to murder Ronnie Cupertine. Like not killing Sal Cupertine when you discovered him in a hospital bed. Like hiding from the law when you know you're doomed.

"Her family knows she's dead. But a couple days ago, I see the ad, and I start thinking, *Well, maybe there's something the cops missed*, so I go online down the rabbit hole of her life. Next thing I'm reading a message board," she said, "that says she was probably abducted by aliens who'd escaped Area 51. That's why they found her car and all her effects but not her body." She pointed up into the darkness of Odessa's ceiling. "She's now in the cosmos, somewhere. With her captors. There's an entire community of people who believe that."

"People just want something to make sense," Matthew said, "even if it doesn't."

"To me," the bald woman said, "that's as dangerous as the people blowing up buildings or beheading journalists. Because it's more insidious. They *know* it's not true, right? Somewhere, deep inside, these people *know* she wasn't abducted, but it's easier to make up a conspiracy than to deal with the hard reality that most shit just happens and it's totally beyond our control. There isn't always a why. At least these religious nuts have some god to take the blame."

The waitress came by, dropped off the woman's bacon and eggs. She tore a piece of toast, dipped it into the egg yolk. "I bring this all up, Agent Drew, to let you know I'm a person who deals in objective reality." She dug into her purse, came out with a business card, slid it over to him. *Special Agent Kristy Levine, FBI Organized Crime & Terrorism Task Force.* "Which tells me there's no fucking way someone on the FBI's Most Wanted list would be hanging out in a place run by the Russian mob, so it must not be you."

Matthew stood up. He had about a foot on Kristy. He could snap her like a twig and then pick his teeth with her arms. But he wasn't going to fight a bald woman. And, sure, he had a nine on his ankle, but he wasn't about to murder a federal agent.

Matthew hazarded a look over his shoulder, sure there'd be five guys with their guns pulled . . . but it was just a couple of strippers coming off the late-late shift, a table of five men in matching sweat suits inexplicably eating a cake, an Asian couple with a baby in the wrong fucking restaurant, and then a couple Russian working girls and their muscle. It was quiet, no one really talking, just eating or looking at their menus. Seven a.m., a block off the Strip, inside a mobbed-up Russian restaurant, you gotta want to be here.

Still, if the FBI didn't have a team inside Odessa, that probably meant there was an assault squad outside, another team over at Gray Beard's RV, and then a full blackout team storming wherever the fuck Sal Cupertine was pretending to be Rabbi David Cohen.

"Have a seat before I have to shoot you," Kristy said, not looking up from her meal. "Lee sent me."

Senior Special Agent Lee Poremba. Matthew sat down. Pondered the situation. If she was going to arrest him, she would have done so already. If Senior Special Agent Poremba sent her, he needed to trust that Poremba hadn't fucked him.

The only person—apart from Sal Cupertine—who knew Matthew Drew was in Las Vegas was Senior Special Agent Lee Poremba, since Poremba had sent him out this way in the first place. When Matthew got tabbed as a serial-killing lunatic, after those bodies were discovered in Portland, he contacted Poremba straightaway, to tell him he'd been framed, that it wasn't true, even if all the evidence pointed directly at him. The police reports for his stalking of the Cupertine family. His attempted murder of Ronnie Cupertine. And, of course, the motive: to avenge the murder of his sister. And then there was the fact that the gun used in all of the killings was his, no attempt to hide it. Matthew had no idea how many more bodies had been added to his sheet, but he imagined whoever was framing him was doing so in a prolific, if measured, manner. Killing only those who didn't have anyone to speak for them.

It was a long-ass list.

What Poremba told him, three months ago, chilled him through and through: "You're safer on the streets. If you turn yourself in, The Family will murder you in prison. Get your own evidence, build your own case, and when you're ready, come to me only. In the meantime, don't get caught." So he'd set him up with a drop—a mailbox at the Postal Express in Summerlin—and sent him cash, burner phones, even a card on his birthday. Matthew wasn't dumb. He knew Poremba was keeping him as a trump card on something larger.

Which is why Matthew went to the only wild card he had: Sal Cupertine, who he found in the hospital in Summerlin, living as Rabbi David Cohen. Sal knew Matthew hadn't killed Ronnie's family. Sal knew how the bodies ended up in Portland, because they came through the funeral home he operated for Bennie Savone first. The one person on the planet who could clear his name was the one person on the planet who couldn't clear his name. It wasn't a catch-22; it was a fucking bear trap. Sal wouldn't move until he found his wife and kid. Matthew couldn't move until he could figure out a way to get Sal safe passage . . . to somewhere. Safe enough to clear Matthew. After that? Cupertine could fuck himself. He'd started all of this, by murdering those three FBI agents and the CI at the Parker. He had to do his time. Either someone volunteered where Cupertine's wife and kid were or Matthew found out himself. Until then, his options were limited. So he'd spent the last months doing what he knew how to do: trying to track down a woman and a child in protective custody. They could be anywhere in America, theoretically, but Matthew knew the truth of the matter—a child like William Cupertine would require a different level of attention, which would include proximity to a university that might have the proper kind of mental health professionals. The threat level meant they couldn't be isolated from a major FBI field office. There would need to be either an organized crime division nearby or a team capable of handling a major assault. Access to a major airport. And having worked organized crime, he had a general idea of where they'd stashed witnesses before. It was just a matter of being methodical and then hoping Poremba might gain intel along the way.

All of which proved challenging, of course, once he was placed on the FBI's Most Wanted list.

"He lets you call him Lee?"

"I've got about eighteen months to live," Kristy said. "I'm trying to be minimalist in all things."

"Cancer?"

Kristy nodded.

"And you're still working?"

"I don't have any friends out here," she said. "It's either I work or I sit in my condo, watching game shows."

Matthew finished off his screwdriver, asked the bartender for another.

"That sounds good," Kristy said to the bartender. "I'll take one, too."

"You get to drink on duty?" Matthew said.

"You never did when you were an agent?"

"I never got off probation," he said. "But you know that."

"Seems to me higher-ups were a little hasty with you," Kristy said. "Top command is all new these days. Could be you find your way back in."

"How many agents go from the Most Wanted list to the Kansas City field office?"

"Depends what kind of collateral you bring. Sal Cupertine would be a big win for the bureau at a time when they really need one. Seems to me, you and Agent Hopper got closer than anyone."

"We were the only ones looking," Matthew said.

"Like I said, top command is all new. You're in Las Vegas for a reason, right?"

Matthew got the bartender's attention again. This time, he ordered a scotch. "Here's what I can tell you. You want to draw Sal Cupertine out," Matthew said, "put his wife on the news."

"What do you mean?"

"Well," Matthew said, "someone blew up her house, her kid shot a security guard in the back of the head, and no one has seen or heard from them since. You really think Sal Cupertine disappeared four years ago and never once got into contact with her? Come on. As long as she's in protective custody, Sal Cupertine will stay hidden. Once he knows where she is, he'll move. All the research Hopper and I did on him, the only thing that proved consistently true was that he loved his wife and kid. Everyone else could get fucked."

"I'm gonna guess she's somewhere with only one road in and one road out," Kristy said, "and it's heavily mined. Anyone looking for her is a bad guy. Even the good guys."

"That's my point," Matthew said. "You want to capture Sal Cupertine, put her on blast."

Before Matthew could continue, a walking steroid sat down on the other side of him. Sweatpants. White tank top. Spiderwebs and barbed wire on his arm. Waved over the bartender. She reached under the counter, came out with an envelope, handed it over. Steroid looked at Kristy. She nodded. He nodded back. What the fuck was going on? "The agent's breakfast is on the house, Svetlana," he said to the bartender.

"Thanks, Mr. Dmitrov," Kristy said.

"Feeling better?"

"No," Kristy said.

"The borscht will remind you of the old country."

"There's a reason we left," Kristy said.

"Svetlana will package up a bowl. You come back anytime, okay?"

"Thank you, Mr. Dmitrov," Kristy said.

"Take care of yourself, Agent. Need you to get that Bin Laden fuck." He looked at Matthew. "This guy bothering you?"

"No," Kristy said.

"You a cop?" he asked Matthew.

"No," Matthew said, "I'm on the Most Wanted list."

"Join the club," he said.

When he was gone, Matthew said, "What the fuck was that?"

"Owner's son," Kristy said. "Nice guy."

"He's a gangster."

"What are you?"

Matthew shook his head. He had no fucking idea anymore.

"How'd you find me?"

"You really want to know?"

"Yes."

"Lee's been sending you marked bills," she said. "He sent me a spreadsheet. It was either here or the Rancho Swap Meet. Where are you living?"

"Nope," Matthew said. "That you don't get."

"I understand." She looked over her shoulder. "There's a whole city beneath Las Vegas," Kristy said, her voice low. "Six hundred miles of storm drains. After 9/11, we walked every inch, because we got a tip there were bombers living in there, getting ready to take down the Strip."

"Find anything?"

"Five hundred, maybe seven hundred locals," she said. "A whole community. Got a mayor and everything." Kristy reached into her purse, came out with another manilla envelope. She slid it over to him. Inside was a band of twenty-five crisp hundred-dollar bills and a cell phone.

"These marked, too?"

"Of course," she said. "If something goes sideways, there's an entrance on Spring Mountain and Rainbow. The Desert Inn Detention Basin. On a sunny day, there's easy access. You find Cupertine, go there, call me."

"Why are you doing this?"

"Lee believes you," she said. "So I believe you."

"I didn't kill Ronnie Cupertine's family," Matthew said.

"It's enough for me," she said. "Pray that Ronnie Cupertine doesn't die between now and then, though," Kristy said. She pushed her plate away, started to gather up her stuff. "You ever been to Russia?" she asked, as if the first part of the conversation had never happened.

"No," he said.

Kristy took one last sip of her coffee. "I always wanted to go. My family, they all escaped in something like 1910. *Fiddler on the Roof* era. Whenever that was. But I think I missed my window."

"Because of Putin?"

"No, no," she said. "Fuck him. He'll be taken out by one of his own sometime. That's how they do czars." She pointed at her head. "Got a ticking time bomb set to go off anytime now. I'm not going to die in Russia, all by myself, where no one knows me. End up in an unmarked grave, my kidneys sold for profit." That made Matthew laugh. Maybe for the first time in a year. "You've got a nice smile, Agent," Kristy said. "Good teeth. Strong prenatal care; that's what my mom would have said."

"I'm not an agent anymore," Matthew said.

"You don't happen to know where Sal Cupertine is, do you?"

"Is this you asking or Agent Poremba?"

"He killed four FBI agents and a CI," Kristy said. "So consider it Abe Lincoln asking."

"My guess?" Matthew said. "We'll never find him."

"Then what are you doing in Las Vegas?"

"I like it here," he said.

Kristy Levine downed her screwdriver and then stood up. She was a tiny thing. Matthew suspected she was unpredictable and fast. "You're a shit liar, Agent," she said. "I don't think you murdered anyone. I want you to know that. And personally? I don't really care if you did put Ronnie Cupertine into a coma. But murder is murder. I believe that."

"I meant to kill him," Matthew said. "Chance came along again, I'd cut his fucking throat."

"Lee cares about you," she said.

"I don't know why," Matthew said.

"Don't make him regret it," she said.

She was halfway out the restaurant when something occurred to Matthew, so he caught up with her just as she was pushing open Odessa's doors into the harsh light of the Las Vegas morning. "That guy who came to the bar. The owner's son. He knew you."

"He does indeed."

"But you said you'd never been here before."

"I know how to lie, too," she said and then she smiled. "If you find Sal Cupertine," she continued, "the FBI upped the reward to a million dollars. Announcement is coming end of the month, for the anniversary. Come buy me a drink at Pour Decisions. I'm there on Tuesday nights."

THREE

"BLOW OUT YOUR CANDLES, WILLIAM," MARYANN SAID. SHE WASN'T JENNIFER Cupertine's mother, nor William's grandmother, but for the last nine months, she'd pretended to be. It was the first warm day of April on Loon Lake, twenty-six miles outside of Spokane. Since William shot a security guard inside Carson's department store in Chicago last August, Loon Lake had been home.

Jennifer could still see it all unfolding.

The security guard tackling her, William reaching into her purse, taking out her gun, and then, very calmly, putting one in the back of the man's head.

Jennifer had tried to keep the man's fate away from William, but Jesus, the man's head splintered and one of his eyes, plus a chunk of forehead, ended up beneath a rack of St. John knits. If Jennifer saw that, it was impossible that William had somehow missed it, since William constantly took inventory of the world.

The guard had, in fact, lived for a little while—a week—long enough for his vital organs to be harvested. His heart went to a teenage girl in need of a transplant; the *Tribune* ran a feature story on it and everything. Key words from the story still pinged in Jennifer's mind, late at night . . . and in the morning and middle of the day, too, if she was being honest: *Leaves behind a wife, Loretta, of Batavia.* And: *The shooter, an under-ten minor from Lincolnwood, is currently under psychiatric supervision.* And then, curiously, not a word about Jennifer. The FBI had done their job. They'd moved her and William into protective custody and even managed to get the newspaper to go along with it.

She'd never trust anything she read in a newspaper again.

"It's not my birthday," William said. They all sat at the red picnic table at the bottom of the long lawn that stretched from the dock to the front door of their two-story Cape Cod. Jennifer was sure they'd picked this house intentionally: the lawn was long enough that it would be impossible to sneak up on them from the lakeside. Navy SEALs could land on the shore, but they'd still need to walk half a city block to reach the house. The racks of motion lights would likely deter them, too.

Jennifer had to concede that it *was* beautiful here, if lakes and trees and fish and birds and bears were your idea of beauty. Jennifer's entire life had been spent in Chicago, so she was still nostalgic for the beauty of high-rise buildings and bombed-out trains and Italian restaurants with peeling wallpaper and the smell of wet cement, but in the months they'd been here, she'd come to appreciate the subtle allure of the natural world. Even her asthma was better.

The woman who was not Jennifer's mother cut her eyes toward her. "Some help, Caroline?"

Caroline was Jennifer's name now. She hated it. But the key was that you never broke character; that was hammered into her every day. *If you want to live*, the FBI told her, *forget your name*. They didn't make clear that "living" meant constantly playing a game where you tried not to fuck up your own identity, lest some mob hit man was water-skiing by and picked up a line of conversation and realized you were not just a woman, but a bounty. Jennifer didn't know what the number was on her and William's heads, but she figured it was probably a pretty decent one considering the number of agents who rotated surveillance.

"I told you," Jennifer said. "He remembers everything."

"In order for this to work, we need your buy-in," Levi said. He was the man who was not Jennifer's father. "You tell him it's his birthday, it's his birthday."

"He's not an idiot," Jennifer said. "Are you an idiot, William?"

"No," William said. "Can I go inside and get my *Guinness* book?"

"Of course," Jennifer said. "Grandpa will take you, won't you, Grandpa?"

"Anything for our boy," Levi said. He took William by the hand. "Let's go find your book. Do you know where you left it?"

"The kitchen counter," William said, "open to page 321. Where the man is eating the plane."

"See?" Jennifer said to Maryann once they were gone. "He's not a child. He understands what you're saying." Two hundred and twenty-seven days they'd lived in this house, and in that time, Jennifer had never felt unsafe, not even after the news reported Cousin Ronnie's entire family had turned up dismembered in a parking lot in Portland.

That was the kind of gangster shit that happened to gangsters' families when they didn't have adequate fear. Jennifer was *always* afraid, but she also felt well protected, enough so that each day she felt comfortable spending a few minutes reminding William about details of their old life, plus things about his father that he should know, so that William didn't lose the sense of his father, not just some vague memory of a man who used to live with them. But also, if something should happen to Jennifer, William should have some knowledge about what it means to be a Cupertine. It had been four years since William had last seen his father. Half of his life. So she tried to be as granular as possible, to keep Sal from growing diffuse.

He buttons his shirts from the bottom up.

He was always getting weird infections, so don't let anything fester. He used to lose a toenail a year!

Dogs always liked him.

He liked you to be called by your full name, so if someone wants to call you Billy, you tell them that's not happening.

"It's the small things that will catch him," Maryann said, evenly.

"You don't want something simple to be the thing that puts his life in jeopardy."

"I'm not going to lie to him about when his goddamned birthday is. He understands the passage of time. He *remembers everything.*"

"Then he's capable of remembering something new," Maryann said.

"I'm still his mother," Jennifer said. "I'm still the decision maker. When I want him to have a new birthday, he'll have a new birthday. Until then, his birthday is December 19. You want to change it, talk to my lawyer."

"You don't have a lawyer," Maryann said.

"That's probably a violation of my rights," Jennifer said, "so maybe ponder that, too."

Jennifer got up and walked down to the end of the dock, sat down, took her shoes off, put her feet into the lake—which was ice-cold, winter over, but only in name, the nights here still frigid and icy—and tried to hit the reset button.

The home she and William shared with these fake grandparents was in a small bay on the lake. On one side was a low hill, a train track cut into the side of it. On weekdays, a train passed through every three hours. On weekends, it was every four hours. Jennifer thinking that, if need be, one day, she could probably grab William, run out onto the tracks, and just leap aboard a passing train. It was a silly fantasy of course, because this placid lake house was also a well-staffed prison: behind the house was an outcrop of granite, a natural wall, and then next door was a guest house where two men with guns stay. How many cameras were about, she had no idea, but she got the sense that somewhere in Quantico, it was some lackey's job to fill out a report about her every movement.

The two men with guns—U.S. Marshals—however, were different all the time. Sometimes they'd be young guys, fresh out of the academy, she suspected, and they'd come and talk to William, ask him about baseball or TV shows. Sometimes they'd ask him about his father, like it was some kind of test. Sometimes the men were older—men a few weeks from retirement doing one last cushy job so they didn't end up getting shot before they could collect their 401(k)s—and they tended to view William with only vague curiosity. They spent their time focused on Jennifer. "You're very pretty," one old-timer told her, but not in a pervy way, just like it was a statement of fact that was universally agreed upon. "You deserve a better life than this." On that point, Jennifer agreed, kind of, because she didn't believe most people *deserved* anything. You earn the good and the bad.

This day, the two men were young and they watched Jennifer from a fishing boat in the bay, shirts off, lines in the water. One of them—he had a mustache, looked like every cop who ever pulled her over when she and Sal were in the car together; Jennifer always afraid of what Sal would do, but he always kept his driver's license and insurance current—waved at her. She waved back. Just a normal spring day in protective custody.

After a few minutes, Jennifer heard footsteps behind her. It was Levi, holding two plates of birthday cake. William was back at the picnic table, reading his book and eating cake with his fingers. "Uncle Steve" and "Aunt Britt" had arrived at the birthday party, with gifts and everything. They were Maryann's and Levi's primary replacements on weekends, and Aunt Britt had also been William's primary homeschool teacher. No one bothered to call them and tell them Jennifer was throwing a fit.

Levi sat down beside Jennifer, handed her one of the pieces of cake. Chocolate frosting on yellow cake, which was William's favorite. They got that right.

"We went to a lot of work to make today special," Levi said.

"It's not his fucking birthday," Jennifer said.

"You made that clear," Levi said.

Jennifer took a bite. "It's good," she said.

"Maryann is quite the baker," he said.

"Really? She made it?"

Levi nodded. "We're trying to help your son." He took another bite. "He's been getting onto the computer at night. After everyone's asleep."

"What's he doing?" Jennifer asked.

"Looking for his father, primarily."

"Join the club."

"He's read a few newspaper articles. Found something about his grandfather's death. We've put blockers on. But you should know. New things pop up."

"He's eight," Jennifer said. "I'm sure he doesn't understand what he's reading."

"You don't believe that," Levi said.

Jennifer took another bite of cake. "No," she said, "I don't."

THAT NIGHT, AFTER DINNER, JENNIFER FOUND WILLIAM IN HIS ROOM, SITTING at his desk, drawing skylines. A new obsession. Back home, he had an old book of Sal's that he loved—*Great Skyscrapers!*—that Jennifer had to scour the internet for once they got settled at Loon Lake.

Jennifer sat on the edge of William's bed. "Sit beside me," she said, and he did. She put her arms around him, kissed him on the top of his head. "I'm sorry about today. It wasn't a very fun party."

"The cake was good," he said.

"Well, that is true," Jennifer said.

"I don't want a new birthday," he said.

"I know," Jennifer said.

"They make you sad," William said. "You always seem sad when you fight with Nana Maryann and Papa Levi."

"I know, baby," she said. "We just don't always see things the same way. But we will. It's not bad when adults disagree with one another. It's just one of those things you learn to accept."

"Daddy wouldn't let them talk to you like that."

He sure fucking wouldn't.

"Daddy's not here. It's just us. And we don't solve problems the way Daddy did. Okay? The way Daddy handled business is the reason we're not in Chicago anymore." Jennifer recognized she was dumping too much on William, again. Knew that if they ever got out of this place, neither one of them would be recognizable if she kept up with this shit. "And you don't need to worry about any of that, okay?" Jennifer brushed the bangs from William's forehead. Stared into his eyes. "I love you so much," she said.

"I know that."

"Your father loves you," she said.

"I know that," he said, "because you've told me."

"He does. I know he does."

"What if," William said, "he's dead?"

What if.

"I'd know," Jennifer said.

"How?"

How do you explain to an eight-year-old boy that some things you just *know*, that you'd feel some shift in reality, that you'd wake up and know he was beyond your reach?

"Do you think he's dead?" Jennifer asked.

"No," William said.

"See? You'd know."

Jennifer looked out of William's open window, which faced the water, and saw Uncle Steve walking across the lawn, pole in one hand, cooler in the other, headed toward the dock.

Uncle Steve dressed in camo and always had two guns on him. One in a shoulder holster, one on his ankle. He was one of those guys who had lots of opinions about the Old Days, which were always better than Today, and which, if the country was to ever get back on track, needed a quick return to, in his opinion, or else The Future Was Deeply Fucked Pardon My Language.

His cover for being geared to the teeth and decked out like he was

taking Normandy was probably not that far from reality in this region: he belonged to a quasi-militia made up of ex-military guys and
people who never made it into the services, who liked to playact revo-
lutions and such. Auntie Britt, she only carried one gun, told Jennifer
that William's intelligence was "off the charts!" and that he was "very
gifted" but that she was exceedingly worried about his propensity toward sudden violence when angry, frustrated, or scared.

There was an incident with hairspray and a lighter.

There was an incident with matches and a neighbor's boat.

There was an incident with a boy at church, back when they were
trying that, where he tried to bite his ear.

"Does Uncle Steve ever catch anything?"

"He doesn't bait his hook," William said.

"Really?"

"I think he just likes to drink beer and pee into the lake."

"I've really fucked up our lives," Jennifer said.

"It's not your fault," William said.

"Look at me, William," Jennifer said, and William did. "It was
always my choice. Everything I've ever done has been by choice. Do
you understand?"

"Yes."

"We will get out of this place, okay? Not today. Not tomorrow. But
we will. And when that time comes, it may not feel like the normal
course of events, okay? Do you understand?"

"I do," William said.

She took his face in her hands. "If I ask you to do something, one
day, that seems crazy, just know that I'm asking you because I love
you. I would never, ever, try to hurt you. You know that, right?"

"Yes," William said.

A cool breeze blew in through the open window, so Jennifer got up
to close it. Which is when she noticed a dozen *Star Wars* action figures
splayed out on the lawn beneath the window.

"What's going on with your toys?" Jennifer asked.

"I've been dropping them out the window," he said, "to see how long it takes for them to hit the ground."

"Oh," Jennifer said. She closed the window, locked it. She'd tell Levi and Maryann to hide the computer at night.

"Can I have another piece of cake?" William asked. He'd already turned back to his drawing.

"Of course, baby," she said. "Every day is your birthday now."

FOUR

"HEY BOSSMAN," LONZO GUIJARO SAID, "CALIFORNIA AIN'T OPEN CARRY. Maybe stow that shit."

Peaches Pocotillo, who'd been dozing in the front seat of the stolen Escalade with a Glock on his lap since they left that gas station in St. George, Utah, six hours earlier, popped his eyes open. Peaches didn't know what he imagined California would look like, but as they wound along a two-lane highway hugging sand dunes and the periodic outcrop of jagged, volcanic mountain, it wasn't this.

"Where we at?"

"An hour out from Palm Springs."

"What day is it?" Peaches asked.

"Saturday," Lonzo said. His phone started to buzz. He looked at it, set it back down. "My kid. She had a soccer game this morning."

"My kids don't play sports," Peaches said. He had three daughters. Three mothers, too. All from different tribes. They were more of an investment than a family, each girl endowed with casino money every month, each getting a nut at eighteen. Peaches in charge of investing it, which meant he took his cut as he saw fit. The mothers had their nuts, too. Eventually, he was going to need to marry one of these women and get rid of the others.

"It's all they talk about," Lonzo said. "Soccer, lacrosse, ballet. Every dollar I make, they spend on fucking shoes and uniforms. Can hardly keep up." He rubbed at his eyes with the palm of his left hand. Peaches saw him do a bump off the same palm before they left the Super 8. The Escalade belonged to the drug dealer. St. George's finest.

Best person to steal from. They have the nicest cars, and they never call the cops. "Don't know what I'd do if Ronnie didn't sponsor the soccer league. Probably have to do freelance hits."

"May his generosity never cease," Peaches said, though he'd look into that when they got back. Fucking Ronnie Cupertine spent so much money trying to look legit that he could have just gone legit. It would have been cheaper.

Lonzo was a Gangster 2-6 OG Peaches inherited from Ronnie, but they'd had a good working relationship even before the Native Mob moved in on The Family. Gangsters didn't live very long, generally, so if you were an OG, it wasn't odd to clique up every now and then, talk shop, partner on drug deals, all of which had been the case for Peaches and Lonzo back in the day, Lonzo being the guy who opened the door to Ronnie in the first place. Now Lonzo was his guy, too. They'd spent the last three days driving from Chicago and hadn't killed each other. A good sign.

Driving was a necessity these days because Peaches Pocotillo wouldn't fly on planes. Wasn't that he was scared. Used to really like it. Even took a few lessons, back when he was learning all aspects of the Native Mob drug trade and considering getting a license to fly crop dusters and Cessnas, but that was back when someone who'd done time could still get into a flight-training program. That wasn't happening now.

In one respect, those terrorists had done Peaches a favor, taking the light off of his business, letting him operate almost out in the open. If you weren't popping civilians on city streets, or selling hotshots to Gold Coast debutantes, and/or making and distributing child pornography, the FBI didn't give a shit.

Run a phony casino?

Fine. As long as you didn't wash any money for anyone named Muhammed, you were going to be okay.

Move H and Oxy throughout flyover country?

Okay. The masses needed opiates. Peaches hadn't heard of anyone getting busted for selling drugs since before 9/11. Not anyone moving weight, that is. Cops might bust a corner, but they weren't tracking up the line. Government wanted the people as dulled as possible.

Kill gang members?

Man, that was no-human-involved shit right there. Go to fucking town.

In another respect, though, if you had a sheet, you could hardly move without somebody running you through Interpol. Get on a plane, TSA is going through your luggage, letting the FBI know you're in transit. Land in a big city, they're picking your face up on the cameras and spinning you through a thousand different databases, logging your movements. They don't arrest you or send a tail, but they know when you were in this town or that town, probably some junior Clarice Starling at Quantico putting you on a spreadsheet. Not that Peaches was Hannibal Lecter. Or even Sal Cupertine, for that matter, though it kind of pissed him off that people didn't realize he was up there with both of them in terms of body count, but whatever.

It wasn't a secret, Peaches was certain, that he was shot-calling The Family with Ronnie Cupertine out of commission, even though Peaches controlled the release of information regarding Ronnie's health like he was governing a tiny Soviet state. Peaches had this idea that controlling The Family was more ceremonial, that underlings kept shit like Ronnie's car dealerships and philanthropic activities handled, but in fact Ronnie was hands-on with everything, hyper-protective of his brand. So the last several months, Peaches had to periodically release statements from Ronnie regarding the various charities he ran, made sure the car dealerships stayed current with their commercials, Ronnie Cupertine still shooting holes in credit ratings with a tommy gun and offering great deals on "Great American Cars!" The advertising agency had enough clips of Ronnie and his tommy gun to make commercials for another two hundred years, and the lot had enough stolen cars to make that a reality.

Peaches hit a button on the side of his seat, came full upright, tipped his sunglasses up, tried to make sense of the world he'd woken up in. "Fuck is this place?"

"Used to be gold and copper mines," Lonzo said.

"No shit?"

"Whole area was filled with precious metals," Lonzo said. "A hundred twenty years ago, you couldn't dig ten feet without running into your fortune. That's the story, anyway."

"What happened?" Peaches said.

"Motherfuckers with shovels is what happened." Lonzo laughed. "And then the government showed up and that's how that goes."

Peached understood *that* well enough. It's why he had a plan to better himself since the first time a jail cell closed behind him. Got interested in real estate, accounting, civil engineering. Got out, took classes at community colleges. Got his real estate license. During the year he spent in Joliet, read a book a day. None of that Tom Clancy submarine shit. Kept that up on the outside, too.

Lonzo's phone started to buzz again. "You mind?" he asked. Peaches waved his assent. He was a good boss, the kind who empowered people. He'd read Iacocca's biography. "The speed of the boss is the speed of the team." He liked that shit. Get people moving how Peaches moved, they'd come up.

When Ronnie was dead, Peaches would do things differently. Keep a lower profile. Be like a ghost, so that when people saw him, they'd be awed by the experience, not sure if they should be scared or filled with wonder. He certainly wouldn't be sponsoring soccer leagues and shit. Less you try to look innocent, more likely you'll do some shit that makes you look guilty.

Fact was, some unforced errors made Peaches adjust his business plan.

Like when Ronnie's wife and kids showed up cut into pieces in a bunch of garbage bags in Portland. Peaches had them murdered and buried in the first place, once it became clear Ronnie was never gonna be much more than a bag of skin, but then Sugar Lopiparno convinced him that The Family had a process for getting rid of bodies that was impeccable, a show of fealty. It was a part of The Family business still fire-walled from Peaches, like the location of Sal Cupertine. Not knowing was smart, in a practical sense: Peaches couldn't get caught up in either situation when they eventually fell apart, and already, that was happening. Two weeks after getting rid of Ronnie's wife and three kids, they ended up on the national news, the *Chicago Reader* going so far as to show a photo of a foot sticking out of a garbage bag, painted toenails and everything.

If Sugar hadn't seemed as stunned as Peaches, he'd be dead already, too. But then the cops traced the bullets in the bodies to Matthew Drew's gun, which Peaches's guys stole from Drew's sister before they killed *her*—which made Peaches feel like the luckiest man alive— so he got to play dumb, too, tell everyone in The Family that Matthew Drew was now their number one focus, killing Ronnie's family, that shit wasn't right, wives and kids off limits . . . which was true to these Greatest Generation Italian fucks, but not to Peaches. He'd kill anyone. He did not give a fuck. So now the FBI, Chicago cops, and the Mafia all had the same target: Matthew Drew. Which gave Peaches some leverage to get shit done.

If it were up to Peaches, he'd let the old guard die. But Ronnie Cupertine's lawyer had paper that said he was to be given every life-saving measure, which meant this fucking guy might live on machines until cockroaches ruled the world. They'd held private funerals for Ronnie's wife and kids, which meant there were still hundreds— maybe thousands?—of cards from friends and family and associates expressing their condolences, which meant Peaches had to then subcontract out the writing of thank-you cards, employing his three baby mamas to do the work, and then getting Sugar and a few of the boys to sign Ronnie's name.

No one told Peaches that being Ronnie Cupertine required so much fucking stationery.

Another result of all this: Chicago was upside down. Bloods and

Crips were doing that Blood and Crip shit, seventeen-year-olds killing one another over streets in LA they'd never visit. Gangster Disciples were at war with Latin Kings over some shit that started in the
pen and spilled to the streets. Gangster 2-6 was beefing with La Raza,
even though both were Latin gangs, to see who could suck cartel dick
faster. Even the Asian gangs, like Hop Sing and Asian Boyz, were at
one another's throats, something to do with heroin, a girl, and someone disrespecting someone else, shit jumping off like it was the Tong
Wars of the 1930s. And where traditionally The Family might step in
and settle everything down—because without The Family, the gangs
didn't have any products to sell, so they listened even when they didn't
want to—Peaches was content to let everyone kill one another.

He knew, in the end, the street gangsters would do something stupid, like light one another up at a White Sox game over who had the
right to wear the black hat, and then he could pick up the business
he was interested in. Sit back in the cut, let the baby gangsters play at
this, and then buy up their houses (Peaches Pocotillo was buying up
gang-infested blocks like it was Monopoly, washing his casino money
into property no one was interested in) and start doing things his way,
until such time The Family revolted, too.

Which would happen. Peaches was 100 percent on that. If he
wanted to avoid that—and he did, now that he was getting deep into
the casino business and The Family still owned the connection on
that—Peaches needed to know how they got rid of their bodies. And
he needed to find that motherfucker Sal Cupertine, eliminate the last
person who might reasonably wrench control away from him, the last
loose end who anyone in The Family felt loyalty toward. No one in The
Family was gonna take Peaches out now, not while he was making everyone money while the boss was in la-la land. But if Sal made himself
known again? Oh, he needed to be ready.

It was yet another reason why Peaches wasn't flying: He wasn't
showing up anywhere without a gun. Too many people wanted him
dead.

Lonzo hung up, shook his head. "Would kill for a son."

"They lose?" Peaches asked.

"Won by four," Lonzo said, "but her best friend was on the other team so now there's beef." He shook his head, like he was clearing the deck, getting ready for the next thing. "What time we meeting your nephew tomorrow?" he asked.

"One," Peaches said. His nephew, Mike, had been in the desert going on three months now, "consulting" with a local tribe on a casino project out in Indio, mitigating some problems between the Mexican Mafia and the Native Mob. Peaches was worried that Mike was on some Fredo shit out here, but his nephew assured him everything was cool. "You book us somewhere nice?"

"The Riviera," Lonzo said. "Elvis and Sinatra played there."

"Elvis doesn't mean shit to me," Peaches said.

"No?"

"Child molester," Peaches said. "I read a book about him. Priscilla was fourteen when he knocked those boots."

"No shit?"

"No shit."

Lonzo shivered. "My girl is eleven. That's fucking wrong, homie."

"What I'm saying."

The two drove in silence for a moment, until Lonzo said, "This meeting, it gonna turn wet? Just want to prepare mentally." Which meant: he'd chop up a few more lines. One line, Lonzo was good company. Two lines, Lonzo was the guy you wanted to be with when shit jumped off. Three lines, Lonzo was fucking Idi Amin. Four lines, better hope he recognized you or that someone hid the automatic weapons and power tools.

"I'm a businessman now," Peaches said.

"Homie," Lonzo said, "no disrespect on this? But I heard you burned down an entire neighborhood in Chicago."

"Who told you that?"

"Streets."

Peaches didn't like that shit being out there. He was in his forties now. The notion of "the streets" spreading rumors about him—even though, in this case, they were true—made him feel like a low-rent celebrity, like some fool at the end of the bench for the Bulls when Jordan was out there killing, some Jud Buechler shit. "Say it's true," Peaches said. "That somehow change your opinion of me?"

Lonzo rapped his knuckles against the steering wheel. "No, no," he said. "But then I also heard it was the Rain Man's house."

Peaches shrugged. "You friends with the man?"

"Blow up a man's house when it's just his wife and kid living in it, that seems like it's outside the game."

"His wife was snitching," Peaches said. "Her son shot a man in the back of the head. Seven years old, popping fools. The point is, these are not good people."

Lonzo remained quiet for a moment, likely doing the math. "Ronnie okayed that?"

"Ronnie ordered it," Peaches said, which was a lie. Ronnie wasn't ordering shit, not even fucking Jell-O.

"Sal Cupertine finds out you blew up his house," Lonzo said, "that's gonna piss the man off."

"He'll never step foot in Chicago again," Peaches said. He hoped he was wrong. That was the whole plan. Get his ass to Chicago. Put him into Lake Michigan, one bone at a time.

"Still. I'd sit with my back to the wall for the rest of my life."

They came over a low rise in the road and nearly slammed into a Cadillac going twenty miles below the speed limit. Dealer plates from "Friendly" Manitoba. A ball cap in the window with the POW logo. Peaches tried to do the math on that. Had Canada even fought in Vietnam? Or maybe it was from a different war, Peaches not totally up on Canadian armed conflicts. The Caddie was bright red, rolling on 22s, one of those new Sevilles. American dream shit. Peaches could work an honest job his entire life and never, ever afford a Seville. And his family was in America before anyone was. Some fucking dream.

"This motherfucker," Peaches said.

"Chill," Lonzo said, "he's about to have a heart attack." Lonzo pressed on the horn, but that just made the Caddie tap its breaks, slow down another five miles per hour.

"Pull up beside him," Peaches said.

"You want me to ride the shoulder?"

"I promise," Peaches said, "I'll pay your ticket."

When they did, Peaches could see that there was a woman in the passenger seat, asleep, and behind the wheel was an old man, maybe eighty, maybe 180, hard to tell with the BluBlockers on. Probably never even heard Lonzo's horn. Probably hadn't even looked in his rearview mirror since the Canadian border. Probably just rode his breaks by habit.

Peaches tapped the horn. The old man startled. Looked Peaches's way. Peaches rolled down his window, said, "Roll down your window, sir." But the old man just stared at him, like he couldn't comprehend how a car had come up on his left on a two-lane road.

"Bossman," Lonzo said, "it's cool. Nothing but open road in front of us. We'll get a new ride in town. Forty minutes from now, you'll be poolside. There's easier ways."

The Caddie slowed, and Lonzo started to pass it. "No," Peaches said, "keep pace."

"Not the lady," Lonzo said. "You don't gotta do that."

"Roll down your window," Peaches mouthed again, and this time the old man did. Peaches picked up the Glock from his lap, extended his arm out the window, and fired two shots. And just like that, they had a new car.

FIVE

THE PROBLEM WITH BEING A JEWISH HOLY MAN *AND* SINGLE, RABBI DAVID
Cohen learned early on, is that whenever something bad happened,
the entire Hebrew world felt like they had to come by his home with a
homemade dish. David broke a toe playing kickball with the Tikvah
Preschool kids, eight briskets showed up at his home within twenty-
four hours. A sinus infection was worth a kugel, scalloped potatoes, a
baked chicken, and a platter of cookies. Even the rumor of illness was
good enough for a casserole or six.

Come home from the hospital with a new face? That was apparently a clarion for matzo ball soup. Already that Saturday, Connie
Blau, Tiffany Friedman, and Zoe Geller had dropped off about twenty
gallons of their very own special recipes, though in each case David
was pretty sure they just came by to view his face. With a full beard,
he wasn't sure how much they saw, though he had patches where hair
just wouldn't grow, which gave him the haphazard look of a man with
a broken razor or a shitty mirror.

And so when his doorbell rang for the fourth time that morning—it was only 11 a.m.—David had the thought that he could maybe
opossum his way out of another guest. Except this time his CCTV
showed FBI agent Matthew Drew alongside Gray Beard, both wearing Cox Cable uniforms and holding clipboards, standing at his gate.
A Cox Cable van idled behind them, Marvin in the front seat. To the
best of David's knowledge, Gray Beard didn't have David's address.
He wasn't surprised he found it, only surprised he used it. Gray Beard
and Marvin had done odd jobs for David over the years. A friendship

had developed, or at least a close business relationship, one that allowed David to make a call from the hospital and arrange a place for Matthew to stay. But that didn't mean you just dropped by to watch a ball game.

"Something I can help you with?" David said through the intercom. David had the high ground here. If need be, he could go upstairs and plug all three using one of his long guns. HOA frowned on brain matter on the streets, so he'd need to figure that part out.

"Got a call about an outage," Gray Beard said.

"Wasn't from me," David said. He trusted that Gray Beard and Marvin wouldn't bring Matthew over to kill him, but . . . still.

"We just need to come inside for five minutes. Adjust some wiring." Gray Beard pointed at Matthew. "Got a trainee who needs to see how things work."

"You think showing up at someone's house without an appointment is a good way of doing that?" David said.

"Emergency situation," Gray Beard said.

Bennie had David's entire house wired. Having Matthew Drew inside of it was not going to work. Never mind that Gray Beard and Marvin in his home would put them all in some jeopardy. But if Gray Beard said it was an emergency, David had to put some stock in that, even if he didn't like it.

"I'll buzz open the gate," David said. "Come in through the side yard. The box is out back." He hit the button to open the gate, retrieved his nine, and went to go wait on whatever was about to happen next.

By the time Matthew, Gray Beard, and Marvin made it into the backyard, David was sitting at a table beneath an umbrella on the far side of the pool. He had a tumbler of scotch, Macallan 30, the good shit, in one hand and his nine in the other.

"Right there is good," David said. He took a sip of scotch. Matthew Drew seemed smaller from this vantage point. The last time he'd seen the former FBI agent was about six weeks earlier, Matthew pretending to be a long-lost cousin to get access in the ICU, but once David was on a more private floor, those visits had to end. Last thing David needed was for Bennie Savone to meet the man. But during their hospital visits, they'd come to an accord. They were both wanted men who could only be helped by the other.

"That a saltwater pool?" Matthew said.

"It is," David said.

"That a Glock?"

"It is."

"Didn't figure you to be Glock guy," Matthew said.

"I like to be familiar with what the cops shooting at me might be using. What are you carrying?"

"Situation like this, I'd probably have a personal Smith & Wesson .380, light, easy to conceal, get up close, do some real damage. And then my service Glock for when I needed to put thirty rounds into you. But today, I come in peace."

"Marvin," David said, motioning with the gun. "Unbutton that big motherfucker's shirt for me."

Marvin looked at Gray Beard, like he needed permission, and then didn't move.

"It don't need to be like that," Gray Beard said. "You want to know if he's got a gun on him, I'm here to tell you he does not."

"Not worried about a gun," David said. "Just want to be sure we're not broadcasting."

"What about those cameras?" Matthew pointed to two security cameras mounted on the house. "And those?" Four security cameras pointed over David's back wall.

"I cut the power. Go look, Marvin."

Gray Beard said, "Check it."

Marvin did, pulling out the sliced power cables from each. "Couldn't have just unplugged them?"

"Never liked them, anyway," David said.

"It's fine," Matthew said. He unbuttoned his Cox Cable uniform shirt, spun around on the patio. Lifted up his pants, showed his ankles.

"I'm clean." He pointed at David. "How about Marvin retrieves your gun and then we can have a brief conversation."

David didn't love this idea. But he did have a butterfly knife in his pocket. But if it came to that, David knew which team Gray Beard and Marvin would play for. "Fine," David said. He flipped his gun around in his hand, so he was holding the barrel. Marvin came over, snapped on a pair of medical gloves, took the gun.

"We leave you alone," Gray Beard said, "you boys going to play nice?"

Matthew shrugged. "If he can find another glass for that nice scotch," he said.

When David came back with a glass, Matthew Drew had his eyes closed and face turned up to the sun. "Feels good," he said. "Not spending a lot of time outdoors, as you might imagine."

"All this shit to avoid jail," David said. He poured two fingers of scotch into Matthew's glass. "What's the emergency?"

"FBI agent rolled up on me while I was eating lunch," Matthew said. "Funny thing, you know her." He told David about his conversation with Kristy Levine, took down most of his scotch in the process. David gave him a refill. Topped himself off, too. It was going to be a long night and it wasn't even noon.

"She's not dumb," David said. "If she looks at your evidence, she'll come to the same conclusions you did."

"I haven't given her anything," Matthew said. "The FBI won't make a move until they have enough for an indictment. Poremba has anything on you, right now? It's inadmissible. He needs to back his way into you. No one is flipping; you have nothing to worry about."

David wasn't so sure about that. All he had keeping him safe with Matthew was that he knew the truth about the murder of Ronnie Cupertine's wife and kids, which had been pinned on Matthew. Namely, that they'd been dug up and sent to Las Vegas for burial, which meant someone in the Mafia—namely Peaches Pocotillo—didn't want them found. And David knew that it was Ruben Topaz who dropped the bodies off in Portland, because he'd ordered it. The only alibi Drew had for those bodies, filled with bullets from his gun, was sitting right in front of him.

"For tonight, maybe," David said. "Have you seen my face?"

"You look like a young Pacino. Like *Dog Day Afternoon*. When he had an edge."

"Never saw that one."

"Sure you did," he said. "You know. 'Attica! Attica!'"

"Oh yes," David said. "Bank robbers."

"Right. Grow your hair out, you could be him. Get a full beard, you'll be *Serpico*. Wouldn't that be dry."

David had worried that Jennifer and William wouldn't recognize him with his first plastic surgery. What about now that he looked like a guy wearing a Sal Cupertine Halloween mask?

"I make this Kristy Levine disappear," David said, "what happens?"

"Five hundred agents descend on Las Vegas," Matthew said, "and we both go to prison. Plus I'd be obligated to come for you."

"After what the FBI did to you?"

Matthew said, "Don't see you fleeing this saltwater pool and mansion. After all the mob did to you, Rain Man."

"Don't fucking call me that," David said.

Matthew put his hands up. "Point being. You can't kill your way out of this."

That was, in fact, David's thinking, too. Not that he was keen to kill her. He liked her. She was part of his congregation. He helped her pick out her grave, for fuck's sake. Since then, prior to David getting his face crushed, she'd become a regular at Temple Beth Israel. David even helped coordinate rides to her chemo appointments.

"I don't suppose you've found my family."

"No," Matthew said. "Poremba's given me some intel. Safe houses in Arizona and Oregon, one in Utah, all come up empty. His chain goes high, but not high enough. Can't break any laws, you know?"

"Shit."

"Hence." Matthew put his arms up. "Here I am in your beautiful home."

"Do you think this Kristy knows . . . something?"

Matthew took a sip of the scotch. "Yes," he said. "She knows you're here. She doesn't know where. Or why. But she knows. What happens when she sees you?"

"She'll see what she wants to see," David said. "She only sees her rabbi."

Matthew stared at David. Ten, fifteen, twenty seconds. "Until she doesn't."

"I'll be ready for that."

Matthew took out a piece of paper from his clipboard, put it on the table between them. "Look who is in the neighborhood."

It was a news release from Gold Mountain Mining announcing the hiring of Kirk Biglione as their new director of corporate security. Gold Mountain was an oil and lithium operation with offices around the world—Australia, Chile, China, Saudi Arabia, and Dallas—and Biglione's hiring landed him in trade publications and corporate newsletters. You want to be serious about your corporate security, is there someone more qualified than the former top FBI agent from one of the nation's busiest offices?

David kept reading through the canned quotes to get to the meat of the news: Gold Mountain's latest venture would be on the shores of the Salton Sea, the ecological disaster forty miles east of Palm Springs. Gold Mountain was breaking ground on their latest geothermal plant, one poised to extract lithium. "The path to being free from Middle East oil interests is a future rich with electric cars, made right here with American lithium batteries," the release proclaimed. Biglione would be based out of the Salton Sea office for the next six weeks.

The Salton Sea was only a few hours away. They could leave right now and be standing in front of Kirk Biglione before the sun went down.

"Why isn't Biglione in prison?" David asked. "How does he have a six-figure job like this?"

"That plant goes," Matthew said, "I'd guess it's more like a seven-figure job."

"He's a gangster, all right," David said. What all the press releases and articles left out, but which David told Matthew about one afternoon when he was still in the hospital, loaded on painkillers and anti-infection meds, was that Kirk Biglione came from a connected family, had even done an internship with The Family before going off to college, and that the rumor in The Family was that he was the very reason they were still in business and The Outfit had melted into nothing. Yeah, the local FBI was going to bust The Family when they did major shit wrong, but Biglione wasn't going to be hauling in Ronnie Cupertine for anything short of assassinating the president, and even then, they'd probably find a patsy first. If The Family kept the ecosystem in control—street gangsters killing street gangsters was fine; mobsters killing mobsters was actually good for local tourism, so that was also fine—everyone stayed busy on both sides of the law. But if civilians started getting lit up, little kids eating drive-by strays and shit? That wasn't going to work. Same with the Mafia. If some mobster killed a wife or a child, that ended up on national news. Kill a cop or an agent? People would start losing their jobs, which in the FBI meant Jeff Hopper and Matthew Drew hit the streets. In the mob, that meant Sal Cupertine got shipped to Las Vegas.

David knew now that Ronnie Cupertine had been snitching on himself all these years, working essentially as an unpaid CI for the FBI since god knows when, and that had worked out fine when Kirk Biglione was the man in charge of the organized crime division. But when Biglione got bumped up and ended up overseeing the entire FBI field office, leaving Jeff Hopper in charge of the organized crime division, well, that shit wasn't gonna fly. Sal Cupertine was supposed to die. Ronnie and Biglione could have closed the doors on their relationship. But instead . . . this shit show.

David wasn't surprised Matthew had this new intel on Biglione. From the moment the cocksucker got charged in the corruption scandal surrounding the FBI's handling of the Sal Cupertine incident—how Cupertine managed to kill three agents and a CI without a backup team within ten miles of the site; how and why the FBI were led to believe a body found in the Poyter landfill was Cupertine; why Jeff Hopper (and Matthew) had been fired for whistleblowing—Matthew had kept eyes on him.

After Biglione pled guilty, earning a suspended sentence, he landed a top corporate-security job outside of Detroit. Not every day an ex-FBI agent lands in Bloomfield Hills, even one with a felony on his sheet. If G. Gordon Liddy got to host his own syndicated talk radio show and own a countersurveillance firm, what was stopping a small fry like Kirk Biglione from becoming a full corporate potato?

"How does he help us?" David asked, though what he actually meant was, *How does he help me?*

"He needs to go down," Matthew said, "but before that happens, he's the one guy who'd know where your wife and kid are. Half his job was probably coordinating with the U.S. Marshals on shit like this."

"How do you intend to get information from him?"

Matthew said, "One toe at a time."

"You ever torture someone before?"

"No. I've only recently become a criminal."

"It's messy and it's time-consuming."

"You have a better idea?" Matthew said.

"Drug him," David said. "Get whatever you can out of him, then kill him."

"Just like that."

"Just like that," David said. "He's not giving up nuclear codes. He's giving up possible safe houses to someone he believes is going to kill people he'd like to see dead. Because if my wife is in a safe house, she's giving up information, right?"

"Right."

"You could probably give him a Hershey bar and he'd tell you, if he's worried my wife will have something on him."

"Does she?"

David thought about that for a moment. By the time they were together, all she might have heard was that Kirk Biglione was crooked in
a good way. She wouldn't have a negative view of the man that had kept
her husband and her friends' husbands out of prison. She'd surely seen
the news reports about the trial and how the FBI faked Sal's death, but
that was all public record. She didn't have anything new.

"No," David said.

Matthew nodded his head, exhaled hard, like he'd been relieved
of some pressing burden. "Kirk Biglione doesn't exist," he said, "my
sister is alive."

"That kind of thinking will fuck you up," David said. "Kirk Biglione dies, your sister doesn't rematerialize. Vengeance is never as sweet
as you think it will be."

"Kirk Biglione doesn't exist," Matthew said, "I'm not hunting you
down for the rest of your life, either."

"Won't happen," David said. "Time comes, I won't make it hard on
you. I'll let you down easy."

"Could be sooner than you think."

David poured himself more scotch then put the cork back into
the bottle, pushed it toward Matthew. "Find my family, get your vengeance, give me a day head start, and we're square. You end up bringing me in, you have my word I'll exonerate you on everything."

"And what if you won't come alive?"

"What if you won't?"

Matthew thought about that. "I'll take a notarized letter. On Temple stationery."

"You're a crazy motherfucker," David said, but it actually made
some sense. He started to head inside.

"What about your bottle?" Matthew asked.

"All yours," David said. "For your service."

SIX

RABBI DAVID COHEN WOKE EARLY ON THE THIRD MONDAY IN APRIL, TWO DAYS after his meeting with Matthew; dressed in the dark; and waited for Bennie Savone, since technically he still wasn't allowed to drive, even though he'd been discharged from the hospital a week earlier. Every anti-infection drug he was on recommended he stay away from heavy machinery, never mind that driving on Klonopin wasn't exactly encouraged. But he was weaning himself, even against doctor's orders, because he needed some fucking clarity of thought for the task at hand.

So he was surprised, to say the least, when he saw on his security camera what looked like a police cruiser pull into his driveway. Except that instead of the Las Vegas Metropolitan Police's logo on the door—which included an unmistakable silver seven-pointed star—it said TEMPLE BETH ISRAEL SECURITY across the door, the *A* in *Israel* a Star of David.

Classy.

David's home phone rang.

"Rabbi? This is Officer Cecil Kiraly; I'm out front in a cruiser."

"I see you," David said. "May I ask what you're doing here?"

"Mr. Savone asked me to come get you," he said. "He's under the weather."

"I'm sorry," David said, "do I know you?"

"No, sir, I'm pretty new."

"Give me just one moment," David said.

When did the Temple get its own cruisers? David zoomed the

security camera in, made sure there weren't U.S. Marshals in the back-seat. Panned over to Officer Kiraly. He wore the standard uniform all the off-duty cops in his employ wore, which is to say he looked just like a cop, except he also had Kevlar on over his uniform, which seemed excessive for limousine service.

The phone rang again.

"David," Rachel Savone said, "you don't have a cell phone?"

"I guess I don't anymore," David said.

"You need a cell phone," she said. "Here's Bennie, hold on."

Bennie said, "The man out front. He's fine. Don't fucking shoot him."

"He's a cop."

"You hired him," Bennie said. His voice sounded scratchy.

"You sick?"

"Got something going on in my throat." Bennie Savone had thyroid cancer a decade earlier. Whenever he got a cold, he started working on his will. "Probably something Sophie brought home. Woke up with a fever. Anyway. Cecil, he's going to drive you today. He's fine. I went to school with his father. Works Metro. One of the good ones. We doubled security today regardless."

"Why?"

"Do you not watch the news?"

"No," David said.

"Jesus," he said. "When you get to the Temple, read *The New York Times* online, okay?"

"Is there a problem?"

"There's a siege at the Church of the Nativity," he said. "Palestinians took it over. You're supposed to be on high alert."

"Church of the Nativity. Is that on the west side?"

"In *Bethlehem*, Rabbi."

"Oh," David said. "Got it. I'll be on the lookout."

"Jesus, Rabbi," Bennie said. "Pretend, okay? Rachel will be by later this afternoon." And then he was gone.

David watched Cecil Kiraly for a few more seconds. It was true: David had hired a passel of off-duty cops to provide security for Temple Beth Israel and the other synagogues in town. He hadn't approved the purchasing of Temple cruisers, however. Four months he was gone and now the Temple had its own armored rides.

Cecil was probably thirty. Buzz cut. Tan. Biceps. Big gold watch. Any other city, he'd probably be a bouncer; in Las Vegas, he was a cop. That's just how it was.

David checked his watch: 7:02 a.m. He had meetings all day at the Temple, plus two funerals. Shit to sign. Things to keep Temple Beth Israel running. All this time pretending to be a straight guy ended with him having a straight guy's job, in addition to everything else. He'd woken up early not because he was worried he'd have to kill whoever showed up at his house that morning, but because he knew he had Excel spreadsheets piled on his desk at the Temple and the mere idea of it all was making him sweaty.

Plus, it was already over 80 degrees. David would never get used to the heat of Las Vegas. This time of year in Chicago, it was still fucking freezing. And then a thought came to him. Four years ago, to the day, he'd wager, he walked into this house for the first time. Back then, he was still Sal Cupertine, didn't know a word of Hebrew, and had the foolish notion that by now, he'd be back in Chicago with Jennifer and William and out of this mess. Was he any closer today than he was then? Still in the desert, staring through a wormhole into his own past.

David grabbed his butterfly knife, slid it into his breast pocket, along with his kippah. This time, he'd be the decision maker. Things went south, he wouldn't wait for someone to do the right thing.

"You can get into the front," Cecil said when David opened the back door of the cruiser.

"I prefer the backseat," David said.

Cecil shrugged, so David slid in behind him and they took off.

"What's with the vest?" David said after a while.

"Heard you've got enemies," Cecil said.

"What are you gonna do if they aim for your face?"

Cecil laughed. "We're on high alert, in light of events in the Middle East. Just a precaution, sir."

"Mr. Savone tells me he went to school with your father."

Cecil looked at David in the rearview mirror. "Yes, sir," he said. "Bishop Gorman. It's where I went, too. Class of 1989."

David nodded. Every Las Vegan of a certain age went to Bishop Gorman. They talked about it like they'd gone to Harvard. David wanted the Barer Academy to hold that kind of weight, but he understood that one day, when David's true story was told, the Barer Academy would mean something entirely different.

"Thing is," Cecil said, "we're Jews, but not Jews-Jews, you know? My mom, she's nothing anymore. Not even spiritual. My dad is Jewish on holidays. Back then, when my dad and Mr. Savone were in school, there was no Jewish high school, so everyone just went to Bishop Gorman. And then when I went to high school, we were a Bishop Gorman family."

"Explain that to the Nazis when they show up," David said.

"Pardon me?"

"Your mother was born Jewish?"

"Yes, but no one can spell *Hanukkah*." He held up his right hand. "And then I've got this dumb shit." Across his knuckles he had a tattoo of Hebrew letters: תָּרֵכ. It was the Hebrew word *kareth*. *Kareth* had different meanings in the Talmud, depending upon what one took literally. It could either mean dying young without children or it could mean you were a soulless motherfucker cut off from your family and the world due to irredeemable sin, or because the sinner simply doesn't give a fuck and is happy with his own iniquity. It was some shit David understood, certainly, but he couldn't imagine getting it tatted up across the knuckles, the mere act of which was probably enough for old-school Jews to cut you off permanently. But David had the sense Cecil was aiming for something like the Hebrew equivalent of *bad motherfucker.* If you had to tell people, though, that usually meant the opposite.

"You're still Jewish," David said. "Even with that ink. Emotion doesn't change identity. It's confusing to know who you are when you're young, but you're a man now, so I will solve it for you. Officer Cecil Kiraly, you're Jewish. Mazel tov."

Officer Cecil Kiraly laughed. "All right then. More days off."

They wound through the streets of Summerlin. In the months David had been in the hospital down the block, nothing of *substance* had changed and yet everything seemed slightly different. Trees and bushes had grown. Grass had expanded. A new Starbucks opened on that corner, a new Baja Fresh on this corner, a new tanning salon was COMING SOON into what used to be the Quiznos, a new Port of Subs was COMING SOON, next to the Coffee Bean. A CVS was COMING SOON a few blocks south of the synagogue. David couldn't imagine who would drink all of this coffee, who would fill these fast-food restaurants, who would need so many prescriptions. The Talmud said that after the fall of the Holy Temple, prophecy was left to the mentally ill and the children.

"What's your beat, officer?"

"Gang unit," Cecil said, meeting David's eyes again in the rearview. "You like it?"

"Don't have to arrest too many of my friends," he said. "Which was a nice change from vice. Appreciate this job, though; we haven't had much overtime lately. Streets have been pretty quiet since 9/11."

"Why is that?"

"Patriot Act has even the Bloods and Crips worried. They all think they're OG enough to get wiretapped without a warrant or that we've got every camera trained on their corner deals. But we're only fishing for whales right now. Sell your weed. Who cares as long as you're not crashing a plane into the Excalibur."

They turned up Hillpointe and there was yet another COMING SOON sign: Kales Assisted Living & Memory Home, a "Sixteen-Acre

Premier Medical and Retirement Destination Featuring Three Pools, a Putting Green, Pickle Ball Courts, and On-Site Five-Star Medical Facilities! Taking Deposits NOW! Live Longer. Live Better. Live."

Cecil pulled into Temple Beth Israel's parking lot, about ten feet from where David strangled Melanie Moss, before ultimately snapping her neck. She was standing there, watching him.

"I'm here all day," Cecil said, which brought David back to the present, "so if you need anything, just call." He handed David one of his Las Vegas Metro business cards. "That's my cell phone on there. And when you're ready to head home, I'm your wheels, Rabbi."

"Thank you," David said. He opened the door and stepped out. Melanie had David's tefillin around her neck, still.

"You okay?" Cecil asked, his window down. "Your color got bad real quick."

"Just stood up too quickly," David said.

"Okay, you sure there's nothing I can do for you?"

David turned to him. "Look into getting that ink off your knuckles if you wish to continue working here," he said, not unkindly. "The survivors here are easily triggered, and that matters to me a great deal."

"I never thought about it," Cecil said.

"I know," David said. "But now you have. You have the inner *sholem* to not hurt someone you've never met. Take that opportunity."

DAVID WAS WRONG ABOUT ONE THING: HIS DESK AT TEMPLE BETH ISRAEL WAS covered in get-well cards, not spreadsheets. Hundreds of them. Handwritten cards from the day school children, fancy Hallmark cards from the parents and congregants. Stacks from the other temples, churches, and mosques in town. Even one from Harvey B. Curran at the *Review-Journal*. The spreadsheets were stacked on his coffee table.

"Everyone has missed you so much," his receptionist, Esther, said. "Mr. Savone had me open them, in case there were checks inside, but I didn't read them."

"Were there?"

"A few," she said. "I deposited them for you." She opened his blinds, flooding his office in light. "I watered your plants every day. Dusted your books."

"Thank you, Esther," David said. He sat down behind his desk. Through the window he could see the Barer Academy, the Temple's K–12 school, and a sliver of the Performing Arts Center, plus the land movers had lined up to start hauling away dirt to build the assisted living facility.

"Mrs. Savone had us replace your computer," she said.

"Why?"

"She said you probably had a bug," Esther said.

"A virus?"

"Right, yes," Esther said, "but she called it a bug. She had us purchase a laptop."

"Such kindness," David said. David flipped open the cover. There was a Post-it Note on the screen that read, in Rachel's schoolgirl script, "Pick a better password."

"Since you've been gone, Mrs. Savone has been here most days, helping Rabbi Kales with the business of things," Esther said. She kneaded her hands. "He's slipped so much, Rabbi Cohen. The stress has had a negative effect on him. And then to lose his contemporaries in town, like Rabbi Siegel, it must have been such an emotional challenge for him. Everyone his age is dying."

To be fair, David had poisoned Rabbi Siegel to get him to go along with the security plan for the local temples. But he would have died, eventually.

"Live long enough," David said, "that's the curse."

"The sorrow of this world," Esther said, and then she just kind of drifted off. She was in her sixties now. Her husband, Paul, had been hit by a city bus years earlier and she'd worked at the Temple ever since, not even drawing a salary, since she lived comfortably off of a settlement that she was not at liberty to discuss.

"Well," David said, "I'm back now." He tried to smile, and, to his surprise, his face reacted with the proper action. "Can you please give me ninety minutes of privacy, Esther? I'd like some time to read the Torah. When Mrs. Savone comes in, please do let me know. So I can thank her."

"Of course, Rabbi," she said. She pointed at the mountain of cards. "Do you want me to start writing thank-you notes for you?"

There must have been three hundred cards.

"No," David said, "I'm happy to do it."

Esther made it to the door and then turned around, David just a few steps behind her. "I like your new face, Rabbi," she said. "You're still you."

"Thank you, Esther. I was worried."

"But if you don't mind me saying so," she said, "you have a much nicer smile now."

David closed the door behind her, then fired up the computer. Four months he'd been in the hospital, he'd been completely off the internet, Bennie of the opinion that bringing him a laptop was only inviting trouble. He was probably right, but the end result was that all David knew about the world was filtered through the journalism of the *Las Vegas Review-Journal*, which was like looking at humanity through the eyes of Sheldon Adelson and Steve Wynn, since they bought all the advertising and therefore controlled most of the coverage, the result being that you believed a holy war was about to take place on the streets of Las Vegas, that the Krispy Kreme on Spring Mountain was an Al-Qaeda training ground, and that United Airlines might be a front for Bin Laden. There wasn't a conspiracy theory one of their dumb-fuck op-ed writers didn't chase down to the root and then leave dangling. Could David Cassidy be leaving his live show to fight the mujahideen? Maybe!

Harvey B. Curran spent his eight hundred words, twice a week, tying everything to organized crime, but with Bennie Savone keeping a low profile, and the casino magnets trying to portray Las Vegas as a place to bring the family even though 9/11 was plotted during lap dances all over town, he'd been forced to focus lately on the arrival of Eastern European and Russian gangsters. They'd been buying up restaurants and nightclubs off the strip, blackmailing Metro cops, and disappearing more people than fucking David Copperfield. Hard to charge someone with murder when no one could find a body.

What David needed to know, however, was more specific. He went to Google and did the one thing he'd avoided doing for the last four years: He typed in his name. Well. His other name. Sal Cupertine.

The first pages that came up were what he expected.

There were the stories in the *Chicago Tribune* detailing the murders at the Parker House, followed by the feature stories on corruption in the FBI, most of which had been given to the paper by Sal himself, pretending to be Jeff Hopper. There were various updates based on news stories and TV appearances. There'd been a rerun of *America's Most Wanted* again, and that triggered what Fresno newscasters called "an amusing story" about the guy who portrayed Sal in the reenactments getting spotted at a local bar where the episode was airing. It was an amusing story, David had to admit. The guy got a free Michelob for his troubles and a nice plug for his appearance in a traveling show of *Death of a Salesman* at the Saroyan Theatre in Fresno.

When all of Ronnie Cupertine's family showed up last December, cut into little pieces, in a parking lot in Portland, killed with a gun tied to Matthew Drew, Sal's name popped up everywhere, the supposition being that his disappearance was somehow tied to these murders. The supposition was probably correct, just not for the reasons they could imagine.

The story in the *Chicago Reader* was the one he did not expect. It was an essay written by a woman named Stacy Elliott, who apparently worked with Jennifer at the Museum of Modern Photography. It was called "The Hit Man's Wife in My Cubicle."

David didn't need to read it to know how it was going to end, the writer finding some epiphany while staring out the window at a floating paper bag. But he kept scrolling, not sure what he was looking for, until he found it: staring out at him from his computer screen were Jennifer and William.

It was a photo he'd taken on Christmas morning, 1997. Jennifer in bed, hair in a ponytail, wearing an old T-shirt from the neighborhood—Bruno's Fine Meats—William snuggled beside her, *Where the Wild Things Are* open between them, the room filled with pale light. David remembered it had snowed the night before, but that morning, the air was misty, giving everything the glow of a memory. They had a rule in the house about pictures—nothing that had to be developed outside the home, owing to the fact that Sal was the most wanted hit man on the planet—but they also were normal parents, or tried to be. So they had a Polaroid and Jennifer had her darkroom in the basement. On Christmas, Sal took stacks of Polaroids, even put a few into the mail for his mother, Arlene, in Arizona, long after they stopped speaking, because he still wanted her to see William growing up, Sal perpetually snarled up about such things.

But that photo, it had gone on the refrigerator moments later, and Sal would see it every day, until he surely took it for granted, until he stopped seeing it altogether. And now he had to wonder: did he remember the photo, or did he remember the moment? The photo must have migrated from the refrigerator to Jennifer's desk . . . and then into the hands of someone at the *Chicago Reader*. And now, it was online, theoretically available to billions of people, anyone who wanted to know what Sal Cupertine's wife and kid looked like. A singular moment in his life, and now David had to share it with the world?

But now David was grateful. He hadn't seen his wife or son since the day he left Chicago. And though his memory was supposedly flawless, he'd begun to lose threads of their appearance. Did Jennifer have a mole on her right cheek or her left? Where was that little birthmark William had that looked like dried honey? Under his right ear? Or his left? And other details in their room, captured in the flat expanse of the photo, began to pull him through time. The clock on the bedside table—an old-school alarm clock, the kind you wound—belonged to Sal's father. It didn't work. But he kept it on his nightstand. At once a talisman and a reminder. You never know when your last day might be coming, so get up, get moving, stay frosty. Where was that clock now?

Gone, he supposed, with .the rest of the house. Burned to the ground by whoever this Peaches motherfucker was. He'd killed Ronnie's family, he'd burned Sal's house down, he'd pushed Jennifer and William into protective custody, and for what? To get Sal to appear? So he could have sole control of The Family?

When David sent Ruben to drop off Ronnie's wife and kids' bodies in public, it was to let Peaches know Sal Cupertine wasn't to be played, that he made his own rules. But now, what did it matter? All David wanted was Jennifer and William. He could give a fuck about The Family. All The Family had ever done was try to ruin his life, from the very moment he saw his father hit the pavement. The Talmud teaches that one Jew is equal to the entire world, that each has the chance to change the world, for better or worse, and for a long time David thought that meant his happiness was the most important thing, that his desires could not be superseded. But then every day he sat in this office, listening to the problems of his congregants, and it became clear to him that the Talmud didn't mean we are each in control of all the worlds, only our own, and that if we are to serve our Maker with joy in our hearts, as the sages taught, then that world had better be worth it. So David had begun to build margins around his world, right up until the day some fucking coked-up MMA fighter punched him in the face.

Sitting in that hospital for all those months, realizing he could die and his wife and son would never know, that he'd be buried under a different name and might never be found . . . it began to chafe against all he'd learned as a rabbi. Rabbi Kales once told him that there was no postwar for him, that he would always be chased, for the rest of his life, and that he must settle that in his mind, and for a time David thought he'd be content knowing that his son wouldn't have that life. But now he knew William was in protective custody, and that part of his life would never stop being true: someone would want to make their bones by killing him. That's just how it was. As long as William was a Cupertine, there was no postwar for him, either.

David hit the print icon and seconds later, he was holding Jennifer and William in his hands for the first time in years.

This.

This was his postwar.

Not in Chicago.

Not in Las Vegas.

Not in a fucking grave beside one another. He knew that for sure. Somewhere else.

There was a knock on his door and then Esther opened it a crack. "I'm sorry, Rabbi, I know you said you need some quiet time, but Karen Weiss is here and she's in quite a state. Her dog, Lefty, was run over. Is it possible to speak with her for just a few minutes?"

David folded the printout in half and slid it into his breast pocket, under his knife.

"Of course," Rabbi David Cohen said. "Let the world in."

RACHEL SAVONE SHOWED UP AFTER TWO. SHE CAUGHT DAVID AS HE WAS walking back from the Performing Arts Center, where he'd done a large funeral for Ace Lampkin, who'd played with Artie Shaw back in the day, and so half the funeral was old men with clarinets and trombones and stand-up basses working through big-band classics and sobbing. It had been one of the most glorious funerals David had ever presided over, the shared mourning of a bassline something he'd never heard but would remember ever more. The Lampkin family rabbi flew in to do the graveside, so David was done for the day when Rachel pulled up beside him in her convertible Mercedes.

"Do you want a ride?" she asked.

David looked up and down the street. Armed off-duty cops were in front of all the buildings the Temple owned. Plus, they had plain-clothes guys cruising in rented Town Cars, what with the siege going on in Israel. Each cop had eyes on David now; David could practically hear them radioing each other: *Godfather on the move from PAC, headed south back to base.* Someone had been too slow to stop David from getting lit up the last time he walked these streets, even if the "official" story was that he tripped at the Performing Arts Center. Sergeant Behen had been right there, had seen everything go down, and though David didn't blame him—how could he?—Behen blamed himself for letting that MMA fighter sucker-punch him, knocking him down the stairs, nearly killing him. Behen resigned, then retired from LVPD, convinced that he was too slow for the job now. He ended up moving to his fishing spot in San Felipe, then sent David a long letter apologizing profusely for not doing the one thing he was paid to do: protect and serve. David wrote him back this afternoon, just five words: *It was my own fault.*

"It's nice to walk," David said. "It's been a long time."

"Then I'll walk with you," she said.

She parked her car on the street but didn't bother to put the top up. If someone was dumb enough to rob Rachel Savone, well, they had their fate coming, David supposed, since the Temple's security guards were all armed and itching to fuck someone up, just like all Vegas cops, ever. Rachel popped the trunk and dropped her phone inside.

"Worried you're being tracked?" David said.

"No," Rachel said, "I stopped being worried about that years ago. The nice thing about paranoia is that you're not surprised when the FBI does have ears on you."

David wanted to laugh. Wanted this whole situation to be funny, because at the bottom, at least, it was absurd.

"How's Bennie?"

"I left him there," she said. "They're going to do a PET scan, just to be sure. It's all probably nothing. Besides, we practically own the hospital now. May as well get our money's worth."

"I want to thank you for everything you did while I was incapacitated," David said.

"It was nothing," she said.

"It wasn't nothing," he said. In fact, Rachel had managed all of his care. Whenever David had any complaint, large or small, it was handled immediately. He didn't like his blanket? A goose-down duvet was delivered from Bloomingdale's. He couldn't sleep because of the noise inside the hospital? A white noise machine appeared on his bedside table. It all happened without a word of attribution, but he knew this was because of Rachel. "Why didn't you visit?"

"I couldn't see you like that." She pointed up ahead, toward the Temple. The parking lot was filling with cars, David could see. Must be the parents coming to pick their children up from the day school. "My father would like to see you this week. If you have a moment."

"Of course," David said. "How did the naming ceremony go?"

"He didn't make it," she said. "He's slipped very far, you should know."

"Okay," David said.

"Which is why I didn't bring him to see you," she said. "I didn't think he should see you like that. I didn't think it would be good for you, either."

"I understand," David said, because of course he was the one who'd charted this course for Rabbi Cy Kales. It was either slip into dementia or slip off this mortal coil. Those were the two choices he'd been presented with, and over the course of the last two years, Rabbi Kales had played the role flawlessly. David was sure Rabbi Kales was as sharp as ever.

"I'm not sure you do," Rachel said. "He doesn't recognize Bennie anymore."

"What about the girls? How are they taking it?" David asked. She and Bennie had two daughters, Jean, who was sixteen, and Sophie, who was eight.

"It's all a holy terror," she said. "I need to get Jean on the pill before she comes home with a bump. And Sophie's wetting the bed again." She shook her head. "Our therapist thinks I should put them both in boarding school."

"You're seeing a therapist?"

"What was I supposed to do?" she said. "You weren't taking appointments in the hospital."

"Does Bennie know?"

"Jean's started cutting, too," Rachel said.

"What? When?"

"It's not your problem," Rachel said. "She did it at home and at school. Roberta Leeb called it in, I guess."

"It was Roberta's duty to report that," David said. He knew Roberta well. She was one of the few teachers at the Barer Academy who wasn't afraid to tell him, constantly, her thoughts about everything. "How'd you keep Child Protective Services out of it?"

"I don't know," Rachel said. "I assume my husband has powers of persuasion that I'm unfamiliar with."

"Bennie didn't tell me any of this," David said.

"Why would he?"

"I guess I just thought . . ." David paused, Rachel staring at him now, the hint of a smile on her face.

"What?" she said. She tucked her arm through his, pulled him close to her, whispered, "That you're a real rabbi?"

"I am," David said.

"You're not even Jewish, Rabbi Cohen," Rachel said.

David pulled away from Rachel, let her pass him on the sidewalk. They were in front of the Aquatic Center now. He'd overseen the final stages of that building, helped raise the last $150,000 to equip the dressing rooms with indoor warm-down pools, what the coaches swore was needed to turn the Barer Academy's young swimmers into Olympic hopefuls. David could hear the voices of children, the whistles of coaches. He could take out his knife and plunge it into Rachel's back, drag her into a thicket of bougainvillea, dump her body, hope for the best for a few hours, then have her in a grave after sundown.

But there, on the light pole, was a missing-person flyer for Melanie Moss, the last woman he'd killed for being in the wrong place at the wrong time, for confusing David, for presenting an obstacle to his freedom, her presence still walking around in his subconscious, and sometimes his conscious, too, like right now. Melanie standing in her government-proper black slacks, blue shirt, and black jacket, her neck crooked from David snapping it.

"Everything okay, Rabbi Cohen?"

David whipped to the right, his knife in hand. One of his security guards stepped out of the shadows between the Aquatic Center and the center's admin offices, David a millisecond from plunging his knife into the man's eye.

"I'm fine," David said. "I didn't see you there."

"That's the whole point, Rabbi," the officer said. He grabbed David's wrist, gingerly, pressed his arm down. "Sir, you don't need that knife. I know you're scared, but all having a knife will do is give a bad guy another way to kill you."

"Yes," David said. "Thank you." He put the knife back into his breast pocket. "I'm not myself these days."

"I know, Rabbi," he said. "Which is why we're all looking out for you. You're on the safest street in America right now, sir."

WHEN DAVID CAUGHT UP TO RACHEL, SHE WAS DIGGING A LIGHTER FROM HER purse, a cigarette between her teeth. "You want one?" she asked.

"You know I don't smoke."

"Just do a little heroin?"

"I don't know what you think you know," David said, "but you're wrong."

"I know who you really are. I was with you when the EMTs arrived," she said. "When they asked for your name, you told them you were Sal Cupertine. You asked them to call your wife, Jennifer. You told them your father was dead, that your mother, Arlene, lived in Arizona, and that you have a son named William. You gave them a home address and a phone number in Chicago." Rachel exhaled a plume of smoke. Stopped and picked a fleck of tobacco from her teeth, looked at it on her pinky, wiped it on her hip. "Everything else I wanted to know is practically public record at this point. You've had quite the life, Mr. Cuperti—" David put his hand up between them.

"Rachel," he said, quietly, "I am not your husband. I am the man who does what your husband won't. So I'd urge you to choose your next words very carefully. They may be your last."

Rachel Savone's eyes were saucers, but she said, "You don't scare me."

"Good. Now. Tell me exactly what happened with the EMTs."

David removed his hand.

"Jesus Christ, Rabbi, I covered for you! I told them you were speaking madness," Rachel said. "That's how I knew you were seriously injured. I don't think they wrote anything down. They were too busy making sure you didn't choke to death on your own blood. They were asking basic questions to keep you alert. It wasn't to snitch you out to the FBI. The next thing they did was intubate you."

"Are you sure?"

"David," Rachel said, "are you in prison right now?"

"How do I know you're not wired?"

"How do I know *you're* not wired?" She took another drag on her cigarette, let out another huge plume of smoke, watched it disappear. "I have much more to lose than you."

"You shouldn't have come here today," David said. "You should get in your car and drive away. Leave the country if you can. Take your children and go."

"I know," Rachel said. "Now you have to kill me and everyone who has ever loved me. I get it." She took one of the burner phones from her purse and gave it to him. "I've been preparing for that eventuality. The only person who has this phone number is me. It rings, it's me. I've programmed my number into it. You need me, you just hit star 1. But if I call, it's not to talk about the weather, so please answer, okay?"

"Why do I need this?"

"Because I'm going to help you get out of here, Rabbi," she said. "And you're going to help me get out of here, too." She stopped, the two of them in front of the funeral home and across the street from Temple Beth Israel. She reached over and adjusted David's tie, swept lint from his coat. "Now, there's about a hundred of your flock waiting inside the Temple, to surprise you. I heard talk of a clown making balloon art. There's cookies and punch and everyone has brought you a dish, so be grateful and kind and accept every single kugel and brisket and trough of chicken noodle soup as the perfect kindness it is, understand? Because your congregants missed Rabbi David Cohen a great deal. To them, you are the very light of Hashem, and in your absence, Temple Beth Israel has been a very dark place. Do you understand, Rabbi?"

David didn't answer, just started to make his way across the street, but then he stopped, looked back at Rachel standing on the sidewalk, watching him.

"Do you know where my wife is?"

"No," Rachel said. "I'm sorry."

A catering truck from the Bagel Café pulled up to the Temple. "Who's paying for this?" David asked.

"My husband," Rachel said. "Indirectly." She pointed at his eyes. "They're back. From the old photos I've seen. You don't look so dead inside now."

"Good," David said. "Maybe my mother will recognize me."

"I've only known David Cohen," she said. "You still look enough like him. Half of Summerlin has had work done by the same plastic surgeon, so they'll just recognize themselves."

"I show up in Chicago unannounced. Stand on Michigan Avenue. What happens?"

"You're a dead man," Rachel said.

David nodded. Melanie Moss was standing beside Rachel, pointing at him. He was losing his fucking mind.

"What if I don't help you?" David said.

"You will," she said. "You're a good man, somewhere."

"I'm not," David said. "If we were alone, you'd already be dead."

"That's your learned nature," Rachel said. "But it's not who you want to be. I know that now."

There was an eruption of music from the Temple. Neil Diamond's "Sweet Caroline." It was going to be that kind of party.

"You shouldn't have told me," David said.

"I know," Rachel said, "but I couldn't have you gutting a bunch of children."

"I meant the other thing," David said.

"So did I," Rachel said. She put out her cigarette, joined David in the middle of the street, put her arm through his again, walked him across the street to the Temple. "Light of Hashem," she whispered into his ear, "Sal Cupertine, that's you."

SEVEN

THAT NIGHT, AFTER OFFICER KIRALY DROPPED HIM OFF AT HOME, RABBI DAVID
Cohen spent an hour working the tactical dummy, snapping jabs,
sharp overhand rights, lefts to the kidneys, then worked his forearm
mashes, did fifteen minutes of elbow strikes, pinpointing his elbow
right between the dummy's eyes each time. Next, he slipped on his
father's brass knuckles and pounded his palms, both sides getting ten
punches, to toughen up his skin, the old scar tissue giving way a little
with each concussion. By the time he was done, he was covered in
a sheen of sweat and his knuckles were torn open and bleeding. He
showered, pulled on a hooded sweatshirt, black sweatpants, and black
tennis shoes, a nine on both ankles, hopped his back wall, and jogged
the three miles to the shopping center on the corner of Sahara and
Fort Apache, his wind for shit. Before the hospital, he could run ten
miles on a summer day.

David went to a pay phone and called the one person in all of Las
Vegas he trusted, then waited for him to show up.

Took an hour, but eventually a FedEx van pulled up, Gray Beard
behind the wheel.

"New ride?" David asked when he got in the passenger seat.

"Had to work fast," Gray Beard said.

David looked behind him at the van filled with boxes. "You gonna
return this? That's about five hundred federal crimes back there."

"Might just deliver them myself," Gray Beard said. "Might find
I enjoy the work." They drove a couple blocks, to the Summerlin Library parking lot, which was lit like Wrigley Field for a night game to

keep the homeless from sleeping in the bushes. David knew the homeless preferred the labyrinth of storm drains beneath the city, anyway, the Temple often going down there on holidays to hand out food and gift cards.

Gray Beard parked in the far corner of the lot, beneath a towering light pole, which flooded the inside of the van with light. Nothing new under the sun, Gray Beard always said, so you wouldn't bother to look hard at what wasn't trying to hide.

He took a penlight from his breast pocket. "Take your hood down; I didn't get to see your new look the other day." David did. Gray Beard whistled. "Nice work. You hurt still?"

"Not too much," David said. "Not like before. Just sore."

"That's gonna be the case."

"How long?"

"Rest of your days." He moved David's chin from side to side. "Good movement, finally. Good, good. Open up, let me see inside." David did, Gray Beard shining the light in. "Never seen anything like it," he said. "I don't think I could work in the field anymore. I can't see how they do this. Like they built the Golden Gate Bridge under your sinuses." He tapped his index finger under David's right eye. "Those cadaver bones?"

"Yes."

"Well. That's ironic." He leaned back in his seat. "You like your face?"

"That's the thing," David said. "It's the one I started with."

"That's ironic, too," Gray Beard said. "What do I owe the pleasure?"

"I've sped up my timeline," David said.

"For what?"

"For getting out of this situation."

"Didn't know that was part of the plan."

"It's part of any plan," David said.

"I guess I just thought we'd all grow old and die together here in Las Vegas."

"Gangsters don't die," David said. "Look around. Bugsy Siegel's alive as ever."

"Same fucking guys, isn't it?" Gray Beard said. "Just in a different suit."

"I had a vision in the hospital," David said.

"You were on some good shit, I bet."

"I saw myself as the prophet Ezekiel, sitting on the banks of the River Chebar for seven days and seven nights," David said. "God came to me and said he didn't want me to die. He wanted me to turn from my evil ways and live."

Gray Beard whistled. "Morphine is a motherfucker."

"Thing is," David said, "I had the exact same dream last night. And the night before that. Every detail; it's all the same."

"Is that what you want? To leave it all?"

Truth was, nothing was stopping David from getting in a car and driving out of Las Vegas. But then what? Mob would be after him. FBI would be after him. Public would be after him. His wife and kid, wherever they were, would be endangered. Bennie and Ronnie would put a bounty on his head, equal to or better than whatever the FBI was offering. As long as he stayed in Las Vegas, under Bennie's thumb, he was relatively safe.

"Not yet. The people I'd leave alive behind, I'd ruin their lives. I'm talking about you, too."

"Me and Marvin, we're a mobile unit. My paper is legit. I can be in British Columbia tomorrow morning."

"I need to figure out a way to make things right for the people I'm going to hurt." Fact was, Sal Cupertine was the mob's most efficient killer because he was precise. He killed those who needed to die and didn't leave a trail of others behind as collateral damage. In his life, he'd killed one person who didn't have it coming, and now she was haunting his ass. But David was also thinking about all the marriages and funerals he performed, innocent Jews who had come to trust him. He needed to figure out how to make those events legit. He couldn't

leave their lives in tatters, too. The other side was that he didn't view
what he did as evil. He worked in a business that necessitated a certain
amount of loss. That's just how it was. Everybody dies. That's not evil;
that's just true. It wasn't evil when race car drivers died. It wasn't evil
when boxers died. Everyone knows the risks inherent in their jobs.
Sometimes, it's taking blows to the head for twenty years. Other times
it's the Rain Man showing up in your house in the middle of the night.
"I need to get right."

"It's not my place," Gray Beard said, "so if you don't like what I'm
saying, you just put a hand up." He leaned forward. "You're a good
Rabbi, I bet."

"I think I am."

Gray Beard pointed at himself. "See, I was a good doctor."

"You still are."

"I love heroin more," he said. "That's the truth. But I'm like Keith
Richards now. I got the balance right. Marvin and me, we got something special." He looked out the front window. "This place? When I
first got to Las Vegas, you could park your car, tie off, watch the world
fly into Las Vegas, trip on the lights, nod out to the coyotes running
behind you. This was nothing but wild desert. I wish I'd known Marvin then. He would have liked it." He shook his head. "The point is
that I'm never gonna be a real doctor again. I get to do some work now
and again, and I find it keeps me from tying a rope around my neck.
What's stopping you from getting rid of the criminal element around
you and just, you know, being a rabbi?"

"I love being a gangster more," David said.

"More than being a husband and father?"

"I'm those things whatever my job is," David said.

"Oh, really?" Gray Beard made an exaggerated look around the
empty parking lot. "They inside the library?"

"The Talmud says you've got to judge things by their ending."

"Meaning what?"

"Say ten men stomp the shit out of a guy," David said, "but it isn't until the last man kicks him in the head that he dies. The Talmud says only the last man is liable for the death. The idea being that if the previous blows were enough to kill the man, they would have killed the man."

"It's not exactly medically sound," Gray Beard said.

David reached behind him, grabbed one of the FedEx boxes. Shook it. "Heavy," David said. He handed it to Gray Beard, who also shook it. "What do you think is in there?"

"Probably twenty pounds of socks," Gray Beard said.

"Could be twenty pounds of gold coins," David said. "Won't know until you open it up."

"But opening it up is the crime," Gray Beard said.

"See?" David said. "There you go." He took the box from Gray Beard, cracked the seal, looked inside. "When they write my obituary, it's going to start and end with me being a gangster. Day I die, even if I'm still a rabbi, I will be a gangster. It's beyond my control."

Gray Beard stroked at his beard, eyes still on David. "What are you telling me?"

"How much more do you need to get out of Las Vegas, permanently?"

Gray Beard sighed. "I'm not great with saving money. I got my problems, too, hoss. They aren't your concerns."

"If you had to disappear," David said. "If you had to make it work."

"If I knew it was my last score," Gray Beard said, "I guess I'd want to get a couple hundred thousand in cash. I got my house covered. I get on a methadone program, that would help. I'd want to leave something behind for Marvin, so he could go to culinary school."

"I bounce," David said, "there's going to be an increased focus on . . . everything. Someone works backward far enough, they'll find you. And that is my problem. I don't leave loose threads. And you're a loose end." Gray Beard swallowed. They both knew what David meant. "Something else happened today."

He told him that Rachel Savone had learned his real identity, Gray Beard listening intently. When David was done, Gray Beard took a pack of Marlboro Reds from his breast pocket, put one in his mouth but didn't light it, just gnawed on the filter.

"That's not good," Gray Beard said eventually. "You think she wants protective custody?"

"I don't know," David said. "I'm the only fish she thinks is big enough to get her whatever it is she wants." There was a roll of packing tape in the center console of the van, so David taped the package back up, set it on the floor.

"You gonna tell me what was in the box?" Gray Beard said.

"No," David said. "You could testify against me."

Gray Beard thought about that for a moment. "Piece of advice?"

"Listening."

"Have something the government wants."

"I'm working on that," David said.

"Your friend," Gray Beard said, "has been an education."

Since showing up at the ICU, Matthew Drew had been staying with Gray Beard and his partner, Marvin. They were the only people who wouldn't ask any questions, but David had felt obliged to let them know they were harboring an FBI agent who also happened to be wanted for murder and was being hunted by both the government and organized crime. Gray Beard had taken it all with a shrug . . . and the promise of cash when David got out.

"Help you streamline your operations?"

"Not gonna lie," Gray Beard said with a laugh. "He's gone most the time, though."

"Where to?"

"He says he's looking for your wife and cleaning out his closet," Gray Beard said carefully. Gray Beard had delivered money to Jennifer once before, and Marvin had done recon in Chicago on Ronnie Cupertine. Though he never said a word about it, David knew Gray Beard had figured out who he really was, not that David had any idea who Gray Beard was, except that Bennie Savone had him handle medical issues off the books.

David thought for a moment. Matthew told him about the recon he'd done on the safe houses in Arizona, Oregon, and Utah. But David knew, foremost, Matthew Drew was not his friend. "You believe him? That he's looking for my wife?"

Gray Beard shrugged. "That motherfucker is a lot of things, but he isn't a liar. Our RV is plenty big, but his anger takes up three rooms, so I've got to know his moods. I bought a pop-up trailer for him. Everyone's life got easier. Says he'll be gone until Tuesday, he shows up Tuesday. Says he'll buy groceries, he buys groceries. Is real respectful of my and Marvin's privacy. So." Gray Beard shrugged again. "Man, we're all criminals, so who knows."

"What's he doing for money?"

"He's not opposed to doing work," Gray Beard said.

"He leaves a print or hair somewhere," David said, "we're all done for."

"He's not been doing that kind of work," Gray Beard said. "But he would."

"Say he finds my wife," David said. "And I kill him. That be a problem for you?"

"Marvin's real fond of him," Gray Beard said, "so he'd help you dig the grave extra deep."

"All right," David said. He reached into his pocket, came out with an envelope. "For our friend's rent."

Gray Beard counted the bills. "You're too generous," Gray Beard said.

David opened the door, got out, but didn't close it right away. He had a long night ahead of him. Now that he knew where things stood. "He leave yet?" If Matthew was good for his word, he'd be in California putting a gun in Kirk Biglione's mouth before the end of the week.

"This morning," Gray Beard said. "Said he might be gone a week. Ten days if things got sideways. Marvin rented him a car. I gave him some supplies. So. Something happens, we'll know."

"Supplies?"

"Can't tell you," he said. "You could testify against me."

David said, "He's back, send a signal. Meantime, let me work on your parachute."

"I told you," Gray Beard said. "Not your problem."

"And I told you," David said.

"Well then," Gray Beard said. "There's something else you should know."

"What?"

"Bennie asked me about a cocktail for his father-in-law."

"Rabbi Kales?"

Gray Beard nodded. "Told him I'd need a week's notice to get it all and that it wouldn't be the sort of thing he could administer himself, that I'd need to be there to do it, which isn't actually true. But I figured you'd want some notice."

"Yeah," David said.

"He called yesterday."

Shit.

"Could be," Gray Beard said, "I delay shipment for a few days. Wait too long, he's gonna be suspicious." Gray Beard looked at David for a long moment, then laughed a funny little laugh, put his van into drive, even though the door was still open.

"What?" David said.

"You look about as Jewish as me, Rabbi," he said.

AFTER GRAY BEARD LEFT, DAVID WALKED TO THE SHOPPING CENTER, WAITED for someone to pull up in either a Toyota Tercel or Honda Accord from the 1990s, got lucky with a couple in a red 1994 Toyota Tercel, the easiest mass-produced car to steal.

Took the butt of his gun to break the driver's side window, one tap, muffled the sound with his hoodie.

Knife into the ignition.

Butt of the gun to hammer it.

Twist.

Fifteen minutes later, he was parked down the block from the rear entrance to the Temple cemetery. Twenty and he was over the cemetery's northwest wall, which was secured by desert and a few rows of full-growth acacias, because in pleasant society, people didn't break into cemeteries. If you wanted to pinch from the dead, you typically weren't in the physical shape to spend four hours digging holes, hoping you got the right one, the average motherfucker with no sense how coffins were staggered, sure everything was at six feet. In the years David worked at Temple Beth Israel, the only people who'd broken into the cemetery after hours were either heartsick or sixteen-year-old Goths wanting to drink in peace. There hadn't even been any anti-Semitic graffiti, which was good, because David would have chased those motherfuckers down to the edges of the earth.

David walked out toward the cemetery's final phase: acres of steadily grading man-made rolling bluffs, Rabbi Kales telling him early on that the goal was to sell the plots at street level on Hillpointe for one price and then slowly improve the view as the cemetery expanded north and west. "This will be like Beverly Hills," Rabbi Kales told him, a place neither man had ever visited, but which Rabbi Kales presumed had wonderful views. At the cemetery, at least, this was true: at its highest point, there were clear sightlines all the way to the lights of the Strip in one direction, a glorious view of the Red Rocks in the other, and then blooming foliage surrounded them year-round, the Temple rotating heirloom, Iceberg, and JFK roses along the base of the walls, filling the air all year long.

Still, when he was selling plots out this direction, Rabbi Cohen was prone to calling it "the penthouse at the Bellagio" to prospective buyers. Jews didn't want to be stuck somewhere that turned into a shitty subdivision for eternity, or however long it took for them to be hit with the dew of resurrection upon the Moshiach's return, before making the long-ass trip to the Mount of Olives in Israel. They wanted a first-class afterlife. They wanted an afterlife that was not available to everyone.

So the plots at the Bellagio started at $10,000. Or $50,000. It just depended on who David was talking to.

It was all just grass and dirt and blind faith. You still went into the ground in a simple pine box and with nothing to preserve you but your finest outfit. And a life well lived.

David stopped when he came upon the graves for Clark and Zadie Zarkin and the plot Kristy Levine had purchased last year. Levine was supposed to be dead by now—she'd come to him last year around this time, a diagnosis for an aggressive cancer in hand—but she'd survived. She was even thoughtful enough to send a get-well card to David after his "fall": Snoopy holding a balloon and then, in Kristy's scrawl, a simple sentence: *We're both hard to kill!* It momentarily gave David a feeling of joy—one person who understood how hard it is just to live—and then he remembered Kristy's most salient facts: she'd moved to Las Vegas to work for the FBI, which wasn't a huge surprise—the Las Vegas field office was one of the largest in the nation. Made sense they had some Jews in their ranks. It was just . . . well, David didn't like coincidences. And now she was scoping out Matthew Drew.

Still, when it came time to hide Melanie Moss's body, he'd picked a spot directly between the Zarkin and Levine plots. No one would be disinterring the Zarkins. No one would be disinterring a dead FBI agent, either. Even if you unearthed every body in the cemetery, it would be years before someone found Melanie Moss.

David fired up one of the three backhoes the Home of Peace kept lined up next to the groundskeeper's shed, rolled slowly over to Melanie's plot, and began digging.

Thirty minutes and he was standing on top of the casket with a crowbar.

Melanie Moss was standing at the edge of her grave, looking in.

David just needed a bone. Something easy to run DNA off of. He needed Melanie Moss to be identified.

All he *needed* was a bone.

Melanie watched him put her head into a canvas gym bag he'd stolen from the Tercel.

"Gotta make a bold statement," David said. "Put all this to rest."

David checked the time. He just needed to refill the grave, drive a few blocks, and drop Melanie off at her new resting place, until such time as he needed her found.

EIGHT

IT WAS 102 DEGREES AND THE SALTON SEA SMELLED LIKE A CORPSE, THE
result of a spring heat wave that pushed the temperature in California's low desert and southern Nevada above one hundred for three
days. In Matthew Drew's experience, the Salton Sea smelled worse
than a corpse, an otherworldly wretchedness that came over him in
waves—as the water crashed, as the wind blew, as birds flapped by,
something new got stirred up. Maybe it was the coastline of dead tilapia. Maybe it was some new cancerous gas rising from the salt basin's unique mixture of water, sludge from Mexico, World War II–era
nuclear-test residue, valley fever parasites, and the fresh round of
meth being cooked out at Slab City. He never could tell.

It wasn't Matthew's first time at the Salton Sea, the vast ecological disaster of California's low desert, about three hours south of Las
Vegas. He'd come out years ago, as a kid, with his late father, Conrad,
driving in from Disneyland one afternoon, his dad mentioning his
brother Morris once lived in these parts in the 1960s, ironically working corporate security, had lost his wife here, and Conrad wanted to
drive out and see the place again, even though he and his brother had
lost touch. Or maybe because of that.

He'd parked the car, gotten out, walked to the edge of the Sea, and
sobbed out a verse from the mini New Testament he kept in his back
pocket. "This is a ruined place," he'd told Matthew that day. "Don't
ever come back here."

And yet here was Matthew Drew dressed in a smart linen suit he'd
picked up at the outlet stores in Cabazon, flowered shirt opened at the

collar, a panama hat shielding his face, his sunglasses, long hair, and five months of heavy beard doing the rest of the work. He felt like he should be going to a nice dinner before a Jimmy Buffett concert, not trying to figure out how he was going to shake information out of Kirk Biglione, set to be one of the featured speakers at Gold Mountain Mining's ground-breaking ceremony that morning. He wasn't sure Biglione would recognize him or not, but it didn't matter.

Matthew needed to know where the FBI might have hidden Jennifer Cupertine. He just needed a location, not even an exact address. And only someone like an ex–station chief would know operational details like that. If he could just find Jennifer and William, he was confident that Sal Cupertine would help him. A part of him knew that was madness—depending on a mob hit man to exonerate him from a series of murders didn't seem legally sound—but it was all he had. And thus far, Sal hadn't flipped on him. He'd half expected Marvin to set fire to the trailer he was living in, or just shoot him in the back of the head while he slept, but even those fears had dissipated over time. There was more honor among these crooks than there had ever been in the FBI. If Biglione was as corrupt as Sal believed him to be, Matthew and Hopper never stood a chance.

Matthew spent four years fantasizing about hurting Kirk Biglione, not just for being crooked, but for being reckless with the life of Jeff Hopper. He let him get killed. And if Sal was right, Biglione also abetted the death of the men Sal killed in the Parker House. Sal Cupertine did his job, but it was Biglione and Ronnie Cupertine who made it all possible.

Matthew parked his rented Sebring—Marvin signed for it, using whatever identity still had good credit—under a billowing white tent and made his way to the seating area. There was an unmanned table filled with "Hello, my name is" nametags—probably a hundred—so Matthew filled in his with the name of his childhood dog and the street he grew up on, and Bruce Appleton, freelance reporter, was born.

The area was covered by a portable pergola that provided some shade from the heat, along with the misters and high-powered fans. It still smelled fucking terrible. After a few minutes, Biglione took the stage in a semicircle behind Glenn Gold, vice president of western development for Gold Mountain Mining—sweat rings pushing through his navy-blue suit—before Glenn finally introduced the full team. "You'll be seeing a lot of us in and around the Imperial and Coachella Valleys these next several months," Gold said. "We aim to become a big part of the community. Fix some of the mistakes of the past with an eye toward our vibrant future!"

There was a smattering of applause, followed by a young woman with a huge pair of scissors bounding onto the stage . . . and then fifteen minutes later, it was all over. The vice president of western development was whisked off in a helicopter, and the assembled masses—in this case, a dozen journalists, a film crew from the local ABC station, officials from one of the local Indian tribes, a bloviating city councilman from Indio, the head of the Coachella Valley's chamber of commerce, and then every middle manager Gold Mountain had flown in—retired back to the tent filled with shrimp and wine and handshakes. Matthew waited until he saw Biglione alone at the buffet.

"Pick your brain for a second?" Matthew said to Biglione, who was rummaging through the last of the meats and cheeses. No one was touching the shrimp. It was too fucking hot. Matthew had only met Biglione once in his life: when he started his assignment at the Chicago field office. He'd been prepared to testify anonymously at the corruption trial—Matthew getting in as a whistleblower—his ass sitting in a Ramada Inn in Springfield for a month, but Biglione had bitched out before Matthew had the chance to help nail him. So he wasn't surprised that Biglione didn't appear to recognize him. Gone was the twenty-five-year-old recruit. Matthew was heavier now, pushing thirty, and his beard had come in speckled with gray, his long hair the same.

"Sure thing," Biglione said. He didn't look up from the buffet right away, his focus on a platter of tiny sausages. He was a big guy, over six foot two, probably pushing 275 pounds, the kind of guy who played small-college football but talked about it like it was the NFL, and knees like anvils. "What can I do you for you?"

"What's the chief security concern out here? Seems like Gold Mountain is bringing in an awfully big gun for a drilling op." Matthew took a reporter's notebook from his pocket, poised his pen, all any stuffed shirt needed to believe someone was a journalist these days.

Biglione "uh-huh'd" through Matthew's question, eyes on his plate. "That's a good question," he said when Matthew finished. "Who is this for?"

"Freelance journalist," Matthew said. "Working on a feature about the new developments out here in no-man's-land."

"Uh-huh," Biglione said again. He finally glanced at Matthew but betrayed no recognition. "Okay. First, there's a local element. This is tribal land. Now we've leased it from the Chuyalla, good people, good people. No problems there. But there's a real sense that if this works, who owns the metals found a mile under the surface? Is that Indian land, too? We've got some litigation going about that. So there's natural concerns about sabotage and the like. It's been like that out here since the 1950s when companies first started mining this area. We're monitoring that. There's sensitive technology that we're using that could be of some use to our enemies around the world, so there's a terror nexus, which is my specialty. And then there's just letting people know what we're doing out here is safe, so a little bit of public relations. People still remember the toxic waste the government left after all the weapons testing. But I'm here to tell you, people are going to fall in love with lithium batteries. You'll be able to drive across the country for the same cost you pay to keep your kitchen lights on overnight."

"What about organized crime?"

"Not a concern," Biglione said a little too quickly. He picked up another paper plate. Loaded it up with pieces of ham and a couple olives, an array of crackers. "I mean, there's nothing here but sand, stench, and lithium. What's John Gotti gonna do with lithium?"

"I thought this whole area was built by crime families."

Two men in blue suits that looked right off a rack at Brooks Brothers walked up. Both wore earpieces and were clearly uncomfortable in their shoes, shined to a spit gloss. Both also had sidearm bulges. They helped themselves to some bottled water and pretzels while Biglione shoved ham in his mouth and waited for them to disappear before he responded, Matthew thinking it was a ploy to give him time to think.

"Back in the day?" Biglione said. "Everything from Palm Springs to Las Vegas was crooked. But this place? More military than mob. We paid millions getting the area cleaned up for human life." He pointed lazily into the distance. "Got some Mexican Mafia couple miles east. Some Native Mob, but I tell you, these are not players. We're talking rigged bingo games and stealing golf carts. Different world out west."

"Yet your two associates are packing Glocks for a press conference," Matthew said.

"They don't work for me," Biglione said.

"No?"

"Tribe has their own private security when their big shots roll out," Biglione said.

"To do what?"

"Prevent kidnappings," Biglione said. "Cartel wants to take one of these executives and start ransoming fingers and toes, they can be across the border in ninety minutes."

"You're not worried about yourself?"

"Not a situation that has anything to do with me."

"What hotel are you staying at?" Matthew asked.

"Sorry?"

"Oh, it's just that, in fact, the mob is still prevalent out this way. Depending upon where you're staying, you might be putting money right into their pockets. Or yourself in harm's way. Go to bed, wake up with some mob hitters in your bathroom."

"I'm staying at the Château," Biglione said. He pointed across the parking lot, to three double-wide trailers set up near the construction site for the administrative offices.

"Only the best," Matthew said. If he did this right, taking care of Biglione was going to be easy. He wasn't a pussy—Biglione was a legit agent, even if he was crooked, worked his way up from an assault team to hostage negotiation to the organized crime division head, and that meant he knew how to use a gun, could use those hands, too. Didn't matter much if someone put one in both your knees, tied you to a chair, interrogated you, and then set fire to the trailer you were living in, which was the fantasy Matthew was operating under now.

"Well," Biglione said, "off the record? This whole place is cursed. You couldn't pay me to live here."

"But you're happy to drill it out?"

"Off the record? All it's good for," Biglione said. "I think this place will be safe from any real problems, that's on the record."

"Didn't even take any notes," Matthew said.

Biglione held up a finger, pulled out a mini digital recorder from his pocket. "I'm always recording, just in case."

"I think that's a felony," Matthew said.

Biglione hit the stop button.

"Then it's a good thing neither one of us is an FBI agent anymore." Matthew could have pulled out his gun and ended Biglione right then. One between the eyes. But then the Brooks Brothers would probably light him up or he'd spend the rest of his life in a federal prison. Neither option sounded terrific. By the same token, Biglione surely didn't want to have to explain the presence of someone on the FBI's Most Wanted list. "I'm getting a drink. You want a drink, Agent Drew?"

That answered that.

Biglione stepped away from the buffet, headed over to the bar, ordered a scotch and water, the bartender sweating through his tuxedo shirt.

"Vodka and Red Bull," Matthew said.

The bartender made Matthew his drink, slid it over. Biglione ducked out of the tent and walked down toward the shore, Matthew a few steps behind him. Biglione stopped a few feet from the water. The sand here wasn't as smooth as a real beach. It was covered in fine pebbles and the desiccated corpses of tilapia. The smell was oppressive.

"What's with the dead fish?" Matthew asked.

"The salt water doesn't get oxygenated enough when the heat jumps up like this," Biglione said. He put on a pair of sunglasses, took a sip of his scotch, motioned out to the sea. "What do you see when you look out this way?"

The Salton Sea was surrounded on both sides by sun-scorched mountains and desert. If the government hadn't let this desolate salt pan flood a hundred years earlier, they'd be staring at the neolithic past. Nothing was fit to live out here. "A boondoggle."

"We start pulling the lithium out, there's money to be made." He turned and looked at Matthew. "I know you're not a murderer, Agent. I know you've been set up. And so I know you understand my situation. Gotta be a way we can work together."

"Your boss had my sister killed."

"What did you think was going to happen, Agent? You think you can maim the head of The Family and just walk away?"

"What happens when he wakes up and finds out that the Native Mob waxed his wife and kids just to set me up?"

"He ain't ever waking up," Biglione said.

"Why didn't you take this as your out?" Matthew said. "All these years and you're still standing here shit-scared of Ronnie Cupertine."

"You think you know me?" Biglione said. "I was a good FBI agent. A fucking great one. I didn't get there because of the Cupertines; I got there despite them." He shook his head. "You know what Hopper's problem was? He didn't leave good enough alone. All he had to do was be a shitty FBI agent for two weeks, a month, go get some therapy for his fuckup, take a desk job, pile on those pension years. And instead, he goes looking for a dead man." Matthew didn't respond. Biglione took down the rest of his scotch, tossed the tumbler into the water. "What are you looking for, Agent Drew? What brought you back into my fucking life?"

"Sal Cupertine's wife and kid. The FBI got them into a safe house. I need to know where."

"You think I just keep a list?"

"You still have friends in the agency," Matthew said. "I'm sure you've still got friends with the Marshals, too. Just get me a town."

"And then what? You're gonna use them as bait, hope he comes looking for you?"

"I catch him, it would help clear my name."

"And what do I get from this?"

"You keep this cozy job," Matthew said, "and I don't tell every newspaper in America how long you've been on the payroll of The Family."

Before Biglione could respond, a young reporter in a red dress along with the local ABC camera crew came tromping down to the beach.

"I need a couple days," Biglione said. "Make some calls."

"That's fine."

Biglione said, "You've got big balls, kid." He took a business card from his breast pocket, handed it to Matthew. "Call me on Saturday."

Matthew put out his hand. Biglione shook it, and for a moment—more than a moment, really—Matthew thought about snapping his fucking wrist right there, popping his radius into three parts, getting all of them to stick out of his skin at right angles, like how they taught at the Academy, put a man into instant shock, bleed him out if you're alone. But he let go, or tried to. Biglione kept hold.

"I shouldn't have fired you," Biglione said.

"No."

"I should have had you killed."

"You could have tried," Matthew said. He'd call in a few days. Give him time to get some gas and zip ties and find a good, lonely place in the desert to dump his fucking body.

NINE

THE FIRST FEW DAYS PEACHES POCOTILLO SPENT IN PALM SPRINGS WERE all about getting the lay of the land, meeting the players, understanding just how badly the mere presence of his nephew Mike had managed to fuck things up. Mike was twenty-six but of the opinion he'd only live to his midthirties, based on something some fortune teller told him, and so his understanding of consequence was not so developed. He ended up killing many more people than needed, just as a general way of doing business. Someone disagreed with him, he killed them. It made less people disagree with him, for sure, but also limited the number of those interested in doing business with him. Peaches was about relationships. What was life without people who understood you?

Today, Peaches had a lunch meeting at a restaurant called Melvyn's. He and Lonzo rolled up in their new Caddie at 12:27, hung a handicapped placard from the rearview, and parked in a blue space, close enough that they could make sure there wasn't a bunch of FBI agents changing out of their windbreakers and Kevlar into resort wear. The restaurant was attached to a hotel called the Ingleside Inn, one of those places that looked like it had been cut and pasted from the 1950s, all sun-dappled patios, Spanish-style bungalows, croquet lawns, square pools, and little nooks where celebrities could fix heroin into their necks.

One hundred and twenty-five years ago? This was Indian land. But then the government and the railroads came and turned Palm Springs into a checkerboard, so that the Indians only got every other mile or so. Melvyn's now sat two inches away from reservation land, and a million years in the distance.

Car after car pulled past Peaches and Lonzo toward the valet station. A Bentley. A 7 Series BMW. A Maserati. A Mercedes. Another Mercedes. Another Bentley. A couple would get out. Sometimes man and woman. Sometimes man and man. Sometimes woman and woman. Sometimes groups of women. Sometimes groups of men. The Venn diagram was plastic surgery. It was like a Tupperware party.

After a while, Peaches knocked on the passenger window with his pinky ring. "Watch the valets," he said to Lonzo. The ring was a new thing. Black amethyst. He was trying on the idea of being a guy who wore rings. He was, as usual, dressed in all linen, tortoiseshell sunglasses, slip-on shoes, kind of like if Don Johnson never left Miami; a peach-scented skin cream on his arms, neck, and face kept him feeling fresh. Peaches liked the look. When you're the baddest motherfucker in the room, you can wear whatever you want.

"What am I trying to see?"

"Just watch," Peaches said.

First car, nothing, the couple loitering a bit. Plate from Washington. Valet parked the car right in front of the restaurant.

Second car, nothing, people coming out of the restaurant. Plate from Nevada. Same parking situation.

Third car, plate from California, no one around. One valet popped the glove box. Did something with his cell phone. Closed the box. Other valet watched the door. Knocked on the window when people came out of the restaurant. First valet drove off past Lonzo and Peaches, parked in a reserved lot, spent some more time in that glove box.

"The fuck he doing?" Lonzo asked.

"Took a picture of the address," Peaches said. "Probably has a homeboy driving by it right now, seeing what's what. If they're staying in the hotel, they'll be making copies of the keys."

Lonzo whistled. "Slick."

Peaches said, "Addict shit."

"Still," Lonzo said. "A lot of risk for some pills and furs. Could be housing whole mansions if they did it right. You think he kicks up to someone?"

"Maybe," Peaches said. Made sense, if there was a big score to be had. Valet could get the drugs, the electronics, but if there was a house to roll, a bunch of cars, a safe, you needed pros with access to buyers other than pawn shops and eBay.

Palm Springs was an open city, which to the Italian families meant you could do whatever you wanted provided you didn't kill anybody or fuck them over too badly. In either case, any revenge on that shit would happen outside the city limits. Because of that, no made guys had been killed in Palm Springs in decades. Yeah, they'd blown a motherfucker up in Evansville. Cut a guy's dick off and shoved it in his brother's mouth during a spa weekend in Scottsdale. And yes, absolutely, they'd put three in Dominic Fortunado's face for some shit down at the Salton Sea, but they waited until he was back in Sicily. All of that was ancient history, storybook shit Peaches heard about growing up. These days? Hardest motherfucker from Palm Springs to die was Sonny Bono, and he got taken out by a fucking tree on a ski run.

Still. That was the rules.

You established something, it was yours; no one was stepping. Mexican Mafia had established the cocaine trade routes out of Mexico. Some minor crews built the girl business, but now that shit was all online, plus Palm Springs had a huge gay population, and there was no business in that. Italians had run the gaming before it got legit, so they still had sway on that, plus the nightclubs and golf courses and some of the older hotels that weren't corporate. Bloods and Crips, they fought over the low-hanging fruit—marijuana, protection rackets in the poor parts of the city, car theft. Peaches could give a fuck about that street business. These days, he was a fucking CEO.

Native Mob? For years, they kept their shit to the reservation lands between Palm Springs and San Diego, running the bingo halls, the powwows, parking lot scams, Ponzi schemes, rackets, arsons, and the occasional off-reservation heist. But now that the tribes had free reign to open Vegas-style casinos, they wanted a bigger slice. Peaches was beginning to think they could have the whole pie, if they did things right.

This open-city shit made no sense to Peaches. Starbucks doesn't give a shit if a coffee shop has been in business for a hundred years. They'd open up right next door, charge more for their coffee, and still make that cash. And if Mom and Pop whined to the news, fuck 'em, they'd build another Starbucks across the street. And yet the Mafia, actual fucking criminals, had a code of conduct that said, in certain situations, don't be a fucking criminal?

The Mexican Mafia and the Native Mob didn't adhere to those rules with each other but had never stepped to the Five Families, until recently. The whole reason Peaches was here was to help smooth over some turf shit between the Native Mob, who had an interest in a casino going up twenty miles east of Palm Springs, and the Mexican Mafia, who ran hard drugs and didn't like the notion that the Native Mob would likely be cutting into their business by building a thirty-story palace right in the middle of their distribution highway, with a captive audience to deal to inside.

The result was that the soldiers on both sides were killing each other at a rapid rate, with the Italians in town siding with the Native Mob. Cops didn't give a shit until some beef at the Fuddruckers in Palm Springs ended up with three Mexican Mafia members bleeding out on top of the salad bar and two from the Native Mob missing their faces in the upstairs bathroom, which could have been swept up as another no-human-involved incident, but they found a seventy-five-year-old man named Paul down from Medicine Hat with one in the gut, bleeding out in the shitter.

Even made the news in Chicago. Kill an old man in the shitter, you get two inches in the *Sun-Times*, no matter where you live. Most people saw that and made different vacation plans.

Peaches only saw opportunity. The Native Mob in Wisconsin and Illinois was amazed by how Peaches had muscled into The Family, and while they weren't cutting him bigger shares of *their* game, there was talk from the Council of Elders that he might get a nice bump up in class, get a couple more guys working for him, in addition to his cousin Mike and The Family soldiers and associates he had running with him now, like Lonzo. Which was just fear on their part. They knew now that Peaches had the juice.

He could run any of them out of the game. And if he could get the Native Mob more involved in the Palm Springs tribes' casino operations, well, then they were steps away from golf courses, and where there were golf courses, there were houses, and the Native Mob was all about the mortgage business these days, moving home loans at variable rates, seizing defaulted properties, moving them again, all of it kind of legal. No one was buying million-dollar homes on reservation land in Indiana . . . but Palm Springs, well, Countrywide didn't have shit on the Native Mob. Peaches Pocotillo could be the resort king of the Chuyalla, running game from the West Coast to the Gold Coast.

Or: Get out from under the Native Mob. Be his own thing. Sovereign Nation of Peaches. Use his power running The Family to make a lasting move. Because being lead dog just meant more ass hounds nipping behind you. The Family was making money, for now. But that would change. And they'd come for him. Or Sal Cupertine would show up and want what was his. Or revenge.

"You ever have a real job?" Peaches asked. It was 12:47. They'd need to get moving if they didn't see Mike soon. Already, this place was making Peaches nervous. All this Indian land, not a fucking Indian to be found.

"One summer," Lonzo said. "I worked at a video store. Made $4.25 an hour."

"How long you last?"

"Until I robbed it," Lonzo said.

"What was your take?"

"Hundred and forty-seven dollars," Lonzo said.

"Big balling," Peaches said. "How much they give you?"

"Six months in juvie," he said, "on account I also assaulted the cop who came to question me." Lonzo shook his head. "Truth? It was the best thing that happened to me. If I'd lived out that summer with my stepdad, I'd have put that fool in the dirt."

"That bad?"

"That bad," Lonzo said. "Got out, he'd already skipped out on my moms. Never saw him again. Good for both of us."

"Look at these fucks," Peaches said. A group of silver-haired golfer types got out of a Range Rover. Red pants. Yellow pants. Checkered pants. They looked like retired clowns. California plate. Good. They'd come home and find all their Viagra gone. Maybe then they'd know suffering.

"If these valets had even a single set of balls," Lonzo said, "they'd be doing home invasions, taking hostages, ransoming anesthesiologists and heart surgeons and shrinks for millions. Cut one finger off of one guy, early on, you'd make ten million before the cops even caught a whiff."

It was an idea, Peaches had to admit.

These people didn't have to hustle to feel safe. They had money. Health insurance paid for the Oxycodone and Klonopin and Dilaudid. No one getting shot at CVS. Many of the tribes up in Wisconsin had their own clinics, their own doctors, so Peaches had a bit in that game, but it was a limited marketplace; they could move pills around the reservations, could seep out into the cities, but it was always to piss-poor motherfuckers. The next level was selling pills to people with money, pills their insurance would typically pay for if they just knew the right words to say to their doctors.

Maybe it was about owning the doctors. Because then there was surgery. In-home care. Hospice services. If you had a doctor telling you something was true, it was true. *You're gonna die. You need a live-in nurse.* Worst-case scenario, miracle, you lived. Live or die, the doctor gets Blue Cross to pay the vig. Yeah. Why was he giving a shit about casinos when health care always had one winner at the end? He only had to look at Ronnie Cupertine in his private room, with his private nurses, with his private doctors, with his twenty-four-hour drip of the best shit, legally, *forever.*

Hospitals never went out of business. Shit, Peaches even had an investment strategy around hospitals that Ronnie Cupertine had taught him, back before he moved into one full time. The Family made millions over the years by buying up real estate near hospitals and penitentiaries, selling the land for huge profits to development companies and then getting the bids to build the houses or sanitation dumps, or getting institutional-cafeteria contracts for shitty meat, running rackets where no one ever thought of having a fucking racket. That was The Family way of doing business and not getting caught: Own things legitimately, then run a con based on need, not want. You want to build a golf course next to Stateville so all the guards and their captains can shoot eighteen after work? Great. You're gonna need to buy the land from Ronnie Cupertine, and you're gonna need to pay him to run it, to bring the food to it, to pave the parking lot, to sell you overpriced golf balls.

But Peaches was a practical man. He knew he couldn't own a hospital, no matter how much money he had. Plus, he didn't want to have to deal with those bodies. But you could own all the things those bodies needed to live.

Because what was keeping hospitals in business wasn't the patients. It was the surgeries and the treatments and the legal drugs. It was the longevity. It was the increased life expectancy. The termination of terror management. People weren't so scared to die anymore because so many outlived the desire to stay alive. All those good drugs that would keep your body alive while turning your brain into a bowl of oatmeal.

Peaches didn't need to control cocaine. Peaches needed a fucking patent. Who did he need to kill to get a patent? Didn't even need to be Oxy or Percocet. Could be some blood pressure medication. Some asthma shit. Hell, Peaches took a pill every morning for his cholesterol. Had for fifteen years. It was genetic. Wasn't even like he ate bad. How many others were just like him? Millions and millions. Some broken strand of DNA that was making someone rich.

Aside from the patent, what Peaches figured he really needed was a clinic. Indian Health Services operated clinics on reservation land all over the country, but then independent doctors also had offices, too, many of them little more than pill farms. There could be a dispensary angle, but there also had to be some legit work happening, get a balance going.

Move pills, pimp elective plastic surgery—tit jobs, nose jobs, chin fillers, eyebrow lifts, all that easy cosmetic shit, no one dying on the table for a new smile—plus some light urgent care. Not so high-end that he couldn't lose a body or two every now and then from a stroke or heart attack. Could be owning a clinic would take care of some of the problems running the Native Mob and The Family presented. Be nice to not have to worry about where to send a guy with a bullet hole in his shoulder. Find a Native doctor to front the practice; one of his baby mamas had to have a cousin he could blackmail. Peaches would provide the real estate, the start-up cash; a big key would be expanding off of reservation land fast. He liked Palm Springs. Lots of old fuckers from out of town who might fall and break their hip or get pushed. Little towns, out-of-the-way locations, spots where he could drum up business if things got slow. Maybe even get a few ambulances.

It was an epiphany Peaches frankly didn't see coming. But that's how it was these days now that he was the boss of bosses. He was fucking enlightened. He could see through black holes.

"Here he is," Lonzo said, breaking Peaches from his reverie, all of this so bush-league he almost didn't notice Mike pulling up behind the wheel of a red convertible Jaguar, some fat fuck beside him, some woman with hoop earrings show dogs could jump through in the backseat.

"Yeah," Peaches said, his future so clear now that he already was picturing Mike in his coffin, because once Peaches's epiphany became real, he couldn't have someone like Mike involved.

Mike was already dead.

Peaches stared at Lonzo, tried to do the math on him. He probably could live.

For a bit.

MELVYN'S WAS THE KIND OF PLACE WITH PHOTOS ON THE WALL—DORIS DAY, Bob Hope, President Reagan, Clint Eastwood, Sonny fucking Bono, and Elvis pedophile Presley. The restaurant was filled with old ladies in white tennis skirts and pink polo shirts with the collars popped, diamond tennis bracelets, and tit jobs that made them look like college girls from the side, horror-movie mannequins from the front.

Everyone in the place—save the men picking up the dishes and then Peaches, Lonzo, and Mike—was as white as a snowflake, apart from their brown liver spots. Peaches had never seen anything like it. Gold Coast fucks didn't bother with all the plastic surgery. They were happy to be old and rich. But also, there were Black people with money in Chicago. Apparently not in Palm Springs.

The two people with Mike—Lori Silausk, from the tribe, and Lester Aquafreddo, from the mob—were already picking at salads when Peaches walked up. He'd left Lonzo at the bar, in case he needed someone to come up from behind. When Mike introduced them, Silausk extended her hand, but Aquafreddo didn't even look up. "Am I interrupting you?" Peaches asked when he sat down.

"Sorry, sorry," Aquafreddo said, "the Caesar is like fucking crack. I'm eating like I'm out on bail." He wiped his mouth with the back of his left hand while extending his right. Hands like canned hams. "Your nephew here, he says you can solve all of our problems."

"You don't want me solving your problems," Peaches said.

"You know Ronnie and me, we have some history," Aquafreddo

said, leaning across the table toward Peaches, his voice just above a whisper, like they were in on some conspiracy. "From back in the old days, when there was no vacationing in Palm Springs. Just the streets and making those dollars."

"I don't know anyone named *Ronnie*," Peaches said. "I know someone named Mr. Cupertine. Is that who you're referring to?"

Aquafreddo chuckled, rubbed an imaginary wrinkle from his shirt, which was pulled tight across his gut. He was one of those guys who liked being fat, like it was a sign he was tougher than a cardiac arrest. Peaches never understood that. He was fit because he respected himself. "All right," he said. "Next time you see Mr. Cupertine, tell him I said hello. It won't get you shot or anything."

These fucking guys and their loose lips, Peaches thought. *The worst secret criminal organization on the planet.* He looked at Lori Silausk. He wasn't used to dealing with women in leadership roles, but it didn't bother him. Most times, women didn't feel like they were planning to kill you where you stood. "You have any greetings to extend, Ms. Silausk?" Peaches asked.

"My cousin," she said, "he's married to a nice Chuyalla girl."

"Oh yeah?"

"Desiree Thompkins," Silausk said.

"Where from?"

"Some shitty town in Wisconsin," Silausk said, trying to be funny. "Over in Lake Country."

"Don't know her," Peaches said. He thought he might. Chuyalla wasn't huge and Peaches had made it a point to know anyone who might have some capital for investment purposes.

"Now she's Desiree Palovich," Silausk said. Peaches did know her. He'd run her credit and everything. "They live in Seattle now. Work in sustainable garments with Nike. Shoes made of hemp. Every couple months, she sends us a bunch of samples to try out. Like walking on knives."

"Palovich. Silausk. Sounds Polish," Peaches said. Looked Polish, too: Silausk had sandy-blond hair and soft-brown eyes.

"Everything gets corrupted," Lori said. "My family, they've been here since this was the shore of Lake Cahuilla."

"I don't know what that means," Peaches said.

"Used to be a lake stretched all the way from here to the Gulf of Mexico," she said. "It's where our band got their name. But my last name? It has no meaning. It's just letters. I mean, what's *Pocotillo*?"

"Originally? I don't know," Peaches said. In Illinois and Wisconsin, people paid respect on it. His father, he'd been an OG, came up with the Cupertines, played high school football with them. But then he got run up with some Outfit bullshit, did time, snitched out some motherfuckers, got out, tried to be scarce, until one day he caught a bullet. His grandfather served in World War II, came back a shooter for hire. An old story. But out here? This fucking town? No one gave a shit. "Probably came from *ocotillo*. From a pretty flower to bad motherfucker in three generations." Out the back window, he could see the San Jacinto Mountains, palm trees, people sitting by a pool. Place like this, in Chicago? Peaches would burn it down for insurance money before he'd dine in it. Plus, he liked to do his own cooking. "Nice place. You come here a lot?"

"It's a safe space," Aquafreddo said. "Owner gives free meals to broke wiseguys. After Gotti got pinched and left a bunch of us out in the cold, word got out you could come here, get a warm meal, a bucket of scotch, and some respect. Hard to start earning when you're seventy-five and your prostate is in a bag somewhere at Cedars." Aquafreddo gave Lori's arm a squeeze, which made her look uncomfortable. She wasn't a gangster, Peaches had sussed that out easily enough, but she also didn't seem to be put off by hanging out with killers and crooks. She had those big earrings, sure enough, but everything else about her seemed moderately conservative. Blue jeans, a white blouse, a wedding ring, one big diamond, surrounded by four smaller ones, platinum setting, maybe $7,000 originally. Someone loved her, all right, but it wasn't someone flashy. If he didn't know she was married to a Native Mob shot caller, he'd guess someone with a business degree. Could be both, he supposed. "Ain't no fucking retirement plan in this job, right, Lori?"

"Okay, Lester," Silausk said. "Let's not get ahead of ourselves."

Peaches looked at Mike, who squirmed in his seat. "Something need to be put on the table?"

"Lester's talking about maybe getting the casino out here unionized," Mike said. "I told him, we don't do that back east. That not even Mr. Cupertine has union sway anymore. All that Jimmy Hoffa bullshit is the old ways."

"And yet you're still looking to bring the Teamsters into a sovereign nation?" Peaches asked.

"Carpenters and Millwrights, actually," Aquafreddo said. "Same guys built half the high-rises in Chicago when you were still in diapers."

"The fuck is a millwright?" Peaches said.

"Heavy machinery," Aquafreddo said. "You know, like building elevators and shit. The union already owns the Riviera down the block."

"Really," Peaches said. He made eye contact with Lonzo. They'd need to move. Their rooms were probably tapped. "How do you feel about this, Ms. Silausk?"

"Call me Lori." She waved over a waiter. Ordered a bottle of champagne. "As you can imagine, there's significant pushback on my side."

"I'm just looking for long-term stability for my family," Aquafreddo said. "We're putting a lot of money into the operation, and I don't have an official 401(k), you know what I'm saying. Up the street, Trump has bought into a casino. So workers there, they feel pretty good. He's not gonna go belly-up and leave them without a pension. Maybe we put our money there instead."

"And then the Mexican Mafia?" Peaches asked. "They want health care? Seems like they could use it if I understand correctly."

"Well, that's the other problem." Lester Aquafreddo started to re-arrange items on the table. "You see the sugar caddy here? That's the Mexican Mafia. They run the cocaine from the border up into LA. They got their leadership housed in Indio. About a block away from where our casino is." He placed the saltshaker next to the sugar caddy. "They bought into the casino early on; isn't that right?"

"They made an early capital investment," Lori said, "back when we were still a bingo parlor. I was fourteen. So. I didn't have any say on it. They continued to provide some needed protection for several years, but that time and that investment are up."

Aquafreddo and Lori kept on with the details of the casino part-nership, which ended up being that the LA families wanted to cut the Mexicans out, which would allow them to run the drugs on the prop-erty, wash their money in the casino, and provide protection, and in exchange they'd unionize, get LA-leadership health care and pensions and other shit they could loot if need be. But the Mexicans didn't want to leave. So now the Mexican Mafia and the Native gangsters were beefing.

"Except Lori's cousins and brothers don't know how to shoot," Aquafreddo said. He shifted forward again, his chest halfway into the bread dish. "So your nephew and I have been taking care of things when we have to." He shook his head. "I'm sixty. I'm not doing fucking drive-bys anymore. I can barely see at night as it is. Which is where you come in to save the day."

This fucking guy, Peaches thought. *All these fucking guys.* If there weren't a hundred people in the restaurant, Peaches would put one be-tween Aquafreddo's eyes right now. Existing on a reputation that was formed in the 1970s and now they were pushing retirement age and didn't have shit saved, so they still had to hustle the pyramid scheme that had been the basis of their business since Capone ran the streets. None of them had the sense of how to run a criminal operation in the twenty-first century, much less understood that robbing banks didn't need to involve a gun and a Citibank branch. All of them threw cash around and kept two girlfriends on the side. They were leeches. Peaches knew he couldn't just start killing them, because their lazy asses kept him protected. As long as everyone made rent, they were content to keep on keeping on, a big score always around the corner.

Mike said, "I told them how you brokered the deal between The Family and then our thing. And how you got all the Native Crips and Bloods to fall in line. How you know how to fix shit so everyone wins."

"The gangster whisperer," Aquafreddo said, "that's what you said."

Mike laughed.

Aquafreddo laughed.

Lori poured a flute of champagne, sipped it, looked off toward something in the far corner of the restaurant. Peaches followed her gaze. Two guys, fifties, expensive clothes, hands like fucking baseball mitts, crooked noses, kinda messed-up eyebrows, the sort of guys who led with their foreheads, with their eyes on her, like Lonzo had eyes on Peaches. Real subtle. Real ready to crack some fucking heads.

Maybe she was a gangster after all. Had Mike and this LA dupe doing her dirty work.

"You kick up to New York?" Peaches asked Aquafreddo. "Sixty years old, still paying freight?"

"Made a choice," Aquafreddo said. "Can't stand cold weather. So I pay my taxes; I just pay them to John's kid now, instead of Uncle Sam. No difference. What about you? You got a W-9 with the Cupertines?"

"Mr. Cupertine is his own man. I am my own man. We're a partnership. No one is anyone's boss. Because I guess I don't understand. Gotti is in prison, will probably be dead soon, you're out here earning, and then, what, you're FedExing cash to someone in New York?"

"Something like that," Aquafreddo said.

"And you're telling *me* how you want to do business?"

Silence.

Mike said, "We're all friends here, Uncle."

Silence.

Mike said, "It's the Mexican Mafia that's the problem."

Silence.

Peaches said, "Don't tell me who my friends are, nephew."

Silence.

Lester Aquafreddo smiled. "There's no want," he said. "It's either how it's gonna be or how it's not gonna be. We're doing business with you, or we're doing business with Trump and the other tribes and you're out here holding your Chicago dicks. Respectfully."

"You wouldn't know respect if it was fucking your father in prison," Peaches said. Loudly. Intentionally. Because Peaches was seeing the world so clearly now. It was as if time slowed down and Peaches was moving fast, fast, fast. He knew everyone's moves before they even thought of them, because everyone in this room was living thirty years ago.

And just like that, Lonzo was sitting between Peaches and Aquafreddo. All the women with faces like cats were turned to him. The men, in their golf pants and polo shirts and oxygen tanks, whipped around. Lori's two guys, halfway out of their chairs. No one speaking, everyone waiting, even the waiters, until Lori grabbed one. "A bottle of wine for every table, please," she said, handing over her black Amex.

"Where's your husband?" Peaches asked, once eyes had returned to plates.

"My husband, Rudy," she said, "is doing fifteen in Corcoran."

"When I did time," Peaches said, "I met Richard Speck. Do you know who that is?"

"No," Lori said.

"Murdered eight women in one night," Peaches said. "This was in the 1960s."

"And John Wayne Gacy did my floors," Aquafreddo said. "What the fuck are we talking about here?"

Peaches put a finger up. "One moment," he said, "and I'll get back to you."

"The fuck did you say to me?"

Lonzo said, "He said he didn't want to hear your voice. You can stay quiet for just a minute, can't you?"

"Or what? You're gonna shoot me in Melvyn's?"

"No," Lonzo said. "I'll stab you in the liver."

That got him to shut the fuck up.

"I bring up Mr. Speck," Peaches continued, "because he was not all that nice. In fact, when I met him, he was a fucking asshole. Happy to tell you about how he'd gutted those nurses and just laugh about it."

"Not a lot of nice guys in prison," Lori said.

"No, no," Peaches said. "Is your husband a nice guy?"

"No," Lori said. "Not in the conventional sense. Just like you're not."

"Prison fucks you up," Peaches said. "Speck got estrogen smuggled into the prison. By the time I met him, he had breasts like a woman and was selling his asshole for cocaine. Here was the worst serial killer of his time, a monster, and all he did every day was suck dicks and get fucked for the joy of snorting the shit Mexican Mafia and Gambino fucks like your friend here get rich smuggling into the prisons. How many years does your husband have left on his bid?"

"With good behavior, seven."

"Bet he's been getting into some shit, though. More lately."

"He's had some troubles, yes."

"Corcoran, that's like a Mexican Mafia gated community. They even clique up with the Aryan Nation on the inside. It's a power-share HOA to keep the other races at bay. Which I suspect makes it real hard to live a peaceful, good-behavior life, especially if back on the streets, you're still calling shots that end up with a bunch of dead Mexicans in a Fuddruckers."

"He got jumped a few weeks ago," Lori said. "Broke his jaw. Tried to carve out one of his eyes."

"That's terrible," Peaches said. "What's the Gambino family doing to help?"

Aquafreddo said, "It's a process. We're getting some money on some guards. We got nobody with any sway on the inside. Everyone has aged out."

"He's alone in there right now," she said. "They have him segregated."

"So I understand," Peaches said, "here in the real world, your husband and this fat fuck have a business agreement to erase the Mexican Mafia's entire business plan in this city, keep them out of all the casinos you're planning to build, and in return, your husband is rotting in a Mexican Mafia–run prison with no backup? Does that make sense to you?"

"When you put it like that," Lori said, "no."

"Twenty-four hours, I can have your husband completely protected. Forty-eight hours, I can have him eating a steak dinner in his cell. Seventy-two hours, maybe I get him a year of good behavior restored."

"In exchange for what?"

"Partnership," Peaches said.

"Fifty percent?"

"Less," Peaches said.

"Why not 50 percent?"

"This is your land," Peaches said. "This is your business. For Mr. Cupertine, this is just a business investment. And then, in a bit of time, I may need a favor from you, from your husband, from his interests in the Native Mob for another can't-miss opportunity. Simple as that." Peaches poured himself a flute of champagne from Lori's bottle, sipped it. "As for you," he said, looking at Aquafreddo, "you get nothing. If you walk out the door now, I will let you live. If you stay in this desert for even one more day, I will blow up your house. I will kill your wife, your children, your dog, your cat, and I will find all your living relatives and kill each of them, too."

Lester Aquafreddo, who'd been in the game since Kennedy was president, who Peaches figured was probably a pretty adept killer back in the day, enough so that he didn't mind riding shotgun while Peaches's nephew popped Mexican Mafia so that he could eventually get the Native Mob shot caller in the region put to sleep in prison, so he could squeeze the Native Mob out of their actual fucking birthright? Who was an adroit enough businessman to get hooked up with the Native Mob years ago, back when the tribes were just getting their gaming rights? Who had waited it all out for this day, when casinos would rise in this desert and he could sit back and make his money? That fat fuck sitting not three feet from Peaches?

He burst into laughter. Motioned over a waiter. "Box up the rest of my salad," he said; then he stood up. Five other guys stood up at the same time. Huh. Peaches hadn't seen them. Or maybe he had. They just didn't look like much. Old men in polyester eating fucking salads never did put much of a scare into Peaches Pocotillo. "This is an open city," Aquafreddo said. "You can't fucking touch me. And you can't cut me out of my own deal so Chicago can slide in. That's not how it works."

"If you don't like it," Peaches said, "you're welcome to go to the FBI."

Aquafreddo said, "I make one call, you're dead as soon you get back to Chicago."

Peaches finished off his champagne. He didn't really care for the stuff, if he was being honest. It gave him a headache. But today was for celebrating. "I am Chicago. I'm the whole fucking tri-state area. And you're a dinosaur staring up at the sky, wondering what the bright light is. You're already dead."

Lester Aquafreddo and his five friends made their way out of the restaurant, a mass of Lipitor making for the door, lugging their doggy bags of salads, mad-dogging Peaches and Lonzo the whole way. It must have been something to see when their eyes weren't so milky with cataracts.

"Uncle," Mike said, "what did you do?"

"Solved your problems," Peaches said.

"These guys are for real, Uncle," Mike said.

"And I am not?"

Mike stood up. "Let me see if I can cool them down," he said, and he made for the door, too, leaving Peaches, Lori, and Lonzo at the table, every eye in the restaurant on them.

"Some Fredo shit," Lonzo said. "You were right."

Peaches shook his head. "He's never even seen the movie; it's just his nature. He wants more and more, wants to work less and less."

Lori said, "I'm going to need to buy another round."

Lonzo said, "Bossman, we need to get our shit out of that hotel."

Peaches said . . . nothing. Because he was already living in the future. Lester Aquafreddo and his five friends were dead. He'd need to get rid of their bodies. And then he'd see where they ended up. He might just travel with their bodies himself. Get some answers about how the fuck Ronnie Cupertine's wife and children ended up in Portland when they should have been in the ground.

His nephew was becoming a liability. Chasing after those Gambino fucks like a puppy dog. He was probably eating their shit straight from their asses.

In the meantime, he now had a wonderful new partnership to celebrate with Lori, who he thought he might have an off chance of sleeping with if he played things just right. Maybe give her a baby, too, and then, of course, he'd need to take care of her husband, after saving his ass. That was a future he couldn't see clearly yet, but the outlines looked promising.

"Tell me, Lori," he said, "your beautiful cheekbones. All yours, or did you have some work?"

Lori blushed. "I guess you could say I got a new paint job."

"Who did the work? Someone local?"

"One of our own," she said. "Stayed local and opened up a small office. Very discreet."

"I see," Peaches said.

Lonzo tapped him on the shoulder, handed him his cell phone. "Bossman," he said, "you need to take this. Big Kirk got a problem."

TEN

BEST BUY DROPPED OFF THE COMPUTER RABBI DAVID COHEN ORDERED JUST before five on Tuesday night, David paying extra for them to hook it up inside his three-car garage, in the wedge of space in front of a sailboat, the one used in the murder of his predecessor, Rabbi Gottlieb. David had turned the wedge—intended to be golf cart parking inside the three-car garage—into a working space away from the cameras inside the house, Bennie not smart enough to install cameras in the garage, or maybe he didn't think anyone would intentionally sit inside the sweatbox. The heat wave made the garage unbearable during the day, but at night, when the sun fell behind the Red Rocks, it cooled down to mildly uncomfortable.

Poor Rabbi Gottlieb. David heard nothing but hagiography since he'd come to Temple Beth Israel, but living in his house taught David a few things about the good rabbi's secrets. There was the porn stash behind the dresser and the monthly deliveries of Omaha Steaks, which always included at least one precooked pork chop dinner, neither meal exactly kosher. Plus the man was a bit of a hoarder. When David was gone, he'd figure out a way to get word to the Gottlieb family. They should know what really happened to their son. It was a *shanda* that they believed their son had been drunk when he drowned.

By 7 p.m., David built, essentially, a false wall around his new computer room, stacking coolers, his portable lathe, moving boxes, stacks of towels, and green garbage bags filled with Rabbi Gottlieb's old paperbacks to the roof, leaving a small opening in the rear. He then locked the house, turned on all the alarms, made sure his guns were secure—he had a hidden place in every room for a firearm; he could be anywhere when the Marshals showed up—and fired up the laptop to do what he'd been doing every night that week: seeking out his wife on the internet.

Tonight, he was reading the stories about the explosion that turned his house into nothing but a charred foundation, how the fire could be seen from miles away, how it ended up destroying gas and plumbing lines down the entire block, the explosion's power so significant the local fire department originally thought a plane crashed into the street. The *Tribune* ran photos that included MapQuest's satellite view compared to the denuded new reality. It was shocking to see, but then David realized something far more interesting, which is that MapQuest had satellite photos going back over the last two years, once every few months.

In the first photos, all he could see was the roof and the general outline of the house, though he could still make out bits of himself, too: the towering blue ash tree in the front yard, where he hung a tire swing for William; the brick driveway, Jennifer's dream, which he laid over the course of a long weekend; the backyard built-in grill, which he'd bought after his first substantial hit—Gil Lomontoli, a city councilman snitching to a cop on the take, the dumbfuck—and which he loved. But it was the third photo from space he couldn't stop staring at.

There was a figure standing on the driveway. Even from outer space, he could recognize his wife. The closer he zoomed in, the blurrier everything got, but still he could see she had her hand to her mouth, another on her hip, and she was staring down the block.

He pulled back on the photo, and there, on the corner, by the Sandersons' house, was William, on a bike, a blur of a boy. On either side of the street is what must have kept Jennifer's equal attention: a police cruiser and a black Escalade, neither of which made sense, unless they were both waiting for Sal Cupertine to come home.

How he would like to walk down the middle of that block, gun in hand. Dare the cops or the feds to say one word to him.

Or anyone.

If he came back to Chicago, he'd be the king of the streets.

But . . . no.

He knew better. What was the point of revenge now? Everyone who mattered was dead or dying. What was he going to do? Peel Lemonhead's cap back? For what? Taking orders like a dumbfuck? Same with Sugar Lopiparno, who the papers said was running half of Chicago, what with Ronnie Cupertine rarely being seen these days . . .

To be the king of his own backyard would be enough.

He clicked through the photos again, loaded the latest satellite photo, checked the date: March 1, 2002. Six weeks ago. No realtor sign. No new construction, either. No weeds. Just . . . land. Someone was taking care of it. That meant they were being paid. He supposed the FBI was used to this sort of thing . . . but why hadn't they sold it yet?

Before David could give it much thought, the home phone rang. He looked at the clock. It was nearly 11 p.m. Had he really been sitting there staring at photos of his wife and child from outer space all night long? He got into the kitchen just as the eighth ring was echoing throughout the house.

"Rabbi Cohen. Oh, thank god." It was Jerry Ford, the owner of LifeCore, the Temple and the mortuary's business partner in their limbs, skin, and body-parts business, legal and otherwise. He was breathless. "I didn't know if you were back yet. I've got a problem." David clicked on his CCTV. Jerry Ford was parked on the other side of his front gate, in his butter-yellow Mercedes. He zoomed in. Was that . . . blood on his sweat suit?

"I'm here," David said. "I can see you on my camera. I feel like you've encountered a problem best left to Mr. Savone."

"He'll kill me."

David should have hung up, walked outside with his gun, and shot Jerry Ford in the face, tossed him in the freezer, stolen his car, and driven as fast and as far as he could.

But for fuck's sake, he'd been the guy on the other end of this same phone call and it upended his life. Maybe he was the prophet Ezekiel. Maybe all of this was foretold. Maybe he lived this life one million times to get to this existential conundrum. A man covered in blood shows up at your home and asks for help. What do you do?

"Mr. Ford," David said, thinking of all the possible people, agencies, and crime bureaus who might be listening in, "why don't you come inside. Have a cup of tea. We'll talk through whatever it is you're feeling."

"I don't think you want me in your house in my condition."

"It's fine," David said. He zoomed in as close as possible. Was he . . . crying? *Motherfucker.* "Please, come in."

David hung up.

He stuffed a nine in his waistband, grabbed a towel, walked outside, sprayed his hose on the towel, hit a button on his key fob, opened the gate. Let Jerry pull up his driveway. Put a hand up to stop him from driving any further. David slid into the Mercedes. Jerry was covered in blood. The soles of his shoes to his forehead. He looked like he been slaughtering cows all day. David took the nine from his waistband, since it was uncomfortable to sit that way, set it on his lap. Handed him the towel.

Jerry wiped his face, his hands, his neck. It didn't look like Jerry had murdered someone. Rather, it looked like he'd gone for a swim in a pool of dead bodies. He also smelled like a combination of decomposition—like if lamb chops were left in the sun and a dog shit iodine on them—chlorine, and dried blood. A wave of nausea passed over David. The blood was everywhere, so David said, "Drive. We can't stay here. You never know who is watching."

"Which way?"

"Are we going to the police station to turn you in?"

"No. I'm not prepared to do that."

"Then it doesn't matter," David said. "Just drive. And get some windows open."

Jerry backed out, exited the Lakes at Summerlin Greens, wound around the streets until he saw the on-ramp to the Summerlin Parkway, got on going south, exited on Rainbow, turned left, drove over to the Best in the West Shopping Center, parked in front of McDonald's, which even at this time of night was bumping. The play area filled with kids. Tweaks and bartenders and working girls eating cheeseburgers and watching them fuck around. That was the thing about Summerlin. Middle of the week, the night owls still kept to their clocks even if they weren't working, everything in this town open twenty-four hours, David wondering if these kids ever went to school and who watched them when their parents weren't around. Whole generation of Las Vegas kids growing up behind gates, being raised by voice mails and Domino's and Rachael Ray cooking meals in under thirty minutes.

"Is this okay?" Jerry asked.

"If you don't mind looking like a blood-soaked pedophile."

Jerry pulled behind the McDonalds, next to the dumpster, a homeless guy already decamped for the night. *Fuck it.* Anywhere outside the lights of Las Vegas was someone trying to get some sleep.

"Rabbi," Jerry said, "I fucked up."

"I see that," David said.

Jerry swallowed, hard. "I don't know . . . what you are, exactly. But I didn't have anyone else I trusted."

"I'm your rabbi," David said. "So you're right to trust me."

"Rabbi," Jerry said, "what the fuck is up with the gun?"

"You're covered in blood, Jerry," David said. "I figured this might be a situation where a gun would make us both more comfortable."

"It is not making me comfortable. Do you even know how to handle that thing?"

"I've killed a hundred men," David said. "Maybe more."

"I don't know what part of the Talmud you're quoting." Jerry popped open the glove box. "So, for my peace of mind, please, stash it in there. You're going to end up accidentally killing us both." David did so. He also had a nine on his ankle and of course the knife. Jerry watched him, then said. "You look . . . not the same."

"I've had extensive plastic surgery," David said. He turned the radio on, filling the Benz with Neil Diamond, again. Everyone in this fucking town playing Neil Diamond lately. He turned the volume up, just in case either the car or Jerry was bugged.

"Whose blood are you covered in?" David asked.

"With you away, I've had to take on new clients in the last couple months. I went to do a pickup tonight and ran into a situation."

"Jerry, when I came to you, asking for help when Mr. Savone was arrested, did you ask any questions?"

"I've never asked any questions, Rabbi. Respectfully. I would *never* ask you any questions. What you do, who you are, whatever, that's your show."

"Good," David said. "Speak in specifics."

"I've got bodies melting through the floor of a dentist's office into a swingers club that opens again in about ten hours."

"And you think I can help you?"

"If this becomes public," Jerry said, "they will eventually find me. Because the smell is . . . the smell is very bad, Rabbi. And the leaking is very bad. It is . . . in the ceiling tiles and walls and I am beyond my ability to cope with that alone. And that means the media will eventually see the work I do with the Temple, and that will eventually lead to a reporter showing up at your house. And you said, from the start, no media. So. I've played this scenario out as far as I can, and it always ends with a reporter talking to you. Cops, for sure. FBI will eventually become involved. I've done the math."

Jerry was right about one thing. Bennie would kill him. Bennie would also kill Jerry's wife. Might kill Jerry's kids. Might invent a time machine, kill his fucking parents. David should kill him, right now, but he didn't yet know where the bodies were.

"Where's your wife?" David said.

"I sent her to our beach house in Pismo."

"When?"

"About forty-five minutes ago."

"She can't come back here," David said. "Not until I tell you it's okay. Do you understand?"

"I understand."

"Who owns this dental office?"

"Russians." Jerry squirmed in his seat. "I met some fellas playing poker. They run with Boris Dmitrov. He owns Odessa, the Russian place over on Paradise. You know him?"

"No." He did, in fact, know exactly who he was. Ran the Russian mob in Las Vegas. Had influence across the entire country. He'd been one of the first Russians to operate on a national level. Not unlike Ronnie, he was so outwardly a gangster that it was now his cover. When travel shows did specials on the most mobbed-up places to get a meal in Las Vegas, it was always Odessa, Piero's over by the Convention Center, and the Venetian restaurant on Sahara. Buses let out in front of those fucking places, letting tourists snap photos.

David looked at Jerry and asked, "Why aren't you at Odessa explaining your problems?"

"He's a nice guy," Jerry said. "But his friends scare the shit out of me."

"You're scared of a dentist?"

"It's not always a dental office," Jerry said. "Like how Temple Beth Israel and the funeral home isn't always . . ."

Before Jerry was done speaking, David had the tip of his knife inside Jerry's right ear and one of his giant hands around Jerry's throat. "Say one more word," David said, "and I will shove this knife into your brain. But I'll do it slow, so you have some time to reflect on how many mistakes have led you to this moment. If you understand what I'm saying, blink twice."

Jerry blinked twice.

"You've had some questions about me over the years. Would that be a correct statement?" He twisted the knife maybe a centimeter, enough to draw blood. "Have you voiced your questions to anyone? You wife, maybe?"

Blink. Blink.

"Your wife is a smart woman. I bet she told you that you've chosen a certain life and if you want to stay in that life, you're going to be in business with people who don't always seem to be who they are. Would that be true?"

Blink. Blink.

"I mean, you are aware that Bennie Savone is a fucking gangster, right?"

Jerry didn't move a muscle. Kept his eyes as wide as possible.

"You can answer that question honestly, Jerry, because the Talmud tells us that we need not let the past destroy our future. You know Bennie is a gangster. You know I am not what I seem. That is all past. What happens next is the future. So. Two blinks if you understand where we are at this point on our journey together."

Blink. Blink.

"Tonight is likely to be the end of our association," David said. "So I'm going to speak in specifics. Before we go any further, I want you to understand that if I help you with this problem, whatever it might be, and if you then ever say anything that isn't complimentary about your working relationship with the Kales Home of Peace or Temple Beth Israel, I will kill you." He dug the knife in. A millimeter. Maybe two. Jerry cried out in a pure atavistic response. Also, it probably hurt.

Jerry blinked about six times.

"However this shakes out," David said, "tomorrow, you're going to put your house on the market. You will take the first offer that comes your way. You're going to lay off all of your employees this week. Give them severance. Continue their health care for three months. Be a fucking mensch, Jerry, do you understand?"

More blinking.

"Good. And if the FBI should ever contact you about anything, even if it's because they think you assassinated JFK, I want you to consider killing yourself before answering them. Because if you ever speak to the FBI, even if you lie to them, you are a dead man. Learn the words 'I take the fifth.' Understand?"

Blinking.

David let go of his throat, because it was starting to seem like maybe Jerry wasn't getting enough oxygen, what with the way his lips were turning blue, but kept the knife in his ear.

"Now, be real still while I pull the knife out of your ear. Because if I perceive you moving in an offensive manner, I might accidentally sever your auditory nerve, and I don't want to do that." David slid the knife out, wiped it on his thigh, not that it was all that dirty, but it seemed like a hard-core thing to do, and David wanted to make sure Jerry had something concrete to take from this. "Now either take me home or take me to this dentist's office."

Jerry spent a few seconds thinking about his particular set of problems, which to be generous had just quadrupled, and opted for the dentist's office, since they pulled out of the Best of the West and headed south.

"May I speak?" Jerry said, after they'd been back on the road for a few minutes.

"Of course."

"I thought we were friends."

"We are," David said, leaving the salient part unsaid: *Which is why you're still alive.*

THE DENTAL OFFICES OF YURI "JACK" BELSKY WERE LOCATED ON THE SECOND floor of a sprawling warehouse that had been carved up into store fronts on the east side of the Commercial Center between Sahara and Maryland Parkway, just above the Red Lantern Swingers Club, a gun-and-ammo shop, and a recording studio called Hollywood Starz. The Red Lantern was open Thursday through Sunday, according to the pulsing sign out front, which also advertised the pricing guide for entrance: $85 for single men Thursday and Sunday night, $125 Friday and Saturday. Couples $100 every night! Single ladies free! A fucking racket, but David saw the wisdom. Without the single ladies, it was just a bathhouse, and there were three of those in the Commercial Center already. This was a part of town David didn't spend a lot of time in, because he was not looking for group sex or a recording contract and he had enough guns and ammo to take on a decent militia.

Back in the day, however, the Commercial Center was going to be the epicenter of Las Vegas, a huge outdoor shopping center set to revolutionize retail with its sheer size and walkability. That was in the 1960s and '70s. The story was that Elvis and Frank and then later Lefty Rosenthal and Tony Spilotro would come in with their girlfriends and buy jewelry, grab a meal at one of the steakhouses, and then race their cars around the massive parking lot—three thousand marked spaces!—and maybe part of it was true—he was pretty sure Spilotro's Hole in the Wall gang had robbed a jewelry store in the center—but David figured it was mostly bullshit like everything else, another story about why shit was better when the mob ran the town.

These days, the center was half empty, most of the storefronts obvious money-laundering operations—Korean nail salons, wig stores, pet shops that sold ferrets and snakes but had never seen a golden retriever, rub-and-tug massage joints, delis and Chinese restaurants, all the kinds of places that could operate without real employees, just the owner and some cousins. They all had signs that said, SINCE 1971! or whatever year they decided to make up to give the people shopping some confidence. Personally, David didn't think the fact that the Golden Sunset Bath House had been in business since 1973 was a good selling point.

The parking lot was mostly empty tonight, save for two rows of F-150s and Silverados lined up like soldiers out front of The Ponderosa, a faux Western saloon a floor and two doors down from the dental office, which wouldn't be anything to note, except everyone knew The Ponderosa was a cop bar, the kind with a mechanical bull and a reputation for late-night shootings that went uninvestigated. Jerry was smart enough to pull around the back of the building, a narrow alley off of Market Street, and when he got out, he immediately removed his license plates, tossed them in his trunk.

David could hear the thumping of music coming from The Ponderosa; Lee Greenwood was going on at some length about how he knows he's free, followed by whooping and chants of "U.S.A. motherfucker! U.S.A. motherfucker! U.S.A. motherfucker!" It sounded like the mixture of a Klan rally and bachelor party.

"You've been doing business next to a cop bar?" David said.

"Boris owns The Ponderosa, too," Jerry said. He was in the trunk, looking for something. Meanwhile, things began to click into place. What was the difference between owning The Ponderosa and employing a dozen cops to do personal security? David supposed it was easier to blackmail cops when you had them on video getting blow jobs from the working girls—because there was indeed a subset of working girls who only frequented cop bars, Las Vegas unique for their niche prostitutes—or had the ability to spike their drinks, get them pissing dirty and off the job.

"Here." Jerry tossed David a sealed plastic bag covered in the LifeCore logo. "Put these on." Inside were plastic booties, an N95 mask, and surgical gloves. "You're going to need them, Rabbi."

Jerry unlocked a back door and directed them into a narrow hallway that led to the locked rear exit of the swingers club and to a stairwell which ushered them upstairs to the dental office. The stairwell smelled like a combination of piss, sweat, chlorine, and like the walls were filled with dead rats. The stairs themselves were either sticky or damp, David thankful to be in near darkness, except for the half-light put off by a single tube of fluorescent light on the ceiling. When they hit the second floor, however, they were in complete darkness, Jerry taking out a flashlight, but David could have figured out their path by following his nose: Those weren't rats in the wall. Once you smell rotting human flesh, it never quite leaves you, and working for four years in a funeral home, plus his previous forty years putting people into the dirt, David knew what was what. David snapped on his gloves, then strapped on his N95.

"The fuck happened up here?" David said, except he was aware he'd left David back in the garage at home. Sal Cupertine was on the job.

"Power went out," Jerry said.

"When?" It was also sweltering up here on the second floor. It had been over 100 degrees all day and was still in the high 80s, at least. Felt like it was about 120 in the building.

"Sometime after Sunday," Jerry said. "Power company said it should be back on after midnight." It was 12:12 a.m. "They're late."

There was a security-system keypad beside the door to the dental office, but with the power out it was useless, so Jerry unlocked the door with a key, and they were inside the waiting room of the dental office, six chairs in a *U*, a table covered in old issues of *People*, a frosted window opening into the administrative office. Jerry unlocked another door, and they were into the clinic, the smell getting worse as they moved through the wide expanse of the floor—past the X-ray bay, past the hygienist station, past six separate treatment rooms, the lab, the accounting office, and the dentist's personal office—to eight-foot pneumatic double doors marked STORAGE/PERSONNEL ONLY/ ABSOLUTELY NO SMOKING. Jerry found another key, unlocked those doors, said to Sal, "This is where it gets problematic."

The doors opened into a warehouse that ran the length of the second floor. It was lit with a few trembling emergency lights that revealed eight-foot shelving units stacked with medical coolers between two and six feet long, the kind the Kales Home of Peace used to store body parts they were shipping out to LifeCore. The difference was that Kales kept their containers in a freezer unit cooled to between 32 and 39 degrees at all times. Anything lower or higher would render the tissue and bones unusable.

It was about 100 degrees inside the warehouse. It was like sitting in the *schvitz* at a Russian spa in Chicago.

Sal popped open a cooler at knee level, looked in.

There were six human heads inside. They'd been professionally re-moved, looked like, not cut off by someone like Fat Monte, who used to like doing that shit.

Sal opened the next cooler. More heads.

The next.

The next.

The next.

He counted fifty heads total. This would be a horror show, but the heads were all sealed inside medical-grade coolers and were jacked full of formaldehyde and glutaraldehyde, which made their skin turn a familiar if otherworldly greenish gray: When LifeCore was going to move product for medical research or university study, the clients would sometimes ask Ruben and Miguel to preserve them in this way, so Sal had seen a row of heads like this in the past. With regular injec-tions, they could sit on these shelves for years, probably, if the cooling hadn't gone out.

What Sal couldn't figure out was how or why this dentist had all of this cadaver stock. Kales kept nothing. What didn't go to LifeCore was either buried with the bodies or disposed of in the legal way, Ruben running a clean operation to stay kosher with Melanie Moss and the rest of the state investigators. Surely the dentist wasn't licensed for this shit. How could he be? How the fuck was he going to get rid of fifty human heads?

That was, it turned out, the least of the problems. Sal closed the cooler and stepped through the maze of shelves until he found Jerry standing in front of double doors marked EMPLOYEES ONLY/FLAMMABLE/NO SMOKING. The floor—concrete throughout the warehouse—was covered in a sheen of pink liquid that ran from be-neath the doors and drained toward the southern wall, where it disap-peared into the drywall.

"The fuck is that?" Sal asked.

"Nothing you want to get on your skin," Jerry said. He pushed the doors open and inside were twenty industrial freezer units used to store materials at or below zero. There was an inch of fluid on the floor, each freezer dripping more every moment, the room broiling hot. On the shelves surrounding the freezer units were buckets and open coolers filled haphazardly with body parts, mostly hands and feet and sheets of skin. Sal gave them a glance. The word that came to mind was *molting*.

"I think before the power went out," Jerry said, "the cooling system must have busted because when I got here, the fan was blowing hot air. I mean, it was maybe 90 degrees in here. I think that caused the defrost, and that knocked the power out. We'd need to get someone out here to look to be sure. I'm not confident this place is even on the grid, to be honest, Rabbi."

"Don't bring anyone in this fucking place," Sal said.

"I wasn't going to call Nevada Power," Jerry said. "Boris, he's got guys. KGB fuckers. All leather coats and hand-rolled cigarettes, I mean, not Jews. The opposite of Jews. What is that word for those fuckers who ran us out of Europe? Not Nazis. The other thing."

"Cossacks."

"Right. Cossack motherfuckers. I mean. They built the warehouse."

"They did a great job," Sal said.

"The dental office was already here. The warehouse was just sitting empty. Dental office is on legit power, of course, but everything else, god knows who is getting juiced for it."

Sal looked down at his feet. "This shit is eating through the booties," he said.

"Yeah," Jerry said. "We shouldn't be breathing this. You get lightheaded, it's time to move." Sal had been light-headed since getting out of the truck of frozen meat four years ago. "I made the mistake of opening the freezers, hoping I could save some of the product, but I couldn't. And then that made everything worse." He shined his flashlight behind one of the freezer units. "The fluids are leaking through the floors. And there's no way the smell isn't filling up the club downstairs. I'm worried these fuckers might have attached the cooling system to the main plumbing of the building, which might then cause problems if someone flushes a toilet."

"Like what?"

"I don't know," Jerry said. "Maybe the streets run with blood and golems rise from the gutters. Who knows at this point."

Sal was surprised there weren't coyotes circling the building. He opened a freezer. There were plastic containers filled with eyes. The sheer volume had Sal confused. How was this possible?

"You do business with these people?"

"You've been gone," Jerry said. "I got bills to pay."

"Where do they get the parts?"

Jerry shook his head. "I don't know."

"Yes, you do."

"These fucking Russians," Jerry said. "They're not like us."

Sal opened another freezer. There were hearts and lungs and kidneys and livers stacked like at a butcher shop, each bleeding into the next.

"Jesus," Sal said. He slammed the door shut. He'd seen all these body parts before. He just hadn't seen them smorgasbord-style.

"I told you."

"No, you didn't. You said they're not like us. You didn't say they had fucking liver cutlets." The next freezer: Long bones. Spines. "Who are you selling this shit to?"

"Mostly overseas," Jerry said. "I go through a guy in New Jersey. I think they ship primarily to Afghanistan and Brazil. Wherever there's a war or elective plastic surgery and they need cadaver bones."

The next freezer: more heads.

"What do they need all these fucking heads for?"

"Scientific study," Jerry said. "Testing new lotions and oils and drugs and such. It's either human heads or cocker spaniels, and people don't like burning cocker spaniels. It's a burgeoning business. All these new FDA regulations about testing on animals, no one wants fucking PETA walking in circles in front of their offices. So they've got sites in Mexico and off-book sites in the United States. It's a real problem."

"They use human heads?"

He shrugged. "People donate their bodies to science. It's science, I guess."

Sal looked at the heads closely. A woman with earrings. A man with a cross on a tight gold chain seemingly melted into the flesh under his chin. A teenage girl with a diamond in her nose.

"Give me your flashlight," Sal said. Was that . . . dirt? The decapitation cuts looked ragged, having just done some similar work of his own, in the dark, and with much more precision. "Are these Russians robbing graves?"

"I don't know," Jerry said.

"Yes you do."

"Rabbi," Jerry said, "I ask them the same number of questions I ask you."

Fair enough. They hadn't robbed the Home of Peace, so it wasn't Sal's problem. This Boris character surely knew that Bennie was involved out in Summerlin and kept his shit to this side of town, on the other side of the tracks.

"How is any of this *your* problem?" Sal asked.

Jerry said, "I was supposed to do a pickup on Sunday. But I didn't end up getting here until today."

"It's not your fault the power went off." Jerry didn't respond, just kept his eyes on his feet. "Is it?" Sal said. "Is it your fault?"

"I own this entire floor. I rent the space to Dr. Belsky. He's been complaining about power surges shutting him down for weeks. I was supposed to get someone out here while he was on vacation. So. Yeah. Maybe it's my fault. Power isn't out anywhere else in the center. Not even downstairs."

Sal stared at Jerry for a moment. He looked scared. He should. "How long have you owned this place?"

"Eighteen months."

"Let me ask you a question," Sal said. "Don't lie. Did you *suggest* this line of business to the Russian mob like you suggested it to me?"

"My wife," Jerry said, "I knew she was unhappy in our marriage. I figured if I had just a bit more capital, I could get us the beach house, we could retire, have that good life."

"The question," Sal said. "Answer it."

"I did, in fact, bring them this business opportunity."

"Is there any way to connect this place to the Temple?"

"I keep paperwork on everything, to be legit," Jerry said. "I get audited like everybody else. So yes. The Temple is on my books. Dr. Belsky is on my books. It's all aboveboard."

"This," Sal said, "is not aboveboard."

"In my books," Jerry said. "It has the appearance of being aboveboard, okay? You think I'm going to memorialize a criminal operation? Everything I put on paper is the real. You have nothing to be worried about."

How much scrutiny could Temple Beth Israel and the Kales Mortuary and Home of Peace take? Cops come sniffing around, that wasn't much of a problem. Half the force worked for the Temple as it was, but more importantly, Las Vegas Metro didn't care about white-collar shit. They certainly weren't looking into financial crimes at synagogues, churches, and mosques. If someone showed up dead on the ground, yeah, they were going to investigate, but short of that, you had to be one dubious institution to draw their attention when every gangster, cartel boss, Russian oligarch, and Al-Qaeda soldier on the planet was landing at McCarran four times a day in G-200s.

But if the FBI showed up again? With subpoenas? And forensic accountants? Men offering deals? How long before Ruben went state's? How long before Miguel told a man in a black suit about that summer when he buried twenty Chinese men missing their pinkies in graves named for Jewish women?

Oh, he had something to worry about, all right.

Sal walked out of the freezer without another word, back through the warehouse, and into the dentist's office, Jerry a few steps behind him. The power was back on, cool air blowing through the vents, the electric hum of machinery ticking back to life. It was close to 12:30 a.m. now.

Sal pulled down his mask, gulped in the fresher air.

"When is Dr. Belsky due back?"

"A week." Jerry yanked his mask off, used it to wipe sweat from his face.

"Ponderosa closes when?"

"Never."

"Never?"

"This is Las Vegas, Rabbi."

Shit. He had to think on this for a moment. Jerry Ford was a dead man. Boris Dmitrov was going to have him killed for this. Bennie Savone was going to kill him, too. It would be a race to see who could get to him first.

Truth was, nothing said Jerry couldn't work with as many crime families as he wanted, but this situation was going to put him in a position to save his ass by going to the FBI and flipping on everyone. It was the only way out. That he'd come to Rabbi David Cohen for help was desperate. Surely it was a thing that seemed like a good idea at the time, because at some level, of course, Jerry knew Rabbi David Cohen was not who he said he was, figured that if he got him involved in this situation, he could possibly save both their asses by, in fact, indicting both their asses.

If he worked on the equation long enough, Jerry would eventually land on the answer to all of this, and it ended with him fucked for life. Jerry would not have an opportunity to get ghost. Jerry was already dead. Now, it was strictly about buying time, for everyone.

Sal should have known this would be his downfall. He could never control this part of the Temple's business. It was greedy and stupid of them to ever get involved with LifeCore. But Rabbi Kales wanted an empire. And Bennie Savone was going to give it to him. That was their plan. That plan took cash.

"What do they use to sterilize everything?" Sal asked.

"An autoclave," Jerry said.

"Show me," Sal said.

Jerry walked him over to the lab, across from the administrative office. The autoclave was a top-of-the-line horizonal Sonz unit, out of China. Four feet tall. Three feet deep. You could sterilize a man in here if you cut him in half. Back in Chicago, in his workshop on West Fulton, he had an old-school industrial autoclave that you could walk into, which was nice, whereas this looked like a particularly nice washer-dryer combo that could communicate to NORAD, judging by the four different digital displays and the sound of the whirring hard drive. He opened the door, looked in. He could pour at least two feet of fluid straight into the machine. Pressure steam everything with gasoline if he wanted.

Yeah. This would work.

"Get me every volatile chemical in this office," Sal said.

"I don't understand . . ." Jerry began, but Sal put up a hand to stop him.

"You asked for my help. If you don't want my help, the time to tell me is right now. Otherwise? No fucking questions."

"This is not a question. Well. It is. But it's the prelude to something else. Don't stab me in the ear, okay?"

Sal set the digital timer on the autoclave. "We have one minute to have this conversation," Sal said, and he hit start.

Jerry Ford said, "You know I went to med school?"

"No."

"Yeah. I was going to be a surgeon. That was my plan."

Forty-five seconds.

"Failed out my second year," Jerry said. "Thing was, I didn't tell my parents for another year. And then I told them I dropped out. That I just didn't think I was passionate about the field. My mother, she was Chicago through and through. She thought I didn't work hard enough, that anything could be accomplished with putting your head down. My father, he's Jersey; all he thinks about is the money wasted on me, four years at Rutgers, another year at Harvard, all that cash for nothing, particularly when he realized I basically stole a year of tuition money from him. That pissed him off. Neither ever asked me what I was going through that made this happen. They didn't just want a son who was a doctor; they needed a son who was a doctor. Part of the big grand plan."

"It was a different time."

"Hmm. Maybe. Rabbi, here's the rub: It wasn't hard to me at all. I went to school every day feeling like I knew more than anyone else. The problem, and I recognized this just in time, I think, was that I didn't care about *the people*. If someone lived or died? I didn't care. Meant nothing to me. That began to work on my brain. You can't be a sociopath and be a doctor."

"I disagree."

"Not a good doctor," Jerry said. "Maybe I should have been a veterinarian, because then you gotta be both the doctor and the patient, you know? Maybe that would have taught me something important."

"That you've thought all this through," Sal said, "and have feelings about it, means you're not a sociopath."

"Huh. Well. Where were you thirty-five years ago?" He clapped his hands together, then flipped them over for the eye in the sky, like a poker dealer. "Anyway. I bring this all up because it's come to me that this? I can't just quit this, can I?"

The timer beeped. All done.

"No."

Jerry said, "Can I get one more minute? I feel like, since this is about the rest of my life, two minutes should about handle it."

Sal added another minute. Hit start.

"That was true before this problem, I guess? This is a job you don't quit."

"Yes."

"I've been fucked since the day you agreed to help me?" Sal met his gaze but didn't respond. "I guess I knew I was," Jerry said. He seemed suddenly resigned. Of course he knew who Bennie Savone was all this time. And that's really what this was about. Who represented who. And Rabbi David Cohen represented Bennie Savone. "If you help me, am I going to get out of this alive?"

"For a time. Time comes, time comes."

"How long, do you wager?"

"We do this right," Sal said, "I can get you two weeks."

Jerry shivered. "Can I talk to my rabbi during this minute?"

"Yes," David said.

"What does the Talmud say about this?"

"Everything dies," Rabbi David Cohen said. "That's a fact. But everything that dies one day comes back."

Jerry actually chuckled. "You dumb shit," Jerry said, "I'm from Jersey. You're singing the national anthem." There was a flicker of amusement in his voice. "It was always bullshit, wasn't it, because no one knows anything anymore, do they?"

"If it ever helped you, it wasn't bullshit," Rabbi David Cohen said.

"Turns out, it never did." He yanked off his booties, tossed them in the trash. "Like Moses said, it's a suicide rap; get out while you're young." Jerry Ford could have run then, got into his car and driven off into the night, but instead he turned heel and went about gathering up everything Sal needed to blow up a building.

FORTY MINUTES LATER, SAL AND JERRY WERE SEATED IN A BOOTH AT THE Marie Callender's just down the block. Sal only realized after they sat down that they were across the parking lot from the Tony Roma's where The Outfit fire bombed Lefty Rosenthal's Eldorado, only to have him inexplicably survive. The Outfit always was dogshit with explosives, even back in the day. If you're gonna blow something up, it's egregious to miss your target, which is why Sal and Jerry were here in the first place. Make sure what was done was done.

"Give me a phone," Sal said. They'd stopped at the Chevron across the street and bought two burners. Jerry slid one across the table. Sal dialed 911, watched out the window. From his vantage point, he could see the exit and entrance into the Commercial Center perfectly, along with the intersection of Sahara and Maryland Parkway, a major artery for the city.

The operator picked up on the third ring, asked his emergency. He shoved his pinky into his mouth, bit down on it, then said, "I'm on the corner of Rainbow and Charleston and I just saw a motorist shoot a cop that had pulled him over," Sal said, his voice calm, measured. Not loud. The only way you can speak when you're biting down on your pinky. "Yeah, a blue Honda Accord, California plate, all I made out was the last three numbers, 812. Yes, ma'am, the cop is down. Rainbow and Charleston, east side of the street. You better get an ambulance quick. I can't stay," Sal said, "I'm late for my shift, but you need me, my number is . . ." and then he turned the power off, pried the phone apart with his butter knife, yanked out the SIM card, and crushed it with the ketchup bottle.

Rainbow and Charleston was about ten miles from where they were sitting. Way Sal figured it, every cop in the city would be flooding that direction in about two minutes. Including every single one inside The Ponderosa. There's an officer-down alert, every motherfucker with a badge gets on the scene. That it wasn't the same for every dead body was how Sal had managed to work in the shadows for so long.

"This going to work?" Jerry said.

"We'll see," Sal said. He waved over a waitress. "How's your New York Strip?"

"Better than you'd think," she said.

"Great," Sal said. "Bring me one of those. Medium rare. And some blueberry pancakes. You want something, Doctor?"

Jerry shook his head.

"He'll have ham and eggs, scrambled together. Four pieces of link sausage. And a short stack," Sal said.

When the waitress left, Jerry said, "How can you eat?"

"Number one, don't be memorable," Sal said. "When you're in a restaurant, order food or else you look like a fucking cop. Number two, shit like this always leaves me starved. Plus, this side of town, I can eat whatever I want without fear of keeping kosher."

A cop car came screaming along Sahara, sirens blaring.

Then another.

Then another.

Then another turned off Maryland Parkway at a high rate of speed, nearly getting loose trying to make the turn onto Sahara.

"Shit," Jerry said under his breath.

"Watch," Sal said. "One, two, three . . ."

Before he reached four, trucks began to pour out of the Commercial Center and directly onto Sahara, only pausing at a red light before pushing through the intersection. "Here we go," Sal said. He stopped counting at fifteen trucks. By the time their meals arrived a few minutes later, the street was quiet again, all the off-duty cops at The Ponderosa capable of driving taking off for Rainbow and Charleston.

"Give me the other phone," Sal said between bites of his steak. Jerry did. Sal called 411 for the number of The Ponderosa, then dialed the bar. "Yeah, this is Mark Ulin from the gas company? We've got a leak reported in the Commercial Center, and we're advising all tenants to get out within the next ten minutes. Just taking as much precaution as possible. Thanks so much."

Butter knife.

SIM card.

Ketchup bottle.

Back to his pancakes.

"What are you?" Jerry said.

"Pardon me?"

"If you're not . . ." He stopped, recalibrated. "Are you like Bennie?" he said.

"No," Sal said. "I'm not a businessman."

"Hmm," Jerry said. "I think you undersell yourself."

"Put it this way," Sal said. "I've never made a dollar that I paid tax on." He speared two sausages. "You said your mother was from Chicago?"

"Yeah, grew up out there. Moved east when she was eighteen for college. Met my father. Married and knocked up by twenty-one."

"Still have family out there?"

"Probably," he said. "Once my parents died, that part of my life disappeared. They left me enough money to start this business. I found some investors. But family to me now is Stephanie's family. You know how that is? You find a nicer family sometimes through marriage. They love you for who you are now versus hating you for the fuckup you were." He looked out the window. "How much longer?"

Sal looked at his watch. "Maybe fifteen minutes." They'd encircled the lab with canisters of oxygen and nitrous oxide, poured gallons of formaldehyde on every surface, and filled the autoclave with enough volatile chemicals to leave a hole in the earth. Sal didn't want to kill anyone needlessly, so he was hopeful The Ponderosa was empty now, hoped the bartender smoking out back was a good hundred yards away, that the janitor catching a nap in his car before his shift had the windows up, that the working girls had gone home for the night.

"Do you have a name?" Jerry asked.

Sal shook his head. "Not for you." He pointed at Jerry's food. "Eat. It's getting cold."

"Is this my last meal?"

"Probably not."

Jerry took a few bites of his ham and eggs. Watched the other people in the restaurant, like he was in a zoo. "You know," he said, working on his short stack now, "I've lived in this town for thirty years and have never even stepped foot in this place. What else haven't I seen?" He took a sip of water. Rearranged the salt and pepper shakers. "I've got a lot of money, Rabbi. It will take me a few days to get it all together, but whatever it is you need, I could help you."

"Jerry," Sal said, "take care of your family. That's what matters."

"What I'm saying is," Jerry said, "does it need to be all or nothing here?"

"Let me tell you the future," Sal said. "First thing, cops are going to round up every Muslim in the city. It's going to be a fucking nightmare. I feel terrible about that. Second thing, maybe two days from now, after they realize Bin Laden isn't inside Circus Circus, the cops are going to arrest the dentist, if your pal Boris doesn't get him off the continent first. Then they're going to start working backward, which is going to lead them to you. By the end of the week, they'll have you in an interrogation room. Now, if Boris is any good, he'll have you out of there quickly, but who knows? What you're going to tell these cops is that you just rent the place to the dentist, you have no idea what he's using the storage facility for, he's a great tenant, pays on time, never expected anything strange, and of course, you're here to help. They'll let you go. You have no reason to bomb your own building, after all, but isn't it odd that a guy who runs a tissue bank has a building he owns inexplicably filled with black market corpses? I mean, what are the odds? By then, Bennie will know all about this, will know that if you owned that warehouse and it was filled with cadavers, well, that's coming back to the Temple at some point, and so now he's gotta worry about that. And Bennie, he doesn't like to worry, so he's going to figure out a way for you to die in such a way that looks like an accident. Probably in your swimming pool. I mean, that's what I'd do. Show up in the middle of the night, knock you out by pressing on your carotid for a few seconds, put you in a bathing suit, carry you outside, hold you by your feet underwater in the deep end, you'll fight a bit but not much, which is good, you need to inhale as much water as possible, and then you're dead. Tragedy. Or, I get to your house and Boris already had his boys gut you like a fucking fish, because Russians don't care about subtlety. You've ruined their business and brought the light of the FBI on them. No sense treating you with dignity. End result, either way, you're dead. Like I said, probably two weeks, beginning to end, which would give you time to make sure your wife is taken care of, at least, but like I said earlier, you're gonna be a mensch and pay all your staff, too."

Jerry was covered in sweat.

Sal took a bite of his ham and eggs. They were getting a little cold. But the ham was surprisingly good.

"Or," Sal said and took another bite.

"Or?" Jerry said.

"If for some reason an explosion doesn't happen in, let's see, seven minutes, there's another path. Five hours from now, janitor shows up to work at the swingers club, finds the walls bleeding, calls 911, cops kick down the door, walk through just like we did, start collecting human heads, and everything happens just like I said, but in addition, every family that's had their graves robbed sues your estate, your name becomes synonymous with some of the darkest shit in human history, and your wife dies poor and alone. If Bennie or Boris don't kill her first. My sense is the Russians would probably ace her out in this situation. Because you didn't have the good conscience to burn the fucking place down, destroying any salient evidence that might be left behind."

"Is there another *or*?"

Sal waved over the waitress. "A chocolate shake, please," he said. "You want one, too, Doctor?"

"I'm lactose intolerant," Jerry said.

"Live a little," Sal said.

"Vanilla," Jerry said to the waitress.

After she cleared off the plates, Sal said, "Last *or*. You call the FBI. Admit everything. Turn yourself in."

"Then what?"

"Bail will be in the millions. They'll segregate you in county, but it won't matter. You'll be dead by nightfall. Between Boris and Bennie, you'd need to be on the fucking moon to be beyond their reach."

"You were me," Jerry said. "What would you do?"

"Ambien," Sal said, "and a bag over my head."

"Yeah?"

"Take Xanax first," Sal said. "Like, ten of them. Chase it with the Ambien. Then put the bag on."

"Okay." Jerry inhaled deeply, placed his fingers lightly on the table. "What if I told you that the FBI has already been in contact with me?"

"About what?"

"I got a subpoena."

"When?"

"Last week," Jerry said. "It's not about the Temple. It's about a firm I do business with out of Florida. A real chop shop. I'm supposed to speak to a grand jury in a few weeks. My lawyer says it's nothing. Just providing some background. I've only ever done legit business with them. This sort of thing happens in this business. If I told you about every subpoena I got, you'd be constantly looking over your shoulder."

"Then why are we talking about it?"

"I don't show up," Jerry said, "it's going to be a real problem. For you. And maybe there's a deal for us, both."

David had to give it up to Jerry Ford. Motherfucker had some moves. "This money you mentioned," David said. "How much we talking about?"

"How much you need?"

"Two million. Cash. No fucking around."

"Not even a pause? You just had that number ready?"

"I've done my math."

"I'd need some time," Jerry said.

"How much?"

"A week?"

"I can get you five days."

"You just had that number, too?"

The waitress set down the milkshakes. "Anything else?" she asked, or at least that's what Sal thought she said when the fireball exploded from the back of the Commercial Center. The concussion swept up the block, dust and debris immediately turning the night sky thick and ashy, the air acrid with chemicals. Sal was aware that people inside the restaurant were already screaming and scrambling under their tables, which was good; they'd learned what to do from the news in the case of a terror attack, and in truth, of course, this was terror inducing, eyeballs spattering against the restaurant's windows, loose arms and legs falling from the sky now, bouncing off the hoods of cars, human heads crashing through windshields.

Sal took all the money from his wallet and set it on the table under the saltshaker, then grabbed Jerry by the collar, yanked him out of the booth. "Time to go," he said.

ELEVEN

TRADITIONALLY, WEDNESDAY MORNINGS IN LAS VEGAS WERE FOR HANGINGS and bank robberies. Wake up in a hotel room, three days since the weekend, all your money and hope gone? Anything could happen. People did desperate shit. Fortunately, Special Agent Kristy Levine was in the business of desperate shit.

Kristy understood the feeling. She should already be dead. She'd even purchased her final resting place at the Jewish cemetery in Summerlin, across from her synagogue, made plans for who'd take her dog—her favorite bartender at Pour Decisions—and adjusted her will.

And then something remarkable happened.

Her cancer didn't kill her. Oh, it tried. The chemo took her hair, three of her teeth, about thirty pounds, and her taste buds, but goddamn, it also knocked her fucking cancer out. Oncologist said it was just short of a miracle, since the odds were the cancer would be back, and vengeful, sometime in the next two to five years. "Live your life accordingly," he told her.

So here she was, six thirty in the morning, wearing a blond wig—she'd always wanted to be a blond—that made her look like she danced weekends at the Wildhorse, still a little foggy from the chemo brain but fucking thankful to be alive, walking through the burned-out husk of the Red Lantern Swingers Club, an N95 strapped to her face, safety glasses on her eyes, booties over her low-rise Cole Haan boots, trying to figure out if she needed to adjust her settings. Maybe Wednesday mornings were now for terrorist attacks? She'd need to move her night at Pour Decisions if that was the case, since she was operating this morning with a low-grade hangover on top of everything else. Working a bank robbery was typically a pleasant, well-air-conditioned affair with plenty of coffee and very little blood. This? This was a horror show.

The parking lot of the Commercial Center looked like the aftermath of a plane crash, body parts scattered in a corona around the blast site. Weird thing was, firefighters hadn't found anyone *whole* anywhere in the vicinity.

It didn't make any sense. The main difference between a fire and an explosion is speed. Everything Kristy was seeing told her there'd been an explosion followed by an accelerated fire. It wasn't like someone left a cigarette burning and it caught a magazine and then there was a conflagration. Something went boom and chemicals accelerated the destruction—that the city had closed off this stretch of East Sahara because of toxicity in the air helped confirm that—but that wouldn't disintegrate all of these people. And if Al-Qaeda had set off a dirty bomb—that was the rumor already spilling across the ticker on CNN this morning—why didn't they set it off inside the Mirage versus a closed swingers club on the edge of town?

The other thing she couldn't figure out: there were about two dozen onlookers down the street, on the other side of the police tape, but there weren't any screaming or crying relatives looking for their loved ones, and yet human heads were all over the fucking place.

Kristy looked up and saw nothing but sky. What had been up there?

She walked through the back of the club, ended up in an alley that was strewn with what looked like . . . industrial freezers? There were three of them, on their sides. She'd seen a few more inside the wreckage of the Red Lantern. They must have fallen through the floor.

"What was up there?" she asked the cop guarding the back. Half a dozen investigators were cataloging every piece of evidence in full hazmat suits, Kristy suddenly feeling very underdressed.

"Dental office," the cop said. He was young, maybe twenty-five, looked like he'd be better suited to guarding a frat house at UNLV. "But I don't know about the rest of it."

"What do you mean?"

"They're saying there was a full warehouse up there, too, but I don't know. Nothing on the mall registry but the dentist."

Kristy tried to imagine the layout in her mind. She'd get the blueprints later. The second floor had largely collapsed into the Red Lantern—there were slabs here and there, hanging perilously—and the roof was gone entirely. But she could imagine it well enough, a dental office and then some kind of vast storage area that had been converted into an industrial warehouse, which was not coded for this area. This was all retail, business, medical, and food, no light industrial at all. If these freezers had ended up out here, they must have been either blown through the roof or out the back wall.

That's a shitload of force. She went around the back of one of the freezers. Still intact, save for the ripped-out wiring and tubing. It was about six feet tall, four feet wide, probably weighed over seven hundred pounds. They'd been scorched, but these were stainless steel; the fire would have needed to burn at 3,000 degrees to melt them. That would take jet fuel and time. Firefighters were on-site within ten minutes, but the chemical nature of the fire kept them at bay for twenty minutes, enough time for the whole place to be destroyed, which was also a good indicator of accelerants.

Why would a dentist need industrial freezers?

"Anyone open these up yet?" Kristy asked.

"Yeah," the cop said. "You got a soft stomach?"

"I'm an FBI agent," Kristy said.

Cop put his hands up. "Everyone here is something. I'm just telling you, don't throw up on the evidence."

Kristy snapped on gloves, pulled open one of the freezer doors, and found about two hundred pounds of fire-grilled human organ meats.

"Fuck!"

Kristy slammed the door shut again. She met the cop's eyes. He wasn't laughing, but he wanted to. "Quit fucking laughing," she said anyway.

KRISTY DIDN'T GET BACK TO HER OFFICE UNTIL AFTER LUNCH, NOT THAT SHE was going to eat ever again. At least not meat. She could see herself becoming vegan, soon.

Her phone started ringing as soon as she sat down. It was Senior Special Agent Lee Poremba. He was in Chicago, or at least that's what his caller ID said. "Just saw you on MSNBC," Poremba said. "Nice hair."

"Didn't consider soot when I put it on this morning," Kristy said.

"I like the way it framed your face," Poremba said.

"When I get off the phone," Kristy said, "I'm going into HR."

"Surprised the office gave you the call," Poremba said.

"They didn't," Kristy said. "I took it." No one in the Vegas shop thought she was ready to be back to work, and maybe she wasn't, but they couldn't stop her from showing up. They could, instead, ice her out, or worse, have her running down joint task forces with the postal cops or the private-railway dicks, who ended up falling under FBI jurisdiction, too. Hobos stealing the mail was a federal crime, after all. But Lee Poremba ran the joint Organized Crime & Terrorism Task Force, which essentially allowed the FBI to use the Patriot Act on domestic targets if they thought there was some terror nexus. And what didn't have a terror nexus these days? He operated primarily out of Chicago, which meant he spent a fair amount of time in Las Vegas chasing down the tendrils of cases involving The Family and whatever was left of The Outfit, the two main crime families operating west of Yankee Stadium, each of whom had long used Las Vegas to wash their money, and then all the 9/11 bullshit. The New York families still had some sway in town, but that was mostly in the girl business, which was beneath the care of the FBI these days.

"What's your impression?"

"Gonna be a bad couple weeks for the mosques in town," Kristy said. "We should get some people on the inside. God knows what might happen."

"And then?"

"And then they'll give up, quietly announce it's an arson job, which it is," she said. "But for no reason I can figure. Dental office upstairs is billing a million five a year, they're renting the space, and every chair and tool in the place is financed. Dentist is in Tahiti on vacation, which is a little convenient."

"Little bit," Poremba said. "What's his background?"

"Here's where it gets tricky," Kristy said. "Came over from Russia in 1989. Almost 100 percent of his clientele are local Eastern Europeans. Dr. Yuri 'Jack' Belsky. Known associates include Boris Dmitrov and about a hundred ex-KGB fucks currently splitting their time between Las Vegas and county jail."

"You don't say."

"So I'm thinking, initially, okay, maybe he owes the Russian mob, maybe they're running a pill business out of his shop, he's about to go to the cops, they blow the place up."

"But that only hurts them," Poremba said.

"Right. But then I start walking the place and nothing makes sense. There's body parts for a mile around—I'm not kidding, a *mile*—but come to find, almost half of them have been embalmed. And the ones that aren't embalmed have been stored in giant freezers. I'm getting the blueprints, but I think most of the second floor was a huge walk-in freezer. Some kind of cadaver farm. Not registered anywhere. So. That's gotta be for a reason. Either that or there's a serial killer operating in Las Vegas on an industrial scale."

"What's the terror squad saying?"

"Crew flew in from D.C. overnight. They've got their heart set on a cell doing a dry run on a dirty bomb."

"And the bodies?"

"They're advancing a notion that the cell wanted to see what the potential damage would be if the bomb went off when the center was full but without hurting anyone first."

"And no one noticed them bringing in a hundred human heads?"

"Dentist has been on vacation since last week. Could have been doing it every night at 3 a.m. It's plausible, if unlikely."

"Any other evidence of this cell's profound empathy?"

"Two calls," Kristy said. "One was 911 on a fake cop shooting, which got every cop and firefighter running across town and away from this explosion. Next was a call to The Ponderosa, the bar downstairs, telling them there was a gas leak and to get out. As it was, the entire bar had emptied out for the man down. All seems part of the plan."

"Let me guess," Poremba said, "burner phone?"

"On the 911, yeah," she said. "Don't have the records on The Ponderosa, but that's what the bartender reported to Vegas Metro." Kristy could hear Poremba sighing. "Any precedent for any cell, anywhere, calling ahead?"

"Defeats the purpose of the whole terror part," Poremba said.

"Tell that to D.C.," Kristy said. "They're bringing in every available agent in the West. If you're not in Tora Bora, you're expected in Las Vegas by 5 p.m."

Poremba fell silent for a moment. "The bodies bother me."

Kristy knew the numbers: Two thousand people went missing every year in Clark County, 99 percent of them resolved with a living person eventually walking through a door. Two hundred fifty people got murdered every year in the county, which made up a good part of the remaining 1 percent. The rest either don't want to be found or they're at the bottom of Lake Mead in a barrel, their killers praying there's not a drought. What they weren't, for sure, was being abducted, killed, and left in freezers behind a dental office on East Sahara.

"Who owns this office space?" Poremba asked.

"It's an LLC registered locally to a Jerry L. Ford. He owns a bunch of office and medical space around town, plus an apartment building or two. No previous dirty bombs, far as I can tell." Her cell phone buzzed. It was the head of the field office, Senior Special Agent Sebelius. "Look, I got Sebelius calling me for a report. So. I'll file all of this and be off. Once they realize it's an arson, Vegas Metro will handle it from here, and it will go unsolved until forever."

"Wait." Poremba said. "The ownership piece. You're positive it's Jerry *L*. Ford?" He put the emphasis on the *L* for some reason.

"Yeah," Kristy said. "Pulled it as soon as the city opened up. Bought it eighteen months ago. The whole space has been leased to the dentist for over a year."

Kristy could hear Poremba breathing. Which was weird. She'd always assumed he was a robot.

"I'm emailing a file to your personal account," Poremba said. "Your eyes only. Download it, get a burger, and call me in fifteen from somewhere busy."

"Really?" Kristy said. "I've been at a crime scene since dawn."

"Fifteen," Poremba said again and was gone.

"And I'm feeling better, thanks for asking," Kristy said to the hum of white noise.

KRISTY TOOK THIRTY AND DROVE OUT TO THE BAGEL CAFÉ FOR SOME COMFORT food, ordering a bowl of matzo ball soup and an Earl Grey tea to help ease her guts. Her maternal grandmother was from Russia, her paternal grandmother from England, and this meal was like sitting with them both. The Bagel Café was nearly empty, the lunch rush over, but there was residual energy floating about, as if she'd walked into a room full of leftover conversation hanging lazily in the air. She half expected to see Rabbi Cohen, since she'd run into him here half a dozen times before his accident, holding court with Rabbi Kales, the two of them always looking so serious until a Temple Beth Israel congregant came to shake their hands, slip them a twenty, and then both men radiated such charm she felt the ions in the room rearranging.

Both knew how to make you feel like they could see into your soul, that they'd anticipated everything you were about to say and had answers at the ready, like when Rabbi Cohen found her at the cemetery last winter.

She'd just started chemo and she was, frankly, out of her fucking mind. She'd broken into the cemetery sometime after 3 a.m. and had gone running through its sloping hills, letting the wind blow through her disappearing hair, only to run into Rabbi Cohen. Literally—he caught her at the bottom of a hill, dressed like the fucking Unabomber, in retrospect. She had no idea what he was doing there, was too stricken with grief and madness to even ask, but he comforted her, told her to focus on finding *mazel*, and she'd done that each day since, looking for some proof of *mazel* even when the world seemed inordinately fucked. Some days were harder than others. She was riding a serious zero for Wednesday thus far.

Her waitress—Penny Meltzer's daughter Lynn; she knew them from the book club at Temple Beth Israel, where both had fallen in love with *The Bridges of Madison County*—dropped off the matzo ball soup and a plate of cheese blintzes, too.

"I didn't order these," Kristy said.

"You look like you could use it," Lynn said. She put down a ramekin of strawberry jam. "When they begin gathering us up, you'll want the carbs."

"Who is 'they' in this situation?"

"Didn't you hear? The terrorists hit the Commercial Center this morning. Supposedly they're going to hit Excalibur next. That's what the radio said."

"Don't believe everything you hear," Kristy said. Why terrorists would *want* to blow up a King Arthur–themed casino was anyone's guess. Why someone would *believe* they'd want to blow up a King Arthur–themed casino when the Luxor was right there for the taking, well, that was just a question for another day. Kristy was too fucking tired.

"My dad keeps talking about buying a gun," she said.

"What's stopping him?" Kristy said.

"Have you met my father? He can't even get the VCR to stop blinking twelve o'clock."

Kristy had, in fact, met her father. He worked at the local NPR station, did a show where he played classical music and interviewed local celebrities about their favorite compositions, every meteorologist in town talking about Tchaikovsky. "Can I tell you a secret?" She motioned Lynn toward her. "That wasn't a terrorist attack today."

"How do you know?"

"I'm an FBI agent. I was there."

"I don't know," she said. "A lot of people say the FBI brought down the Towers, so it's all very confusing." She set down Kristy's bill. "The blintzes are on the house."

Kristy waited for Lynn to leave before she opened her computer, read through the file Poremba sent, drained her bowl of soup, then called him.

"What am I looking at here?" she asked.

"You in public?"

"I'm in a deli, currently eating a blintz. Not sure where in the tradecraft book they suggest this, but, sir, I am ready for the briefing."

"Casino deli or freestanding?"

"Freestanding."

"Good," Poremba said. "I picked something up on surveillance. Six, nine months ago, when you were out."

Kristy scrolled through the file with a sense of . . . not quite doom, but wild unease. She pulled up a photo of her own funeral plot at the Kales Home of Peace. "Lee, is this that shit you had set up in Summerlin? I thought you pulled this wire?"

Poremba had legally miked up a house on the other side of the Kales Home of Peace cemetery, working a hunch about the disappearance of Sal Cupertine, since Cupertine was—at least theoretically— last seen in a frozen meat truck that made a delivery to Temple Beth

Israel, owned and operated by Rabbi Cy Kales, the father-in-law of Bennie Savone. Poremba was convinced Savone had something to do with Cupertine's disappearance, but he'd thus far found no connection whatsoever, even after Special Agent Jeff Hopper had come out here and made, seemingly, the same connection and ended up missing his head. He'd even sent out Matthew Drew and turned that poor fucked-up kid into a ticking time bomb.

Four years Poremba had tried to find something. Four years he'd come up empty.

In fact, the only thing Poremba picked up of interest was Kristy and her rabbi talking about her cancer while she surveyed her plot. That was a year ago. Since then, Poremba had become her . . . friend, of a kind. If it was possible to be friends with Senior Special Agent Lee Poremba.

"I did," Poremba said. "This is more of a homemade deal. Something I did on vacation."

Now she understood where this was headed, why she wasn't in the office.

"I think we call that *inadmissible*," Kristy said.

"It's not illegal to rent a home," Poremba said, "and set up a recording device to pick up birdsong. Do you know anything about birdsong?"

"Not a thing."

"I've started birding. It's about the only activity I do these days that isn't directly involved with the very worst people on the planet. Las Vegas is an excellent place for birding." He paused. "Summerlin alone has over three hundred species of birds. Did you know that?"

"I hope to never know that."

"You can see why one might rent a home and train a camera on the surrounding foliage. If one were very into birding. Which I am. Scroll to page 63."

Kristy did. There was a photo of a van marked LifeCore pulling through the front gates of the mortuary, time-stamped 9:02 a.m., another time-stamped 12:19 p.m., another at 4:17 p.m., another still at 9:45 p.m. "What am I looking at here?"

"LifeCore is a tissue bank," Poremba said. "They use the mortuary to harvest organs and tissue for donation."

Something began to tickle at the back of Kristy's mind.

"That's illegal?"

"No," Poremba said, "that's legal."

She kept scrolling. Ran into pages of invoices. That didn't seem right. Kristy knew well enough about the black market for major organs—the urban legend of coming to Las Vegas and waking up without a kidney wasn't started out of the blue. At a different time in the late 1990s, Russian and Chinese gangsters had set up chop shops in the desert, using call girls as the lure for young, healthy men with good bones and organs. It was some horror-movie shit, but it was true. These invoices were from companies all over the country, plus some overseas. That couldn't be right. These people couldn't be so stupid as to put their criminal enterprise on paper . . . and then, it appeared, pay taxes on it. Or maybe that was the way to do it. Pay taxes, hope no one notices. "These bills and invoices to third parties, what are those?"

"LifeCore can't sell body parts per se, but they can charge for the harvesting, storage, prep, cleaning, delivery, everything but the actual human form," Poremba explained. "They can then pay the funeral home for their time and work."

"Who is their white market?" she asked.

"Companies that make surgical implants. Plastic surgery supply companies. Hospitals doing major transplants. All the way down to companies that make wigs from human hair."

Kristy pulled the wig from her head. Looked at the label: "Made with real human hair. Product of India." The company's name was Enchanted Hair Enhancements. She'd paid a grand for it, online. She dropped it into her purse.

"Dental offices?" Kristy asked.

"Of course," Poremba said.

"Shit," she said. "Okay, where does it all fall apart?"

"Say X company needs a bunch of good femurs, but so does Y company, because maybe they have a government contract, putting soldiers back together. LifeCore goes out to bid for their harvesting services, and suddenly it's a competitive situation. Who is willing to pay the most for good, clean, young femurs? Could be a plastic surgery operation jumps in, too, and then they start offering performance bonuses."

"That happens?"

"That happens. You get us five hundred good donors, we'll pay you an additional $5,000 per donation. Maybe $10,000. Maybe $15,000 for some really good corneas. Tissue bank wants to make money, they need volume. Because the regulation is on the tissue bank's side, not the supplier's side. Supplier can sell almost anywhere once they've turned a donation into some other product. Cadaver bones for hip replacements can be sold overseas, as long as they come from a legitimate firm. So they need bodies. But the fact is, that's all mostly legal. Unethical, but mostly legal."

Kristy whistled. "How'd you get on this?" she asked.

"We busted an outfit out of New Jersey called BioSciTech that was suspected of funneling money to Al-Qaeda."

"Were they?"

"They were Muslim. At this point, it's enough to get a warrant," Poremba said. "Plus their visas were out of date and so now they're in Gitmo getting waterboarded twice a day, so who knows."

"We're about a week from them opening camps, Lee."

Poremba said, "What do you think Gitmo is?"

Kristy was Jewish and her whole family had been military, her father teaching them that they were fight-in-the-streets Jews, not hide-in-the-attic Jews. It was an important distinction even today. What she saw happening to Muslims in the country had her worried. The mob always came for the weakest part of the social order, and Muslims were already fairing horribly. Two mosques in Las Vegas had been burned in nine months. This thing at the Commercial Center wasn't going to make life any easier, for anyone.

Kristy kept clicking. More photos. More invoices. A transcript of a recording, all of it redacted. *Oh boy.* "What's the organized crime nexus?"

"BioSciTech was getting bodies from some shady figures, including the Russian mob, who were robbing funeral homes and cemeteries and university research labs, going in at night and cutting out whatever it was BioSci needed. They'd retrofitted a warehouse, turned it into a giant freezer, filled it with body parts. Sound familiar?"

"Oh my god," Kristy said. "How'd it get found?"

"They hired a janitorial service," Poremba said.

"No."

"Seventy-two-year-old Guatemalan lady walked into the police station with a bag of human heads," Poremba said. "Thing about BioSci, the guy who ran it, he was smart. He had a for-profit side and also a nonprofit, moving body parts for research and educational purposes, which isn't regulated. So while he's in Gitmo, his sister, she's still running the nonprofit business, and we can't touch her because instead of moving parts to transplant firms, she's selling spines to Harvard for medical research. They don't have the same volume as they had before, but for the research and education, it's about quality, not quantity, and they've got a nice deal going with a funeral home in the good part of town. High-class skin."

"I'm gonna tear that pink sticker off my license. No one gets shit off of me."

"I already did," Poremba said.

"How's LifeCore involved?"

"Well, BioSci used them, primarily for corneas and long bones. That side of the business appeared to be mostly legit." *Mostly.* "But it was enough to get a subpoena for records."

Kristy was looking at tax records now. LifeCore's revenue in 1998 was $3 million. In 2001, it was $17 million. "What happened between 1998 and 2001 that they started making so much money?"

"The only substantial difference in LifeCore's business since 1999," Poremba said, "is that they started using the Kales Home of Peace in Summerlin as a harvester."

"How much would the funeral home take on that?"

"Looks like they've paid Kales Home of Peace between 15 and 20 percent of their total revenues," he said. "At least according to what they're putting out on actual invoices. But I think there's work happening off book."

"What's the official number?"

"Four million dollars."

"Since 1999?"

"No," Poremba said, "per year."

That couldn't be right. Kristy took out a pen, started scratching numbers on her napkin. They'd need to be moving about a thousand bodies per year to be making that kind of money. That seemed impossible. Particularly for a Jewish funeral home and cemetery.

"How many Jews die in Las Vegas every year?"

"Five hundred, give or take," Poremba said. "We'll be overly generous and say maybe 60 percent are donors."

"So we're at three hundred," Kristy says. "And then they'd all need to come through this one particular funeral home. Plus whatever overflow work LifeCore is bringing them from the hospitals."

"If it's high value," Poremba said, "hearts, livers, lungs, hospital is doing it right there; they're not sending a bus to Summerlin. So we're talking low-priority work. No one is clamoring for a seventy-five-year-old hip bone."

There was no way those numbers would line up. No matter how inflated the cost of corneas. Something was absolutely amiss. Kristy clicked a file on her computer, opened up a copy of her life insurance policy. She crossed out a line for secondary beneficiaries, right where it said Temple Beth Israel, her synagogue. She scrolled back through Poremba's file. All the way to the first page again. Why wasn't this official business yet? Or, moreover, why was it unofficial?

"What am I missing, Lee?" she asked. "How does this tie in to Sal Cupertine?"

"Ask me who owns LifeCore."

"Who owns LifeCore?"

"Local paperwork shows the CEO to be Jerry L. Ford," Poremba said. "Who, I should note, belongs to Temple Beth Israel."

"Tenuous," Kristy said.

"Hold on," Poremba said. "Do you know what the L stands for in Mr. Ford's name?"

"Can't say I do."

"He is Jerry Lopiparno Ford."

"That doesn't sound Jewish," Kristy said.

"It's not," Poremba said. "He's 100 percent Italian. Doesn't mean he couldn't have converted for his wife, the former Stephanie Katz, but Lopiparnos came over on a boat in the 1880s. Settled in Chicago."

A tingle began to work its way up Kristy's spine.

"Same boat as the Cupertines, in fact," Poremba said. "One hundred and twenty years, Cupertines and Lopiparnos were so close, they're cousins now. Jerry Ford's mother, the late Giovana Lopiparno, second cousin to Thomas Cupertine, Ronald Cupertine's father."

Kristy was shit with ancestry, but she understood what this meant. They were all family. They were all The Family. Just like how the Mafia had infiltrated food service by creating companies that became vendors for restaurants, they'd created a company that became a vendor for a source they were uniquely qualified in supplying: bodies.

"You think Ronnie Cupertine owns LifeCore?"

"I know it," Poremba said. "Now I just need to prove it. Somewhere, there's the movement of money between the two. We'll find it."

"How long have you been working off book, Lee?"

"Since the FBI let Sal Cupertine kill Jeff Hopper and get away with it," Poremba said.

"Did you think Matthew Drew would find Sal and make this right for you? Because you've got no probable cause for any of this shit. Not even with what happened today."

"Where do you think the funeral home is getting all their bodies, Agent?" Poremba asked.

"Las Vegas mobsters aren't disappearing people on this scale, I can tell you that," she said. Since coming back, she'd been working on the Eastern Europeans and Chinese, a few Russians, and their game was all tech shit and mortgage fraud. Bloodless, since their victims weren't in the game, for the first time ever. These were civilians they'd never meet, stealing their money one pixel at a time.

"What do you know about Bennie Savone and his crew?" Poremba asked.

"Not enough," Kristy said.

"We're not talking about nice guys," Poremba said. "They don't care if someone is in the game or not. They'll beat down a tourist. Savone is a thug pretending to be a legit businessman, using his wife's Judaism to get straight looking. Same with Jerry Ford. He's using Temple Beth Israel; he's using the mortuary and the funeral home, I promise you."

There was a pause on the line and Kristy heard barking. "Are you walking your dog?" she asked.

"Yes."

"Are you on vacation?" Kristy said.

"I haven't taken a vacation in twenty years, Agent Levine."

"That's the difference between you and me," Kristy said. It wasn't the only one; she knew that much for sure. "You need to assure me I'm not gonna get into some rogue shit where I end up losing my pension. If I survive this cancer, I need it to live on, eventually."

"You won't."

"Everyone you sent here is either dead or on the run," she said.

"You solve this, you won't have to worry about pensions. They'll build a statue for you in Chicago. You'll be the person who finally ended The Family once and for all."

TWELVE

JENNIFER CUPERTINE DIDN'T DREAM ANYMORE. AT FIRST SHE THOUGHT IT was the Ambien, but then she weaned herself off the prescription and her nights became bouts of intermittent blackness broken up by sitting straight up, gasping for breath, a metallic taste in the back of her mouth, her heart beating so hard she could feel every vein in her face. After a few weeks, she was convinced she'd die like this, stuck in blackness forever, vaguely aware that she should be somewhere else, content to be quiet for just a few hours, but even in the blackness always the feeling of something lurking, waiting, and she knew, in some way, that it was every man her husband had ever killed. *You love a monster; you are a monster.* She couldn't hear it, but in the blackness, it was the message. And so she'd pull herself out from it, clawing for lucidity, only to find herself back in the real world. Where was this sense of peace everyone felt when they were slipping off this mortal coil, only to be yanked back to life? Every documentary she saw, it was the one universal: this feeling of remarkable peace and joy followed by the message—usually from a mother figure—that said your job in this realm was not done yet, that your child needed his mother. And then the imagery of a rock garden or a flowing river or the gentle sounds of a summer rain.

All Jennifer got was her terrified gasping, gulping air like water.

Every doctor she'd visited in the last year had told her she was in—surprisingly!—excellent health. These were government doctors, though, so Jennifer never knew what to believe. Would they tell her if she were in congestive heart failure? They told her to track the experiences, see if there was a pattern. For two weeks, she kept a note-book and a pen beside her alarm clock.

Bed: 11:12 p.m.

Wake: 1:41 a.m.

Wake: 3:33 a.m.

Wake: 4:46 a.m.

Out of bed: 6:34 a.m.

Was the house waking her up? Was something going off at that same time every night? The carbon monoxide detector? The neighbor's dog? An agent's alarm?

Bed: 12:33 a.m.

Wake: 1:13 a.m.

Wake: 2:19 a.m.

Wake: 4:02 a.m.

Out of bed: 7:02 a.m.

Nothing. No pattern. At least the Ambien kept her asleep.

What she missed about dreaming was easy to pinpoint. It was the only time she was allowed to be with Sal without feeling the pressing walls of the world's judgment. The FBI agents and U.S. Marshals were unfailingly kind to her—and they tried with William, they really did—but she knew that if Sal knocked on the door tomorrow, they'd put one between his eyes. They were the only adults in her life and yet she could never talk to them about the pain she felt, every single day, the void in her life that was her husband, because she knew they'd have to fake compassion. Her husband had killed at least four FBI agents. Her husband had probably killed another hundred men. Her husband had disappeared into the real world and was living his life, somewhere, and here she was, locked inside a house on a lake twenty-five miles out of Spokane. Maybe someone's idea of paradise, but for Jennifer, a city girl through and through, this was like living in the 1800s. And yet, she could imagine living here with Sal, in this house, their back a mountain, their front a body of water, one road in, one road out, a feeling of safety or imprisonment, depending upon the day.

But that was a dream, too. One she didn't let herself have, unless she had a few glasses of scotch before bedtime, something that was happening too often these days, bedtime getting earlier, the scotch becoming more plentiful.

And so, on this third Friday in April, she willed herself to stay up until 11:30 p.m. watching the news in bed, William asleep beside her. It had been like this for the last three nights, since Levi and the two agents on security detail got a call and then disappeared—Jennifer didn't know where, only that they were gone within the hour—leaving only Maryann to watch over them. Now, with all this shit happening in Las Vegas, it was pretty clear that the president, or whoever was in charge of this sort of thing, conscripted every available FBI agent to help with the investigation. Jennifer didn't figure that government thought of her and William as high-priority assets, so it made sense they would yank people off her detail. But William was now scared, obsessively checking the windows and doors—like he needed one more thing to obsess over—even made the three of them walk the perimeter of the property after dinner, just in case.

"He's always watching you," Maryann told her once they'd come inside, Jennifer washing dishes, Maryann drying them. "There's going to come a time when you two are apart, and I worry about how he'll react to the freedom."

"When's that going to be?"

"I don't know," Maryann said. "I'd guess that in the next few months, the Marshals will try to resettle you in a place where he can go to regular school. You can get a job. That sort of thing. This situation here isn't permanent. It never is."

"If I'd known how hard it would be," Jennifer said, "I might have tried to stay out on our own."

"Honestly? You'd both be dead. You're in a good situation here, Jennifer. I know it's hard to see it from this angle. And the information you've given about how The Family operates has saved lives. I know it feels like stasis. Sometimes, it's as simple as purchase orders being approved before a move can be made. You're still important. You're just inside a vast bureaucracy now. Next year at this time, I wouldn't be surprised if William was somewhere getting the help he needs in an environment that is healthy for you both. Palo Alto or Ann Arbor or even Austin. All would be good options for the programs at the universities."

Jennifer knew this was true. She knew that William needed help. This sweet boy with his head in her lap, snoring from his mouth, both of his thumbs twitching, surely playing video games in his own dream life. In some ways, he was still a little boy, scared of things like thunder and lightning—plentiful in these parts—and then in other ways, he was completely unknowable. He memorized everything. She had to hide certain books because it was impossible for him not to memorize passages and then repeat them back to her. But also, he could tell you—verbatim—the warning label from a bottle of antifreeze. And then there were the facts he'd digested. His latest obsession was about the speed of a falling body. How long did it take a body to reach terminal velocity?

She slid William's head off her lap, straightened him out in her bed, watched him for a few moments. Eight years old, going on infinity.

JENNIFER WALKED INTO THE KITCHEN. MARYANN SAT AT THE KITCHEN TABLE in a nightgown, reading a book, a cup of coffee and her .357 on the table beside her, still in its ankle holster. The TV was on in the attached family room, filling it with a familiar blue glow, the sound off, Jay Leno talking to Justin Timberlake.

"You don't need to stay up all night," Jennifer said. She filled up a glass of water.

"It's fine," she said. "I catnapped during the day. Steve and Britt left this morning, too, so it's on me for twenty-four hours. Tomorrow afternoon, the field office will send a patrol every couple of hours; I'll catch up then. Don't worry."

"William is in my room again."

"Okay," she said, and she forced out a frown. "You'll miss that at some point." Maryann was supposed to be William's grandmother, which meant she was supposed to be in her sixties, but Jennifer knew she dyed her hair gray and caked foundation in the lines around her eyes and mouth, bringing out what would be more subtle wrinkles. She wore clothes from the Goodwill, a size too small in some cases. Maybe she was fifty, fifty-five.

"Should I lock us in the room?" Jennifer asked.

"No, no," Maryann said. "I'll be right here."

"Can I ask you a personal question?" Jennifer asked.

"You can try," Maryann said, not unkindly. It was just the way it was.

"Do you have a husband? In the real world?"

Maryann started to answer, then stopped herself. "Let me put it this way," she said. "In the real world, it's a 100 percent impossibility."

"Ah," Jennifer said.

"In this life here," she said, "Levi is more than enough. And he's a good man, you should know."

"I know," Jennifer said.

"Why do you ask?"

"I just wondered," Jennifer said, "these months you've lived with us, how you've done it."

"Oh," she said. "That's easy." She got up from the table, went back into the kitchen, where the pot of coffee was beside the stove. She re-filled her cup, took a sip, added some sugar. "Your son's safety is more important to me than my own comfort."

Maryann returned to the kitchen table, opened her book again. For a few moments, Jennifer stood there, watching her.

"I appreciate that, I do," Jennifer said. "But what about mine?"

"You chose this life, Mrs. Cupertine." Maryann didn't even look up from her book. "William didn't."

JENNIFER DIDN'T THINK SHE'D SLEEP THAT NIGHT, WAS CERTAIN SHE WASN'T asleep at all, her mind spinning with a mixture of rage and grief, until she sat up, gasping, bangs stuck to her forehead by a sheen of sweat, her T-shirt drenched. William was curled into the fetal position, asleep beside her. At some point, he'd thrown off all the sheets and blankets so that they were piled on top of her; no wonder she was broiling and dying of thirst. Jennifer touched the tiny mole on the back of William's neck—she had one in the same place, this secret thing they shared—and his skin was cool, so she pulled a sheet over him. She reached across him for the glass of water she kept on the nightstand, but it wasn't there.

She turned on her reading light and saw that the glass was shattered on the hardwood floor, a puddle of water spreading beneath the bed. It was 3:32 a.m.

Of course. That's what must have woken her. She'd get another glass of water, plus a towel and broom, from downstairs. Clean up the mess.

Jennifer made her way downstairs, the only light coming from the kitchen and family room at the bottom of the stairs, the air for some reason freezing. When she reached the bottom of the stairs, she figured out why: the front door was blown open. Even though it was April, nights on the lake were still frigid, dipping into the thirties. The house was old. Every windowsill needed to be repaired, air, water, and spiders leaking in regularly. Was Maryann out there smoking or something?

Jennifer poked her head out the door. "Maryann?"

Nothing.

She took a few steps out into the darkness. The moon was high up in the cloudless sky, its reflection shimmering on the lake. Jennifer trembled, wrapped her arms around herself, walked out onto the lawn, the wind blowing hair into her eyes. Normally, there'd be a man either in a boat or on the patio across the way, watching, but everyone was gone. She looked behind her, at the house where "Uncle Steve" and "Auntie Britt" lived. It was dark. They were in Las Vegas, too.

Must have been the wind.

She closed the door and turned the dead bolt, flicked on the foyer's light, headed into the kitchen.

Maryann's holster sat on the kitchen table, empty. Her coffee cup was on the counter, empty.

"Maryann?" she said again.

The family room, which was sunken by two steps, was dark except for the blue glow cast by the TV. The volume was too loud, Tommy Lee Jones screaming at Harrison Ford in the rain, Maryann watching something on the VCR. Jennifer stepped into the room and saw the agent was asleep on the leather recliner in the far corner, her head on her chest.

Jennifer switched off the TV. "Maryann," she said, "you fell asleep." She shook her foot, propped up on the attached footrest. "The front door was wide open."

She turned her back to Maryann, thought she heard a low yawn coming from the FBI agent, went back into the kitchen, filled a glass of water from the sink, stared out the window above the rack of dishes, gulped it down. Outside, visible in the moon's glow, the wind rippled the water. "It's practically white water out there. We should have Levi look into some better doors, don't you think?"

She turned back, thinking Maryann would be up now, wiping sleep from her eyes.

Except.

No.

Jennifer dropped her glass in the sink.

Maryann's gun was on the kitchen floor, just before the steps, dropped next to a stack of newspapers for recycling. She must have missed it in the dark.

She walked over, tentatively, felt the gun.

The barrel still warm.

Maryann wasn't asleep at all.

Jennifer saw that now.

With the light on in the family room.

The spatter of blood on the wall.

The hole in her head.

She'd been shot above her left ear. The bullet had gone straight through, a hole in the wall, blood cascading down the drywall, pooling on the floor. How had she missed this?

The darkness. Being barely awake. The last four years. That's what she'd tell herself for the rest of her days.

Hadn't she heard her sigh? Hadn't she just made a noise? Jennifer touched Maryann's neck to check for a pulse. Her skin was still warm, but Jennifer felt nothing. She took Maryann by the wrist, pressed her thumb hard against the radial artery. Did she feel something? Or was that her own pulse?

The front door slammed open.

She dropped Maryann's wrist, crouched low, moved through the family room, picked up Maryann's gun. What was she going to do?

Whatever it took.

She'd chosen this life. And now someone was here to take it from her.

A voice came into her head.

Never let anyone into our house.

"Mama?"

Jennifer turned around, half expected to find the intruder standing in the kitchen, but no one was there.

She grabbed Maryann's car keys from the dish on the counter. Maryann's cell phone.

She walked into the foyer.

"Mama?" William called again. He stood at the top of the stairs.

"Keep quiet, sweetheart," she said. "Don't make a sound."

Calm.

Cool.

The front door banged against the wall, the dead bolt still out.

She turned off the foyer light.

Frosty as could be.

But if they come, never let them leave.

"Mama, I can't see you."

Now. Run.

"I'll be right there," she said.

"Mama!"

More plaintive now. Anyone still in the house could hear her child, easily find her child.

No drawers were open. Nothing was taken. This was a hit.

Professional. Silent. Deadly.

Take out the FBI agent.

Make sure no backup was coming.

Finish the job.

Baby, the voice in her head said. Except it wasn't just any voice. It was Sal. Like he was standing right behind her.

Baby.

Listen to me.

Run.

THIRTEEN

MATTHEW DREW'S ROOM ON THE SEVENTEENTH FLOOR OF THE FANTASY Palms Resort Casino in Indio faced west, which gave him a panoramic view of the entire Coachella Valley. At dawn, with the sun rising behind him, the valley glowed fuchsia, pink, and orange, cloaking everything in hues that reminded Matthew of an old Polaroid photo, as if he were already in the middle of a memory. Wouldn't that be nice, then all this madness would be done. Barely six in the morning and already Matthew knew today would be a long-ass day. Could be he didn't walk away from it. Could be he walked away from it with a body on his sheet.

Either way, he was going to put some shit to bed, which would be a nice change. Matthew tried all night to get some rest, but he woke up every fifteen minutes or so, sure someone was bursting into his room, even though the name on it wasn't his own. Marvin gave him a Nevada driver's license and a Mastercard for someone named Jarret Keene, told him it was good enough to pass muster at a hotel but not to show it to a cop if he didn't want to end up in a gunfight.

Still, he barred the door, stationed guns around the room, and tried to close his eyes.

It was no use.

So he got up, showered, conditioned his beard, put his long hair into a ponytail, and stared out the window, drinking coffee while planning how to kill Kirk Biglione, if it came to that.

The last time he was in the desert, he and Jeff Hopper were searching for Sal Cupertine. While Jeff humped through Las Vegas,

Matthew went door to door between Palm Springs and Indio, stopping anywhere that had a contract with Kochel Meats, the company in southern Illinois that aided in Sal's escape, shoving him in the back of a truck to get him out of town. In fact, it was just a few miles from here, at the Royal Californian motel, where he found out Jeff Hopper was missing. Of course, that wasn't true, Matthew knew now. Jeff was dead. Sal Cupertine killed him. And now Matthew was back, doing Sal's bidding in hopes of clearing his own damn name. It was senseless.

There had to be a way to break this cycle. He would find Sal's wife and kid. He'd deliver Sal to them. He'd bring down The Family and the Native Mob. Cupertine would surely go state's and get protective custody, because he wasn't the decision maker, he was just the tool, and the government was predictable in how they dealt with tools. And then, maybe five years from now, maybe ten, maybe fifty, Sal Cupertine would be walking down a street somewhere in Arizona or South Dakota or Rhode Island and a sniper would take him out from fifteen hundred yards away. And Matthew would pack up his gun, toss it into a river; the scales would be even, Hopper could rest in peace, Matthew's sister could rest in peace. All the fucking bad guys would lose.

He made another pot of coffee, watched the shadows stretch across the desert, then called Kirk Biglione from his burner, told him where to meet, gave him an hour, and hung up.

THE NORTH SHORE BEACH AND YACHT CLUB WAS ONLY A FEW MILES, AS THE pelicans and seagulls flew, from where Gold Mountain Mining was set to begin looking for lithium just south of Salton City, but it was a good four decades in the past. It opened in 1959 as part of the Salton Sea's original business grift, gangsters like Ray Ryan and Chicago Outfit hitters developing a toxic pit with the idea of turning it into an inland riviera, the Beach and Yacht Club where the Rat Pack could perform, where Desi Arnaz could sip scotch at sunset, where poker games could go all night, until it all went south a few years later.

Today, though, the club was a living wreck sticking out over a two-foot-deep expanse of water, desert where the sea used to be. Over the years, the Salton Sea had receded so dramatically that the marina was now three hundred yards from water deep enough for boating, leaving it useless. The modern design of the club had persisted through time, but the garish yellows and bright blues of the original paint job were long gone, leaving the building dull.

Biglione was already there, sitting at a table on the dilapidated patio of the club, smoking a cigarette, like he was Dean Martin, reincarnated. Matthew thought that if he got out of this mess in one piece, maybe he, too, could graduate to some meaningless corporate security job that paid well and gave him some peace.

"Nice joint," he said when Matthew got out of his car. "There's not even a place to piss."

Matthew said, "Stand up, lift your shirt up, and do a turn for me."

"You think I'm wired?"

"Empty out your pockets, too," Matthew said. "I don't want you making any calls while we're out here."

"Let me know when you see a cell phone tower," Biglione said, but he did as he'd been asked. "How about you do the same?"

"I didn't ask you to dump the gun you got on your ankle," Matthew said. "And I'm not gonna dump the one I got on my belt or the one on my ankle, so let's just call it even. Pretty sure I'm not wired up, seeing as I'm a wanted man."

"Fair enough." Biglione tucked his pockets back into his pants, sat down.

Matthew made his way up the stairs to the patio, made sure there wasn't a strike team hiding inside, not like there was anywhere they could have hidden their cars, since there was nothing but water and desert for miles around. He looked into the sky, made sure there wasn't an Apache descending from the clouds, but only saw birds. Out on the water, he could make out a few fishing boats, a couple people on Jet Skis doing lazy figure eights, not much more.

Biglione held a thin manilla envelope. "I got what I could," he said and pushed it across the table. Matthew dumped the contents out. There was a faxed photo of a one-story cinder block house—white with blue trim—with a carport, a black Ford Explorer inside. There was a semicircular driveway made of crushed shells in front of the house, a mature oak tree sitting in the middle of a well-tended lawn. Second faxed photo showed the rear of the house from above, which was an open field leading to a canal, which fed into a bell-shaped lake. There was a double-wide trailer as well, pushed off to the southern portion of the field. The faxed photo was fuzzy, but the trailer looked new. Like where they'd put a Marshal or FBI team.

"Where's this?" Matthew asked.

"Land O'Lakes, Florida," Biglione said. "Thirty miles north of Tampa."

Made sense. Tampa field office had a significant organized crime division, plus community access to keep a single mother and child as comfortable as possible. The house location made sense, too, backing up to a lake. No one was going to surprise them. One less direction mom and kid could run if they decided to do that, too.

"You get the names they're living under?" The picture of the house had a street number—837—but not a street sign. It would take some work, but that was fine. He had nothing but time.

"Be happy with what you have," Biglione said. "Wasn't cheap." A flock of egrets flew above them, landed on the shoreline. Must have been forty of them. White as snow.

"Good you still got people you can pay off," Matthew said. He slipped the photos back into the manilla envelope. "What can I do for you?"

"Keep your word," Biglione said.

"I find Jennifer Cupertine at this house," Matthew said, "I'll keep my end. She's not there, I'm coming back." He stood up. Looked out to the Sea. The Jet Skis he saw earlier were speeding toward the marina now, racing. It looked like fun.

"I know," Biglione said.

"Wait here for twenty minutes," Matthew said. "Can't have you following me to my hotel."

"I'm just gonna enjoy the view."

Matthew began to back away from Biglione. He trusted him, kind of, but not so much he'd give him the back of his head. He was down the stairs and just a few feet from his car when the roar of an engine came from the Sea. Matthew saw two men on Jet Skis skidding into the marina. Did they realize how shallow it was? They disappeared for a moment behind the flock of egrets, which were spooked and taking flight, a wall of white filling Matthew's vision. He saw Biglione reach for his ankle, realized the setup, the men from the Jet Skis sprinting up the beach toward him, guns out. Matthew ducked low, came up with guns in both hands, firing at Biglione, firing out toward the mass of white, taking one in the leg, the shoulder, the other leg, the stomach, the back, Matthew on his side now.

I should have brought backup, Matthew thought, waited for another bullet to hit him. *I should have brought the fucking Rain Man.*

But nothing happened.

Matthew tried to sit up, tried to run, tried to shoot his guns, which he could see at the end of his hands, but for some reason the messages weren't going through.

He saw two sets of legs moving toward him from the beach. Soon, another pair of legs joined them. A man knelt beside him, looked into his eyes.

"Can you speak?" Peaches asked.

Matthew tried to say, *Yeah, motherfucker; I'll be waiting for you wherever you end up.*

"He's past that, I think," Biglione said.

"You want me to finish him?" the second man asked. He was younger than the other, smaller, had on a backpack.

Peaches put up a hand.

"I want you to know that when my nephew Mike here killed your sister," Peaches said, "she called to you. Over and over again. With each finger Mike cut off, she called to you. When he dug her eyes from her head, she called to you. Your name was the last thing she said when he pulled her tongue from her mouth and shoved it down her throat. And you never showed up. You never even looked for her. You spent all that time looking for Sal Cupertine and not one minute looking for your sister." Peaches grabbed Matthew's jaw. Didn't squeeze. No pain. Matthew thinking he was being very gentle. "I owe you," Peaches continued. "What you did to Mr. Cupertine has allowed me to rise up in this organization and get rid of loose ends that have been dragging us down for decades. But there's one thing I still don't know: the location of Sal Cupertine."

That's what this was all about. Matthew understood now, better than ever before, that it was not Jeff Hopper who was the center of everyone's anger about this case. It was Sal Cupertine, the man who got away with it. The last living Cupertine.

"No matter. We'll backtrack you. I'm sure you've been sloppy. Sal Cupertine will be dead by the end of the week." Peaches stood. "Sit him up."

Biglione lifted Matthew by his shoulders, his mouth close to his ear, whispered, "Be calm, Agent; it's almost over." Matthew could see the Salton Sea again. The egrets had settled once again on the beach.

Mike took a plastic bag from his backpack. Inside was a gun. Matthew had purchased it himself. A Glock 19. First paycheck from the FBI, made it his personal handgun. Bought in a shop in Bethesda, day after Christmas, place called the Pied Sniper, his mom with him. The gun he'd given his sister the night she disappeared. The gun used to kill Ronnie Cupertine's wife and children. The gun that made him the most wanted man in America.

Matthew Drew understood then that these were his last moments.

Matthew Drew also understood that he'd won.

He'd found Sal Cupertine.

He'd accomplished something no fucking gangster, cop, or fed had ever done: He'd caught Ronnie Cupertine slipping. He'd hobbled him, turned him into a vegetable.

Kirk Biglione had done him a solid, of a kind. He always imagined he'd go down fighting, but in the end, what was the use? Everybody dies. He could barely remember what these men had said, words drifting off of him now, falling into the sun-dappled water.

The little one, Mike, put the gun in Matthew's right hand, which was useless now, a mop at the end of his arm, pinned his trigger finger to the side of the gun, swept Matthew's arm straight out, toward the sea, and fired, twice, then let the gun drop to the ground.

Egrets filled the horizon.

A billowing cloud, moving.

Like heaven filling the sky, undulating whiteness.

It was beautiful.

Kirk Biglione, the man who'd shaken his hand and welcomed him to the FBI, the man who'd fired him, the man who'd in 1973 watched Sal Cupertine's father plummet off the IBM building and done nothing, the man who for forty years had been unable to buy himself out of that one piece of knowledge, a frozen moment that had come back to him every day since, picked Matthew's stolen gun up off the ground, said, "Sorry, hoss," and shot Mike in the face—Matthew thinking, *Surprise, motherfucker*—before he put the gun to the side of Matthew's head and fired once. Maybe twice. Matthew wouldn't ever know.

FOURTEEN

RABBI DAVID COHEN HAD HIS TORAH STUDY GROUP AT 11:00 A.M. ON Saturday, so he slept in, took his morning jog at nine o'clock, figuring most of the chemicals would have burned out of the morning haze by then. Bennie told him to be ready by ten thirty; they needed to talk before the ride over to the Temple.

Already the manicured streets inside the Lakes at Summerlin Greens were packed. On the sidewalks, women pushed babies in street-legal strollers that looked like they were rolling on dubs. Men in shitty casino tuxedos sat on their front porches or stood against their SUVs, smoking cigars and reading the *Review-Journal*, every douche in the city acting out scenes from *The Sopranos* before their degenerate-gambler shift at the Palace Station. Meanwhile, on the golf course, landscaping crews fanned out, making sure each blade of grass was the same length, assuring not a single biting insect was anywhere near, the itinerant Mexican workers modern-day coal miners, except instead of dying from black lung they'd get unique cancers from the tanks of malathion on their backs, and they'd have no recourse to sue, since half of them weren't really even here, officially speaking.

It was like this behind every gate in the whole goddamned town. The gates provided the illusion of privacy and exclusivity, but really it was just a bunch of prisoners walking the yard, twenty-four hours a day, seven days a week, everyone greeting each other with the same silent nod, no one engaging in anything close to personal interaction. Which was just fine by Rabbi David Cohen. But if you kept your holiday decorations up too long or ran your sprinklers at the wrong hours or parked your car too far from the curb or, worse, failed to ask permission of your neighbors to paint your own house, the Snitch Brigade would have the jackbooted HOA motherfuckers on your lawn, assessing fines, threatening to take your house, all manner of shit that, if they'd ever chosen to visit David on the wrong day, would end with one of them in a non-HOA-approved shallow grave. It amused David that the Rambo fantasies he knew his neighbors harbored—everyone a trained killer in their imagination—was how he'd lived most of his life. He didn't believe that might made right, but he knew he was capable of violence and would not be caught, that he could live that way.

Jennifer had changed him. His son, William, had improved him. The value of their lives outweighed his own desires. He would do what he *had* to do, not what he *wanted* to do. It made it possible to believe he would find them again.

This week made it clear he'd need to leave a trail of bodies to get there. But today, after Torah study, he was scheduled to bury half a dozen of them. David didn't know how many were real and how many were fake and, at this point, it didn't really matter. Bodies needed to get in the dirt, so David practiced the Kaddish as he ran, getting the Hebrew familiar on his tongue again.

David made the turn at Pebble Beach Way, heading toward Sawgrass Street—his usual route except he was going at about quarter speed and could feel every breath like he was inhaling shards of glass—and encountered precisely what he hoped to find: a "For Sale" sign wedged into the lawn in front of Jerry Ford's butter-yellow McMansion. A box of flyers was attached. David pulled one out.

MOTIVATED SELLER
WINE CELLAR
SOLAR PANELS
STEREO SOUND
INDOOR & OUTDOOR HOT TUBS!
$2.1 MILLION

Not exactly priced to move.

The gate in front of their home was wide open, so David walked up the driveway to the front porch. David rattled the lockbox on the front door, heard the key bouncing around. Normal situation, he'd pick the box and be in the house in minutes, but it was like I-15 on the streets right now; someone was probably on the phone to the HOA already.

David walked across the front lawn, peered into one of the six-foot-tall picture windows, where the blinds were parted slightly. The only illumination was coming from a single overhead light in the foyer, but that was enough: the house was empty.

Good.

"Help you, sir?"

David looked at his reflection in the window. Standing about ten feet behind him, hand on his gun, was one of the private security guards David—and everyone else in the Lakes at Summerlin Greens— paid $740 a month in HOA fees toward. They could have paid a little less for guards who weren't armed, but everyone in the Lakes at Summerlin Greens was unified in their desire to have an armed response to doorbell ditchers, Mormons, and Canadian renters.

David turned his head, tugged his hood off his face, so that he could see the guard from his peripheral, make sure it wasn't some Family hitter playing dress-up. But in fact it was a slightly overweight young man called Lavar that David had met before. Lavar worked full time in the HOA office by the front gate. Some days he did security, some days he worked the concierge desk, some days he probably cleaned the fucking pool.

"It's me, Lavar," David said. "Rabbi Cohen. I'm going to turn around slowly. Please don't shoot me." David faced him completely now, hands up, what passed for a smile trying to escape the darkness, David's new face not much better than his old one at accepting orders to relay kindness.

"Rabbi, I didn't recognize you," he said. "When did you get back?"

"A couple weeks now." He pulled his hood all the way down and walked down the lawn, hands still up, in case someone got to the motherfucker; you never could be too sure these days. "I had some work done, as you can see."

Lavar cocked his head, like he was trying to line up David's features. "Oh, yeah," he said, unconvincingly, but he did take his hand off his gun. "I heard there'd been some unpleasantness at the Temple?"

"I was having surgery anyway," David said, "and then unfortunately I took a spill. Now here we are."

"You fell?" Lavar said.

"That's not what you heard?"

Lavar opened his mouth to speak but stopped himself, David able to see the rotors and motors grinding to a halt, the homeowner always right at the Lakes at Summerlin Greens. "That's what I heard, yes," Lavar said. "Are you looking for Mr. Ford?"

"Yes," David said. "Thought I'd invite him to Torah study today."

"His windows are alarmed," he said. "If you tap on them, cops will be here in minutes."

"Well we wouldn't want that," David said. "When did Mr. Ford put his house on the market?"

"Sign went up yesterday."

"Did Mr. Ford leave town?"

"I couldn't really say," Lavar said.

"You couldn't say," David said, "or you shouldn't say?"

"I guess I don't know the difference?"

"Did he leave a forwarding address?" David asked.

Lavar brightened. "Yes! Yes, he did."

"Then you *can* say," David said.

"I guess I never know what is supposed to remain private."

"Things not done in public," David said. "But as you can see, we're standing in public."

Lavar looked over his shoulder, like he thought others might be coming up behind him. "Mrs. Ford went to their beach house. Don't know where Mr. Ford is staying, I'm afraid. Real sad, though; I guess they're going their separate ways?"

"Marriage is a series of discussions over contested emotional agency," David said. It was something he told his congregants regularly. It made them feel like the worst parts of their marriages were simply contractual issues between equal parties, which they never were, not to the person who filed first, anyway.

Lavar's radio squawked, so he held up a finger and slid his earpiece in, and said, "Go ahead."

Lavar was maybe twenty-five or twenty-six, wasn't really an officer at all but had a patrol car, a fancy polyester outfit, a fake-ass badge, and a real-ass gun on his hip. Two men pretending to be something they weren't talking about a third man who reconstituted the dead for the living. Wasn't that something.

"Ten-four," Lavar said, then slid the earpiece out of his ear. "Sorry about that, Rabbi. Looks like either a hit man or a flower delivery for Mr. Tinch. Do you know him?"

"No."

"He lives on the other side of the course, in the new houses over on Mickelson. Really nice guy. Anyway. They don't have a pass, so I have to give my approval." David had never heard of anyone named Tinch, not in the Lakes or anywhere else. The other side of the golf course, which was a good two miles from David's front door, was another fucking universe, with its own clubhouse, book clubs, ladies' bunco. Lavar took a couple steps toward Rabbi David Cohen, lowered his voice. "They say Mr. Tinch is mafia. That's why the HOA office thinks he could be a hit man."

"Really. Who else is mafia?"

"You know, you wear a nice suit and blow-dry your hair, there's going to be questions," Lavar said. "My dad? He used to run errands for Moe Dalitz. Do you know who that was?"

"I do," Rabbi David Cohen said.

His radio squawked again. "Well, I better get moving. You have a good day, Rabbi. Don't touch the windows."

David followed Lavar back to his car.

"May I ask," he said, "what they say about me?"

Lavar shrugged. "They all want you to marry their daughters." He looked down, seemed to get embarrassed, David thinking he had him now; that was good. "Or date their sons."

That was a twist.

"It's nice to be admired," David said.

"And some think you're Mossad," he said, "but I think that's just because of 9/11. Everyone wants to feel safer, you know? So now their rabbi is an assassin."

BY THE TIME DAVID WAS OUT OF THE SHOWER, HE COULD SEE ON HIS CCTV that Bennie's Mercedes was idling in the driveway, the Israeli kid who'd been with Bennie at the hospital behind the wheel, which meant Bennie was somewhere in the house. That was the thing about Bennie Savone. He treated everything he owned the same. No locked doors. He had keys to everything. It wasn't even a fucking metaphor.

David walked downstairs, saw the sliding glass doors to the backyard open, cigar smoke wafting in. He found Bennie relaxing on a chaise lounge, a glass of orange juice on the table beside him, a cigar burning in the ashtray, Ray-Ban sunglasses pressed close to his eyes, sun on his face.

"Make yourself comfortable," David said.

"You've got a nicer pool than me," Bennie said. His voice sounded scratchy, like maybe his cold was getting worse. "I told Rachel we should get a saltwater but she was against it, said the maintenance costs were double. I was like, baby, I'm a rich man. She said, 'You want a bunch of strangers coming to the house twice a month to keep it clean? Or do you want to be able to hire some kid from the neighborhood?' I mean, she had a point. Then we bought this place for Rabbi

Gottlieb; first thing she does, gets a saltwater pool installed." He took a drag from the cigar, poofed his cheeks full of smoke, then blew it all out, careful not to inhale. "But we got a better view."

"That's true," David said. He dragged another chaise lounge over, sat beside Bennie. "Also, your house isn't a prison."

Bennie laughed. "Try spending a year there on house arrest." He pointed at the cameras perched on the block-wall fence surrounding the property. "Noticed you unplugged those."

"I like to swim nude," David said. He also didn't want Bennie to know when he was going for his walkabouts. He'd unplugged other cameras in the house over the years, a few mics. Bennie claimed to have a safe house where all the video was being kept, but the longer David worked with him, the more this seemed improbable. Bennie Savone operated just like everything else in Las Vegas: the perception of danger was just enough to keep most people in line.

"You're an odd man, Rabbi," Bennie said. He cleared his throat. Or tried to. "I need to go out of town for a while."

"Where to?"

"Rochester, but in Minnesota," Bennie said. "You ever been?"

"No," David said.

Bennie said, "Me either," and took another drag of the cigar. Again, didn't inhale.

"What's out there?"

"Mayo Clinic," Bennie said. When David didn't respond, he said, "My cancer's back."

David pointed at the scar across Bennie throat. "I thought they took your thyroid out?"

"They did," Bennie said. "It's metastasized to my throat, my lymph nodes, there's a spot on my prostate. I've been shitting blood for a month." He took another sip of orange juice. "This place, it's supposed to be the best in the country for this sort of thing. So I'm learning to become a person who takes vitamin C."

"It's good for your immunity," David said.

"Once it's in your fucking lymph nodes," Bennie said.

David waited for Bennie to continue, but he didn't.

"When do you leave?"

"Doctors wanted me there yesterday," Bennie said, "but we gotta get housing set up, all that shit. I'm gonna fly out tomorrow night. Bring a couple guys with me. Clinic has housing, but that won't work long term. So I need to find somewhere to set up shop. Rachel will be there for the surgery this coming Friday and then she'll come back and forth, I guess."

"What about the kids?"

"The *tsuris* this is causing me with the kids is out of this fucking universe," Bennie said. "We can't just pick up and move to fucking Minnesota. Summer break, Rachel will bring the girls out for a couple weeks. Once we know everything is in order. But Jean is so fragile right now. They're here until the foreseeable future."

"Kids don't need that stress," David said.

"I'm trying to live a more honest life, Rabbi," Bennie said, "but the girls don't need to see me shitting in a bag. My pops? When he went? I was sitting with him when he died, and let me tell you, part of me is still sitting in that room. I want to avoid that."

"You're not going anywhere."

"They got me set up for a minimum of three months of chemo, then radiation, then I guess if that doesn't work, they send me to the Space Station. Let me live in zero gravity." He shook his head. "You're gonna need to take care of some things for me."

David started making a mental list:

1. He'd want Rabbi Kales dead.

2. He'd want Jerry Ford dead.

3. He'd probably want one more local rabbi dead, to ensure a membership bump in 2003.

"First thing," Bennie said, "my girls, they need to be protected. These fucking Russians? You see the shit they did this week? Mother-fuckers can scream Al-Qaeda all day, but Boris Dmitrov owns that

208 TOD GOLDBERG

whole corner of Sahara. Whoever did this did it to send him a message. Some motherfucker sees an opportunity to come in here and
become somebody by taking out my wife and kids? Someone with a
beef from the Old Country that Rabbi Kales boned out in 1909 with
their kugel recipe? That's not happening. Rachel's cousin, he's been
living in the house. But when they're at school, I need to know you're
willing to jump into the fray. You're the only person I trust on this
shit. Comes down to it, no rental cop is taking a bullet for Bennie
Savone's kid, you got it?"

"Of course."

"Rachel can handle herself, a little bit, but someone steps to her,
I expect you to put them on their back. Second. I want you to run a
clean shop. I need to get this assisted living facility off the ground.
That can be a real earner for us. Once we get the building up, get everyone licensed and certified, get it approved by the fucking state,
we're looking at two years, and that's if everything goes A-plus all the
way through. You hear what I'm saying?"

He did, but he couldn't believe it. "Nothing crooked? You gonna
turn the strip club into a monastery?"

"You let me worry about the Wildhorse. Everything else, nothing
with a fucking dent in it. The Temple and the mortuary need to be
clean. This is fucking important. Because I'm on the funeral home's
insurance. I lose my fucking Blue Cross because of some shit, that's
it, okay? That's fucking *it*. I've already told Ruben; he's 100 percent on
board. He voiced some concerns about your ability to take the same
order."

"Ruben thinks he knows me," David said. "He doesn't know anyone like me."

Bennie watched David for a few seconds, a smile working its way
across his face. "No," Bennie said, eventually, "he does not." He put
his sunglasses on, leaned back in the chaise lounge. "How long you
been here now?"

"Four years."

"Tell me something," Bennie said. "How many times did you wish me dead?"

"You or the idea of you?"

"Let's go with the idea," Bennie said.

"Every day since the doors to that meat truck opened and you were standing there with Slim Joe."

"That's reasonable."

"Wasn't personal. I would have felt that way about anyone."

"Ronnie saved your life," Bennie said.

"My cousin," David said, "killed my father and set you up, too. If he had his way, you'd probably be dead."

"Look where that got him," Bennie said. He tried to clear his throat again. "Listen. Rabbi Kales's gotta go. I ordered a cocktail from our friend the doctor. I'd planned on doing this myself, but that's on you now, Rabbi. I can't trust Rabbi Kales to keep his mouth closed. Half the time he talks, he's on another planet. Have you seen him since you been back?"

"No."

"Go see the old man," Bennie said. "You're his proudest achievement. Talks about you like you're his son. I think while you were in the hospital, he lost a lot between his eyes because he didn't have you to talk to."

"Maybe," David said, "he just got old."

"Maybe," Bennie said, slowly, to make sure David heard him precisely, "someone told him to fake it and he got too good at it."

"Maybe," David said, "someone was trying to save your life."

"Maybe, maybe," Bennie said. "Anyway. Go see him. Wait till I'm gone to do the other thing."

David nodded. "What if some of your clients don't take no for an answer?"

"Try not to get into a shooting war with the Triads," Bennie said.

"That's not who I'm worried about. There's some people out there I don't want to be showing my face to."

"Let Ruben handle it," Bennie said.

"All of it?"

"He'll do what needs to be done," Bennie said. "He didn't get that thirteen tattoo on his chest because he's *not* a killer. Need be, Barrio Naked City will earn their keep on the fucking payroll."

"What about Jerry?" David said, testing the waters. David had wondered why he hadn't heard from Bennie about the explosion. Now he understood. Hard to give a fuck about shit down the road when you're facing your own dead end.

"Most of what he does is legal," Bennie said. "You'll speak to him. He'll understand." Bennie took another puff of his cigar but this time inhaled it all the way down, held it, then exhaled a huge plume of smoke into the air. Took down half of the orange juice, wiped his mouth with the back of his hand. Took a tiny bottle of cologne from his pocket, sprayed it all over himself. "If Rachel smells cigar smoke on me, she'll fucking flip."

"Drive with the window down and your head out the window, like a dog."

"I've tried that. Doesn't work." Bennie pointed at David with his index finger and pinky, something he did, David had noticed, when he was trying to convey emotion without looking like a pussy. "Last thing, then we don't talk about it in front of anybody. This whole thing. Everything we've been doing." He lowered his voice, muttered, "Fuck." Took his last sip of orange juice. "I know you don't see it the way I do, but we built some shit out here that's gonna last. Shit that's good for the Jews, right? That's the legacy I want to leave for my girls. That their fat fucking gangster of a father, who died with a limp dick, choking to death, bald as a fucking cue ball, in the end, he was making life better for them, specifically, but better for the Jews in general. That's how I want them to think of me. If it weren't for you, that wouldn't be possible, is what I'm trying to say."

"Don Corleone, I am honored and grateful," David said.

"Shut the fuck up," Bennie said. He stood up, brushed ashes off his pants, made his way through the sliding doors. He put out his cigar in David's sink, tossed the butt down the disposal, let it run. David followed him inside, locked the sliding doors, tried to figure out this new algebra. With Bennie gone, it might be slightly easier to get out of town. But Bennie dying—and not by David's hand—things got a lot more complex.

Bennie disappeared into the guest bathroom, presumably to go shit blood, so David spent a few minutes staring out the front window, watching the Israeli kid futz around in the front seat of David's car. Moving the seat back and forth. Opening and closing the moonroof. Thumping the bass, lowering the bass. He was what stood between the Jews and the hordes?

"The fuck is that kid's name?" David asked when Bennie came out.

"Avi."

"He's really IDF?

"Killing for your homeland for five years now."

"Rabbi Kales takes a fall," David said, "he's not gonna come after me?"

"He's not a cop," Bennie said. "His loyalty is to whoever is paying his bills. Currently, that's me. So, any troubles outside your purview, let Avi know. He can help. He knows you speak for me."

"I didn't even know that," David said.

"Anyone need to tell Spock he was number two?"

"I'm a *Star Wars* guy."

Bennie shook his head. "Always have an answer, don't you? Rabbi Kales teach you that?"

"Streets taught me that."

"I wish the streets had taught you to be an oncologist. That would be more helpful."

"How long, you think?"

"I don't think I'll ever come back here," Bennie said, "except in a box."

"My advice then is find a suit you like," David said, "then get six more just like it."

This made Bennie actually laugh. "Time comes," Bennie said, "*you* put me in the dirt. *All* of me, clear?"

"Time comes," David said. "Every last bit of you."

"And then get out of town, because I won't be able to protect you anymore."

"I didn't realize you were."

"Don't be naïve," Bennie said, "it doesn't suit you, Rabbi." He headed for the front door, David behind him. "I look all right?" he asked before they stepped outside. "I got sick in your bathroom."

"Yeah," David said.

"I'm going to die, aren't I?"

"Not today."

Bennie stepped out on the front porch, looked into the sky, took another deep breath, which then unfurled into painful-sounding hacks. He spit a gob of blood onto the pavement, wiped it with his shoe.

"The Talmud says if you see a house on fire in the distance, do not pray that it isn't your house."

"What's that supposed to mean?"

"It's either your house or it's not," David said. "God can't change it. You're gonna die. It's how you continue living that matters. That's what I take it to mean."

Bennie hacked another gob of blood onto the pavement but didn't bother smudging it away. "My house is on fire, no doubt about that." He waved Avi to pull up closer. "Get in the front, Rabbi. May as well get used to the view."

FIFTEEN

SOME SHIT *IS* FORETOLD: THE TORAH STUDY GROUP RAN LONG BECAUSE THE Torah study group always ran long. Rita Wolfe did not understand the notion of redemption through kindness and spent the last twenty minutes talking about all the times her family "shit on her" when she was being kind—and how they still talked about her like she was a convert because she'd, briefly, had an affair with a Mormon congressman from Reno.

"Rita," Rabbi Cohen said, as the other eight ladies in the group gathered the remaining butter cookies and mint Milanos into their Tupperware, "my advice is that perhaps if you keep doing the same thing and are unhappy with the results, stop doing that thing."

Rita Wolfe burst into tears. "You're telling me I'm crazy, aren't you?"

Rabbi Cohen waited a moment to see if any of the other women would comfort her. He got the impression, after about ten seconds, which is an eternity when someone is sobbing, that the other congregants didn't think much of her.

Rabbi Cohen said, "Rita, you misunderstand me."

"You just told me I'm the very definition of insanity," she shouted. "You can be a real golem, Rabbi. I thought I missed this group, but it turns out maybe I just missed the ritual. Well, you won't need to worry about my descent into insanity any longer."

He waited another ten seconds. Nothing from the women. Susie Helms actually peeled a Milano apart and licked the mint, eyes on the show.

"If that's how you feel," Rabbi Cohen said, "we'll miss you." Kristy

Levine caught his eye, shook her head almost imperceptibly, as if to say, *It's not worth it*, then sat down beside Rita.

"Rita, what the rabbi is telling you is that you're too good for these people. You're trying to redeem *them* with your kindness. He's telling you to redeem yourself with your kindness. Do you see the difference?"

Rita dug in her purse. Came out with a Kleenex, blew her nose, dropped the Kleenex on the floor, then kicked it under the table. "I do," Rita said. "Thank you."

"I'm sorry you're upset," David said.

"No you're not," she said. She stood up, picked up the last remaining plate of butter cookies, and dumped them all into her purse. "You should sue to get your old jawline back. You look twenty years older."

"I APPRECIATE WHAT YOU DID BACK THERE," DAVID TOLD KRISTY ONCE everyone else had emptied out of the community room.

"It was nothing," Kristy said. She took off her baseball cap and set it on the table, scratched at the stubble on her head.

"Your hair is growing back nicely."

"That's kind of you to say," Kristy said, "even if it's a lie." She cocked her head, curiously. "I like your new jaw, by the way. So don't take what Rita said personally."

"My mother came to see me in the hospital and burst into tears," David said. "Said it looked like they'd removed all the Ashkenazi from me. Wanted to know if the doctors were all goyim."

"Were they?"

"Half and half," David said. "I've had a deviated septum all along, apparently. So for the first time in my life, I can actually breathe. A tiny mitzvah."

"Your mom still staying with you?"

"No, no," David said. "She's back east."

Kristy stretched her arms above her head and let out a little yelp of a yawn.

"You look tired."

"You're not supposed to tell women that."

"You *seem* tired," David said, "am I allowed to say that?"

"Bad week," she said. "My lung function isn't good, and I breathed all that shit in the air all week long."

"Were you working . . . whatever that was?"

"I can't tell you," Kristy said, "that I was working on the corner of East Sahara and Maryland Parkway, no."

"I see," David said. David had a fondness for Kristy Levine that he couldn't quite place. He knew she was an FBI agent, but he also knew that like Bennie, she was staring at the dead end of life, even if her road was perhaps a little longer than Bennie's, but who could tell? "Perhaps you can also *not* tell me if I need to keep all of this extra security?"

"Who are you worried might show up?"

"Terrorists?"

"Rabbi," Kristy said, "if terrorists wanted to blow up the Temple, they would. Worse than we saw at the Commerce Center."

"Vivid," David said.

"I just want you to know what the reality of the situation is, Rabbi. Do the armed guards stop your average Carson City skinhead who wants to kill a Jew? Yes. But does it stop a terror cell from killing all the Jews? Not even a little bit."

"Then who should I worry about?"

"Are you running from the Russian mob?"

"Not at present."

"Good," she said, "because half the guys patrolling your grounds are on their payroll."

David walked over to the window. It faced the playground of the Tikvah Preschool, which the Temple kept open all weekend long, so the kids could come and play in a safe environment. There was a guard about twenty yards away, walking a slow figure eight on the lawn, another watching from his car in the parking lot. In the car, they were strapped for war: AR-15s, flash grenades, enough tactical gear to dress a battalion. On their person, two guns: a service revolver on their hip and a Glock on their ankle. "What about these two?"

Kristy stood beside David, close enough that he could feel her breath coming fast from her nose. "They're clean," Kristy said after a while. "But the guy standing in front of the mortuary? If he invites you out for drinks, tell him you're busy."

That was Officer Kiraly.

"I'll keep that in mind," David said.

"What's it like," Kristy said, "to look different?"

"What did it look like to you when you shaved your head? Lost your eyebrows? Had your eyelashes disappear?"

"I finally understood why people get cremated," she said. "I looked like a corpse. Unrecognizable."

"Do I look unrecognizable to you?"

Kristy said, "No, of course not."

"Nor to me," David said. "This work has taken away a persistent pain. I miss my chin a little, but my nose? Not so much." He smiled. "I'm a vain man, Kristy, and I happen to think I look better now. Despite what Rita said."

There was a knock on the open door. David turned around, found Ruben standing in the doorway. "Excuse me, Rabbi?"

"Yes, Ruben?"

"You have a funeral in thirty minutes. Just wanted to make sure you had time to meet with the family first?"

"Of course," David said. He pointed at Kristy Levine. "Have you met Ms. Levine?"

"No, I don't think so," Ruben said. He walked across the room, confident as ever, and shook her hand. "I am Ruben Topaz, the executive director of the Kales Mortuary and Home of Peace."

"Please," she said, "call me Kristy."

"The family is waiting for you, Rabbi."

"Thank you, Ruben," David said.

"Makes you want to die, that one," Kristy said, once Ruben was gone.

"You'd be surprised." David checked his watch. "Unfortunately that means I need to leave you to clean up the rest of this. Can you stack the chairs for me, Kristy? Or just drag them into the storage closet?"

"Of course, Rabbi," Kristy said. "Are you locking up anytime soon?"

"No, no, as long as there are kids here, we'll keep everything open," David said.

"So it would be okay if I stayed? I just find it very peaceful here."

"Of course," David said. "It is your temple."

"Thank you, Rabbi," Kristy said. David was almost out the door when she added, "Do you really believe kindness can redeem a person in the eyes of God?"

"I have to," David said.

THE LAST BODY RABBI DAVID COHEN WAS SCHEDULED TO BURY THAT DAY WAS someone named Lon Levy. Sixty-three, no spouse, lived at the new Sun City Anthem in Henderson, died two days ago, so he was on a deadline to get in the ground, Jews real strict about getting into a pine box and under a shovel of dirt in three days. But since the service was scheduled for 5 p.m., David had a pretty good idea old Lon was going to be some Chinese gangster transported from San Francisco, since Jews were not big with evening funerals. Bennie told David about the business he'd been getting from the Woh Hop To lately, a Hong Kong Triad gang that was looking to colonize in Las Vegas.

Bennie's cellie up in Carson City had been a Woh Hop To OG named Simon, and the two had hit it off. Basically, the Woh Hop To were keen to capitalize on the lack of state taxes in Nevada, the easy incorporation laws, and the opportunities to run mortgage fraud, everyone looking for a less violent future. So Bennie helped broker a land deal, even got Simon and his homies a place to live, over in the

Rivers-Upon-Craig, a new European-style development going up on Craig Road, which was still the hinterlands but wouldn't be for long. In the meantime, Bennie told him Simon had been good for three dozen bodies while David was stuck in the hospital.

"All pristine," Bennie told David. "No blown-out eyes, no knife wounds to major organs. No one set on fire. I told him, for our purposes, best thing you can do is cut their throat and bleed them out like a deer, pack 'em in ice and head out." And so that's what they'd done, particularly since the active street war with the Wah Ching had escalated into high-profile kidnappings and extortions, except no one ever got anyone back, their bodies disappearing into the manicured graves of Summerlin. These fuckers didn't give a shit about who they took, either. It was men, women, children, and pets. Bodies were bodies. All of which were profitable for Bennie, save for the bunnies and spaniels.

Yet, when David got back to the morgue, he was surprised to find not a Chinese teenager on the table but a sixty-something white guy with a giant barrel chest and prominent beer gut, his salt-and-pepper hair caked with blood from the hole in the middle of his forehead. David admired the work for a moment. One shot. Professional. A pleasure to see.

"We've actually got two for this burial," Ruben said absently. He was at the sink, washing his hands. "So we might not get this going until five thirty. We'll send Miguel to speak to the mourners if need be." The mourners were some old fucks from Sun City brought in for these kinds of services. Each got paid fifty bucks plus dinner. Old friends of the Savone family.

"Are they able to fit in the same coffin?" David asked. The man was at least 285 pounds.

"He'll bend."

"You sure?"

"We'll make it work. We've got a backup in the coolers. The boss says he wants us done with everything this week."

"Yeah," David said as he picked up the man's right arm. "I heard." He had a tattoo of the ace of spades on his wrist, another of Italy on his forearm. David half expected to find an eight ball on his bicep, just like David had until they carved it off when he arrived in Las Vegas, but instead he had five dots—one in the center of four—which either meant he'd done time or was an OG. Either way, old white guy with legacy tats was not a good fucking sign. He tipped the body on its side, so he could get a look at the man's back. In five-inch Old English lettering across his shoulders it said AQUAFREDDO.

Shit.

There'd been some Aquafreddos in Chicago back in the day. Some Gambino cousins. Brothers that got sent out west to find their fortune or some shit. By the time David heard of them, they were a West Coast connect, guys you could get weed from if you needed a lot of it, like a truck's worth, and then lately they were always talking about making their fortune in Indian bingo, some shit Ronnie was morally opposed to. You didn't rip off grandmothers to make your nut. Gambinos saw the world differently. They'd periodically beef, but for the most part, it was what it was. McDonald's don't give a fuck about Taco Bell. Last David heard, there was only one Aquafreddo left; the other three had ended up in prison or dead.

"Where'd this guy come from?"

Ruben said, "Palm Springs. Picked him up on Friday."

"Where's number two?"

"Got some choices. Check the freezer. We'll take the smallest guy."

In the last two years, the Kales Mortuary and Home of Peace had expanded from six freezers to eighteen to accommodate all of their business, which was good since when David began opening doors, over half held bodies, one whole row was just for the cremation services, and the last two were for guys with holes in their faces. First guy had a single shot through the right eye, blew out half of his skull all over his black Adidas sweat suit. Hollow point. Nice.

Second guy had put up a fight. Gutshot, one in the shoulder, then maybe a hatchet to the face. Still dressed in pajamas. Half of his face was somewhere else. He was a couple inches shorter than the other.

David checked them for tattoos.

Ace of spades.

Italy.

Five dots.

Hatchet face had ZANGUCCI on his back. The other guy also had ZANGUCCI. Brothers or cousins, each with the same dumbfuck artwork as their local boss.

Used to be, Five Families fucks didn't get ink. But like everything else in the culture, that shit began to change once tattoos moved from the poor to the rich. You want to prove allegiance? Put a permanent mark on your body.

These guys? Fucking Gambino soldiers, maybe the big guy a capo, by now. Fuck. He's a guy who would be missed. They all would be. Seventy-two hours. Maybe less.

All the time David had been in Las Vegas, laundering bodies for the mob, not once had they put someone from the Five Families in the ground, unless they'd died legitimately in Las Vegas and wanted to get buried out in Summerlin. Which happened, periodically. Lotta OGs ended up retiring out here, never returning to the old neighborhood, not even in death. Shit, there hadn't been an unsanctioned Five Families killing in Las Vegas in twenty years. Palm Springs? Maybe fifty years. That place was an open city, just like Las Vegas, but it was treated more like a sanctuary spot. Even Ronnie used to go there for vacation, play golf all week on the same course as a bunch of Outfit twats, everyone on time-out, drinking scotch at the nineteenth hole, telling lies, all that Frank Sinatra/JFK/Sam Giancana shit they read about in history books, or told people they read about.

Bodies from Palm Springs weren't anything new. They'd been getting Sureños and paroled Mexican Mafia, plus dudes without obvious affiliation, by the hearse-load ever since Bennie hatched some deal with the local Native Mob. If New York found out Bennie had these boys? Gulfstreams filled with mooks would be landing in Henderson and then it wouldn't matter what Ruben wanted. The right thing to do would be to hold the bodies, have Bennie make some calls, make sure everyone was square, keep the peace, and take no cash. If he wanted to keep things straight while he was in Minnesota, they couldn't have these fucking guys in the freezer.

"Hold up," he told Ruben when he came back to the morgue. He had the big guy bent in half already, his body like a *V*, and had his electric bone saw out. "We can't put these guys in the ground."

"We can't have them in the freezers looking like that much longer, Rabbi," Ruben said. "Wrong person opens those doors, they're gonna wonder why they didn't read any new stories about any Jews getting a hatchet to the face."

David considered this. "You picked these bodies up?"

"Met a guy out in the desert," Ruben said. "Standard practice."

"Anything weird about it?"

Ruben thought for a moment. "Same guy as it's been for a bit," Ruben said. "Indian dude."

"Like from India?"

"No," Ruben said. "Native. Name's Mike."

Growing up in Chicago, Native Americans weren't thick on the ground. You had to go up to Wisconsin to see them, and even then, the ones David knew were all gang related. Native Gangster Disciples or Native Crips—reservation gangs that essentially paid franchise fees to use the iconography of prison and LA street gangs—but more likely outfits like the Four Corner Death Warriors, shitty little reservation gangs running drugs and guns for someone higher up the chain, half of them inexplicably named Junior.

"Anything weird? Strange vibe or anything?"

Ruben thought for a moment. "Had his uncle with him."

"Some old-ass man?"

"No, maybe ten or fifteen years older," Ruben said. "Dude seemed chill. Just watched. Mike said he wanted to see the operation, that's all. Had another guy that drove. Big Mexican OG-looking fool."

"And you were cool with that?"

"I got two choices," Ruben said, "be cool, or try to kill three guys. So. I was real cool."

"You catch the uncle's name?"

"Naw," Ruben said, "wasn't real chatty."

"These bodies," David said, "will kill us both. Is what I'm trying to say."

"We don't got a return policy, Rabbi. So we either bury them or burn them. Which you want?"

"Who knows these bodies are here?"

"You," Ruben said, "me, Miguel, and whoever fucking killed them."

"You have any more pickups scheduled for this client?"

"Sunday morning," Ruben said. "We meet in the same spot every time. Out in the Mojave."

"What time?"

"Three thirty a.m."

"Pack those bodies to go back."

"Are you fucking kidding me?"

"And I'm coming with you," David said, "to inform them our business relationship does not include these fucking guys."

"I don't think that's a good idea," Ruben said.

"I don't pay you to think," David said.

"You don't pay me," Ruben said.

The last time David saw Ruben alone was inside this very exam room, a bag of bones representing Ronnie Cupertine's wife and children between them, David telling him to drive to Oregon, dump them there. That must have been some drive. Turned out the bodies still had bullets from Matthew Drew's gun in them, turning the ex–FBI agent into a fugitive, which was a good thing. If he wasn't a fugitive, David would already be dead.

"You want money? Fine. I'll bring you money."

"You owe me an apology," Ruben said.

David spent his entire life in the employ of criminals. Ruben was no different. He'd been banging until Bennie installed him at the funeral home. Problems always settled the alpha-dog way. Whoever was the baddest motherfucker, you did what he said. You wanted something different? You come for the crown. But you don't ask for an apology.

"Christmas night," Ruben said, "having dinner with my in-laws, right? Dan fucking Rather is talking about those bags you had me drop off. Telling me the FBI and the ATF and DEA were on that shit because those bodies were fucking Ronnie Cupertine's missing wife and children. You know who the fuck Ronnie Cupertine is?"

"I am familiar," David said.

"There's fucking websites devoted to how that motherfucker kills people. They did an HBO documentary and shit. Dude from *The Sopranos* narrated it. Last four months, I've been waiting for some motherfuckers with tommy guns to light my house up. Dan Rather was talking about me. On fucking Christmas."

"Keep your voice down," David said.

"Who is gonna hear?" Ruben said. "Everyone here is dead."

"Look," David said, "you're protected."

"From The Family? They been in business since the 1800s. Where exactly is safe for me? They're in the prisons, they're on the streets, they're in fucking government. How am I protected?" He inclined across the body. "And then there's the fucking private detectives looking for information about Melanie Moss. The fuck, man. Every day, someone else has a question."

"I understand you're mad," David said.

"I'm not *mad*," Ruben said. "Mad would be normal. Mad is you lay off Miguel and now I'm working Tuesdays. Mad is you build this new assisted living place but don't give me a raise. This is a whole other level." Ruben stripped off his gloves. Yanked his scrubs off. "Did you do something to Melanie's grave?"

"What?"

"Melanie's grave. I went out there this week, put some flowers down, and it looked *fresh*."

"I had to get something."

"What the fuck could you possibly need from her grave?" David didn't respond. Would never respond. You could put him on the fucking rack and he wouldn't respond. "Fine. Fine. Maybe I call the cops, let them know someone is fucking with our graves. How about that?"

Miguel walked into the exam room just as David was about to take out his knife and stab Ruben in the eye. Miguel was just coming onto his shift, so he had a backpack with him, with a change of clothes, his lunch, and probably a couple paperbacks.

"Sorry I'm late," Miguel said, setting his stuff down on a counter. "Got stuck on the Spaghetti Bowl for like twenty minutes. Always forget that my Monday is everyone else's Saturday . . ." He looked up, saw that David and Ruben were poised like fighters in the middle of the room, a corpse between them.

"Oh," Miguel said, "am I interrupting? I can come back, Rabbi."

"You work for the rabbi or you work for me, Miguel?" Ruben asked. He paused. "I guess I work for you, Ruben."

"That's right," Ruben said, "so stay right here. This evening's funeral is canceled. I'll let the mourners know. While I'm gone, bag up Mr. Levy, put him back in the freezer. Turn the temperature down to 20 degrees on those units that have bodies."

"That will make them too cold to work with easily," Miguel said.

"Miguel," Ruben said, "just do it."

Ruben stormed out, leaving David and Miguel alone.

"What's going on, Rabbi?"

David liked Miguel. He did. Sensitive kid. Hard worker. Never said a cross word to David in four years. Yeah, David almost killed him once, but they managed to pretend it never happened, like a shared delusion. "Do your fucking job, Miguel," David said, and he went to find Ruben.

SUNSET WAS STILL AN HOUR OFF WHEN DAVID SPIED RUBEN SITTING ON A stool and smoking a blunt behind the gravedigger's shed in the Bellagio. Melanie Moss's unmarked grave was about twenty yards away. David killed Jeff Hopper about a hundred yards from here. If he'd let that man take him into custody that day, where would the world be? Would it be better? Probably, he had to admit. All this time he spent protecting himself for the possibility of being reunited with his wife and kid, he'd done nothing but make the rest of the world a fucking cesspool. It was like the butterfly effect, if the butterfly spread doom around the world with a single flap of its wings.

Ruben took a hit then offered David the blunt.

David took a hit, let the weed fill his lungs. He hadn't been high since the day he killed those feds. But that was heroin. Weed usually just made him want to take a nap. This was some good shit, though, and almost immediately, he started to feel it.

"What is this?" he asked.

"Sativa," Ruben said.

David took another hit. *Damn.* "This isn't the shit I smoked in high school."

"Naw," Ruben said. "That was probably parsley and nail clippings. I grow this shit myself."

"In your yard?"

"Naw," Ruben said, "I got a house. Over by Bennie's crash pad. Out past Durango and Craig."

"Where all the cops live?" There were articles in the *Review-Journal* about how cops were moving farther and farther out of the city, building plush homes on cul-de-sacs backing up to the open desert in view of Lone Mountain, where they could shoot their guns and abuse their wives in peace, David assumed.

"Turns out," Ruben said, "they're pretty good neighbors. Nobody calls the cops."

It was, admittedly, some fucked-up logic that had its own reality-defying truth to it. The other point, more saliently, was that David didn't know Bennie had a crash pad. Well, that wasn't true—he didn't *believe* Bennie had a crash pad, because that meant there really were computers filled with video and audio of him inside his own home and wherever else Bennie had placed bugs. It would take him five minutes online to find it if it was in his name.

Ruben took another hit, offered the blunt back to David, but he turned it down. Two hits and he was already feeling capable of making some big fucking mistakes. "Look," Ruben said, "I know who Bennie Savone is. Okay? I know. And I'm going to be loyal to him until the end; you can bet on that."

"Good."

"But I don't know who the fuck you are," he said. "You don't even look like the motherfucker who got me tossed up anymore. I know you ain't a rabbi. Not for real."

"What's real, Ruben?" David said.

"Dan Rather," Ruben said, again. "Talking about how this was the start of some shit the likes of which was only in the movies. Homie, I ain't fucking seen *The Godfather* before that. I rented it from Blockbuster. I do not need that shit. What we did to Melanie, that's real." He paused. "When Miguel walked in, you were going to kill me, weren't you?"

"I was," David said.

"Why didn't you?"

"Honestly? I didn't want to kill Miguel, too."

"Guess I'll give him that raise, then," Ruben said. He hit his blunt again. Exhaled. "You don't have much of a problem with killing, do you?"

"None at all."

"How'd you get that way?"

"Practice," David said. "Repetition."

"I killed someone once," Ruben said. "I was fifteen. Walked right up on the motherfucker in the food court of the Meadows Mall and stabbed him like, twenty, thirty times, blood all over the glass at Sbarro, families screaming. Blood in the lemonade at Hot Dog on a Stick. A fucking scene, man."

"Who was it?"

"Some dude wearing the wrong shit," Ruben said. "He was Twenty-Eighth Street, I was Naked City. That's all that mattered. I don't even remember his name."

"You're lying," David said.

"Alejandro Espinoza."

"You get caught?"

"Naw," Ruben said, "his family was illegal. Twenty-Eighth got them out of the country, back to Mexico, no one said shit to the cops. But I ended up in juvie a month later anyway on a B and E beef. That's where Mr. Savone found me. Killing that dude, that fucked me up. But this job? I feel like, in a way, it evens the scales."

Ruben took another hit. David took one also.

"If I could grant you three wishes," David said, "what would they be?"

"Homeboy, you are high."

"I am," David said.

Ruben pinched off his blunt, carefully wrapped it up in a plastic bag he pulled from his pocket, dropped what was left in a small Tupperware container, then dug a hole underneath the stool, buried the Tupperware, covered it up with dirt. "To be legit," he said after a while. "To run this place the way I want to run it. Kales and Topaz Home of Peace. No more of this gangster shit. Be out from under Bennie. See you out the door. Deal with real Jews. They're good people. They deserve better than this shit you're running." When David didn't say anything, Ruben went on: "One day, maybe me and my sons do it together. One day, make it Kales and Topaz and Sons. Or just Topaz and Sons."

"I deliver that," David said, "we're square?"

"It's a job you gotta respect," Ruben said. "Right now, I'm just employed. All this shit I'm not proud of? That's following orders. That's providing for my family. But when it's my name on the door? I won't abide no fucking around. So yeah, you come through? Me and you are flat. But I don't want to see you again. Ever."

Ruben stuck out his hand. David shook it. A deal. "You owe me a wish," Ruben said.

"I'm sure you'll think of something," David said. "I need one more favor."

"Every time you ask for a favor," Ruben said, "my potential sentence gets another ten years."

"I need a body," David said.

"Whose?"

"Male," David said. "Natural causes. You got one in the freezer marked for cremation that seemed fine."

"That's Mr. Bodi. He'd already been in his house a week when they found him."

Which is why David wanted him. "Everything goes according to plan, you'll get him back."

"I don't want to know."

"You're in luck," David said, "because I'm not going to tell you. And I already had him picked up. You'll get me at midnight?"

"This shit," Ruben said, "is going to turn sideways."

"It won't," David said. "Something might happen, but it won't happen to us."

He started back to the Temple. He had calls to make. A plan to execute. Plus, he'd told Rabbi Kales he'd bring dinner to the nursing home.

"Rabbi," Ruben said, "I did think of something else. About the uncle from the pickup."

"What's that?"

"He smelled like a stripper. Like he'd been bathing in peach body wash."

SIXTEEN

EARLIER THAT AFTERNOON, OUTSIDE OF IDAHO FALLS, WAITING IN A
Starbucks inside a Target while William used the restroom, Jennifer
spread out a map. She knew when they got into the car eight hours ago
that they needed to go south, but she didn't want to take a desolate
route, in case someone was on her tail. She wanted to hug cities, be
within a few minutes or so of a town, or at least a gas station, figuring
whoever was going to kill them wouldn't do it in, say, the parking lot
of the Target in Idaho Falls. So instead of shooting down from Spokane toward Oregon on I-5, before cutting down through Utah into
Arizona, she'd wound southeast, across Idaho, then into a sliver of
Montana, before toggling back down into southern Idaho. Now, she
searched for a town on the map where they could spend the night,
somewhere in Utah, so that tomorrow's drive wouldn't be so long. She
knew only one person alive who might take her and William in, and
she was in Sedona.

Jennifer ran her finger down the map, avoiding towns that reminded her of the shitty Westerns her father used to read or places
that sounded like they were being run by a polygamist cult. Cottonwood? No. Ephraim? No. Cottonwood again? No. Burrville? Elysian
Hope? Fish Lake? Beggar's Pass? No.

Torrey.

She'd gone to school with a girl named Torrey Harris. Kind of girl
who was nice to the disabled kids, who when someone new came to
school, Torrey showed them around on their first day; the kind of girl
who you knew was going to end up being a pediatrician or social worker.

She circled Torrey, Utah, on the map. They could get there by the evening. Find a place to stay. She took out her cell phone, dialed 411, asked for the library in Torrey, Utah, got patched through. Within five minutes, a librarian named Crystal, who only worked there on the weekends, told Jennifer that her cousin Hanna owned a bed-and-breakfast inside an old schoolhouse on the outskirts of town. That would work. Jennifer scratched down the number.

William came out of the bathroom and, for a moment, seemed panicked—he took a few tentative steps into the store, gripped the bottom of his shirt in his tiny fists, a thing he did when he was nervous. She'd been able to shield him from the mess in the family room, from Maryann slumped there, her brains on the wall, grabbing him up and running to the car in the garage, scooping up a basket of clothes from the laundry room on the way out. He slept for the majority of the drive and when he wasn't asleep, he stared out the window in the backseat, repeating things he'd memorized—lists of prepositions, that mushrooms reproduce via spores, that Death Valley and the Salton Sea are two of the ten lowest places on Earth but you'd have to stack them on top of each other four times before they'd be as deep as the Dead Sea. When he asked her where they were going, she told him the truth: to see Grandma.

Jennifer thought: *No one knows us here. I should call the police and they will help us.* But what could she say that wouldn't end up with William in Child Protective Services and her on a forty-eight-hour hold? *You see, we've been living in protective custody for about a year because my husband is a hit man for The Family and I finally went to the government for help when I became afraid someone would try to kill me to get to him. My son? He killed a security guard in Chicago, but he was just trying to protect me. So. The government is trying to figure what to do about that. Or was. We woke up this morning and our handler was dead.*

Forty-eight-hour hold? More like seventy-two. With that story, she might never see William again.

Jennifer waved, caught her son's eye. He let go of his shirt. Re-laxed. "I didn't see you," he said when he sat down. He was teary-eyed. "I got worried you left me behind."

"I'd never leave you behind," Jennifer said.

"Never?"

"Never." She reached across the table and swept his bangs from his forehead, so she could see his face. He hadn't had a decent haircut since they'd ended up at Loon Lake, Jennifer taking it upon herself to do the job with some dull scissors in the backyard until she just . . . stopped. He now looked shaggy and overgrown, like a dog that hadn't been properly cared for.

"Do you remember that number I told you to memorize?"

"Grandma's?"

"That's right," Jennifer said. "Punch it into my phone." William did. She took five dollars from her purse and gave it to him. "Go buy yourself a brownie from the nice barista, okay? I'll be right here. I'll be watching you the entire time."

After four rings, Arlene Cupertine, who Jennifer hadn't seen in years, said, "Hello?"

"Mom," Jennifer said, "I don't have much time. I need your help."

SEVENTEEN

SATURDAY, APRIL 20, 2002

LAS VEGAS, NV

IT WAS AFTER SEVEN BY THE TIME RABBI DAVID COHEN FINALLY MADE IT TO
The Willows, the assisted living and memory-care facility where
Rabbi Cy Kales was living out what would be the last days of his life,
whether David killed him or not. It was located on Rampart, just past
West Lake Mead, and directly across the street from Desert Shores, a
gated community built around a man-made lake.

"Just drop me off in front," David told Avi. "I'll get a cab home."

"You sure?" Avi asked.

"I'm sure," David said.

"Mr. Savone," Avi said, then corrected himself, "Cousin Bennie,
he always makes me wait. I don't mind."

"The Talmud says waiting for family is easier than waiting for
a stranger," David said and got out. He opened up the back door,
grabbed the bags of food he'd picked up at the Bagel Café.

"It does?" Avi asked.

It didn't, not as far as David knew. "Look it up."

RABBI KALES'S APARTMENT WAS ON THE SECOND OF FOUR FLOORS, AT THE
end of a long hallway that smelled like cooking onions and Chanel
No. 5. There were a dozen apartments on the floor—most doors were
adorned with mezuzahs; like everywhere else, the Jews liked to con-
gregate together—as well as a library filled with books, board games,
and DVDs, the back wall devoted to a flat-screen TV, plus a bar serving white zinfandel and chardonnay in plastic cups, ice optional. This

evening, six people sat on an L-shaped leather sofa watching a Tom Cruise movie. David and Jennifer had caught the flick at a theater by Navy Pier and walked down toward the water after, despite it being the middle of December, barely 20 degrees outside. They'd had a sitter for the evening; they were going to take advantage of it.

"The only thing I didn't find realistic," Jennifer said, her head buried in his arm, "was his epiphany. You don't change like that overnight. He was a scumbag and then he wasn't because of one bad deal? You ever had a day at the office that changed you completely in, like, fifteen minutes?"

Sal stopped walking in the middle of the sidewalk. "What?" Jennifer asked. They were a few feet apart, their frozen breath meeting in the distance between them.

"I could change," Sal said.

"But here we are, Sal," Jennifer said.

"You want me to quit? I'm out tomorrow."

"And then you're dead, what, day after tomorrow?"

"They could try."

"They *would* try," Jennifer said. "They wouldn't stop. Ever." She took out a Kleenex. Blew her nose. "I'm freezing, baby. We don't need to have this conversation right now."

"Our house is probably bugged," Sal said. "This is the best place to have this conversation."

"I don't want to have it," Jennifer said. "I just want to have a date night with my husband and not worry about anything real. Can't we do that for one night?" She stepped into his arms. In his memory, they stood like that for a long time, holding on to each other as the wind whipped around them, Lake Michigan lost in blackness. The truth is the moment was probably fleeting: they held each other, he kissed the top of her head, apologized for whatever he could apologize for, and then went to find their car. They'd had that moment before and they'd have that moment again, when Jennifer's fears and doubts showed up and Sal would lie to her.

She spoke the truth. He could never leave. Even now, thousands of miles away, in an entirely different life, he was still so deep in the game that it seemed impossible there'd ever be a final score.

RACHEL SAVONE OPENED THE DOOR AFTER DAVID KNOCKED THREE TIMES AND then called Rabbi Kales's phone. "Sorry," she said. Her hair was tangled up and she had folds in her face from sleeping on something patterned. "I fell asleep watching TV."

"It's fine," David said. "I brought more than enough food." He opened the bags, showed her the Styrofoam containers of corned beef sandwiches, soup, and bagel chips.

"Looks good," she said. David set the food down on the small kitchen table inside the apartment. "Is it poisoned?" she asked.

He opened each of the containers, popped a piece of meat from each sandwich into his mouth, and smiled.

Rachel said, "Tell me something. You killed Rabbi Siegel, didn't you?"

"How would I kill a man who died of pneumonia?" David asked. He had, in fact, poisoned him. Wasn't trying to kill him. He just needed the man to agree that all the synagogues in town should pool their money and get better security. He wasn't sorry for that.

"The last place he visited was our Temple," Rachel said, "for your sewing circle of Rabbis. One day he's well, and by the end of the month, he's buried in our cemetery."

"Well," David said, "first, he was eighty. Second, he should have built his own cemetery. Third, he will return, and he will be perfect. So don't stress too much, Rachel. It's all been foretold."

Before Rachel could respond, Rabbi Kales walked into the kitchen. David expected him to look as he always looked—dressed either in a suit or slacks and a pressed shirt, his gold Rolex on his wrist, reading glasses in a leather case somewhere nearby—but he wore a cream-colored robe, done up tightly at his waist, over pajamas, perfect hair mussed up a bit, like maybe he, too, had fallen asleep.

"Terry," he said, sitting down at the table, "you didn't need to come all this way."

David met Rachel's eyes. She put up her finger, exhaled.

"Poppa," Rachel said, carefully, "that's not your nephew. That's Rabbi Cohen."

"Oh," Rabbi Kales said. He squinted up at David, then took his hand in his, patted it, let it go. "Rachel, sweetheart, get me my glasses."

When Rachel left, David said, quietly, "Laying it on pretty thick these days."

Rabbi Kales shook his head. "I don't understand what you are saying, Terry." He opened up the boxes. "What is this?"

"Corned beef," David said.

Rabbi Kales stuck his pinky into the sandwich, lifted the bread up. "Would it kill them to put some mayonnaise on it?"

"That's not kosher, Rabbi," David said.

"If I was going to die from not keeping kosher," Rabbi Kales said, "I'd already be dead." He went to his fridge, took out a jar of mayonnaise, then slopped a gob of it onto his sandwich. He looked pleased.

"That's how I like it, too," David said.

"That's why I love you, Terry," Rabbi Kales said, "no bullshit. Tell me. How is the law practice?"

David slid his seat next to Rabbi Kales, so that they were only inches apart. "Rabbi," David said, his voice not much above a whisper. Who knew who was listening? "You don't need to pretend, okay? Rachel knows who I am. We can just be . . . who we are, all right?"

Rabbi Kales took a bite of his sandwich, then a spoonful of potato salad, seemed to consider everything David said. "Terry, I think Rachel is trying to kill me."

"No," David said, "no. Rabbi. Rachel is not trying to kill you."

Rachel walked into the kitchen, Rabbi Kales's glasses in hand. She opened them up, slid them onto his face. "Now you can see the real world."

Rabbi Kales touched Rachel's cheek. "There's that beautiful *punim*," he said. "The most beautiful girl in the whole world. You never age a day, sweetheart." He turned to David. "Your wife. Is she as beautiful as my wife?"

"All wives are," David said.

"That's the right answer," Rabbi Kales said. "The Talmud. Do you know what it says about wives, Terry?"

"No," David said.

"It says a man should love his wife more than he loves himself," Rabbi Kales said. "It tells us to honor her life more than we honor our own, and if we do so, we will be wealthy beyond all compare. And look at me, Terry. I must sleep in a bed of gold."

"Eat, Poppa," Rachel said. She looked at her watch. "Shit. I'm late." She looked up at the ceiling, as if God might show up in the dry-wall, but in fact she was trying to stop her tears. David handed her his handkerchief. She did that thing women always do—she dabbed at the corners of her eyes—and then tried to give it back.

"Keep it," David said.

"It's monogrammed," she said.

"A couple years," David said, "sell it on eBay, put the kids through school."

Rachel folded the hanky, dropped it into her purse, which was sitting on the counter, then squeezed her father's shoulder. "Poppa, I have to go. Terry is going to walk me out, but then he'll be back, okay?"

"We have much to discuss, Terry," Rabbi Kales said.

"Of course, Rabbi," David said.

RACHEL LEANED AGAINST HER CAR, SMOKING AND SOBBING.

"How long has he been like this?" David asked.

"Every day he's worse," Rachel said. "The nurses take wonderful care of him. But the progression is startling."

"Jesus," David said. "I don't know if I can go back in there."

"You have to," she said. "He'll eat until he's sick otherwise."

"So he can pull up the Talmud," David said, "but he can't remember you're his daughter?"

"His book," Rachel said, "has lost its narrator. He needs someone to tell him what's going on. Sometimes it works, sometimes it frustrates him, sometimes it frightens him, so, I think, well, what does it matter? Let him believe what he wants."

"For how long?"

Rachel took a step back. "What do you mean?"

"If you intend to disappear when I leave," David said, "do you have a plan for him?"

"Who said disappear? I just want out."

"There is no out," David said.

"My husband," Rachel said, "is going to die. His cancer is Stage 4."

"That could take five years."

"Jesus Christ, Rabbi, I don't *want* him to die. I'm just saying it's time for me to be free of this. If I can help you, don't you want that?"

"What? You're just going to take his children and slide into protective custody while he's sucking radiation? You think the FBI helps you with all that and nothing happens to your husband?"

"I don't know, Rabbi," Rachel said, "I've never gone into protective custody. Have you, Sal?"

Hearing his name in her mouth was like having a cat scratch. Harmless, but it pissed him off.

"I had a friend growing up named Paul Bruno," Sal said. "Was gay, which was, you know, hard in an organized crime family. But he found his way. Spent, I dunno, ten years snitching out The Family, but in a kind of wink-wink way, my boss in Chicago used him to get rid of people, so it was like he was a sanctioned gossip, probably saved some lives in the process since if Bruno snitched you out, that meant the cops were gonna roll you up and that was that. He decides to get out, ends up moving out of state, gets a new job, nothing flashy, FBI is supposed to be protecting him, I guess. Lost track of him for a few years. I thought, good, maybe he's happy. Last time I saw him, he was dropped off at the mortuary without fucking eyelids. And this is a guy they *liked*. What the fuck do you think they'd do to you?"

"I've got something bigger to give up," Rachel said, which meant, of course: him.

"You do this, Las Vegas is done to you. Your father? He is done to you. As soon as you go to the feds, you belong to them, forever."

Rachel flicked her cigarette out into the darkness. Lit up another one. Sal assumed that was her way of saying, *Maybe I hadn't thought that part through.*

"You flip when Bennie's in treatment, they are going to pluck him out of there, toss him into a prison. This will not be a bail situation. If he's lucky, he'll have enough federal crimes on his docket that he might, maybe, get into a federal prison hospital, but I wouldn't guess they'll go light on him. And whatever information you give the feds to get Bennie jammed up? If it's so good as to put you into protective custody, it's good enough to have him shanked in the showers. Then they'll find you. You won't see fifty."

"Who is 'they' in this situation?"

"Me. Or someone like me."

"I want to show you something." She opened up her purse, and in what was supposed to be a smooth move she yanked out her Lorcin .380, put it right up against David's forehead . . . except that in the process, she fumbled out her compact and her cell phone clattered onto the pavement and she caught the hammer on the zipper. But she didn't notice any of that. Rachel Savone's awareness was not, it turned out, as good as a hit man's. "Don't fucking threaten me, okay? I will kill you and people will cheer on the streets of Chicago. I know who the fuck you are. I know about all the men you've killed." She stopped. "Why are you smiling?"

"Rachel," Sal Cupertine said, "look down." Sal already had his knife pressed into her side. She was already bleeding. He'd sliced right through her blouse and punctured her flesh, directly below her left rib cage, blood running down her leg, dripping onto her shoes.

"Oh Jesus. Why don't I feel that?" she said.

"Adrenaline," Sal said. "Now, move that gun or I'm going to carve out your kidney and serve it to your father with eggs in the morning." Rachel didn't move, not because she didn't want to, but because she was transfixed on the pool of her own blood.

"Am I going to die?"

Sal snatched her wrist with his left hand and took the gun from her, let her see him there: a gun in one hand, a knife in the other, no fucks to give. "You wanted to know Sal Cupertine, here he is."

"It wasn't even loaded," Rachel said.

"I know," Sal said. "Also, the safety was on."

"You stabbed me."

"No," Sal said. "I cut you. You're not gonna die. You might need a Band-Aid."

Rachel unlocked her convertible Mercedes, sat down in the driver's seat. "I've never seen this much blood."

"Get my handkerchief out of your purse, apply pressure to the wound. The bleeding will stop."

She did as she was told. "It wasn't even loaded," she said again.

"Get a real gun if you're going to start pointing it at people. I still can't believe Bennie bought you a .380." He handed it back to her. "And then load it. Next person you point an empty gun at is liable to beat you to death with it."

"I bought it for myself, asshole," Rachel said. "And I was worried my daughter would find it and blow her brains out, so I took the magazine out." She put it back into her purse. "Jesus. Do you hear me?" And then she was sobbing again.

Fuck. How had it happened that for the first thirty-odd years of his life he'd managed to avoid crying women, but now, four years into being a fake rabbi, all he ever did was comfort crying women? He got in the passenger side of the Mercedes.

"Listen to me," David said. "I have a plan. It's coming together. But it doesn't include you leaving with me. Your father needs you.

Temple Beth Israel needs you. But I can help you. You have to trust me."

"Why would I ever trust you?" Rachel said. She reached into her backseat, found her gym bag, David watching her in case there was a shotgun inside of it, but instead came out with a pink Juicy zip-up hoodie. She unbuttoned her blouse, balled it up and tossed it on the floor, put on the hoodie. Sat there, panting. "Jesus. I can't even breathe."

"Also adrenaline," David said.

"Have you apologized to me?"

"I'm not sorry," David said.

"Want to hear something funny? Just to put a cap on this whole fucking surrealist nightmare?"

"Sure," David said.

"I don't look anything like my mother. For years, I thought maybe they'd adopted me. But what I really don't understand is why he thinks you're Terry. You don't even look like the man you actually *were*." She reached past David, opened his door. "Get out, please. I don't like having you this close to me." David did as he was asked.

"Rachel, you're in shock."

"From the blood loss?"

"No," David said, "because part of you knows you should be dead."

She started the engine. "We leave on Thursday. Bennie doesn't want the kids there, but if he doesn't make it through surgery, I'd feel sick if they were at home alone."

"The surgery won't kill him. That's not what happens."

"Okay," Rachel said. "I'm bringing them because I want them with me, okay?"

"Okay," David said. "Whatever choice you make, it's the right choice."

"You need to promise me something," she said.

"You want someone you don't trust to promise you something," David said.

"Let me talk to the other guy. The one who stabbed me."

"He's right here," Sal said.

"Kill my father before I get back," she said. "Don't let him suffer like this."

"He's so far gone," Sal said, "anything he says will be viewed as gibberish. You and Bennie have nothing to worry about."

"I don't care about that," Rachel said. "All of us deserve the dignity of not withering to absolute shit before we die. I've said goodbye to him a hundred times, and each time, he is further and further away from me. When I see him now, he's a speck in the distance. Barely familiar. Don't let me come back and find him swept away. I couldn't take it." She put her hand out. "Please, take my hand." He did. "He got lost in his apartment this evening. He couldn't get out of his own walk-in closet. The horror on his face, it was incalculable. Every day, every single day, he gets closer to oblivion. You wouldn't let a dog suffer the way he's about to suffer. Promise me you will do this."

Sal said, "Don't make me do this, Rachel."

"It's you or it's someone like you," Rachel said. "Isn't that right? Let it be someone he loves."

EIGHTEEN

SATURDAY, APRIL 20, 2002

LAS VEGAS, NV

WHEN DAVID MADE IT BACK TO RABBI KALES'S FLOOR, THE GROUP WATCHING
the Tom Cruise film had doubled in size. Judging by the din, the white
zin was flowing.

David was halfway down the hall when someone shouted, "Rabbi,
is that you?"

He turned around to see Shoshana Friedman a few feet behind
him. Or was it Shoshana Hall? Or was it Edelmen? She'd been married and widowed at least twice during his time at the synagogue. He
couldn't remember the order of names now because his brain was
occupied with figuring out a more difficult mystery: On Shoshana's
arm was an apparition. A memory. Fat Monte Moretti's mother, Lana
Moretti. At least eighty, the skin on her neck looked like crepe, but her
lipstick was the same bloodred she wore every day of her life, her eye
shadow frosted blue, her hair so high it tickled God's feet.

David smiled, made sure his mouth opened all the way, and said,
"Yes, hello, Shoshana, how are you?" He grasped her hands, held them.
"I'm just on my way to see Rabbi Kales."

"Of course, of course," Shoshana said. She turned to Lana, who
looked like she too was witnessing a ghost.

Lana said, "You're Dark Billy's son. He killed my husband. And
because of you, my son is dead and my nephew Neal is dead, you fucking cocksucker."

She was right. Word was Dark Billy iced Germaio Moretti the night
before he tried to skip town. Fat Monte punched his own ticket after
Jeff Hopper and Matthew Drew fingered him in Sal's disappearance,

but she probably didn't realize Fat Monte was the one to ace out Neal, though Sal would have done it if he'd had the chance, since Neal drove Sal to Kochel Farms on the night he got disappeared.

"I've been busy!" David laughed. "I'm sorry, I didn't catch your name?"

"I'm so sorry, Rabbi," Shoshana said. "She probably needs to move to the memory care unit."

"Shut up, you cunt," Lana said, "my memory is just fine. This man is no rabbi. He's Sal Cupertine. A button man for The Family. I've known him since before he was fucking born." She stomped toward David, stopped mere inches from him. "Don't pretend you don't know me; it's disrespectful. I fed you a thousand lunches when your mother was too depressed to get out of bed, even after my husband died." She spit on the ground between them. "Salvatore, you were my son. I bathed you. I know every birthmark on your body."

"I'm so sorry!" Shoshana said again. She grabbed Lana by the elbow. "She watches these mafia movies all day long. Come on, Lana, please. Let Rabbi Cohen go on his way." She tried to pull at the old woman, who stiffened, dug in her heels.

"No, no, it's all right," David said, his eyes fixed on Lana's, to let her really see him. "I have experience with this. Why don't we go for a walk?" David put an arm over Lana's shoulder and squeezed, which is to say he lifted her a few inches off her feet and carried her down the hallway, away from the library, toward a sitting area with two leather chairs, a stack of People magazines, and a view of the parking lot. He learned toward her. "This man you think I am, if he were standing in front of you, and you said these things about him, what do you think he would do?"

"Shoot me in the back of the head," she said. "All that bullshit about shooting people in the back of the head, all this Rain Man shit about you never forgetting anything, you were a myth. But my boy? He was real. He should be running The Family now, not some Chuyalla fucking Indian from Wisconsin. You ruined The Family. Now here you are. So pretty in your suit, while my son rots. I should claw your eyes out." She was practically panting now, her face beet red. If she kept at this much longer, she'd probably stroke out.

He set her down in the chair beside the window. Then, very quietly, Sal Cupertine said, "Lower your fucking voice."

"Or what?"

"Or I'll throw you out the fucking window."

"You kill women now?"

"I've made exceptions in the past."

"Your mother would be horrified by you."

"My mother *was* horrified by me," Sal said. "So that's not the insult you think it is."

They sat for fifteen, thirty seconds until Lana said, "So you're not dead. The papers were right."

"First time."

"You know what happened to my son?"

Happened was a bit of a misnomer. He shot himself and his wife, except his wife lived, at least for a while. "I want you to know, Monte was fair to me. He could have killed me and he didn't. He was like a brother." *A deeply fucked-up, sickly violent, hard-drug-abusing, steroid-ingesting piece-of-shit brother, but a brother.* "What happened after that night is all on Ronnie. Ronnie snitched us all out, Mrs. Moretti. Whatever Monte thought he had to do, that's on my cousin."

Lana put a finger on Sal's chest. "You were the spark. Everything was fine until you killed those agents."

Lana began to cry.

How many was that today? Three?

"What are you even doing here?" she asked.

"You wouldn't believe me if I told you," Sal said.

"People think you are a rabbi?"

"Consider it like witness protection," Sal said, "but without the feds."

"I wish my Monte had known this was a choice," she said.

"I had no choice in the matter," Sal said. "And what are *you* doing here?"

"I wanted out of the cold," she said. "Half of Chicago is here now."

"What do you mean?"

Lana listed the mothers of nearly every fucking soldier in Chicago and the Las Vegas retirement community they'd settled into. The fathers were all dead or in prison. This was not good.

"How long have you been here?" Sal asked.

"I don't know," she said. "Eighteen months? Two years? I barely leave the building. My COPD is killing me." She let out another sob. "I just miss Monte and Neal so much," Lana said. "Do you know what they did to Neal? Is he possibly alive, too?"

He'd been dumped in a Chicago landfill, along with Chema Espinoza, the night Sal was disappeared. They never found his body. What Mrs. Moretti didn't know was that her son shot him. She could live the rest of her life without knowing that.

"He's long dead," Sal said. "I'm sorry."

"You used to babysit him; do you remember?"

"I do," Sal said.

"He and Monte were my last family," she said.

"What about his son? Out in Springfield?" Fat Monte had a kid with the granddaughter of the owner of Kochel Farms.

"That whole family is in prison for what they did to you," she said. "Boy is in the system now. Probably has a different name. Do you see? All of this. Because of you."

"Because of Ronnie," Sal said.

Lana took a Kleenex from her pocket, blew her nose, wiped at her eyes. "Let me tell you something, Salvatore. You can blame Ronnie for all the bad things in the world. But you never walked away. You made your choice."

"I don't walk away," Sal said. "That's who I am."

"Macho bullshit," Lana said. "It's the opposite of who you are. It's what your cousin Ronnie wanted you to be, and you were so weak, you let him turn you into that. You preferred being the Rain Man to being a real man." She spit again, but this time into her Kleenex. "Your father was trying to walk away. He killed my husband so he could walk away. So you could have a better life."

"Is that true?"

"Of course it is," she said. "Your mother never told you?"

"No," Sal said. But it all made sense now. The money and the guns in the trunk. His mother's shock. Dark Billy had done one last job, and it was to save his family. And in the end, he'd died trying.

At the far end of the hall, Rabbi Kales's front door opened. Light and the sound of CNN flooded the hallway for a few seconds, until Rabbi Kales walked out—completely nude, a sandwich in one hand— dragged a chair out, sat down, and began to sing. Was that . . . "Hava Nagila"?

"Oh, shit," Sal said.

"You better help," Lana said.

"Yeah," Sal said. "Do I need to worry about you?"

Lana said, "What can I do to you?"

"There's a reward," Sal said. "Wrong person finds out I'm here, they might try to collect. That would be bad for them and bad for you."

Lana said, "I'm just an old woman. No one will believe Sal Cupertine is a rabbi in Las Vegas."

BY THE TIME RABBI DAVID COHEN AND A NURSE NAMED PERRY MANAGED TO wrangle Rabbi Kales back inside his apartment, he'd started in on the Neil Diamond catalog. David found Rabbi Kales's robe in the kitchen sink; then he and Perry put Rabbi Kales into bed.

"All right," David said, once Perry was gone. He tucked Rabbi Kales in. "Are you comfortable?"

"Yes, Rabbi," Rabbi Kales said. A smirk.

"Oh," David said, "you know I'm a rabbi?"

"I know you think you're a rabbi." A smile. And then a deep belly laugh. "Nice of you to come visit, Rabbi. I've been pretending for so long, I don't know if I'm myself or not."

"You motherfucker." Had he faked . . . all of this? All these months?

Rabbi Kales pointed at the small sofa beside the bed. "Sit." David did. Rabbi Kales put on his glasses, went to his closet, came out in pajamas. "Turn on the lamp. Let me see your face." Rabbi Kales sat beside him, inches away, and examined David's face. "And this is the original you?" he said.

"Close enough," David said. Then he told him what had just happened with Lana Moretti.

"She's a strange woman. I've had breakfast with her too many times. She puts mustard on her eggs."

"My father killed her husband," David said.

"She hold a grudge?"

"No, he had it coming. But I'm not confident she'll keep her mouth shut."

Rabbi Kales took off his glasses, slid them into the pocket of his pajama top, like he was wearing a suit. "What are you going to do?"

"I've got two options," David said. "Kill her and every single person from Chicago who steps foot in Las Vegas, or just get out of Las Vegas. Which do you advise?"

"Have you located your wife and son?"

"Not yet," David said. He hadn't told anyone about Matthew Drew because it was all so desperate. It put everyone's life in jeopardy. David wasn't foolish enough to believe Drew wouldn't double-cross him, not when the reality was that David—or Sal—killed his friend, killed those three CIs and their informant, and all the others. He wasn't so desperate that he didn't have some contingencies in case Drew failed. "I've got a guy on it."

"What does that mean, David?"

"Can I tell you a secret?" David asked.

"I am your rabbi," Rabbi Kales said, "and I have profound dementia, so I think you should be fine."

David explained the existence of Matthew Drew to the rabbi, how he ended up beside David's hospital bed, how they entered into a de facto partnership to find Sal's family and save each other's hides.

"When was the last time you spoke with this man?"

"A week ago."

Rabbi Kales fingered the Star of David he wore around his neck. "David, this man, Benjamin doesn't know of him?" There was a tinge of worry in Rabbi Kales's voice.

"No," David said.

"Does he know of him in principle? As a person wanted by the FBI?"

"Maybe," David said. "All this shit went down with Matthew, Bennie was in lockup or under house arrest. Don't know if he was paying close attention."

"He will kill you," Rabbi Kales said. "This deal promises his demise, David. You must see that. It promises all of our demise."

"You don't think I know that?" David said. "Trouble comes, trouble goes. I have no problem not keeping my word to him."

"It's beyond your control now." Rabbi Kales got up from the couch. "Come with me."

"SIT," RABBI KALES SAID. THEY WERE IN THE SMALL LIVING ROOM, THE anchor on CNN going over the weather. It was a minute before nine o'clock. "Watch. Do not change the channel."

Rabbi Kales stepped into his kitchen. David could hear him putting water into a kettle. At the turn of the hour, CNN led off with an update on the terrorist attack in Las Vegas, a woman in a CNN windbreaker standing across the street from the Commercial Center, an N95 over her face. "Sources tell CNN," she said, "that fingers are beginning to point away from an Al-Qaeda cell to a possible lone-wolf attack. Is it possible one man could do this much damage?" The mayor came on. Said Las Vegas would rebound and come back even stronger.

Siegfried and Roy were interviewed. Talked about the indomitable spirit of the people of Clark County.

There was a segment about a Chinese airplane crash, killing 128 people aboard, and then something about an old Hollywood star getting arrested for murdering his wife, and then, "A strange story out of California, where one of the FBI's most wanted was brought to justice by his former boss. Kai Amberg from our sister station KESQ in Palm Springs reports from the Salton Sea."

The teakettle whistled.

It was 9:07 p.m.

Rabbi Kales set down his tea service at the very moment Matthew Drew, his body covered in a white sheet, was pushed into the back of the coroner's van.

"Matthew Drew has lived for the last several months on the FBI's Most Wanted list," Kai Amberg said. "Until today, when he tried to ambush mining executive and former FBI station chief Kirk Biglione at what was once a popular tourist spot along the shores of the Salton Sea . . ."

"How long have you known about this?" David asked. Kirk Biglione was on the screen now, his shirt spattered in blood.

"It has been on the news all afternoon and evening."

Kirk Biglione said, "I knew how dangerous Matthew Drew was; I trained him myself."

"Did you tell Rachel?"

"No."

"Don't fucking lie to me."

"I only speak babble to my daughter," Rabbi Kales said.

"Did you know he was out here?"

"No, no, of course not. But I knew he was connected to you. That he supposedly killed your cousin's family."

"And so you looked into him."

"I kept abreast," Rabbi Kales said.

How closely were the feds monitoring Matthew Drew on the

internet? Were they pinging on searches of him from Las Vegas? Were they triangulating him?

Probably not.

Not while they were so busy not finding Bin Laden.

On the screen, Kirk Biglione was talking about how this assault went all the way to the ganglands of Chicago, David waiting now, sure he'd hear it, and then, there it was: "This man might have been working with Sal Cupertine, for all we know." And then there he was, the same fucking photo they'd been using for years—waiting in line at Subway in Chicago, picking up lunch for Jennifer and William, getting himself a tuna sandwich, as he recalled—and his Chicago driver's license. He was mostly a smudge in a trench coat in the Subway photo, a still from their black-and-white security cameras, but it showed his full height up against the door, which was important since his driver's license said he was only five foot seven, Sal never changing it from when he was sixteen, a good joke that turned into a good diversion. He was thirty in his driver's license photo. Ten years ago.

"Would you know that's me?" David asked.

"No," Rabbi Kales said.

David clicked over to *Headline News*. Waited. Then: his face. MSNBC. Fox. His face.

Shit.

This wasn't local news.

This wasn't on some dumbfuck *Unsolved Mysteries* at midnight.

This was repeating all night on cable news in prime time, which meant it was also on ABC, CBS, and NBC nightly news.

Kirk fucking Biglione.

And then, a starker truth began to show up in Sal's mind: *I'm never going to find Jennifer and William.*

If Peaches was running The Family now, that meant Peaches was involved in this setup of Matthew Drew, however it had really gone down.

They were coming closer.

If they knew how to touch Matthew Drew, they were steps away from finding Sal Cupertine. They'd already dumped those Gambino fucks on Ruben, probably just to see what would happen. It made sense that they'd let Biglione claim this death versus just dumping Matthew's body. It helped burnish Biglione's name and made Matthew look even *more* guilty. The police probably had his gun to match to all those bodies.

Sal Cupertine wasn't going to wait around for either of these motherfuckers to show up on his front porch. He'd be goddamned if Kirk Biglione was going to watch him die, too. That was not fucking happening.

Sal clicked off the TV, stood up. "I need to go."

"Sit," Rabbi Kales said. "Drink a cup of tea."

"I don't want a fucking cup of tea."

"I know," Rabbi Kales said, "which is why you will sit here and drink a cup of tea with me." He slit open an envelope of Earl Grey, dropped it into a cup, poured in hot water, then handed it to Sal. "Let it steep." When Sal didn't move, Rabbi Kales said, "Rabbi, in my home, that is who you are."

Sal went to the window, half expecting to see Las Vegas Metro lined five deep, but there was nothing but an In-N-Out wrapper scooching across the blacktop. This whole building was in the wide open. Attackers could come from all points. "It's not safe here," Sal said. "If they can't find me, they'll start working through the people I care about. We need to move you."

"For what? My safety? You know as well as I do that in a week's time, you will kill me. I know how my son-in-law thinks. And Rabbi, I am settled to this fact."

Sal said, "Rachel wants you dead, too."

"I know. Her desire comes from kindness. Bennie's comes from fear. The end result is that both are probably right."

"Listen," Sal said, "everything has turned sideways. I'm not sure I can protect myself, much less have time to kill you." A cop car came screaming down Rampart, lights and sirens, kept going. An ambulance, no lights, pulled lazily into the parking lot of The Willows. Two EMTs got out, snapping on gloves, grabbing duffel bags. "There a good reason for an ambulance to be here?"

"Every night," Rabbi Kales said, "someone needs 911. I try to go to bed by this hour so that I can have something to surprise me in the morning. Was the siren on?"

"No."

"Then it's probably a catheter problem."

Sal closed the blinds. Looked up at the ceiling. There were water stains in the acoustic tiles. How many people had come and gone from this apartment over the years? How many ghosts were watching the two of them right now?

"Rabbi," Rabbi Kales said again, "leave the hit man at the window." *There's no difference anymore.*

Rabbi David Cohen sat down on the sofa, took a sip of tea, too bitter, poured in some half-and-half, dropped in a square of sugar. Took another sip. Let the warmth wash over him. Here was Rabbi Cy Kales, the most honest bad man he'd ever met. All this was put into action because of him. He wanted his synagogue. He wanted his Home of Peace. He wanted a place in the desert that celebrated the Jewish faith. He saw the history of Moe Dalitz, Bugsy Siegel, Meyer Lansky, saw the streets that bore the names of their hotels and imagined, in its place, streets named for him and for his family. Imagined a Las Vegas where a bad Jew did some good versus those bad Jews who simply washed their money in tourists' losses and called it philanthropy. Rabbi Kales had done mostly good. Rabbi Cohen had done the rest. Which is why Sal Cupertine ended up here in the first place.

And, in the end, wasn't that the final existential conundrum Sal Cupertine had to face? If Rabbi Kales had never let his daughter marry into the mafia, Sal Cupertine would already be dead. Talk about *mazel*.

"Can I give you a piece of advice?" David asked.

"Of course."

"Run," David said. "Trouble is about to come down, and you're going to end up in prison. Tomorrow, pack a bag, buy tickets to Israel for you and Avi, and as soon as Bennie is gone, go."

"I'm an old man, David."

"Avi will protect you," David said. "You have family there. They will also protect you. You once told me that if I found myself in trouble, I should surround myself with Jews. Give yourself the same respect, Rabbi."

"David, I fear you're being rash."

"Your name is on everything," David said. "You've been running an extremely lucrative criminal operation, and the only reason you're not already in prison is that Bennie hasn't opened his mouth. But if your daughter goes to the FBI in hopes of getting away from her husband, you'll be implicated. You'll be dragged through everything. That's the truth, Rabbi. I know the man who killed Matthew Drew. He saw my father die. He did nothing but ascend to the top of the FBI in Chicago. He is bought and paid for by the same gangster who tried to own me for my entire life. If he figured out how to kill Matthew, I'm next. I don't have much time. With or without my wife."

"You're scared."

"No," David said, "I'm realistic."

Rabbi Kales stood. "Well. There is but one thing left to do, Rabbi." He went into the kitchen, came back with a butcher knife. "Are you ready?"

"Rabbi," David said, "I'm not gonna kill you. If you want to die, I'll give you a bottle of pills, but I'm not putting my hands on you."

"No," Rabbi Kales said, "that's not what I meant." He walked into his bathroom, began to run a bath, then came back into the living room, still holding the knife. "Do you want to save your soul, Rabbi?"

"We're beyond that."

"We're never beyond that," he said. "If you want to walk through the Mount of Olives hand in hand with me, you must convert. That's all that's left. Draw your blood, bathe in the mikvah, and take a Hebrew name."

"I don't think I can observe all six hundred thirteen of the mitzvoth," David said.

"We do our best, David."

"I will let you down."

"You are a Maccabean warrior, David. You will bring woe to anyone who insults the Torah, will you not?"

"If someone insulted a Jew near me," David said, "I would gut them like a fish."

"I know." Rabbi Kales frowned. "Can I tell you something, David? You are a better Jew than me. Because you have the rest of your life to do right if you so choose. I have sold my life. Every good deed I have done as a rabbi is counterbalanced by the tremendous woe I have left in this world. You, David, beginning today, can be the best of us. You are a good man who has done terrible things. But you did those things outside the faith. Today, I can give you the faith. And for the rest of your days, how you live as a Jew is finally your choice."

"I've . . ." David began, but then stopped. Did he want to say this? "I've been having visions, Rabbi."

"Of what?"

"Two things," David said. "In one, I'm the prophet Ezekiel. Or at least I am seeing the world through his eyes. And God is telling me to repent. In the other, I see a woman I killed."

"I see," Rabbi Kales said. "And what does this person say?"

"She doesn't speak. Her intent is clear enough." He motioned over Rabbi Kales's shoulder, where Melanie Moss was pointing at him. "She's by your kitchen door now."

Rabbi Kales glanced over his shoulder. "I don't see her," Rabbi Kales said, "but that's not proof she is not there."

"If I do this," David said, "if I commit fully, do these visions stop?"

"I cannot tell you that, David," Rabbi Kales said. "What I can tell you is that I see my wife every day. I don't know if her spectral presence is real or a manifestation of my desires or a memory or just an old man who can see the end of life, but she comes to me and we talk and it is pleasant."

"Can you ask her?"

"It's not like that, David."

"I don't believe in God," David said.

"Yes you do," Rabbi Kales said. "You don't believe in a god who watches you. You don't believe in a god who plays a role in the outcome of football games or traffic jams. But you have shown me that you believe in something beyond yourself. God can come in whatever form you choose. He is not an old man in the sky. He is all around us. He is you and he is me and he is the memory of your father and the hope to once again see your wife and son. He is where you go when the world has lost shape."

"No," David said. "Where was God when those planes hit? Where was God when the camps were being built? Torah says fare well and you'll have a long life, but that's bullshit, Rabbi."

Rabbi Kales groaned. "We suffer because of evils that we have produced ourselves of our free will," he said. "Maimonides wrote that. We are good, and we are evil. But your free will, your choice to become Jewish tonight, can begin to balance that." Rabbi Kales transferred the knife from his right hand to his left. "I need to draw blood, David, if we are to do this."

David knew well the conversion ceremony. He'd done a dozen of them, usually right before a wedding, always with the husband changing teams. The drawing of the blood was to symbolize the circumcision since everyone was circumcised these days, but it was also the point at which conversion wasn't just a notion, an idea, a thing you told your wife you believed and then went back to putting mayonnaise on corned beef. Your flesh was cut. Your people were my people. The act was more like some omertà shit. Gone was living by the gun and the knife. Join the company of lions rather than assume the lead among foxes.

And there it was. An honest, simple truth.

He turned his palm to Rabbi Kales.

"Then I'm ready, Rabbi," David said.

Rabbi Kales cut him, just a nick, a bubble of blood rising up on his palm. "The Ethics of Our Fathers says, 'Distance yourself from a bad neighbor, do not cleave to a wicked person, and do not abandon belief in retribution,'" Rabbi Kales said. "Do you believe that, David?"

"All this time," David said.

"Retribution," Rabbi Kales said, "is your calling, David. You are a warrior. You have always been a warrior. You have served terrible leaders. What I am giving you now is a chance to serve yourself, in the word of the Torah. Is that what you want, David? Because the tub is filling." He smiled. "I must know only one thing about you. Your given name."

"My name," David said, "is Salvatore William Cupertine."

Rabbi Kales pressed his thumb over Sal's wound, stopped the bleeding. "Salvatore William Cupertine. There are but three things you must know in this life. Know from where you came, where you are going, and before whom you are destined to give a judgment and accounting. From where you came: from a putrid drop. Where you are going: to a place of dust, maggots, and worms. And before whom you are destined to give a judgment and accounting: before the supreme King of Kings, the Holy One, blessed be he." Rabbi Kales smiled faintly. "I know, Salvatore, that you do not yet believe in the Holy One, that you have pretended all of this time for the good of your congregation, but I also know that you have found him in the small things, that you have found him in your darkness, and that he calls to you in visions and dreams. He exists in your countenance, returned to you, Salvatore. One day, you will walk beside him in faith."

Rabbi Kales led Sal to his bathroom, to the tub filled with water. Rabbi Kales turned the water off, tested it with his finger. "Now, Salvatore, remove your clothes and get into the tub."

Sal did as Rabbi Kales had instructed. He knelt in the tub and then immersed himself completely, laying himself flat to cover his head, and then rose up, Rabbi Kales beginning his prayer, "Blessed are you, God, Majestic Spirit of the Universe, who makes us holy by embracing us in living waters."

Sal dipped himself twice more and then sat up, he and Rabbi Kales praying together, "Blessed are you, Adonai, Ruler of the Universe, who has kept us alive and sustained us, and enabled us to reach this day."

Rabbi Kales took Sal's hands. "You have earned the Hebrew name David, if you so wish to keep it."

Sal knew the meaning of his name. David, the second king of Israel. David, from the Hebrew *dod*, meaning *beloved*. The Star of David, the symbol of the faith. "I do," Sal said.

Rabbi Kales said, "May the one who blessed our forefathers, Avraham, Yitshak, and Ya'akov, Moshe and Aharon, Yoav ben Tsruyah, and Mordekhai ben Yair, may Hashem bless this man and let his name in Yisra'el be David, with good luck and in a blessed hour; and so may it be your will, and let it be said, amen!"

"Amen," David said.

Rabbi Kales reached around his neck and undid the necklace he'd worn every day since David first met him at the Bagel Café. It was a chain with a simple Star of David, originally gold but time had dulled it, tarnishing the shine away. He clasped it around David's neck. "This was my father's," he said. "And now it is yours. Maybe one day it will be your son's."

"Rabbi," David said, "I can't take this."

"You already have, boychick," Rabbi Kales said. He put his hand on David's cheek. "Tradition says you may now choose a prayer of your own. You may recite it aloud, you may recite it in your heart, but it is to be done alone, so I will leave you."

For almost five minutes, Rabbi David Cohen sat quietly in the tub, felt the warm water wash over his body, and tried to remember the last time he felt peace.

Ten years old.

In the backseat of the DeVille.

Chicago.

Summer.

His whole life in front of him.

His mother, Arlene, "I've got a feeling about today, baby. I've got a feeling today changes everything." Fixing her hair in the mirror. Spraying a bit of perfume on her neck.

And then.

A Cadillac pulled in front of them.

A Cadillac pulled in behind them.

Mom said, "No, no, no."

Three Black men got out of the first Caddie and disappeared into the building.

One Black man got out of the Caddie behind them. "Morning, Arlene," he said. Everyone called him 8 Ball Randall, because he sold eight balls, had an eight-ball tattoo on his chest, the personalized plate on his car said 8Ball, and every Gangster Disciple on the planet knew you didn't want to be behind the 8 Ball. Sal thought he was the coolest man alive. Dark Billy and 8 Ball went to high school together. Played football. Now they ran the city, the prisons, the world, as far as Sal knew. "What's up, Big Sal?" he asked.

"The IBM building is fifty-two stories," Sal said.

8 Ball Randall looked up. "Maybe fifty-one and a half right now," he said.

"What do you want, Randy?" Arlene said. She always called him that, just to piss him off.

"Pop the trunk," he said. "And you can call me Randall now; I ain't eleven."

"I ain't eleven either and you're not the cops," she said, "so I don't have to do anything."

"You'll wish I were the cops," he said, "if you don't do what I ask."

"Billy will be down in a minute," she said. "Until then, fuck off, Randy; you don't scare me."

8 Ball Randall grabbed Arlene by the throat with one hand and pinned her head against the seat. "You got a mouth," he said, then opened the glove box with his other hand, hit the yellow button to pop the trunk, and noticed the gun. "Look at that," he said. "Got a license for that, ma'am?" He let go of her, stuffed the gun in his waistband. "I'll hold this, just in case."

"Fuck off, Randy," Arlene spit out again. 8 Ball Randall was already inspecting the trunk, yanking shit out and tossing it on the pavement.

8 Ball closed the trunk, walked over to Arlene. "You going off to war, girl?"

"I don't know what Billy keeps back there," she said.

"I'll tell you," he said. "An arsenal and a bunch of money that don't belong to you." He looked up at the top of the building, then back at Sal. "Fifty-two stories? How many feet is that?"

"Five hundred and sixty-two," Sal said. "Give or take."

"That's pretty high." He smiled at Sal, reached over, mussed his hair, then turned his attention back to Arlene. "Sorry about your throat, didn't want to get rough, but you made me." He patted the hood of the car. "Don't be trying to leave, all right? This'll all be over in a minute."

8 Ball stood against the building, lit up a cigarillo, winked at Sal.

"Stay in the car," Arlene said, but then there was an otherworldly caterwauling, a scream that Sal would hear for the rest of his days, on birthdays and funerals, during those colicky early nights of William's life when he cried for hours, in the back of that frozen meat truck as he bounced across the Midwest, as he came out of surgery four months ago, as he dunked himself in the tub minutes ago, the sound of a life ending and beginning all at once, the sound of no turning back, the sound of the end of his peace, forever.

It stopped when Dark Billy Cupertine met the pavement at terminal velocity.

He'd hear that, too.

His entire life had been about terror management. How not to

think about what it must have been like to jump or be thrown from
a fifty-two-story building. How not to constantly be counting out six
seconds, because that's how long it takes to fall fifty-two stories. How
not to know, absolutely, that he'd met his father's gaze a millisecond
before he hit the ground, how he'd seen the last of him in his entirety,
how he looked . . . at peace? Was that possible? Or was that memory
fucking with him? It could be all those things, he understood, because
that's what terror management was all about, making the ends of this
life seem tolerable.

And so Rabbi David Cohen prayed.

To find his wife.

To find his son.

To not lose himself in the process.

He stood. Let the water drip from him. He cataloged the scars on
his body. He could take a few more, if need be.

He adjusted his necklace, centered the Star of David.

And then he prayed for retribution: *If I walk in the midst of dis-
tress, keep me alive; against the wrath of my enemies stretch out your
hand, and let your right hand deliver me.*

NINETEEN

DAVID CAUGHT A CAB HOME, GRABBED HIS NINE, MADE A CALL, THEN DECIDED, fuck it, and got into his Range Rover and drove across town, to the McDonald's down the block from Lorenzi Park, where Gray Beard and Marvin parked their RV. The doctors were right: his depth perception was for shit, and driving the car made him feel light-headed and a little sick. So he went inside, ordered a chocolate shake.

David found a table adjacent to the PlayPlace, watched twenty kids bouncing between the vibrantly colored slides and tubes and that disgusting vat of typhus they called the "ball pit," David thinking that what was going to bring down the world was not greed and violence, but probably some virulent super flu born in the bottom of that fucking thing. But this was Vegas at ten thirty on a Saturday night—a bunch of feral kids running crazy, not a single adult to be found.

Before too long, Marvin sat down at the table next to David's. Opened up his bag. Set out a quarter pounder, fries, a Coke. Took a couple bites.

"What's going on?" David asked.

"Wanted to make sure you weren't being watched," Marvin said. "So we split up."

"Smart," David said.

"The news right on this shit?"

"You know as much as me," David said.

"Don't seem real. All I seen in the world, you'd think I'd be impervious. But I liked him. Weird to see his big ass under that sheet."

"I need to go through his shit," David said.

"We figured," Marvin said. He was wearing a Lakers jacket, which he took off, set down between them. "Put that on. You look like a cop in that suit. People gonna remember you." David stripped off his jacket and tie. Put on Marvin's coat, which smelled like weed. "Fire alarm is gonna get pulled in about five minutes, so we can clear the streets a bit. Go out the back door, walk through the parking lot, turn right at Party City, you'll see there's a hole in the fence leading into the park. Fifteen minutes over by the Senior Center. You're late, we're on the move."

"I understand." He put out his hand, but Marvin looked at it like it was a rattlesnake. "Shake my hand, Marvin."

Marvin set down his burger, shook David's hand.

"Thank you for your help," David said.

"Wasn't a thing."

"You could have flipped on me anytime," David said.

"Bro," Marvin said, "you made us rich."

"Good," David said. "Listen, I want you to know, I will never look for you." A cop walked into the play area. He set out two cheeseburgers, a Coke, his radio. Marvin glanced his way, gave him a head nod. Cop flashed the peace sign. Weird fucking town. "But if you ever come looking for me, I will kill you. We good?"

"We good," Marvin said. "Ask you one question?"

"One."

"What's it like?"

"What?"

"Being mobbed up. Is it like in the movies and shit?"

"No," David said, "because movies end."

GRAY BEARD'S RV WAS PARKED RIGHT WHERE MARVIN SAID IT WOULD BE. THE RV was black with a swoop of gold along the side. Thirty feet long. Pop-out sides. Tinted windows. It was a Thor Cyclone, top-of-the-line shit. Probably retailed for just under $200K. David couldn't imagine that Gray Beard bought it through legit means, but who knows? They were, indeed, rich. David knew it wouldn't last. This was the problem with mob fix-it guys. They didn't have savings accounts. They didn't have health insurance. They had money and pipe dreams.

The passenger-side door opened as David approached, and there was Gray Beard, except his beard was gone. "See what you've made me do?" he said by way of greeting. He looked both ways, then stepped aside, let David into the RV, which was half medical practice, half home. A real upgrade from when Gray Beard first operated on David's face while sitting on a chair inside the tiny Winnebago shower.

"Where you headed?" David said.

"I was stationed out in San Diego; that's home to me. Plus, Marvin's mom is there. Hasn't seen her in a minute." He took David into the rear bedroom, where they had a king-size bed, surrounded by wood paneling, and a mirror on the ceiling. There were two large duffel bags on the bed.

Gray Beard said, "That's all his shit. Soon as I saw the news, I burned his clothes and sundries. One bag is full of notebooks, charts, graphs; sure it has some meaning to you."

"Okay."

"Other bag, I figured, maybe someone could get it to his family. Photos and books and shit. Diplomas. That sort of thing."

"Okay," David said again.

He went into his closet, came out with a bag marked Hospitality Animal Care, handed it to David. "Syringes and enough pentobarbital to put down whatever you need to put down. If there's a problem, also got enough morphine to do the trick, but autopsy will look for that."

"How long does it take?"

"Fifteen minutes."

"You done it before?"

"Desert Storm." He paused. "Then Marvin's dad, a few years ago, by request."

"Does it hurt?"

"No one's come back to say so," he said.

David put the drugs into the duffel of Matthew's personal items, hefted the bags up.

"This is the way to go," he said, "travel light." He checked out the RV. It was pretty fucking nice.

"You get to missing a yard," Gray Beard said and ushered him out of the room. "You and your wife ever make it to San Diego," he continued, "keep going south; you'll find me where the lobster's most plentiful."

"Leave a couple for me," David said, and then Gray Beard did something David never would have expected: he hugged him. "Do your jaw exercises. I can see your bite is already off again," Gray Beard whispered. "I hope to never see you again."

"Same," David said. He patted him on the shoulder.

Gray Beard opened the passenger door and Marvin was standing there, waiting.

"Adios, Rain Man," Marvin said, David knowing he'd made a mistake letting these two live, knowing that he fucked up his own training, knowing none of it mattered anymore. The sword comes to the world for the procrastination of justice, the corruption of justice, and because of those who misinterpret the Torah, David knew, but it said nothing of letting a friend who knew too much walk away with their life.

TWENTY

IT WAS A LITTLE PAST 10 P.M., BUT THE WRECKAGE OF THE COMMERCIAL Center was illuminated like Dodger Stadium. There were klieg lights set up in the middle of the vast parking lot and along four city blocks of East Sahara, cops and agents walking the grid, looking for evidence and body parts. Special Agent Kristy Levine had been on her shift for over an hour, inside what was left of The Ponderosa, when Jacob Dmitrov was allowed past the yellow tape. She'd never seen him outside of Odessa, much less in paper booties and gloves and a zip-up disposable hazmat suit.

"This is necessary?" he asked.

"Depends," Kristy said. She was also in full gear. "You want your skin to fall off?"

Jacob shook his head. "I have relatives in Chernobyl; they're fine."

"For now," Kristy said. "Your father couldn't make it?"

"He's not a big fan of meeting with the FBI." Jacob peered around the burned-out bar. "No way we can rebuild this, yeah?"

"Once they find the last eyeball and tooth," Kristy said, "my guess is they level this entire wing. The bomb scattered so much hazardous material, plus the human remains. There's no chance for these buildings. Be a nice insurance payout."

"That's one time," Jacob said. "You don't just build another bar and hope all the cops and hookers start coming. That's a generational thing. Habit, you know? You ever come here?"

"No," Kristy said. "I'm a Pour Decisions gal."

"Nice place," Jacob said. "Wouldn't sell to us." He shrugged. "So, what? I already told the cops what I know, which is nothing. We're not in the habit of burning down our most profitable businesses, you know?"

"I don't care about who burned this down," Kristy said. "I want to know what was going on in the warehouse attached to the dental office."

"Talk to the dentist."

Kristy said, "We already detained him at McCarran coming home from vacation. He said to talk to you." She flipped through her notebook. "Direct quote, was 'Talk to those KGB fucks.'"

"Well, that's not me."

"But it is your father."

Jacob was silent for a moment. "I need a lawyer?" he said eventually.

Kristy took her hood off. Unstrapped the N95 from her nose and mouth. Looked directly at Jacob. "You see me?"

"Yeah."

"Honestly, I don't give a shit about what you do, Jacob. I don't give a shit what your father does unless it hurts regular people. You do your gangster shit to each other, fine. But a couple blocks away, little kid, ten years old, finds three eyeballs in his front yard. Goes running into his backyard to tell his mother, and there's a human head floating in the pool. So now, Jacob, it's my problem. You didn't burn this place down? Great. You're paid. But who pays that kid?"

Kristy's cell phone rang. It was Poremba. "Give me ten minutes. You think on that question, and then we'll see if you need a lawyer."

KRISTY FOUND THE ONLY PLACE TO TAKE POREMBA'S CALL THAT SHE WAS sure wasn't under surveillance or being filmed by one of the twenty news crews staked out around the Commercial Center: her car.

"I don't have much time," she said. "I'm about to break Jacob Dmitrov."

Poremba said, "Matthew Drew is dead."

"What?"

"He tried to ambush his former station chief, Kirk Biglione, and ended up getting shot in the head with his own gun." Poremba so matter of fact, he could have been talking about getting his toilet fixed.

"Where?"

"The Salton Sea, this morning. It was all over the news. Where were you?"

"A Torah study group at Temple Beth Israel," she said. "Jesus. What was Drew doing?"

"I don't know," Poremba said. "It doesn't add up. Tell me what you saw at the Temple."

She spent the entire day at Temple Beth Israel. Peered into every open door. Spoke to as many people as possible. Walked the entire campus of the Barer Academy. Circled the Performing Arts Center. Dipped her toes into the pool at the Aquatic Center. Even saw the Blue Room inside the funeral home, where grieving families could wait for their funeral to begin, met a nice man named Miguel who gave her a croissant and a map of the dead. Thousands of names. Maybe ten thousand. Including her own.

She watched a van from LifeCore pull up around 6:30 p.m., depart fifteen minutes later.

Business as usual.

Everyone very happy that Rabbi David Cohen was back.

"We need to get into the funeral home," Poremba said. "Hold on. I'm going through TSA."

TSA? "Are you coming here?" she asked after a moment.

"I land in four hours," he said. "Go pick up Jerry Ford."

"For what?"

"Arson," he said. "Jaywalking. Figure it out. We need to get him off the streets before something bad happens. Get Dmitrov to say his name. That's all you need." He paused, lowered his voice. "Next week, I'm going to be appointed the head of the joint Organized Crime & Terrorism Task Force out of Las Vegas," Poremba said. "His name is connected to that shit in New Jersey. I want him off the street and in an interrogation room by the time I get to Las Vegas."

"Wait," Kristy said, "why are you flying here now?"

"Two disgraced former FBI agents got in a gunfight," Poremba said, "and the one thing they have in common is Sal Cupertine. They'll backtrack Matthew to Las Vegas by morning if they haven't already. We need to make sure we're clean on this."

"We. You said we."

"I'm sorry," Poremba said. "You were right."

Shit.

"None of this is making sense. Tell me what happened."

He told her what he knew, which was little more than the news reported. Matthew Drew ambushed Kirk Biglione at the Salton Sea, where Biglione was running corporate security for Gold Mountain Mining. Biglione disarmed him. Took him out.

"You knew Biglione?" Kristy said.

"Yeah."

"He capable of that? Of disarming Matthew?"

"I don't know. He was a top agent for a long time. It's possible. But he's in his fifties now."

"You're fifty," Kristy said. "Could you take Matthew?"

"He'd break my fucking neck."

"Why would Matthew Drew attack Kirk Biglione?"

"Revenge?" Poremba said. "He was ready to testify against him in his corruption trial. Biglione pled out and walked. Drew held him responsible for Hopper's death and, by association, his sister's."

"Drew was qualified for assault-team work. He could have plugged Biglione from a thousand yards away. Could have blown up his car. Lee, this doesn't add up. What did he *need* Kirk Biglione for? If he was out here searching for Sal Cupertine, doing the job you gave him, what could Biglione possibly have for him?"

Poremba stayed silent, thinking. In the background, Kristy heard a baby crying, an announcement for a flight to Tampa, and bits of mundane conversation as Poremba walked through the airport. Everyone going somewhere. No one aware of the world crumbling around them, all the time, every day. All of life was practical avoidance, making sure you didn't think about all the terrible things working in the background.

"Why did you believe Matthew was framed for those murders?" Kristy asked.

"Because he had a code," Poremba said. "He wasn't a serial killer. He wanted Ronald Cupertine dead, and he was upset that he'd failed, but he had no reason to go after his wife and children. He was a good agent, Kristy. A good man. This case turned him inside out. He wanted Sal Cupertine to make it right for the family of those dead agents, so they'd have some sense of closure. And he wanted to avenge Hopper's death. He wasn't going to kill a family, bury them, dig them back up, and dump them two thousand miles away."

"Okay," Kristy said. "The only forensic evidence we have is that those people were killed using Drew's gun, right? What else?"

"He stalked that whole family. We have an entire file of evidence. I wouldn't be surprised if he stalked Biglione, too."

"But why would he want to kill him? If he had evidence against him, wouldn't he be better served getting him arrested?"

"That already happened. He walked," Poremba said. "Biglione was crooked. He protected Ronnie Cupertine for years. Protected the whole Family to keep the ecosystem in balance. Kept the cartels from moving in, kept the Russians from having too much influence, took out guys who needed it. Even controlled the prisons to an extent. This wasn't revolutionary thinking. New York and Boston operated this way for years."

"What changed?" Kristy said.

Poremba said, "Whitey Bulger and John Gotti. Bloods and Crips. Terrorists. Twenty-four-hour news. Take your pick."

"Wait. Go back to something. You said Ronnie Cupertine's family had been buried and dug back up?"

"Yeah," Poremba said. "They were covered in dirt."

"Dirt from where?"

"Forensics narrowed it down to half of southern Illinois."

"But they were found in Portland, Oregon?"

"Affirmative."

"Who could possibly move a bunch of body parts across state lines with no one noticing? Or caring? Who wouldn't be afraid to do it?"

"That's why I want you to arrest Jerry Ford."

"Right, right," Kristy said, but then a Jenga tower started to come together in her mind, she could see it, block by block, stacking up . . . but it was teetering in the center. What was missing? "Or anyone who works for a funeral home and might want to send someone a message. Agent Hopper thought something was sideways. We know that he conducted interviews there, right?"

Poremba said, "That's public record. I have no idea what he found. He never got in the place, but that's why I encouraged Matthew to go back. We know there's something wrong there. Money laundering, at the very least."

"Hold on," Kristy said. She dug into her purse, looking for the papers Miguel had given her this afternoon, the list of names buried at the Kales's Home of Peace. "I went to the cemetery today, and they gave me a map to all the people buried there. Lee, there's ten thousand names. Do you know how much money that is?"

"Millions."

"It could be $100 million. My plot was $10,000. That doesn't include a funeral. What if the reason the numbers don't line up with LifeCore is because they're not laundering money, they're laundering bodies?"

Kristy thought about Ronnie Cupertine's family, how maybe they'd been sent to the Kales's Home of Peace, not to be harvested, but to be buried. They ended up in Portland because someone wanted them to be found. Wanted the world to know they weren't missing. Wanted The Family to know their boss's wife and children were chopped up like firewood. Wanted the FBI to investigate how the bodies got there in the first place.

Who would want that?

Not Jerry Ford. He wouldn't want the FBI in his business.

Not Bennie Savone. Same reason.

"No," Poremba said. "No. You've got it backward. LifeCore isn't laundering bodies. The funeral home is."

"If that were the case," Kristy said, "they'd need to have the complicity of the Temple leadership. I don't see that happening."

"Why not?"

"Well, for one, Rabbi Kales is two hundred years old, and Rabbi Cohen is the most decent man I've ever met. How would they be getting the volume? You think Rabbi Kales and Rabbi Cohen are out on the streets collecting bodies?"

"No," Poremba said. "Divorce yourself from your beliefs. Look at what we know about Temple Beth Israel. We know that it was the last place Jeff Hopper was seen. We know that Bennie Savone paid for its construction and that Rabbi Kales let him marry into his family, which isn't exactly how most devout Jews work. We know that the rabbi previous to Rabbi Cohen was found floating in Lake Mead. What do you know about Rabbi Cohen?"

What did she know? He was about forty. His family was military.

"He's just back from the hospital," she said.

"For what?"

"He fell," she said. "And had to have plastic surgery to fix his face."

"Are you hearing yourself?"

She was. Even before the fall, he'd looked . . . different. Like his face had been made of puzzle pieces jammed into the wrong spots.

"I guess I don't know much of anything."

"Run him," Poremba said. "Find out who did his plastic surgery. Get every driver's license he's ever had. Are you hearing me? I want to know where Rabbi Cohen went to elementary school. I want to know how his grandparents met."

"Are you saying," she said, "that Sal Cupertine has been here all along?"

"And Matthew figured it out," Poremba said. "What other reason would he stay in Las Vegas? What other reason would he have to go after Biglione? He must have thought Biglione had something Sal needed."

"I don't see it," Kristy said. She didn't want to see it. Couldn't imagine it.

"Sal Cupertine learned at the foot of Ronnie Cupertine," Poremba said. "He was his father figure for the last thirty years of his life. So what did he learn? That if you snitched on yourself, you could control things. Those bodies of Ronnie's family come through for burial. He sees them. He realizes Chicago has turned upside down, that if they're killing Family members, someone is coming for him. So he has them dumped where they'd be found as a message. Come fucking get me. Not to the FBI, but to the killer. Killer knows where the bodies are supposed to be. FBI has no idea." Poremba actually laughed. "It's brilliant, really. Ronnie Cupertine's wife and children were four bodies—how much were each worth? How much was it worth to the Native Mob or whoever in The Family iced them to have their hands clean, forever? Not have some bones pulled out of a housing development in Peoria in thirty years, scientists find a dot of foreign DNA on a scrap of clothes, you get yanked out of the assisted living facility to do the rest of your life in federal lockup, three hots and a cot and a catheter until the day you die. Priceless. That shit was priceless. And what better way to get rid of bodies than to bury them in a cemetery, two thousand miles away, where no one would ever look for them?"

"But the volume."

"You saw the warehouse," Poremba said. "Russian mob can hardly piss straight. A guy like Bennie Savone, a good real businessman, he's probably franchising bodies. Don't think about what's been done before. Think about the next level. Twenty-first century. You're a gangster. How do you make money with a cemetery?"

"You bury bodies," Kristy said, "for whoever really needs to get rid of a body."

What did it take to disinter a body?

Next of kin. A court order. Probable cause. That could take

months. Years. And whose body, exactly, would you be disinterring? How would you ever know? They'd need to go one by one, through every name. And who is to say that there weren't other bodies, not named?

Jews didn't preserve their bodies. Simple pine boxes and a suit of clothes was all that stood between the dead and eternity.

And right then, Special Agent Kristy Levine saw through Jeff Hopper's eyes. Saw him driving up to Temple Beth Israel, meeting with Rabbi David Cohen, asking him questions about Sal Cupertine, maybe looking out at the expanse of construction going on—the day school for preschoolers, the high school, the Performing Arts Center, the Aquatic Center, the expansion of the Jewish cemetery across the street—and knowing. Because Jeff Hopper understood Sal Cupertine wasn't dead. Sal Cupertine hadn't disappeared. Sal Cupertine was sent somewhere, to do a job, that only he could do, with his flawless Rain Main memory, with his penchant for killing without getting caught, and with Ronnie's desire to have him out of the picture entirely.

Rabbi David Cohen wasn't a cover.

Rabbi David Cohen was a job.

No one ever reported dead gangsters. It was outside the code. You left a body somewhere, it was because you wanted them found. Were Bennie Savone, his father-in-law, and Sal Cupertine operating a members-only cemetery for the underworld? Was that even possible?

"I'll get Ford," she said. "You figure out how to get the warrants to save my pension." She paused. "And Lee? I know you cared about Matthew. I'm sorry."

"He was a good agent," Poremba said, "and we destroyed him."

JACOB DMITROV FOUND THE ONLY NON-BROKEN BOTTLE OF SCOTCH IN THE Ponderosa and poured himself two fingers. "You want some?" he asked Kristy when she returned.

"I'm working," she said. "Did you wash that glass?"

"Alcohol will kill the germs." Kristy didn't think that was true, strictly speaking, but Jacob clearly looked like he was going through some shit. "That story, about the boy, is that true?"

It wasn't. "Probably see it on *20/20* next week," she said.

"Me? I don't get down with that shit, you know that." Not anymore, anyway, Kristy did know that much. Jacob's girlfriend disappeared under mysterious circumstances a year before. Since then, he'd been off of Kristy's radar entirely, save for when she went to Odessa for a meal. "My father, that's his business. I'm trying to live a better life now."

"I'm not asking you to flip on your father," Kristy said.

"I give you a name, you work it around a bit, you'll get what you need, but you and me, we're done. No more free lunches. Someone will blow up Odessa and then that will be war. Anonymous tip."

"Fine," Kristy said.

He took her notepad and pen, flipped to a blank page, wrote something, closed it, downed his scotch, stood up. "This place was a dump," he said. "I'll miss it."

Once he was gone, Kristy found Jacob's chicken scratch: *Jerry Ford.*

LIFECORE WAS LOCATED ON THE CORNER OF BONANZA AND LAS VEGAS Boulevard in the husk of an abandoned Safeway, only half a mile from Las Vegas Metro headquarters. Kristy could see the ghost of the grocery store's logo embedded in the terra-cotta beneath the organ bank's blinking blue neon sign, even medical facilities needing that hint of bling these days. The parking lot was stone empty, except for a tilting palm tree planted in a concrete island, a box marked "FREE Clean Needles!" on the ground beside a towering streetlight, and Jerry Ford's Mercedes, parked diagonally across three spaces in front of the clinic. It was nearly midnight. Kristy had called Ford's home number, but when there was no answer, she took a gamble and came to his office.

Kristy hadn't spent much time in this part of town, which was surprising since it was only three miles from the FBI field office, but she didn't have much of a reason to hang out in the city's old graveyard district, miles of dead Las Vegans interred on what used to be the edge of town but was now smack in the middle. Once, though, she stopped to check out the grave of Sonny Liston, her father's favorite boxer. Kristy thought it would be some ornate affair, but it was just a flat gravestone carrying Liston's given name—Charles "Sonny" Liston—his dates—1932 to 1970—and a simple statement: *A Man*. There were fresh flowers and an American flag resting on the grave.

The Jews held prime property in the old joints, Moe Dalitz made sure of that, but now, instead of rolling sand dunes, they stared at the Neon Graveyard and a skate park covered in North Town Gangster Crips and East Side 13 Killers tags, the two gangs fighting for streets they'd never own, streets that in a few years would probably be condos and townhouses and Quiznos franchises. Could be Las Vegas would do like San Francisco and move all the graves out of official city limits, or at least the headstones, pave this shit over and build a stadium.

Shitty as it was, this area was only five miles from the fountains of the Bellagio, ten miles to Temple Beth Israel, thirteen miles and you were swimming in the deep end of the pool at Kristy's condo, but right here? You could be in any city in any state. Chicago. Rochester. Detroit. Didn't matter. They all ended up taking on the same veneer. Kristy used to not care about such things, but now it seemed like another symptom of the world's bigger problems. She spent years in military intelligence battling drug cartels around the world, ended up in the FBI taking on organized crime in all its guises, and now . . . they were giving away clean needles in a parking lot in Las Vegas. There was no drug war. Not really. It was just people trying to earn a living, earn a dying, or earn an imprisonment. It was useless. It would always be useless.

Kristy got out of her car, walked over to Jerry's Benz, half expecting to see Jerry slumped over with a bullet through the back of his head, but all she found was a box of Krispy Kreme donuts, a Styrofoam cup of coffee in the holder, and Jerry's cell phone charger sitting on the dash.

Kristy put a hand on the hood.

Cold.

"You with the Jews?"

Kristy looked up. Next door to the old Safeway was a five-story apartment building called the Silver Suites, which wasn't silver, and Kristy doubted the *suites* part, too. A young man stood out front wearing a puffy white-and-red UNLV jacket, even though it wasn't cold. He walked across the parking lot, stood on the other side of the Mercedes.

"You could say that," Kristy said.

"Mr. Ford said you might be by. This is for you," UNLV said. He had a slight accent, like maybe he'd come over from Russia as a kid and still hadn't lost the lilt of the language. He slid a manilla envelope across the hood, Kristy catching it before it hit the ground. Kristy opened it up. It was filled with cash. Maybe fifty grand. "Said it was a bonus for February."

"When was this?"

"Couple days ago. Friday."

Shit. It was Sunday morning now.

Kristy stared at this kid. He was maybe twenty-two. So not a kid. A young man. When Kristy was twenty-two, how many bodies did she have on her sheet? A dozen? Twenty? Four years of service at that point. All of it legal, of course, but it didn't stop her from thinking she'd done some horrible things for the government, if not by her own hand then by saying, "Kill this man." "Kill this woman." "The subject can be found here. He should be neutralized." She'd do that and then get dinner afterward, and it was just a day at the office.

She imagined killing this kid. Of having the easy compunction to take a life, even now.

It was impossible. And yet, Matthew Drew was dead. A man she talked to days ago. Sal Cupertine was out there, somewhere, still putting bodies in the ground. There were ten thousand bodies in a cemetery that should only have a few hundred, maybe a thousand. Where was the value of a human life?

Now this kid. Who thought she was a bagwoman for flesh.

"Anyone else show up?" Kristy asked.

"Nope."

"You've been sitting here watching, 24-7?"

"I got spotters," he said. "Someone showed up, they'd get me."

Kristy looked past the kid. A window on the third floor was open. A little girl, maybe eight, watched, a camera in her hands.

"That your kid?"

"Niece."

"She takes a photo of me," Kristy said, "I'm going to have everyone in that building under arrest before breakfast."

The kid put two fingers in his mouth, eyes still on Kristy, and whistled. The window closed. The blinds went down.

"You a cop?" he asked.

"You a UNLV student?" When the kid didn't answer, Kristy said, "How do you know Jerry?"

"I do favors for him."

"How long?"

"Couple years."

"What kind of favors?"

"Come on," the kid said. "You know."

"Where you from?" Kristy asked. "Your accent."

"Ukraine. But it was still USSR then."

"Ah," Kristy said. "Do you also work for Mr. Dmitrov?"

The kid looked surprised but said, "He got us here. So I do favors for him, too. You know him?"

"I know him," she said. So Jacob was right. "Have you seen Mrs. Ford? Is she somewhere safe?" Kristy asked.

"Mr. Ford said she left him."

"Yeah," Kristy said, "but I'm asking if she's safe."

"Yo," the kid said, "I don't do favors like *that*."

"What's your name?" The kid hesitated, so she said, "What do your homies call you?"

"Pool Boy," he said.

"You stay in the Silver Suites?"

"I manage it." When Kristy seemed dubious, he said, "Mr. Ford owns it. I get to stay for free if I fix shit."

"Okay," Kristy said. "Mr. Ford. He inside?"

"Guess so."

"You sure he didn't leave?"

"Pretty sure."

"You hear something?" Kristy asked.

"Naw," Pool Boy said. "But you get close enough, there's a smell."

Kristy looked back at the former Safeway. It was huge and filled with old body parts. It wasn't necessarily true that it was Ford's body making the smell.

"Did he leave you keys?"

Pool Boy reached into his pocket, took out a key ring, jingled them. There was one for the Benz, one for the house, one for LifeCore. "Told me if you didn't show up, I could take the car."

"You been inside?"

"Naw, ma'am."

"Be real honest with me," Kristy said, "because if you left DNA in there, you're going to have a problem."

"Might have looked around, seen if there was anything worth moving, you know. Found some weird shit."

"Touch anything?"

"Naw, I got out quick." He pointed over his shoulder. "My niece used the bathroom."

"You let your niece in?"

He shrugged. "If she was with me," he said, "I could talk my way out of it." Not a bad idea, actually. "I took a laptop."

"One?"

"Two."

"Two?"

"Okay," he said, "like five."

Jesus fucking Christ. She counted out $10,000, folded the bills up, handed them over. "Dump the laptops," she said. "And I need the keys. I want you and your niece to go on a long vacation, okay?"

Pool Boy pocketed the cash, handed over the keys, but then said, "What about your DNA?"

"It's okay," she said, "I'm an FBI agent."

KRISTY WALKED THROUGH A MAZE OF EMPTY CUBICLES—MAYBE THIRTY OF them—family photos, coffee cups still in place. It was like the staff of LifeCore had been raptured. Computer screens still glowed blue in the dim fluorescent light of the old Safeway. Phones periodically rang, even though it was the middle of the night. The dead, they don't keep a clock, Kristy supposed. Copy machines and printers clicked and hissed and sighed. Somewhere, a fax spewed out pages. Sweaters hung off the backs of chairs.

The stench was overwhelming.

She only smelled anything like this once, a few days ago, when she opened that freezer. The facilities were not being maintained, and that meant it was little more than a corpse farm.

And yet, everywhere, signs of life.

A bulletin board announced a company softball game at Bruce Trent Park in Summerlin against the Palm Northwest Cemetery Workers and a potluck for Emily's birthday, and then, smack in the middle, was a bright yellow Missing poster for Melanie Moss, which shouldn't have been a surprise. They were on every streetlight and telephone pole in the city, her face smiling out into forever, alive and well.

Which is perhaps why Kristy had the distinct feeling she wasn't alone. Kristy didn't believe in ghosts, not really, but as she made way her way toward Jerry Ford's office, the stench of death getting more overpowering with each step, she couldn't stop feeling . . . what? Residual energy? Maybe it was thirty years of people walking around Safeway picking up the sustenance of their lives. Or maybe it was that LifeCore had transformed Safeway's intricate system of freezers into housing for a jambalaya of the dead: arms, legs, sheets of skin. Eyes, livers, kidneys. All the stuff that made a human a human? It was all stored in what used to be the meat lockers and frozen-food storage, T-bones and Swanson's chicken dinners replaced by the very parts of human life.

Which was an unsettling notion.

She stole a glance over her shoulder. Nothing but cubicles.

Kristy unlocked Jerry Ford's office and found his body on a fake leather sectional, across from his desk and an entire wall of ancient CCTV monitors, none of which were turned on. He'd been dead for a while. Three days at least, judging from the decomp. There was a plastic bag zip-tied around his neck, his face either purple or disappearing, the poor son of a bitch more meat than man. Kristy stared into Jerry's now-sunken and clouded eyes, tried to imagine all the turns in his life that had led him to this moment.

Jerry Ford, though, was long gone. Not that she'd ever known him. She'd seen his wife at Temple plenty of times. Stephanie even picked her up from the infusion center one day and they talked about their favorite old characters on *General Hospital* back in the day, Stephanie going on about Rick Springfield, Kristy more of a Jack Wagner fan. The kind of conversation you have when you think you're going to die.

So Kristy did the only thing that seemed right, even though she knew Ford wasn't really a Jew: she picked up a pair of scissors from Jerry's desk, pulled her blouse out from her jeans, snipped the corner of the garment off, rending it, as was Jewish custom, in grief and anger at the dead. The body would rot away. The body was already rotting away. The soul would continue, somewhere. That was the Jewish belief. But it didn't quell in Kristy the anger she felt toward Jerry, what all this might mean.

Kristy put the envelope of cash on Jerry's desk, then sat down on the other side of the sectional, where it seemed Jerry'd been living, a stack of Styrofoam food containers on the low coffee table in front of it, a colony of coffee cups, clothes, medication, including an empty bottle of Ambien, which Kristy figured was in Jerry's dried-up bloodstream, and a stack of legal paperwork. Including, she saw, an unopened letter from the FBI's field office in Chicago.

Jerry's cell phone was on a small coffee table. She grabbed a Kleenex, picked it up; one bar left. She scrolled through his calls until she found Stephanie's cell phone, which she dialed.

"Baby?" Stephanie said by way of greeting. She sounded relieved.

"No," Kristy said, "I'm sorry, ma'am, this is Special Agent Kristy Levine."

"From . . . Temple?"

"Yes, ma'am," she said, "but I'm not calling in that capacity."

"What's wrong?"

"Ma'am," Kristy said, "are you in Las Vegas?"

"No."

"Where are you, ma'am?"

"Jerry told me not to tell anyone," she said.

"Ma'am," Kristy said, "you know me. You know I'm an FBI agent. I'm trying to help you."

"He told me I couldn't trust the FBI," she said. "That there are corrupt agents trying to get him. And then I see the news and it's nothing but corrupt agents. So. No. I'm fine. What do you need, Agent Levine? Why do you have my husband's phone?"

"Ma'am," she said, then stopped. "Stephanie. Stephanie, listen to me. Your husband has taken his life. I'm worried your life is in danger. Your husband is in business with some very bad people. And some very bad things have started to happen because of it. You need to tell me where you are so I can send someone out to protect you."

She pulled the phone from her ear.

Stephanie Ford had hung up on her. She redialed. Straight to voice mail, which was full.

Poremba wouldn't be landing for another two hours.

If she called this in now, she'd be out front doing interviews all morning, then stuck in a conference room explaining how she ended up inside LifeCore, would probably be on paid administrative leave by 5 p.m. Sal Cupertine would be long gone.

Kristy grabbed the envelope filled with money and headed outside.

SHE FOUND POOL BOY ON THE THIRD FLOOR OF THE SILVER SUITES. HE WAS walking out of his apartment with two suitcases. At least he could take direction.

He set his bags down, put his hands up. "I'm leaving, like you said," he said.

"That's good," she said. She peered into his apartment. His niece was asleep in front of the TV, which was playing *The Wizard of Oz* on DVD. She handed him the envelope filled with cash and the keys. "Why don't you hold on to these things."

"For how long?"

"For as long as it takes you to spend the money."

"What do I have to do for it?"

"Anyone asks, I was never here."

"I'm not gonna be here, anyway. And I don't know your name."

"Lotta bald ladies come around this way?" In the apartment, the flying monkeys were beginning to rain across the sky in search of Dorothy.

TWENTY-ONE

THE MOJAVE DESERT AT 3 A.M. WAS NOTHING BUT BLACKNESS AND

abandoned history. Hollowed-out mining towns; darkened mountain ranges and dormant volcanos; skeletons of World War II military installments. The Mojave used to prepare the troops for duty in North Africa, airfields carved into the desert floor, left behind like petroglyphs, old bases marked by obelisks in the dirt and faded bronze plaques.

Baghdad. Fenner. Cádiz. Siberia.

The Dead Mountains.

The Devil's Playground.

The Amboy Crater.

The Camp Ibis memorial.

Now, in the air between the marine base in Twentynine Palms and Fort Irwin, flying low: An Apache helicopter. An F-16. A bomber. Making training routes in the darkness, lights off, and then suddenly above you. The Mojave lousy with known and unknown training bases, still, preparing to attack this or any desert. Could be Afghanistan tonight. Could be Iraq. Could be Kuwait.

And then: nothing. Just a two-lane road off Highway 40, cutting through the desert, no lights forward, no lights coming from behind, David thinking, knowing, understanding: *You could die out here. Look at this place.* And then a sign, to spur hope: Salt Lake City 599 miles. Yuma 280 miles. Los Angeles 192 miles.

"You come out here every time?" David asked. They'd been driving for three hours, since Ruben picked David up in the parking lot of the

Bagel Café, the safest spot he figured he could leave his Range Rover and Matthew's belongings in case he didn't make it back. David spent most of those hours thinking about what he learned from Matthew's notebooks, but also doing nothing but staring into the vast nothingness. If he was a man prone to metaphor, he'd really be fucked.

"Mr. Savone says it's been used by the families forever," Ruben said.

"Ever bring anyone with you?"

"Depends who I'm meeting. If it's someone I know, I might bring my kid to keep me company."

"What about Miguel?"

"He's not ready for it. I mean. He can handle himself. But he just got married, you know? He should get his life established first."

"So he's got something to lose?"

"Less likely to fuck up," Ruben said. He wasn't wrong. Ruben hit the brights. "Not much longer now. You see a boulder painted pink, that's where we turn."

They were in the hearse SUV, a retrofitted black Ford Expedition that could hold up to six caskets, and in the back were three bodies. David did some research online, figured out that the fat guy with Aquafreddo across his back was probably Lester Aquafreddo, judging from the photos in the *Los Angeles Times* and *NY Post*, when he was younger, skinnier, and had all of his head. He'd been out in LA for years, first as a porn producer, which just meant he was washing money through X-rated films, then as a gaming consultant for Native American tribes opening up bingo parlors, which just meant he was washing money through old lady's bingo cards, then as general manager of a night club in Palm Springs called Freddo's, which just meant he was washing money through his fucking bar, and then, finally, as a consultant, again, to a tribe in Palm Springs going full Vegas-style gaming. Whenever he appeared in the paper, he was always called a "reputed Gambino crime figure," but he never did any time and never

sued anyone for defamation, which meant he didn't want to enter dis-
covery on that shit.

The other two, the Zanguccis, were local muscle to Palm Springs.
Chaz and Kiki. Fraternal twins. They ran a gym called PowerHaus
that seemed mostly to be a front for selling steroids, at least according to the arrest blotter in the *Desert Sun*. David doubted they were
even made, despite their tattoos. Probably did whatever Aquafreddo
wanted, but who knows. Maybe all three were keeping omertà in the
trunk of a tricked-out Ford Expedition.

If David was right, Peaches killed them as part of the Native Mob's
expansion into California, but also because he wanted to learn about
The Family's network for laundering bodies, in light of what happened
to Ronnie's wife and kids. David had no idea if Peaches would be at the
drop-off tonight, but he had to hope. Because he had a little something
for him.

Plus, the only reason Jennifer and William would seek protection
was if Peaches threatened them. He knew that. No one in The Family
would have ever stepped to Jennifer, even with Ronnie out of commission. They knew she could have them all arrested with one phone
call. They knew if Sal ever came home, they'd be met with prejudice.
If they were smart—which was a big if—they'd figure out that Peaches
set up Matthew Drew to take Ronnie out by getting him hired to run
security for the Chuyalla casino, where Peaches knew Matthew would
absolutely get a chance to take the motherfucker down.

Ever since this Peaches showed up, shit turned upside down. David admired the efficiency with which Peaches worked. Game respects
game and all that, but that didn't mean David wouldn't put two in the
back of his head and another two in the front.

"We get there," Ruben said, "let me do the talking."

"It's your show," David said. "I'm just here to watch."

"You say that," Ruben said, "but you're the one holding two guns
and a knife."

"You don't got a gun?"

"That's not the point," Ruben said.

Up ahead, the headlights caught a glimmer of pink in the darkness. The road bent into the desert, and the pink was gone. "We're close," Ruben said, and twenty seconds later, the boulder came into full view, on the left-hand side of the road. Ruben turned across the two-lane road into the desert, the road paved by use but not anything else.

"The fuck is this place?" David asked.

"Ragtown," Ruben said. "Used to be a mining village. Southern Transcon ran through here back in the day."

"How the fuck do you know that?"

"I listened in school," Ruben said. He ran his finger in a circle. "Everything out here, all the mountains, was gold and silver and bronze. Used to camp here in the winter with Boy Scouts. We'd go exploring all the old mines. It was cool. Brought my sister to look for gems, found some, too. Plus arrowheads and seashells and shit."

"You were some kind of Boy Scout?"

"Homie," Ruben said, "you don't know shit about me but what you see with your eyes."

The dirt road took a dip down and they were moving across what David thought might be a dry riverbed. David peered out the side mirror and the road was gone, they were in total blackness, and yet Ruben knew exactly where they were going. They swept south and then climbed before coming to a plateau, David making out structures in the distance. An old barn? A couple lean-tos? And then, parked among the Joshua trees, parking lights on, was another black hearse SUV, this one smaller.

"We work with another funeral home?" David asked.

"Naw," Ruben said. "We did so much business with the Native Mob, we gave it to them. As a thank-you. Less chance any of us get caught."

Made sense. No one ever pulled over a hearse for speeding, or any other reason. You could dump two thousand pounds of cocaine in a coffin and a cop would need a court order to open it. The only better cover was driving a cop car or fire truck.

"This what you were expecting?" David asked.

"Yeah, all kosher," Ruben said.

David couldn't tell how many people were in the other hearse. They were supposed to be dropping off one body, but they didn't know three were being returned in the process, which David assumed might be a problem. There could be fifteen guys in the back of that hearse, each with an AK-47, all with an opinion on the situation, in which case this might be David's last stand, though Ruben seemed calm. David took down his window. The air was cool, maybe 60 degrees, the high-desert climate cooler than Las Vegas, which is why David had changed into a black hoodie and jeans. He smelled damp creosote, exhaust, and weed smoke.

"Pull into the clearing," David said. "Make them come to us. They get pissed off about us giving back the bodies, we'll want a clear exit."

"Only one way in and out," Ruben said.

"Then we want to be in front."

Ruben made a clicking sound in his mouth, thinking. "This is going to tell them something is different."

"Fine," David said. "Let them worry about it."

RUBEN PARKED THE HEARSE IN THE OLD TOWN SQUARE, LEFT THE ENGINE running. In the headlights, David made out the ruins of a church— not much more than a cross and the frame of a building—with a well, surrounded by a three-foot-tall rock wall, directly in front of it. To the left of the church were the remnants of smaller buildings, dilapidated walls and exposed foundations encircled by hitching posts. The field of Joshua trees extended back and to the right of the church, dying in the blackness of the hills.

"What now?" Ruben asked.

"You said you wanted to do the talking," David said. "Talk."

Ruben reached into the glove box, took out a Glock, checked the magazine. "I only got fifteen."

"You think there's twenty guys in that hearse?" David asked.

"Could be motherfuckers coming down the hills."

Shit.

David gave him one of his two extra magazines and then both exited the SUV. Stood in the glow of the headlights, let whoever was in the other hearse see them. Across the dark expanses of desert, the driver's side door opened, and a man walked out, headed toward them, hands open, arms loose at his sides. He was about six feet, wore a black Adidas sweat suit. David still couldn't make out who was in the passenger seat.

They headed toward him. Friendly. Normal night.

"You recognize him?" David asked, quietly.

"Guy I've been dealing with was half his size," Ruben said. "This is the OG I told you about."

"What's his name?"

"Lonzo," Ruben said.

Shit.

"You sure?"

"Could be Alonzo, but yeah."

Ronnie's Gangster 2-6 triggerman, now working for this Peaches fool. Was Ronnie's guy on the streets for years. Middled every deal they made since the early 1990s, took care of any street business that Sal was too busy to take on. A pro. A good guy, in David's estimation, who still would have killed Ronnie's wife and kids, would have had no trouble putting Matthew Drew's kid sister to sleep or signing up to work alongside Peaches. Followed the money.

David tugged his hood low on his face, looked down.

"What up, dog," Lonzo said.

"Chilling," Ruben said. "Where's Mike at?"

"You'll be dealing with me now. Mike is out of the picture. In fact, he's in the box." Lonzo motioned over his shoulder to his hearse. Just one of those things. "You got a problem with that?"

"Can't say I do," Ruben said. "But look. This is gonna be our last run for a bit. We've got some heat on us, so we gotta take a hiatus."

"How long?"

"Could be three months." Ruben making shit up as he went along.

"What kind of heat?"

"Yo," Ruben said, "I'm just driving."

"All right, all right," Lonzo said. "No worries."

"Another thing," Ruben said. "Mike gave us some bad cargo last time. You gotta take it back."

"The fuck you mean?"

"We don't put New York families from an open city into the ground. Rules are rules. Your boss knows them."

"Rules?" Lonzo said and started laughing. "You out here in a hearse, in the middle of the desert, talking to me about *rules*. How about this, bossman, you do what you've been paid for, we all keep quiet." Not apologizing, David noticed.

"It's the principle," Ruben said. "I got cash in the car to pay you back right now on the three bodies; we'll take the one you got on credit. And then we're square. You got a problem, take it up with my boss." He pointed at David.

"Who the fuck are you?" he asked David.

"I'm the rabbi." His hands were inside the front pocket of his hoodie, guns in each.

"You make the rules?"

"No," David said. "I enforce them."

"Last time we had a big order, it somehow ended up in Portland and on the fucking evening news," Lonzo said. "If *my* boss doesn't like this shit, it's beyond my control," he said. "I'm being real level with you both." He kicked at something on the ground between them.

"This isn't a negotiation." David took down his hood. Stared at Lonzo straight in the eyes. Let him get a good look. Then he shot him twice in the chest. Walked up two paces, said, "This is for Ronnie's kids," and put two more in his face.

"What the fuck!" Ruben screamed. Lonzo was bent back grotesquely, snapped at the knees, which would hurt if he wasn't already dead. "Why the fuck did you do that?"

"It's what I do," David said. "Stay down."

David didn't wait for Ruben to respond. He stalked across the desert, toward the other hearse about fifty yards away, guns in both hands, body crouched, moving in the space between the two lights. When he was within twenty-five yards, he started shooting at the hearse, until the windshield was gone. Did no good to shoot at the body of a car. It wasn't like TV. They didn't blow up. You just fucked up a car.

Five yards in front of the hearse, David didn't see anyone in the front seat, just a shitload of broken glass, the jacketed hollow points doing some work. Could be Peaches was shot dead and was now slumped under the glove box, oozing brains. Could be he was about to pop up with an AR-15 and put a hundred rounds into David. Could be it didn't matter, because this was going to be the day for one of them.

David slid around the front of the SUV, then popped up in the driver's side window.

Empty.

Except for half of an ear—the bottom—which was a mangled bloody mess on the passenger seat.

So he did hit him.

David peered through the back of the hearse. There was a single coffin in the back, spattered with blood, and there was a bloody handprint on the side window, too, and the rear hatch of the SUV was up, another bloody handprint on the window. So that's how he got out.

Peaches couldn't be far.

David was surrounded by the grove of Joshua trees, a thousand men with their hands up in the darkness. Maybe two thousand. Peaches might come out from behind one of them, try to get a shot, but it wouldn't be clean. He'd need to get bullets that could bend around trees.

David bent low, looked at the dirt, found what he was looking for.

Blood. It led away from the hearse, toward the abandoned church, David following the drips and smears in the sand, moving slow, both guns out, ready, when he heard two gunshots in rapid succession, then: an almost inhuman yowling, a sound that came from deep inside a wounded animal, wordless, atavistic, and unmistakable throughout time. Pain. Profound pain. David sprinted out into the clearing, hugged the well for cover, stopped.

Peaches Pocotillo stood beside the driver's side of the SUV, staring straight ahead, gun in his left hand. He must have made a dead run as soon as David started shooting. Ruben Topaz was splayed against the rear driver's side wheel, directly at Peaches's feet. He was missing the left side of his face, most of his jaw blown off. Must have turned his head at just the last moment. If David wanted to shoot Peaches, he'd need to shoot Ruben, too.

"Your friend got shot," Peaches said. "Gonna need some dental work." Peaches wore a white linen suit that was now covered in blood, his and Ruben's. The right side of his face looked like someone had taken a sledgehammer to it. His ear was gone but so was a good part of his cheek. Must have been grazed, which sounds like nothing until you get grazed in the fucking face. His right arm didn't look great, either. Like a chunk of his bicep was missing. He'd tied his belt around it. Ruben tried to crawl away. Peaches stomped on his leg. That scream again. "Good news. He's still alive." Another scream. A coyote, somewhere in the distance, answered. If Ruben could just slouch one more inch, David would have a shot.

Maybe.

"Your friend is already dead," David said. They were about twenty, twenty-five yards apart. Not a good distance for a gunfight.

"He wasn't my friend."

"He was Ronnie's," David said. "You're gonna need to answer for that."

"I don't answer to anybody."

"Gangster 2-6," David said, "don't quit. I were you, I'd stay out of Chicago. State prisons, too."

Peaches cocked his head. "So it is you," Peaches said. "Don't know if you saw, I blew up your house."

He loved that fucking house. If he got the chance, maybe one day he'd rebuild it just so he could bury this motherfucker in the foundation.

"You should call 911. Get that award money." Another moan from Ruben, then a high-pitched whine, like air leaving a balloon. "How's my guy?"

"Breathing," he said. Then: "You really remember every face you've ever seen?"

"That's right," Sal said. He had no idea if that was true. He doubted it.

"So you know me."

"Did you used to have two ears?"

"Joey the Bishop," Peaches said.

"The fuck is that?"

"You killed him," Peaches said. "House in Batavia, 1990. Tried to pin it on me."

Sal barely remembered. Joey B. was a bookie The Family used a million years ago. Must have been seventy years old. Had literally been around when fucking Capone was in business. Ronnie sent Sal to take him out, so he did. Didn't remember this fucking guy involved with it. Sal had never tried to frame anyone. He claimed his kills.

He worked his mind. A detail from the news reports showed up. "You were hiding in the closet," Sal said.

"That was his wife," Peaches said. "We had a whole conversation. I was working for your cousin. Delivering luggage. Then you fucking set me up."

Sal said, "If someone tried to pin that murder on you, it was

Ronnie. I was doing work for my family. If all this shit is about something you think I did to you twelve years ago? Homeboy, I tell you, I do not recall it."

"I'm the boss of your family now."

Ruben lurched forward; his legs started to twitch. Maybe cardiac arrest? He couldn't let Ruben die. Not like this.

"You can have The Family." Sal held up both of his guns. He hadn't gotten this close to getting out just to die in a fucking Old West shootout. "Way I see it, we both have a pretty good chance of dying out here tonight. You prepared for that?" Peaches didn't respond. "You *might* kill me," Sal said. "Then what? I die, so what? I'm already dead."

Peaches leaned forward. Listening.

"Say in the process, best case, Ruben dies in the next twenty seconds, and I run up on you and your bitch ass runs away and I put two in your spine and now you're in a wheelchair for the rest of your life. Plus whatever is going on with your arm and your face. You think Sugar is gonna take orders from some motherfucker can't even stand up to piss? Can't hear unless his head is turned just so? He'll push you off a fucking dock. You'll be dead by Christmas. Because if we don't come to some kind of accord, I'm going to open on you, and the odds are, I'm going to fill you up. And then all this shit, everything you've been working for, will mean nothing. That what you want?"

Peaches said, "What kind of accord?"

"My guy alive?"

Peaches looked again. "My experience," he said, "he's got an hour."

Ruben screamed. His actual voice. Not some animal. Sal pretty sure he heard the word, "No!"

"My experience," Sal said, "you're gonna lose that arm you stay out here much longer. I wouldn't fuck with that ear, either. So, you start walking east," he continued, "I get my friend and drive west. Thirty minutes, you walk back this way, get your car, find a clinic that takes your insurance." When Peaches didn't respond, Sal said, "Maybe see if Kirk Biglione knows first aid."

"He's been more trouble than he's worth."

"Yeah," Sal said, "not a guy to trust."

"And you are?"

"Gotta have faith in the game."

"Then what?"

"Then maybe one day you catch me slipping," Sal said. "But that's not today."

Peaches said, "You really don't remember me?"

"I told you."

Peaches shook his head. "You will now," he said and fired a shot into Ruben's leg, and then he disappeared into the darkness, Sal running toward Ruben now, but by the time he got to the hearse, Peaches was gone, somewhere in the ruins, or in the Joshua trees, or maybe he was never there to begin with, Sal beginning to think he was out here fighting ghosts.

Ruben was splayed on the ground, the left side of his face blown off, blood pulsing from where his jaw used to be. His tongue was gone. His left eye was ruined, but his right was wide open. It darted back and forth. His right leg gushed blood from the thigh. Shit. Probably the femoral. Fuck. Blood everywhere now, rushing like a river in the sand. They were two and a half hours from a hospital.

Rabbi David Cohen took Ruben's left hand. Held it. Tried to calm his noises, the convulsions.

The Talmud teaches that a man does not tell lies in the hour of death, so David said, "The wheel always comes full circle, Ruben, for all of us. You were always going to die. I do not know if it was always going to be like this, but know, Ruben, you will see the face of God and he will already have forgiven you."

Ruben blinked. Tried to turn his head to face David, what was left of his mouth attempting to make some sound, but nothing was happening, no sound was coming, just the wheeze of air and blood in his esophagus.

David kept hold of Ruben's left hand, said, "Look into my eyes,

Ruben." He did. "You are the righteous. And the righteous are greater in death than they can possibly be in life. You do not need to suffer. Please," David said, "let me relieve you of the pain."

Ruben reached out and touched Rabbi David Cohen's face, gently, and David realized he was already somewhere else most likely, that this world was almost gone to him, but still, any second of pain he could spare him was a gift.

"Close your eye," Rabbi David Cohen said, and then he shot him once, in the back of the head.

TWENTY-TWO

AT 4:46 A.M., PEACHES POCOTILLO PARKED HIS HEARSE BEHIND THE LONG John Silver's in Victorville, loosened the belt around his arm, tried to flex his hand, the blood pumping out of him again, getting everywhere. He'd done this every fifteen minutes for the last hour while he drove to the spot Kirk Biglione picked, figuring that way he wouldn't lose his fucking arm, but also he didn't want to bleed to death. He hadn't lived this long so he could die in a gunfight in the middle of the fucking desert with the most proficient hit man in the mafia. He certainly hadn't lived this long to die behind a fucking Long John Silver's, either, so he was relieved when Biglione pulled up beside him.

"Where to?" Peaches asked.

"Follow me," Biglione said.

They drove up Highway 395 for another mile, then cut into the desert, the city lights disappearing behind them, Peaches following Biglione another ten minutes, until they hit an expanse of fence that was mostly missing. Biglione stopped his car, got out, popped his trunk. Peaches parked a few yards away. The spot was littered with charred junk. A bed. A refrigerator. A trailer. An old station wagon.

"Where are we?"

"BLM land," he said. Biglione stared at him. "The fuck happened to you?"

"Rain Man shot me in the face," Peaches said.

"What about your arm?"

"Also shot me in the arm," Peaches said. "Did you bring me what I asked for?"

Biglione dumped a handful of pills into Peaches's hand. "That's Oxy. Doctors gave it to me today. Go easy." Dug around his trunk, hefted out a gas can, set it on the ground between them. "Sure about this?"

"Positive," Peaches said. He chewed up three Oxy, took the can, dumped it over the hearse, poured it over the casket in the back, set the can down, lit a match, tossed it. The hearse went up in flames. Peaches watched for a moment, made sure that the casket began to burn, since Mike was inside and he was still, nominally, responsible for him. He'd left Lonzo in the desert. Coyotes would take care of that.

"Will it blow up?" Peaches asked after a while.

"No," Biglione said. "It will just burn." He examined Peaches's face and arm. "You need a hospital."

"How long can I wear a tourniquet?"

"Five hours," Biglione said. "Plus or minus." He leaned closer. "That ear is going to be a problem. You're gonna need plastic surgery."

"Yeah," Peaches said. His new friend Lori Silausk would know where there was a friendly IHS clinic. Soon, he'd have his own; situations like this firmed that in his mind.

"You finish off Cupertine?"

"No," Peaches said. The flames were inside the casket now. The smell was not one he'd encountered before. It was like charcoal and melting copper and sulfur all at once. "We came to . . . an accord."

"Fuck does that mean?"

Peaches said, "We agreed you had to go."

Peaches kicked over the can. Gas splashed on Biglione, pooled around him, Biglione about to say something, but it was too late. Peaches had lit a match, tossed it, and Biglione was a torch, the big man running, screaming, flailing into the desert, Peaches thinking he'd put the fucker out of his misery and put one in his back, but it turned out he didn't need to. Biglione collapsed, set fire to the creosote around him, the fire dancing from body to bush and back again, screaming, and then nothing but the sounds of cooking meat.

Peaches checked his cell phone for service.

Four bars.

Good.

You could die out here without a phone.

Got into Kirk's car. Adjusted the seat. Drove out of the desert. Hit the 395. Opened his windows, let the desert air get the smell of Biglione and his cousin Mike off of him, chewed another couple Oxy, the pain in his face getting a little further away, the pain in his arm still throbbing with his heartbeat, the tourniquet doing its job. Hit the radio. Found a song he liked, Johnny Cash singing about prison. He'd get to Palm Springs, get his arm taken care of, get his ear fixed, or maybe keep his ear that way if it looked badass, he'd need to figure that out, but fuck Chicago, he didn't need that place, he could run The Family from somewhere sunny, maybe make his move on Lori Silausk sooner than later, maybe get her husband washed right quick, Peaches Pocotillo flying high now, everything cool, everything in focus, everything real cool.

TWENTY-THREE

SEVEN IN THE MORNING, SENIOR SPECIAL AGENT POREMBA CALLED KRISTY
Levine, told her to meet him in an hour behind the Smith's super-
market on West Lake Mead, five blocks from Temple Beth Israel, to
be dressed for tactical work, and then he was gone. So at 8 a.m., when
she pulled behind the store, she expected to find Poremba waiting for
her by himself, but instead there were sixty agents in Kevlar, checking
their AR-15s, adjusting their wraparound sunglasses, drinking coffee from Styrofoam cups. She found Poremba in his SUV, watching
everything.

"The fuck is going on?" Kristy asked.

"We've got four strike teams hitting the Temple, the funeral home,
Rabbi Cohen's home, and Jerry Ford's home, soon as we have a warrant." He checked his watch. "Which should be in five minutes."

"Why didn't you tell me?"

"What did you find on Rabbi Cohen?" Poremba said.

"Nothing," she said. It was true. She'd been up until 3 a.m., trying
to find anything she could on the man she'd told all of her personal
secrets to, the man who had cooled her fear of death, and learned that
there are thousands of Rabbi David Cohens in the world, that it was
like looking for a needle in a stack of needles, but there was no proof
that *this* David Cohen had ever existed, which she told Poremba.

"It's because he doesn't exist," Poremba said. He reached over,
picked up a file from his passenger seat, handed it over. Inside were his
medical records from Summerlin Hospital, which included his name
and social security number, none of which Kristy had been able to

get the previous night. "The social security number belongs to a gen-tleman named Joe Delotta, Bennie Savone's nephew, who hasn't been seen since 1999. Surprisingly no one has reported him missing. Bill at the hospital was paid by the Temple, weekly, which gave them a 15 percent discount. You want to guess the cost for reconstructive plas-tic surgery and three months of around-the-clock care? $1,601,924.29. And then the Temple bought their own wing, another ten million."

Kristy thumbed through X-rays. "How many times has he had plastic surgery?"

"At least three, according to the records," Poremba said.

"I can't get a prescription for Percocet from CVS without them running a full background check on me," Kristy said. "And he just walks into a hospital with someone else's social security number?"

"Pay with cash," Poremba said, "anything is possible."

Money plays. The age-old Las Vegas edict. Kristy tried to assemble all these facts in her mind. "Why did you have me looking," she said, finally, "if you were going to go behind me and get this?"

"He was your rabbi, Kristy," Poremba said. "I didn't think you were inclined to believe he was anyone but the man he purported to be. You would look for proof that you weren't a dupe, and I didn't have that kind of time."

"I had no reason not to believe him," she said. She handed the file back to Poremba. "You sure he's Cupertine?"

"No," Poremba said. "That's why we're here."

"Ford is dead," Kristy said. "I found him with a bag on his head at LifeCore last night. I would have told you, but here we are. Maybe send Vegas Metro over to do a wellness."

"You sure you saw what you saw at LifeCore?" Poremba asked.

"Hard to miss a dead body," she said.

Poremba put a stick of spearmint gum in his mouth, inhaled, took stock of his surroundings. "Hopper had him. Cupertine."

"So did Matthew," Kristy said. "He must have."

Poremba shook his head, sadly. "We're going to dig up every single grave in that cemetery until we find Hopper's remains. We'll run DNA on those remains for thirty years if we have to. He's coming home."

"They could be in someone's hip replacement by now," Kristy said.

"No," Poremba said. "Cupertine made sure his head was left in Chicago, where it could be found, identified, and given proper burial. Cupertine respected the game. Hopper's bones are out there. We bring in Cupertine alive, I bet you five bucks he tells us exactly where Hopper's buried."

Poremba's cell phone rang. He answered, listened for a few moments, then said, "Thank you, sir," and put his phone back in his pocket. "You ready?" he said to Kristy.

"What am I doing?"

"It's your case, Agent," Poremba said. He picked up a bullhorn from the backseat, handed it to her. "Go solve it."

Special Agent Kristy Levine, who should be dead, who could be dead in less than a year, she knew that atavistically, could feel it every morning when she woke up, that she was living on bonus time, considered why she was still here. Maybe it was to learn more about her culture, maybe it was because her cancer was advancing faster than science, maybe it was that she finally understood a pillar of the faith, of *her* faith, words she now repeated silently to herself: *It is not incumbent upon thee to complete the work; but neither are thou free to desist from it. Faithful is thine employer to pay the reward of thy labor. But know that the reward unto the righteous is not of this world.*

"All right," Kristy said. She clicked on the bullhorn. "Agents. Let's go get these motherfuckers."

KRISTY STOOD BEFORE RABBI DAVID COHEN'S OFFICE INSIDE TEMPLE BETH Israel. Down the hall, agents were in the Temple's business office, boxing everything. Outside, agents had the entire Temple and funeral home staff zip-tied, including the off-duty Metro cops charged with keeping everything secure. Until they could prove every single person's identity, no one was going anywhere. Though the synagogue had not yet opened for the day, the Jews of Summerlin had already begun to gather beyond the yellow tape. The time would come, soon, when Kristy would have each and every one of them questioned, but that morning they gawked, sipped coffee, and called everyone they knew.

Kristy tried the door. Locked. She radioed for a tactical door ram. Five minutes later, two junior agents arrived, looked at the door. "You don't want to look for a key?" the one named Stallings said.

"No," Kristy said.

The agents shared a look. Shrugged. "All right," Stallings said. "Stand back, just in case."

Kristy stepped around the corner. The two agents grasped the ram, took five steps back, and then smacked the door. The doorframe splintered, and the door swung open. The two agents pulled their guns, swept the room, stepped back out. "All clear," Stallings said.

Kristy dismissed the agents. How many times had she sat with Rabbi Cohen in this office? Ten times? Twenty? Thirty? It seemed so much larger in those visits. She'd sit across from him at his desk, Rabbi Cohen always offering her the more comfortable sofa, but she always refused. She liked her meetings with Rabbi Cohen to feel like business, but in truth she always left feeling like she'd heard from God himself, even if she wasn't sure she believed in God.

What she did believe in was Rabbi Cohen. Believed that he understood her. Believed that he cared about her soul. Believed that long after she was gone, he would keep her grave clean. She'd even considered asking him to care for her dog, if it came to that.

All of it a lie.

Kristy walked around the desk and sat down in Rabbi Cohen's chair. Saw the world the way he did. Imagined herself sitting across the desk. How yearning she must have seemed. How lost. And this kind man with his words of faith and goodwill and the living hope of peace was nothing more than a hit man, a murderer, a liar.

She opened the desk drawers. A pair of shiny silver scissors. Pens. Pencils. Files. She pulled out a stack, thumbed through them. The Teen Fashion Show. The Tikvah Scholarship. Expansion plans for the assisted living facility. Private security contracts. All the things he should have.

She turned on his computer.

Password protected.

She'd get IT on that.

Beside his desk was a low bookshelf filled with knickknacks.

A porcelain figurine of three people dancing the hora.

A single teacup.

His engraved diploma from Hebrew Union College, in a glass frame, propped up on a silver stand:

TO ALL PERSONS BE IT KNOWN THAT

DAVID COHEN

HAVING COMPLETED THE PRESCRIBED STUDIES AND SATISFIED THE REQUIREMENTS FOR THE DEGREE, YOUR DIPLOMA HAS ACCORDINGLY BEEN ADMITTED TO THAT DEGREE WITH ALL THE RIGHTS, PRIVILEGES, AND IMMUNITIES THEREUNTO APPERTAINING.

Kristy pried the back off the frame, slid out the parchment. Ran her fingers over the embossed logo of the university . . . except it wasn't embossed. It was flat. Neither were any of the words, in fact. She held it up to the light.

"Son of a bitch," she muttered.

She licked her finger, rubbed the university's golden logo . . . and smeared ink across the pages.

A fake. An ink-jet fake. Not even a decent fugazi. Just card stock and the free printer you got with the Dell desktop.

Motherfucker.

She leaned back in David's chair. Out the window, she could see the Barer Academy playground and, in the distance, the high school, and beyond that, the Red Rock Mountains. A view of the future, the present, and the past all at once. There was a sofa and two chairs across the room, a coffee table where Rabbi Cohen kept an antique samovar and tea set, and then three walls of bookshelves. There must have been hundreds of books. Maybe a thousand. Kristy's eyes tracked up the bookshelves from the ceiling to the floor. On top of the bookshelves were fake plants shoved into ornate vases. She'd noticed them a thousand times but never thought much of them, until today, sitting at this angle, where she could see the electrical cords running from the backs of the vases.

Kristy couldn't reach the top shelf, so she started yanking books off the shelves—*Modernity and the Jews*, *The Holocaust in History*, *The Burning Bush*, *A Book of Jewish Thoughts*—tossing them onto the floor, one after another, until she found the cord running behind them. She pulled it down and a vase clattered to the ground. Buried inside the fake plant was a camera. And it wasn't even particularly small—a standard Sony, the kind you could get at Lowe's for home security. That it also had a microphone was the disturbing part.

She knocked more books off the shelves, found more cords, more cameras, more mics.

There were three paintings in the office: one behind Rabbi Cohen's desk, one beside the window, one by the door. Kristy ripped all three off the walls, found more cameras, more mics. The whole room was bugged. Every single conversation she had in this room was recorded.

Every single conversation anyone had in this room was recorded.

Every private word, every fear, every hope was cataloged . . . somewhere.

Kristy picked up the porcelain samovar and hurled it against the wall. It exploded into pieces. She swept the entire tea set onto the floor, stomped on it until it was little more than shards, tipped over the coffee table, where she found another microphone, snapped off the legs, jerked down a bookshelf.

"Agent!" Kristy turned and saw Lee Poremba in the doorway, an open laptop in his hands. "What are you doing?"

"Every word," Kristy said, "was a lie." She was breathless. Covered in sweat. "Every single kindness a fucking lie." She dropped onto the sofa. "Every word every person in this temple told that man was stolen from them. This entire room is bugged."

"The entire synagogue is bugged, Kristy," Poremba said. "Even the bathrooms." He sat down beside her, handed her the laptop. "We got into their network. This is the good rabbi's search history."

Poremba clicked on a link and there, in full color, were pictures of Jennifer and William Cupertine and an article from the *Chicago Reader*.

And like that, Kristy Levine found Sal Cupertine. Now, where the hell was he?

TWENTY-FOUR

BARRIO NAKED CITY SHOT CALLERS LIVED A FEW BLOCKS OFF THE STRIP IN the shadow of the Stratosphere Casino, literally: the sun rising in the east cast the entire West New York Avenue neighborhood in the tower's shadow, its highest point dying inside a low-slung two-story, L-shaped dingbat. The building had a flat roof and was surrounded by an exterior stair that was trying to be a floating staircase but looked cheaper than that. Its exterior walls were stucco but painted a surprisingly elegant blue-gray, and all of the aluminum windows had been replaced with vinyls. Unlike every other apartment complex on this side of town, this one was being taken care of: there were only six apartments in the dingbat, and each had a reinforced metal security door. The building was surrounded by a six-foot wrought iron fence, spiked at the top, and the two entrances had sophisticated keypad entries.

Inside the fence, the lawn was deep green and looked like it had been cut using scissors. There was also a kiddie pool and a tricycle parked in the shade. Four brand-new cars parked in the lot out front—matching black F-150s, a black Mustang, and an Audi—somehow lacked the dents and scrapes of everything else in the neighborhood.

A garbage-strewn vacant lot on one side of the building stretched for two city blocks, David making out abandoned grocery carts and piles of burnt things. Across the street, surrounded by nine-foot chain-link fencing, were buildings belonging to the Culinary Union, their logo ten feet tall. Only three blocks behind the dingbat, down on Industrial, was the Wildhorse, Bennie's strip club. That's how old Las

Vegas was. You could be in a place like the Wildhorse, with every ac-
tor, rapper, visiting athlete, and fucking bachelor party and insurance
conventioneer in town getting their dicks teased by barely legal girls,
or you could be going to work for the most powerful union in town,
and then, one right turn away, a street completely owned and operated
by a violent gang.

That most people didn't realize Summerlin was the same way was
an irony David couldn't help but ponder, even on a morning like today, with Ruben Topaz in the back of the hearse.

David had been in these parts a few times with Bennie, when Bennie had errands to run, David his muscle of choice. They'd pick up
money, or guns, and once they collected photographs of a guy running for DA, Barrio Naked City always solid to help him out on shit
he couldn't trust his own soldiers to do. Not unlike the Gangster 2-6
back home, an alliance that got Chema Espinoza dumped in a landfill
the night Sal got out of Illinois, and had ended Lonzo's life just a few
hours ago, both for being in the wrong fucking place at the wrong
fucking time.

David parked his hearse perpendicular to the F-150s, Mustang,
and Audi and sat on his horn until someone came out of an apartment. A woman wearing a tank top, shorts, and a scowl came from a
first-floor apartment, gun in hand, and not some shitty little thing,
a real .357, shouting in Spanish.

David rolled down a window. "*No habla*," he said.

"Who the fuck is you?" she said.

"I work with Bennie Savone," he said. "I need to talk to whoever
is in charge."

"This motherfucker," she muttered then disappeared into the
apartment. She came out five minutes later in a sweatshirt, holding
a baby, and unlocked the gate from the inside. "Come on, then," she
said.

"You're the boss?"

"Dora Lechuga," she said, "boss bitch. Look it up."

"Why don't we stand out here," David said.

"You don't come to my home and tell me where to stand," she said. She shifted the baby to the crook of her right arm. "Come inside or get the fuck out."

DORA LECHUGA'S APARTMENT WAS FILLED WITH LEATHER FURNITURE—TWO leather sofas, a leather recliner, a leather ottoman—and framed photos of her and a man at Disneyland; at the Eiffel Tower, except not the one in Paris, the one about a mile away; and in front of the Golden Gate Bridge from the deck of a cruise ship. And then there was one giant photo, maybe two feet tall, of the couple on their wedding day, barefoot on a beach, kissing, a big orange sun crashing into the Pacific behind them. Dora's husband was a huge motherfucker. Six foot six, maybe, all muscle and ink, the kind of guy who looked like he enjoyed fighting, was probably good at it, and also probably would be dead from a steroid-induced heart attack before he turned forty-five. The portrait hung over the mantle of a fake fireplace filled with candles. Toys were scattered over the floor of the small family room. The apartment's kitchen was vintage 1969, right down to the yellow linoleum, but it was clean.

"Don't touch nothing," Dora told him when she went to put her baby down. "I don't want your fingerprints on my shit."

So David sat on his hands until, a few minutes later, Dora returned to the kitchen, opened the fridge, took out a Coke, put it on the table, then went to the sink, ran hot water on a towel, reached under the sink for a bottle of hydrogen peroxide, handed both to David.

"You're covered in blood spatter," she said.

David wiped his face, his neck, his hands, ran the towel over his hair, too. Dipped each of his fingers into the hydrogen peroxide, got the blood from his nails, Dora watching the entire time. He cracked open the Coke, took a sip, felt it burn down his throat, the caffeine hitting just right. He'd planned to go home before all of this, but that was impossible, he knew, from the helicopters hovering over Summerlin . . . and the message he received from Officer Kiraly, informing him he wouldn't be able to pick him up today because the FBI was detaining him at the Temple, and if at all possible, could he please come by and explain everything?

Money well spent.

At that point, he could have dumped Ruben's body on the side of the road and headed east.

At that point, he probably *should have* dumped Ruben's body on the side of the road and headed east.

But he couldn't.

The Talmud told him: *If I am not for myself, then who will be for me? And if I am only for myself, then what am I? And if not now, when?*

He did manage to dump Aquafreddo and the Zangucci brothers, however. Left them right in the church in Ragtown, just in case they were Christians.

David pointed to the portrait hanging over the fake fireplace. "Where's your husband?"

"My guess would be chow. Or walking circles in the yard."

"Where?"

"Lovelock," she said. A prison, located between Reno and Winnemucca, not a bad place. Mostly minimum and medium security.

"How's that?"

"Easy time," she said. "Thanks to Mr. Savone. You see him, give him my thanks."

"I will," he said. "What's he in for?"

"Strong-arm robbery."

"Five?"

"Seven," she said.

"He must be good at it, then."

Dora shook her head. "Too old now," she said. "He should let the baby gangsters handle that shit, but he still liked the rush, you know? He's about your age."

"You get to liking it," David said, "you're never too old."

"Mr. Savone paid for his lawyer and everything."

"That's why I'm here," David said. "Mr. Savone needs a favor."

"I see that," she said. "You missed a spot on your forehead." She licked her finger, wiped a smudge over David's right eye, dried her finger off on the towel.

David said, "Ruben Topaz, you know him?"

Dora's cheeks flushed red, but all she said was, "Since he was a peanut."

"He's dead," David said. "And I need to get his body to his family. But when you see the situation, you're gonna have a lot questions and I can't give you any answers, except to say that he died like a soldier."

Dora Lechuga reached across the table, grabbed David's Coke, took a sip. "Who killed him?"

"One of the questions I can't answer."

"How do I know it wasn't you?"

"Because I would have left him in the desert to get picked apart by coyotes and I'd be halfway to Paris by now."

She seemed to consider this. "Is that his blood?"

"Honestly? I don't know. It's been a long night." He pointed out the window, to where the hearse was parked. "He's in a coffin. No need to open it. Not ever. Okay? Bennie's going to take care of his family, and we're going to make sure the people who did this pay, but right now, I need you to do this and do it quickly. I need to count on you to take it from here. Can I count on that?"

"He in pieces or something?" Dora asked.

"Or something," David said.

She made a noise, unsettling.

"I've got ten minutes to get this taken care of."

Dora walked over to her kitchen sink and threw up. Wiped her mouth off. Threw up again. Drank water from the tap. Took a deep breath. Cracked her neck. "All right," she said. She took out a cell phone, made a call. David heard a phone ringing in the apartment upstairs. Dora spoke in Spanish to whoever was on the line, tears running down her face. David heard movement, doors opening and closing. She set her cell on the kitchen counter, took two more deep breaths, then said, "We got a storage unit in the back. It's secure. Back your hearse up." Down the hall, the baby started to cry. "Shit," she said. "You need anything else from me?"

"You have any bullets?" David asked. "Jacketed hollow points, preferably."

Dora opened a cabinet door, moved around some canned food, brought out a box. "Anything else?"

"No," David said.

She started down the hall, then stopped.

"Did you really know Ruben?" she asked.

"I worked with him every day," David said.

"Was he a good man? Because he didn't come this way anymore. Mr. Savone made him promise. Like that was a condition of his parole or some shit. I never even met his wife."

"He was . . ." David paused, looked then at Dora's hands, saw that she had topaz rings on every finger, except for her wedding band, saw the tears running down her face, saw then a familiar nose, the same lips, saw how he'd always be in this moment in Dora's memory, that these seconds would be her new eternity, that she'd probably need to change apartments, that she'd never sit at that kitchen table again without remembering that as the place she learned her brother was dead. "Ruben was a light in the darkness."

TWENTY-FIVE

THE SCHOOLHOUSE IN TORREY, UTAH, WAS AN OLD THREE-STORY REDBRICK structure turned into a bed-and-breakfast. The night before, the manager told Jennifer that the herb garden out front was where they got the ingredients for their homemade breads and salads, including the rolls William was already wolfing down from the basket of warm treats each guest received upon check-in. The fruit trees that lined the property helped with their fresh pies, which Jennifer could smell baking when they pulled up to the otherwise empty place. The manager was named Hanna, probably a year or two younger than Jennifer, but had such an easy personality that she seemed timeless, as if she'd minded this property since the early 1900s, when pioneers first came through these parts.

Not much had changed since then, Torrey a dot in the road, a place where three hundred people lived hard against the Capitol Reef National Park, their livelihoods predicated on whether or not people could still get excited about seeing the living past. Places like Capitol Reef made Jennifer uneasy. Seeing the footprints of dinosaurs in ancient sediment, or the cave-wall scrawling of native peoples, gave her feelings of vast insignificance. Here she was, in the middle of this gangster shit, and she'd be lucky to even be remembered by this woman explaining the schoolhouse's Wi-Fi, lactose-free and soy milk options for breakfast, and how to operate the DVD player. You could manipulate a picture—it's what Jennifer used to do at work all day—in such a way that you could stare into a person's eyes and almost imagine yourself as them for a moment, could see yourself on that street in 1906 while the earthquake crumbled San Francisco, standing in that field watching the Hindenburg burn, pointing at the back of the car where Kennedy's skull landed. Those people lived recently. But dinosaur tracks and cave drawings were like messages from an alien society. It made everything seem sad and small comparatively.

Jennifer wondered if she could live in a place like this, where the present and the past looked the same, frozen in the shadow of the mountains, only the periodic hum of a car on Highway 24 breaking up the dream. Could she find some old building and turn it into a business? An artist residency? A dance studio? A place to house dogs and cats once their owners died? Where she did something good?

"Do you love your job?" Jennifer asked. They were walking up the stairs to the Arithmetic Room, their space for the night.

"That's a funny question," Hanna said. "I guess so far so good. It's nice knowing you're someone's good memory, you know?"

"I was just thinking that," Jennifer said.

"Living in a small town is more crowded than you think," she said. "I can't avoid the people I really want to avoid. Different than living in Salt Lake or something. If you want to disappear, a small town is not for you."

They reached the second floor, and Hanna unlocked the room. There were two queen beds, a bathroom, two large windows that faced out to an expanse of field, native grass about three feet high, an old yellow school bus rotting in the distance, about a hundred yards away. There was also a single tree in the field, Jennifer making out a tire swing dangling from a branch. Hanna opened the windows, let fresh air in.

"Do you get rattlesnakes?" William asked.

"We do," Hanna said. She gave Jennifer a subtle wink. "They're delicious. But they don't grow on trees. We usually only find them under beds."

"Rattlesnakes can live twenty-five years," William responded. He'd gone through a snake phase right after his dinosaur phase,

Jennifer hoping he'd become interested in golden retrievers or gerbils next, anything less lethal.

"Is that so?" Hanna said.

"But not if you kill and eat them," William said.

"Well," Hanna said, "next snake I find, I'll find out their age first." She turned to Jennifer. "Will this work for you?" Hanna asked.

"This will be great," Jennifer said.

"Got the call from your mother-in-law, so you're all settled up," Hanna said. She pulled back the covers on both beds. Fluffed the pillows. "Do you need help with your bags? My brother Dale will be back in just a bit and can drag them up for you."

"No," Jennifer said. "We're good. Traveling light."

"What about you?" Hanna asked William. He was standing in the doorway, hadn't crossed one step into the room.

"Is this room haunted?" he asked.

"William!" Jennifer said. "Apologize."

"No, no," Hanna said, "it's fine." She gave Jennifer a little smile. "I don't think so. Why do you ask?"

"There's a girl sitting on the bed," William said.

Jennifer and Hanna shared a look. *Kids.* But Jennifer's look also meant to convey: *Help me.* But Hanna didn't see that, Jennifer supposed, because how could she know anything about their life?

"She's very nice, I promise," Hanna said. She turned to Jennifer. "Do you want another room?"

"No, no," Jennifer said, "of course not. My son's imagination is enormous."

"I'm not imagining anything," William said. "She seemed happy." He walked in, plopped down on the bed. "She's gone now."

IT WAS THE WORD *SEEMED* THAT KEPT JENNIFER UP ALL THAT NIGHT, NODDING off only for a few moments at a time, because the fact was that William was scaring the living shit out of her.

You're being crazy, she kept telling herself.

What if William walked downstairs, turned on all the gas, and blew this whole building apart?

Stop.

It was the kind of thinking that cycled through her brain at 3:30 a.m., worrying about everything they'd been through and its effect on her young son, but by the time the sun was up she needed to get out of bed. Even if the day was going to be a shitstorm. She hadn't seen Sal's mother in years, hadn't talked to her in longer, even if she did try to send photos of William when Sal wasn't paying attention.

On the phone yesterday, Arlene was calmer than Jennifer imagined she would be.

"Well," she said to Jennifer, "I guess I always knew this day would come. Is William safe?"

"Yes," Jennifer said. "He's not fine, though. Neither one of us is. It's a very confusing time, Mom."

"Mom," Arlene repeated. "I haven't been called that in so long."

"Do you want me to call you Arlene?"

"No, of course not." She cleared her throat. "Tell me what needs to be done." Jennifer gave her the B and B's information, asked her to cover the bill for the night, and Arlene agreed. "I should tell you, my husband passed," Arlene said.

"Oh no," Jennifer said. "When?"

"Two years ago. Hung himself."

"My god, why?"

"He took that answer with him," she said. "I've been thinking of moving into one of those assisted living facilities. One where they cook and clean for you. How bad could that be? Be like a cruise ship, wouldn't it? Maybe I could find a new husband who could outlive me for once."

Jennifer didn't have the heart to confess she couldn't remember the man's name. When did she forget? She'd known it for twenty years and now it was gone, replaced with data about reality television and the terminal velocity of falling bodies, perhaps. The last time Jennifer saw Arlene was in a Target in Chicago, after she'd come back to town to sell her house, and since then she'd just been an address, a phone number, the notion of a lifeline.

"I appreciate your help, Mom," Jennifer opted to say. "We'll figure it out when we see you."

They both hung up without saying goodbye, as if they knew there was nothing good about this situation at all, not even the leaving.

Jennifer crept over to the window and looked out at the rising sun—a sliver of gold to the east—and then down at the garden. She found Hanna out there, sitting in an Adirondack chair beneath a tree, sipping what looked like a hot cup of coffee or tea, the steam rising from it in the cool morning air, and reading the morning paper.

And then a thought: Could she just walk away from her life? Could she sneak out the back, get into the car, and instead of driving to Sedona just keep going, hit the Mexican border, disappear into a new life? Wouldn't William be better off? Wouldn't his chances of a normal life increase?

Sal had done that. Was his life better? How could it be worse? Wherever he was, he was *living*, which was different from what Jennifer and William were doing, all this time. They were surviving and barely holding on at that.

Jennifer took a knee beside William's bed, brushed his bangs from his forehead so she could see his face. His eyes fluttered open. "Go back to sleep," Jennifer said.

"Don't let them take me," he said.

"I'd never let anyone take you," she said.

JENNIFER FOUND A POT OF COFFEE ON THE LONG KITCHEN TABLE, ALONG WITH several sweet rolls, so she grabbed a cup and a roll and stepped outside. When Jennifer reached the back end of the garden, Hanna dragged a second chair over, and asked Jennifer to join her.

For a while, they made small talk about the garden—*More work than I ever imagined!*—how busy the summer months typically are— *So many Swedes! It's really something. I guess they just love to vacation together?*—and the state of the world—*Well, I thought it was going to be Al-Qaeda, too, but now they're saying it was an arson? That's what they said on CNN. You know they didn't find any whole bodies! Isn't that gruesome, but I guess there's labs like that all over the country, it's how medical science operates now, can you believe it?*—Hanna ending every sentence with a question that begged no answers.

"I thought more about your question."

"Yeah?" Jennifer said. "What did you decide?"

"I do love my job," Hanna said. "I'm at work right now, and we're having a nice conversation, and in theory, I'm getting paid for it. I'm outside, and I'm drinking pretty good coffee, and that's so much better than what I used to do."

"What was that?"

"Lawyer," she said.

"I could use a lawyer," Jennifer said, almost to herself.

"I was a public defender," she said, "so probably no help for you. What is it? Divorce? I still do business mediation in town because who else can, you know?" She put on a pair of eyeglasses that were in her breast pocket. "Okay. Ready to hear your case."

Jennifer took a sip of her coffee. "My husband," Jennifer said, "is a mafia hit man, and my son and I have been living in protective custody for almost a year. Two nights ago, someone murdered the FBI agent watching us, and so we fled in the middle of the night. I think we're being followed and are in great danger. Later today, we'll be at my mother-in-law's house in Sedona, and then after that, I guess I don't know what happens. I need to keep my child safe, but I have no idea how to do that. I just don't want us to die a horrible death, so that my husband never learns what happened to us. So. What would you do, counselor?" She took another sip of her coffee.

Hanna smiled at her. "Watch fewer Lifetime movies would be my advice," she said. She clapped her hands and started laughing. "Can you imagine? I couldn't handle that level of drama."

Something moved in Jennifer's peripheral vision, so she turned and saw William staring out the window. She waved. He pointed out toward the field.

"How old is he?" Hanna asked.

"Eight."

"That's a good age," she said.

"You have children?" Jennifer asked.

"I had a daughter," Hanna said, except she said it in such a way that invited no follow-ups, which Jennifer understood completely, in light of the ghost girl on the bed. She pointed to the school bus in the field. "She just loved playing on that. It was her favorite place in the world, which is why I've never had it hauled away. I like to come out here and imagine she's playing inside of it and will be coming in soon." She smiled, not happily. "It is a coping mechanism, because *soon* is always right around the bend, isn't it? She's always right around the bend."

A flock of red-winged blackbirds took to the sky, lifting up from the field en masse. "Oh," Jennifer said. "I didn't even see them in the grass."

"Something must have spooked them," Hanna said. She picked up her newspaper, folded it over, stood up, looked south. "Looks like it might rain today."

William banged on the window, pointed again.

"You think so?" Jennifer stood up. Looked out at the field again. The tall grass waved in the breeze.

"This time of year," Hanna said, "the weather changes every few minutes."

Jennifer took a few steps, so that she stood on the edge of the garden. Something moved against the school bus, a shadow, maybe a cat?

"Do you get animals out here?" Jennifer asked.

"Birds mostly," Hanna said.

Jennifer looked back at the schoolhouse. William was still in the window, but now he was looking north, his face pressed against the glass.

Jennifer walked to the opposite side of the garden, followed William's gaze. Another field of natural grass, trembling. On the edge of the field, a white van, parked, exhaust coming from its tailpipe, rear doors open, a football field away.

"Who is that?" Jennifer asked.

Hanna stood beside her. "I have no idea," she said.

William pounding on the window now. Pointing in every direction.

The grass came alive. Ten, fifteen, twenty men, guns out, running toward Jennifer, screaming at her, Jennifer running into the schoolhouse, sprinting for her son, crashing through the door and into the muzzle of an AR-15.

TWENTY-SIX

KALES MORTUARY AND HOME OF PEACE KEPT METICULOUS RECORDS, RUBEN Topaz running a tight ship. Senior Special Agent Lee Poremba appreciated the attention to detail, particularly now as he walked the graveyard, working his way through a multicolored spreadsheet that showed the activity for the week Jeff Hopper disappeared. There were seventeen funerals that week, twelve performed by Rabbi Cohen, five either by rabbis brought in for the occasion or by a "Nonaffiliated Entity," which Poremba guessed meant a civilian. The funerals were spread across the entire land known as the Home of Peace, three in Zone 1, four in Zone 2, six in Zone 3, etc. Poremba printed out the spreadsheet, picked up a map of the cemetery, and headed out after meeting with Kristy. He didn't know what he was looking for, only that he wanted to see the plots with his own eyes.

He'd imagined this place so many times, learned to identify the birds in its trees by their songs, viewed photos of it, from the street and from outer space, but he'd never smelled the freshly cut grass, never felt the humidity settle onto his skin, never been surrounded by so many Jews, if he was honest, living or dead.

What faith Lee Poremba had left in this world was focused on one thing: justice. He'd given up God years before. The fact was, Senior Special Agent Lee Poremba—soon to be the head of the joint Organized Crime & Terrorism Task Force in Las Vegas, where he'd be busy every goddamned day of his life, the city filled with visiting strangers being afforded any courtesy money could buy—kept his inner life for himself. He gave the federal government everything else—he was ready to die for his belief in the ideals of the country, a vow he couldn't believe wasn't shared by every American alive—and in the process, he'd lost his marriage, lost good friends, and, as it related to Matthew Drew and Jeff Hopper and their pursuit of Sal Cupertine, much of his better judgment. But he'd never wavered in his pursuit of justice. Sal Cupertine murdered three FBI agents and a confidential informant in a hotel room in Chicago in 1998, and if Lee Poremba had to chase him to Mars to arrest him, Lee Poremba would build a spaceship by hand in his garage.

Poremba walked up a low rise—on the internal map, it showed him leaving Zone 2 into Zone 3, though the signage within the cemetery said he was leaving Tranquility and entering Serenity—and found himself on a wide plateau, filled with densely packed graves. Poremba had a sense of why: The view wasn't that great, since they were essentially in the middle of the cemetery, so that you could hear the water feature in Zone 4 but couldn't see it, you could smell the massive rose garden on the edge of Zone 2, but it was too far away to be a selling point, and even the massive shade trees and benches littered throughout the cemetery were fewer here in the great inland empire of the dead.

The pre-dead seemed to know this, since families were lumped together in exacting rows, only a few feet apart from one another, whereas in the higher-rent districts, you had a little elbow room.

Poremba unfolded his spreadsheet of the funerals from that week in 1999. This area had seen the most action.

Burl Meltzer, 1919 to 1999.

Josef Barer, 1923 to 1999.

Sherri Morgan, 1953 to 1999.

Sol Cohen, 1906 to 1999.

Jennie Fishmann, 1975 to 1999.

Megan Berkowitz, 1959 to 1999.

He walked by each grave, hoping to see some hint, some guide-post, but of course Sal Cupertine was smarter than that, so Poremba left a stone on each headstone, said the only prayer he remembered from childhood—the twenty-third psalm—and then sat down on one of the few benches, watched the thick white clouds that had formed this morning burn slowly away to reveal a deep-blue sky.

It was in these moments that Poremba wished he possessed some kind of clairvoyance other than recognizing the awful truth of it all: that in the end, he'd be in a place just like this, too, and without children or a wife or even siblings, he'd be just as lost, just as gone, as the body of Jeffery Hopper. Because of that, Poremba always imagined he'd ask to be cremated, but he was changing his mind about that. He sort of admired the notion that he could disappear into eternity, his usefulness, his desire for justice, feeding the earth.

He looked toward the Strip, though he couldn't see it from this angle, his view blocked by trees and houses, and imagined what it must be like for the people in those casinos, going about their life on vacation, not once turning on the news today, never knowing or caring about that which had obsessed Senior Special Agent Lee Poremba for four years. Sal Cupertine would be caught. Sal Cupertine *had been* caught. And in the end, how many people died because of it? What a waste. What a terrible waste.

"There you are."

Poremba turned and saw Kristy Levine walking through the headstones.

"Sorry," Poremba said, "I should have let someone know where I was going."

"It's fine," Kristy said. "I tracked your phone."

"Really?"

"No, I just looked on the security cameras. They're out here, too."

Poremba took his phone from his pocket. Thirty-seven missed calls. Kristy sat beside him. Pointed off into the distance. "My plot is over there, if you'd like a tour."

"I shouldn't have come here," Poremba said.

"Probably not," Kristy said.

Poremba said, "Jeff Hopper was kind of a shit. You ever meet him?"

"No."

"You might have hated him," he said. "He was never wrong. Not once. He was so headstrong when he started, he actually thought he was going to bring down the very notion of organized crime. And when that didn't happen, he was sure it was a conspiracy."

"Isn't it?"

"We need bad guys, Agent," Poremba said. "If we didn't have any, we'd start arresting good guys instead. Become an authoritarian force. In the absence of evil, we'd create it."

"You honestly believe that?"

"I do," Poremba said. "It's why history never sleeps. No one is ever content with happiness." He gestured to the graves. "Why doesn't anyone ever come back to tell us how wonderful heaven is, make all of this worth it?"

Kristy laughed, somewhat ruefully. "Wrong cemetery, Lee."

Poremba turned his ringer back on. Two seconds later, he had a call. He let it go to voice mail. "What's the update?"

Kristy took out a notepad, ran through what they had and what was missing: Bennie Savone was on a plane to Minnesota; agents would greet him at the airport when he landed. Rabbi Cy Kales had booked a red-eye the previous night, departing from McCarran to Tel Aviv at 1:10 a.m. They didn't yet have any crimes to charge him with, but they sure wanted to talk to him.

His phone rang again. His boss at Quantico. He turned the phone to show Kristy. "We're national news now." He silenced the phone again. "Where do you suppose Cupertine is?"

"We've got eyes on the 95, 15, 215, 515, and 11," Kristy said, "going in and out of the city and the state. We've got air support to the state line. Checked the border crossings, nothing. Checked the agricultural checkpoints in Yermo, Blythe, Truckee, and Needles. Nothing."

"When was the last time we had eyes on him?"

"Security at his gated community has his Range Rover exiting the main gate last night at 11:52 p.m. We're working on getting a photo, see if anyone was with him."

"He could be anywhere," Poremba said.

"One other thing. Ruben Topaz is missing. His wife says he never returned from a pickup last night. She hasn't heard from him since midnight. I suspect they're together."

"A pickup? What does that mean?"

"I asked the other worker. Miguel. He had no clue."

"You believe him?"

"Kind of. Unlike Topaz, he's not some reformed gangster."

"What about Topaz's wife?"

"Not real forthcoming. Said if we had any more questions, we could talk to her lawyer. Vincent Zangari."

"Zangari represents every mobster Oscar Goodman had to give up when he got elected."

"Right." She flipped through some pages. "So, we've got a BOLO on the Kales Mortuary hearse, which is what Topaz was driving. His own car is parked behind the mortuary. You'll be surprised to know that the security system here that films everything records absolutely nothing on-site. It's all going somewhere else. It's not networked to a security company. It's private."

"Stunned," Poremba said.

"Cupertine's house is the same way. Bugged up the wazoo, all of it feeding off-site. It's going to take us a while to figure that out."

"House turn up anything?'

"An arsenal," she said. "All of them registered to Bennie Savone."

"Do it all legal," Poremba said, "less chance you'll get nicked for some stupid shit. It's smart."

"Other than that, a lot of beautiful suits. A shit ton of books. A tremendous amount of yogurt and scotch. Nothing useful."

"Keep looking," Poremba said. He got up from the bench, walked over to the closest row of graves, set down some more rocks. Got down on one knee, wiped dirt off a headstone. Peter Copeland, 1997 to 2001. "Do you know the Copelands?"

Kristy walked over. "I don't think so," Kristy said.

"This boy died when he was four," Poremba said. "Where was God then, Kristy?"

"I think he's never stronger than then," she said. "The Talmud says, we live our life in deeds, not years. Rabbi Cohen taught me that. That boy must have been loved tremendously and must have loved tremendously."

"Rabbi Cohen taught you that?"

Kristy nodded. "He's a good rabbi," she said. "He gave my life purpose when I needed it."

"Does *he* believe that?"

"I've been wondering that all day," Kristy said.

Poremba walked a few more steps, stopped in front of one large headstone:

Beth Hertz 1961–2000   Neil Hertz 1959–

"Do you think it's a comfort to the husband to have his name already engraved on the tombstone?" Poremba asked.

"I guess it prevents him from falling in love with someone else," Kristy said.

Poremba found a stone in the grass, placed it above Beth Hertz's name, an idea coming clear. "You have any friends in local media?"

"I dated an investigative reporter on Channel 8 for two nights until he wanted to talk to me about the aliens being held out at Nellis."

"Give me his number," Poremba said.

TWENTY-SEVEN

THE PALM TIKI WAS ONE BLOCK OFF THE STRIP, WHICH WAS AS CLOSE AS David ever got to the Strip during his time in town. Before 9/11, there were more surveillance cameras in Las Vegas than almost anywhere; now it was a virtual police state. So he never stepped one foot inside the Bellagio or the Mirage or even the dumps, like Excalibur and Circus Circus.

But the Palm Tiki took cash and didn't really care if your ID was real or not, which made it the perfect place for Jerry Ford to hole up while David figured out how he was going to keep him alive. A harder proposition now than it had been a few days earlier.

So even though he called Jerry and said he'd be there in twenty minutes, David showed up in ten, because he wanted to case the place, make sure Jerry hadn't gone soft on him. The plan Jerry and David had cooked up after the explosion so far worked—it would be at least a week before anyone realized the body they pulled out of LifeCore wasn't Jerry Ford, which was good because the Russians would be coming for him, the FBI would be coming for him, and, if he gave a fuck, Bennie Savone would be, too—and that meant Jerry had enough time to grab his wife and get out of the country or hope the feds gave him some kind of deal, which he'd need now that everything was falling to shit.

David parked between a dumpster and a light pole, turned on the local NPR, listened to some asshole prattle on about how if you wanted to really understand real estate investing, you had to first understand kabbalah numerology, that the truth of life and making money was found in the four hundred life-path combinations and their resonant vibrations.

"If you're just joining us," the warm-oatmeal voice on NPR said, "we're with an up-and-coming Southern Nevada leader, Yehuda Stein from the Kabbalah Center on Sahara. He's got some fascinating notions about investing, which we'll explore even more deeply after this short break. You're listening to Faith, Finance, and the Future on KNPR."

Fuck no. If David weren't feeling so charitable about the faith, he'd drop by KNPR on his way out of town, get Yehuda's home address, and show him the number nine pressed against his fucking face.

Instead, he switched to an all-news AM station, KXNT. David closed his eyes.

He'd been awake for over twenty-four hours.

He'd killed two men.

He'd maimed one man.

He'd become a Jew.

Not a day he could have predicted.

David opened his eyes. He was pretty sure he opened his eyes. Most of Melanie Moss was sitting in the passenger seat. He hadn't forgotten her.

David opened his eyes, again, and there on the light pole was a Missing flyer for Melanie Moss. He put down his window, reached out, yanked the flyer down. It was a newer one, which included the bounty from Temple Beth Israel. There was a number to call with a 775 area code. Carson City.

David pulled out his burner. Dialed the number. A man picked up. "This is Trevor," he said. Who answered their phone like that? David had the notion it would be a police station, or a private detective.

"Hello?" Trevor said while David was still trying to figure out what the fuck to say.

"Don't hang up," David said eventually. "Do you have a pen?"

"I'm sorry, who is this?"

"A friend," David said. "You've waited too long. Do you have a pen?"

"Is this about Melanie?"

"Yes," David said. "Do you have a pen?"

"Yes, yes, I have a pen."

"You will find Melanie's remains in the pond directly behind Bennie Savone's home, located inside a community called The Vineyards at Summerlin. This is in Las Vegas. You'll need to have the pond drained. It's very murky and deep, but you will find what you're looking for. She was killed because Savone is operating a criminal enterprise out of Kales Mortuary and Home of Peace." He paused. Melanie was watching him. "She figured it all out. She should be considered a hero. And Trevor, you must know she didn't suffer." A thought came to him. "Are you recording this?"

"Yes, everything is recorded."

"Though I discovered this information, I don't want the reward. It should go to you. Temple Beth Israel will pay. Make a claim." The back door of the Palm Tiki opened and Jerry Ford walked out, wearing a Hawaiian shirt, a straw hat with a huge brim, and cargo shorts, pushing a luggage cart with four duffel bags, each big enough to conceal a small child. "She didn't deserve what happened to her. I'm very sorry."

David ended the call. Got out of the hearse, unlocked the back doors. Jerry pushed the cart to the back of the SUV, looked inside. "You're lucky we live in Las Vegas. It's almost impossible to get ransom money in Boise." He wrinkled his nose. "What's the smell?"

"You don't want to know," David said. He unzipped the first bag, looked inside. Stacks of hundreds. Good. Tossed it in.

"Ruben must be slipping. He keeps this baby pristine," Jerry said. Then Jerry saw the dried blood on the bumper. Getting Ruben from the ground into a casket was a journey. "Where *is* Ruben?"

"Moved to a farm in the country," David said. He unzipped the second bag. More stacks of hundreds. Tossed it in back.

"You're not gonna count them?"

"I trust you," David said.

"That's fucking weird," Jerry said. He unzipped the third bag himself, reached his hand in deep, came out with a stack. "You should at least cut a random one open, make sure it's not a hundred on top and then filled with singles." Which is what he did. All hundreds.

"Good," David said. "Keep two bags for yourself."

"What?"

"Get out of town, Jerry," David said. He closed the back doors, locked them, headed to the front seat. "FBI is onto everything. It's all over."

"I need to get my wife."

"Then do that," David said. He got back into the hearse but didn't close the door. "Autopsy will take a good five days. You're not a priority. Probably longer, since Stephanie won't be calling to hassle anyone. So right now, you've never been freer. You can get far away using your own ID. But if you can't get to Stephanie by tonight, you'll have to leave her behind."

"I can't do that."

"Yes you can," David said. "The feds will have someone on Stephanie tonight. I promise you. And if the feds don't, the Russians will. I'd have her get into a car and meet you in the desert. If she doesn't make it at an appointed time, you'll know she's either been picked up or killed."

"Or what? Get on a slow boat to China?"

"I'd go to Ukraine," David said. "No extradition. Most everyone speaks English. Get settled. Then in a couple months, send for Stephanie. Have her fly to Romania, enter Ukraine from there. A million dollars will go a long way in Eastern Europe."

Jerry looked pained. "You should have told me who you were," Jerry said.

"When?"

"The first day we met," Jerry said. "Would have solved a significant number of problems for both of us." Jerry checked down the block, made sure no one was around. "You're on the local news. They said your name."

David figured as much.

"You realize you're about to be a very wanted man, too."

"I sense that," Jerry said. "FBI called Stephanie in Pismo yesterday."

"What did they say?"

"It was Kristy Levine, from the Temple? She said I was dead and Stephanie was in danger, so Stephanie hung up on her."

"Kristy Levine?" David said. "You sure?"

"She and Stephanie are friends. Well, Temple friends. Play canasta together or something. I don't know."

"She ever met you?"

"I try not to meet FBI agents, buddy."

"You should take my advice," David said. "It's a good plan, Jerry."

"All due respect, Rabbi? I'm not like you. I can barely tie my shoes without Stephanie." David looked down. Motherfucker was wearing slip-ons. "I'm going to spend the rest of my life either in jail or waiting to get killed. That's what you're telling me?"

"Yes."

An ambulance pulled into the parking lot behind the Palm Tiki.

"This normal?" David sank down in his seat.

"Every day about this time," Jerry said. "Maids start making their rounds. If they find a body, first call is the EMTs." Two men stepped out of the ambulance, both in their thirties, shuffled into the Palm Tiki, moving at a pace usually reserved for those walking to an electric chair. "LifeCore gets a lot of clients from this block. We've made a lot of money from these people."

"You did," David said.

"You just made a million dollars, if I remember correctly."

A police cruiser came slowly down the street. David pulled out his gun. Put it on his lap. But the cruiser kept going. It probably wasn't unusual for a hearse to be at the Palm Tiki, as normal as an ambulance, anyway.

"I need to get off the streets," David said.

Seconds later, another cop car came down the block, but this one pulled into the parking lot behind the Palm Tiki, no sirens, but with a K-9 in the back. David had never killed a dog before. A cop no older than twenty-five got out of the cruiser, looked right at David, right at Jerry, said, "Doing a pickup?"

"Down the way," David said, "just waiting on the call."

Cop nodded. "Sundays are always terrible in this city. Makes me want to move somewhere safe, like New York." He laughed. David laughed. Jerry laughed. "Have a good one, gentlemen," he said then disappeared into the hotel.

"Get in the fucking car," David said.

THEY DROVE A FEW BLOCKS AWAY, TO THE PARKING LOT FOR A NEW CITY park under construction. It was to boast two full artificial-turf soccer fields, a water feature, pickleball courts, whatever the fuck that was, basketball hoops, barbecue areas, a lactation station, and shaded study areas. But at ten thirty on Sunday morning, it was just concrete, mounds of dirt, about an acre of grass, and a series of 1950s-era one-story buildings that at some point had been set on fire, but not recently. There were six rotting buildings in total. The construction site was surrounded by a chain-link fence riddled with huge holes, likely cut by the homeless or anyone interested in stealing copper wiring from the massive stadium lights being installed.

For fifteen minutes, David and Jerry sat in the hearse listening to the all-news station. They kept repeating, every five minutes, that the FBI was raiding half of Summerlin, looking for a mass murderer. It was, frankly, a categorization that David did not appreciate. He wasn't fucking Pol Pot. He killed criminals, 99.9 percent of the time. An argument could be made that he'd made the world a better place.

David said, "How much did the TV news say about me?"

"Your real name, like I said," Jerry said. "Showed your photo, from when you were a kid, I guess. You still had baby fat in your cheeks. Said you were armed and dangerous. Said the public should not approach you. Said you were wanted for at least four murders, suspected of hundreds. Said your wife and kid were reported missing . . ."

"Wait," David said. "What was that last part? About my wife."

"I don't know. They were looking for your wife and kid, too, threw up photos of them. At that point, I was already feeling kinda like I was at the bottom of a well."

But then, a new update, from the perky host of the local news show, whose name was never mentioned: "Now Charles, this is crazy, we're hearing from sources in the Jewish community that the mass murderer they're looking for—this Sal Cupertine—has been living in this region for *years*, embedded in the Jewish community as a rabbi!"

"No!" said Charles, whoever the fuck that was.

"We're going to be joined by Harvey B. Curran from the *Review-Journal* at eleven with the full story. This is a bizarre one. Apparently, he and the rabbi are very close friends."

"Only in Las Vegas!" said Charles.

"We're quickly becoming Florida," said the perky one, who then cut to a commercial.

David said, "I need some air."

"HARD TO IMAGINE THIS AS A PARK," JERRY SAID. THEY DUCKED THROUGH A hole in the fencing and were walking through the grounds, toward the burned-out buildings, David feeling like he should enjoy some freedom while he still had it. "This was a VA clinic for years. During the Gulf War, someone threw a Molotov cocktail through a window. Place went up like tinder. Been sitting here ever since." He pointed in the distance, to a gleaming four-story white building that loomed over the neighborhood, blocking out the view of the mountains that encircled the city. "That was built a few years later. Guess they knew they'd have more veterans." They approached one of the buildings and

Jerry peered inside. "Stephanie's father used to volunteer here. World War II vet, one of those tough-ass Jews you read about. Growing up, I thought all Jews were pussies."

"You're not Jewish, are you, Jerry?"

"You learned my secret," he said. "But that's not because I don't believe in the Torah or dislike a good kugel. It's because I don't believe in *anything*." He tried a door. It opened, revealing an old closet that mostly smelled like piss. "I didn't know you were Sal Cupertine until about an hour ago."

David did not like hearing Jerry say his name. He didn't like the ease with which it rolled from his tongue, like he wasn't scared.

"No one did."

"Not true," Jerry said. "Ronnie knew. For decades." He closed the closet door. Leaned against it. "Which means you're not Jewish, either."

David stared at Jerry for a few seconds, tried to figure out if he was having some kind of stroke, if both of them were having some kind of stroke.

"You fucking wired?" David said.

"If I were," Jerry said, "we'd already be in prison."

He had a point. But still. "Take off your fucking shirt," David said.

Jerry said, "Rabbi, why don't you first look to see if my cell phone is on. Wouldn't that be easier? Who needs to be wired anymore?"

"I'm old-school," David said, "show me both."

Jerry unbuttoned his Hawaiian shirt, did a little twirl, then handed David his phone. "Satisfied?"

He wasn't, not in a general way, but as it related to this issue, yeah, he was fine.

"What the fuck are you telling me?"

"I didn't know you were a Cupertine," Jerry said. "My mother, she was a Lopiparno. Ronnie Cupertine fronted me to get started in the business. I mean, he's like my cousin. When I dropped out of med school, he was the only person who understood."

"He *is* my cousin," David said.

"I know," Jerry said. "I mean, Sugar used to talk about the Rain Man like you were Batman."

Sugar Lopiparno. Ronnie's guy in Detroit, who came back to work in Chicago after Sal's fuckup. Who became Ronnie's number two after Fat Monte kicked his own bucket of shit.

"We ever meet?"

"I don't think so," Jerry said. "By the time you were old enough to matter, I was already in college."

David didn't know what to make of this.

"When did Bennie come to you with this idea to launder the bodies?" David asked.

"No, no, you got it all wrong," Jerry said. "I can't tell you how many times I asked Ronnie to help *me* with Bennie Savone, but he said he couldn't, it wasn't the right time, that he was out of Las Vegas. I kept telling him that we could make some real money out here if we had a rabbi who could make shit happen. That we could hit a lick in the multimillions, David. The multimillions. And then one day you showed up and I told Ronnie, never mind, we had a guy, and he just played fucking dumb, I guess."

Ronnie was good at playing dumb, David knew. But in fact he was the smartest motherfucker on the planet, if he'd actually orchestrated all of this shit. David was sure he had, that he'd planned it for years, figured out how to franchise his people across the nation, by becoming *mostly* legit and working with people who either feared him or didn't know they should.

Bennie Savone thought he had one over on him but didn't realize he was working for Ronnie all along.

And whenever he wanted, Ronnie could have pulled the plug. Bennie would be stuck holding his dick and a murderous hit man.

"You let the mafia invest in your business, Jerry?"

"I let my cousin stake me," Jerry said.

"Let me guess," David said, "he took 80, you took 20."

"If that."

"You talk to him lately?"

"Not since whatever happened to him."

"But before that."

"Weekly." He paused. "Daily, when it started blowing up." He shook his head. "I think I got you here. I think I'm responsible for all this. I brought it on myself. Every dollar you made, you made five for Ronnie."

And now, David presumed, Peaches. If he wasn't dead already.

"You shouldn't have come here," David said.

"I should have fucking stayed in med school, is what I should have done."

"Why did you come to Las Vegas in the first place?"

"Ronnie," Jerry said. "He said I'd be his guy here. I guess I didn't know what that meant."

"Yes, you did," David said.

"I'm not that type of guy, Rabbi. You know that. It's been eating me up all morning," Jerry said. "I'm a fucking dead man, aren't I? You tried to save me, but here I fucking am." He closed his eyes. Took a deep breath. "What are you gonna do?"

"See if I can find my wife," David said.

"And what? Turn yourself in? Would that save my ass?"

David tried to figure out ways in which Jerry Ford might come out of this situation alive. The problem was that he wasn't safe in prison, he wasn't safe on the streets, and he wasn't really the kind of guy they put into witness protection. He had enough money to pay for his own security, which only meant he had enough money to feel safe without actually being safe. No one was taking a bullet for anyone these days. David doubted heavily that the Secret Service was lining up to protect George W. Bush, everyone shit scared about being found out and targeted by some fucking terror organization. Back in the day, you didn't worry the Soviets were coming for you personally, but now, who the fuck knew? End up getting beheaded just for knowing a guy? Fuck no.

"You're fine, Jerry," David said. "You're just fine. Once I leave, either get out of the country or call the FBI, turn yourself in, make sure they get Stephanie, and you'll both be safe."

"That wouldn't piss you off?"

"Of course not," David said. "You have to do what you have to do. Maybe I'll be in Ukraine by then."

"Oh, Jesus, David, thank you. Thank you. I won't say your name. We never met. It was all Bennie. That's what I'm gonna tell them."

"Everybody dies," David said. "That's a fact."

"Yeah, yeah," Jerry said, and he pointed a finger gun at David, "like that. No one needs to blow up the Chicken Man!" He walked past David, headed toward the hearse, his whole demeanor lightened by his admission, a life of promise stretching out wide before him, because Jerry Lopiparno Ford just made a deal with the Rain Main, saved his own life in the process, secured a future with Stephanie where maybe they'd need to pinch a few pennies, but he was humming a Bruce Springsteen song when Rabbi David Cohen shot him once in the back of the head.

TWENTY-EIGHT

DAVID STOPPED TO CATCH HIS BREATH A HUNDRED YARDS INTO THE DESERT
Inn Detention Basin storm drain, hauling a million dollars in duffel
bags more strenuous activity than he'd thought, each bag weighing
about fifteen pounds, which shouldn't have been a problem, but he did
not have his wind, having not slept or being in any kind of shape since
his time in the hospital. He'd also dragged Jerry Ford's body into one
of the burned-out VA buildings and took his wallet, placing Jerry's
driver's license in his mouth. Some motherfucker might roll a dead
man, but they weren't going to poke around his orifices.

But now, an hour later, his back was on fire, his wrists were killing
him, he was starving, and he needed to figure out what was happening
with his wife and son.

He'd been down in these drains a half dozen times over the years
with the Temple during the winter, dropping off food and clothes for
the homeless, but in the spring and summer, it was just too fucking
hot, David already sweating through his clothes. What he knew about
these drains he knew from Miguel, who'd been the person to suggest
they go down there and help out in the first place.

"When I was a kid," he told Rabbi Cohen, "we lived there whenever my mom didn't have the rent money. There's good people living
in the storm drains. It's safer than on the streets, so we had our place,
and when she got some cash, we'd find another aboveground place to
live."

"How long ago was this?" Rabbi Cohen asked him. They were in the mortuary, Miguel getting a body ready for donation, this time an actual dead Jew, Billy Pelz.

"Well, I'm twenty-six," he said. He cut open the body using a *Y* incision, the room filling with a smell like defrosting meat, something metallic, and old shit. "Last time was, I guess, senior year in high school."

"Where's your mom now?"

Miguel shrugged.

"You don't know?" David asked.

"She wasn't a real good mother, Rabbi," Miguel said. He walked around the body, his fingers lingering on a hand or foot, depending upon where he was standing. "Did you know him?"

"A little bit," David said. "He was an optometrist."

Miguel said, "Not a lot of bad news in that job." He picked up the order. "We're going to remove his lungs, Rabbi, and you don't want to be here for that."

"Okay," David said. "Can I ask, Miguel, how did you get here?"

"For a little while, my mom danced at Mr. Savone's club. We waited in the car for her. Mr. Savone would come out sometimes, bring us food. He was real nice. Told me to come see him for a job when I was older. So I did."

Now, David hefted the bags back up, walked another fifty yards, to an area they called the Art Gallery, the walls covered in old newspaper clippings painted over in garish colors, Mayor Goodman's face now bright orange, Wayne Newton a phoenix rising, Joe Pesci, from some movie, in a clown suit. Every inch of available wall, another piece of art, dating back years now, plus the requisite gang graffiti, though there wasn't much in these parts, gangsters just as scared of the dark as anyone else. The walls didn't quite reach the roof, leading up to a manhole that opened onto Rainbow Boulevard. The cavity was illuminated with a pinhole of sunshine from the manhole, enough to make art by, the whole spot ethereal in the afternoon glow. Almost pleasant if you could excuse the stench of sewer water, exhaust, and time.

David lifted a bag over his head, shoved it up between the wall and the ceiling, then the other. They disappeared into the darkness.

"Is there anyone here?" David called out. He waited. The roar of traffic above made this spot impossible to sleep in, the cacophony constant, but David wanted to make sure no one would fuck with his money.

He walked another ten yards down the tunnel, calling out, but there was nothing. When they'd feed the homeless, they usually found them a few blocks away, directly under Davis Park, where it was quiet, there were bathrooms, and, at night, the children could play on the jungle gym and the adults could sit under the stars, forget about their problems, at least for a little while.

DAVID CAME OUT OF THE BASIN AND INTO DAVIS PARK. HE FOUND A SPOT OF shade, sat down, tried to slow his heart rate, and then did something he hoped he wasn't going to regret: he called Miguel.

He answered on the first ring.

"Miguel," David said, "this is Rabbi Cohen. Are you somewhere safe?"

"Yes, Rabbi. The FBI let me go home. Should you . . . be calling?"

"No," David said, "I should not be." That was Miguel. Ever helpful.

"Is it true, Rabbi?"

"What part?"

"That you're . . . not a rabbi?"

"No," David said, "I am a rabbi." He was now. He believed that honestly. He'd done the work. Passed the tests. "The other stuff, whatever they said, is probably true."

"Yes, Rabbi," Miguel said. "I guess I've always known to some extent. But, Rabbi, I loved my job; I felt like I did good work. Whatever you and Mr. Savone and Ruben did, that was your thing. I took care of those people like they were family. Every day."

"You did," David said. "You have nothing to feel ashamed about."

"I'm sorry," Miguel said, "that it was a lie."

"Listen," David said, "I need you to do two last things for me. Okay?"

"I'll try," Miguel said, "but I got a family, you know?"

"I know," David said. "First thing, tell the FBI everything. Turn state's evidence. I know you feel you need to be loyal to Mr. Savone. The way to do that is to be loyal to yourself, first. Do you understand?"

"Yes, Rabbi."

"Second thing. I've left something for you in the storm drain. In the Art Gallery. Two, three feet from Rainbow manhole, in the ceiling. Once everything is clear, move out of Las Vegas, Miguel. Find a small town in the middle of the country. Somewhere with shitty weather, so there's not a lot of tourists or gangsters. Go to mortuary school. Then open your own funeral home. Because you are very good at your job."

A pause. Then: "Yes, Rabbi." Another pause. "Will I ever see you again?"

"Probably not," David said. "I appreciate you, Miguel. Have a good life."

"You too, Rabbi. And I'm very sorry about your wife and son."

David bolted upright. "What?"

"What I saw on the news just now. About them being missing and presumed dead."

Presumed dead.

"Tell me exactly what the news said, Miguel."

"They said that they could confirm your family has been missing since December." Miguel paused. "They showed your son, Rabbi. He was beautiful. I didn't know you had a family. I'm so sorry. They said that they believe they've been killed."

Miguel kept apologizing, but David couldn't hear him, not with the world tipping upside down, the sun falling from the sky, the hand of the Lord upon him, dragging him through the Valley of Dry Bones.

TWENTY-NINE

THAT RABBI DAVID COHEN WAS A CHICAGO HIT MAN NAMED SAL CUPERTINE had ceased, over time, to be a problem. At least to the congregants of Temple Beth Israel having the Early Bird Dinner at the Bagel Café.

There was Mark and Claudia Levine, in marriage counseling twice a week for an infinite amount of time, David never once sure what either was upset about, each ending their sessions with the same fucking question that David was forced to answer within the context of the faith: *Does that make me a bad husband?* or *Does that make me a bad wife?* No, David always told them, *that* is not what makes you a bad husband or wife. They never asked a follow-up, and David never offered.

There was Phyllis Rosencrantz, always obsessing about the Teen Fashion Show for the Homeless. With the big-box department stores going out of business, who would sponsor the show this year? With everyone worried about terrorism, should we make the show a 9/11 benefit? Will you go golfing with the general manager of the new Burberry store opening at the Forum Shops? If we could get them on board, Rabbi, it would make a huge difference!

There was Michael Solomon and Naomi Rosen—she kept her last name, after all—dining with both sets of parents, as they did every Sunday night. Michael was a fucking piece of shit, started cheating on Naomi a month after their wedding, came to David in tears, asking him what he should do. David didn't admit what he hoped would happen—that Michael would have a sudden and profound allergic reaction to the Drakkar Noir he wore that would kill him, fast—but instead pled with him to change his behavior. If he couldn't change his behavior, then he should ask for a divorce, immediately, not prolong the facade. Michael never showed his face at the Temple again.

There was Clara Jaffe and Esther Barer and Leona Siegel and Violet Epstein and Marie Granek, who called themselves The Widows Club, sharing two sandwiches and a platter of blintzes. Widowed over twenty years now and carried themselves with profound grace and elegance. They were everyone's Nana, in their St. John knit sweaters, Chanel No. 5 perfume, and coral lipstick. But David knew them differently. David knew that each saw their dead, still, in various forms. Clara's husband was found in the whiff of cigar smoke on a spring day. Esther's husband sat beside her in movie theaters, where she spent most of her free afternoons, laughing and sharing popcorn. Leona's husband sat on the edge of the tub each morning and told her how beautiful she looked before she went off for her nine holes of golf. Violet's husband didn't appear at all, because she never loved him, but her special friend Julie did, each night, in the California king they were never able to share. Marie Granek's husband was in a tiny vial of hair she wore on a necklace, but no one knew that, not any of the Widows, just David.

Fifty-two tables, Rabbi David Cohen counted, with his people.

And there, sitting in his corner booth, alone, was Rabbi Cy Kales. He wore a suit and tie. Hair impeccable. David slid in across from him.

"Rabbi," David said.

"Rabbi," Rabbi Kales said. "I thought I saw your car in the parking lot."

"You should be in Tel Aviv," David said.

"God created man for incorruption, David, and he failed. There is no running from that truth. So I sent Avi instead. Let him fight for Israel." He pushed a plate of lox toward David. "Eat."

"I can't stand that shit," David said. "You should know that by now."

Rabbi Kales gave David a wan smile, then handed over half of his corned beef sandwich, waved over his waitress, asked for a bit of mayonnaise. "Now," Rabbi Kales said, "eat."

David did.

"Why so dressed up?" David asked after a while.

"I have a funeral to attend," Rabbi Kales said.

"My wife and son are dead," David said.

"I know," Rabbi Kales said. "I'm sorry, David."

"Since December," David said.

Rabbi Kales straightened his tie. "You don't want to hear what I have to say."

"Say it."

"You and I have chosen to put everyone we love in the way of bullets. We have been selfish with their mortality. And so now we have come to a crossroads with a golem standing at the end of all the roads and we are surprised." He tsked. "We should have been strong enough to say no, David, and so, now, I will. What else is there for me to do?"

"What's your plan?" David asked after a few bites.

"Sleeping pills."

"Imprecise," David said. "You'll more likely throw them up."

"Do you have something better?"

He rolled Gray Beard's syringe across the table. "I was going to use this myself," he said, "but I can share."

Rabbi Kales examined the syringe for a moment, then put it into his pocket.

"You're a young man, Rabbi," Rabbi Kales said, "you have much to live for."

"My wife and child are dead," David said again. "I've been fighting to get back to them when they were already gone." He shook his head. "The things I've done. The people I have killed. Useless. Everything." David looked across the Bagel Café at his people, since they were all he had left. "I have let each and every one of them down. To make Bennie Savone and my cousin Ronnie rich. I have been a fool."

"My wife is long dead." Rabbi Kales reached across the table, took David's hands, squeezed them. "My child is lost to me. And here I am. Do you know why, David?"

"I don't," David said. The truth was, David was in shock. All the world had come to a halt a few hours ago. He wanted to kill everyone. He wanted everyone to know his pain.

"Tell me their names, David."

"Jennifer and William." When was the last time he'd said their full names out loud? "Jennifer Dawn Frangello Cupertine. William Robert Cupertine."

"Adonai is their guardian, David. Adonai is their shade. The sun cannot touch them in the day; the moon cannot shine upon them in darkness. Adonai does not sleep. He cares for Jennifer and William. Their memory is a blessing."

"They weren't Jews, Rabbi."

"What were they?"

"My wife and son," David said.

"Iron breaks stone, fire melts iron, water extinguishes fire." Rabbi Kales let go of David's hands, picked up his knife, spread some cream cheese on a piece of lox, sliced it in half, popped it in his mouth, chewed thoughtfully, the way he always did when he was trying to make a point but didn't want food to go to waste, David thinking it was some shit rabbis first learned when food was scarcer; now it was in their genetic code. "The clouds drink up the water, a storm drives away the clouds, man withstands the storm, fear unmans man, wine dispels fear, sleep drives away wine, and death sweeps all away." He paused, ate the rest of his lox, took a sip of water. "It is the foundation of our faith, David," he said. "Death comes for us all. God protects all."

"I have lived these years *only* for them," David said. "For the chance to see them again."

"It need not be tonight, David."

"Then when? How many more people do I need to kill? How many more people need to try to kill me? Isn't it time, Rabbi?"

"Time," Rabbi Kales said, "is flexible in our faith, Rabbi. Your wife and son will not be waiting fifty years for your soul to arrive. Your soul is already there. You are already in the arms of your wife and son.

We celebrate Passover not to commemorate the Exodus, but to *be* the Exodus. Your wife and son are as alive today as they were yesterday; you are as dead today as you will be in two thousand years. You must understand this, Rabbi, you must."

David tapped on the window. "Tell that to the FBI and the mafia, out there looking for us both," he said. The restaurant was still buzzing and full. A single black SUV pulled into the parking lot, government plates, just as David knew it would. Special Agent Kristy Levine stepped out. "If you're going to leave," David said, "do it now. It will take fifteen minutes."

Rabbi Kales picked up the syringe. Examined it.

"Is there an antidote?"

"It's not poison," David said. "It's medication. You'll be asleep in seconds. And then you will be gone."

Rabbi Kales took a sip of tea. Ate another bite of lox. A bite of pickle. A single bagel chip. Took a pinch of salt, placed it on his tongue. Smiled. "You knew they would come here, didn't you, Rabbi?"

"I had Ruben Topaz's son call in a tip," David said. "Figured he could use a million dollars in reward money."

"You're a mensch, David."

"I have tried, Rabbi."

"Yes, you have."

Rabbi Cy Kales slid from the booth and stood up, brushed a hair from his suit. Took a yarmulke from his pocket, placed it on his head.

"I am going to the bakery, David, and I'm going to get a black-and-white cookie, maybe some rugelach. And then I am going to sit in that nice red banquet and take a long, happy nap, and when I awake, we will be together with our families walking through the Mount of Olives. All will be Israel again."

David rose and took Rabbi Kales into his arms, whispered into his ear: "*Oseh shalom bi-m'romav, hu ya'aseh shalom aleinu v'al kol yisrael, v'imru amen.*" He who makes peace in high places, he will make peace for us, and for all of Israel, and let us say, amen.

"Amen," Rabbi Kales said.

David watched Rabbi Kales glad-hand his way through the packed restaurant, a shoulder squeeze here, an elbow squeeze there, a kiss on the cheek, a slow handshake, a touch on the back, and then he disappeared into the mobbed bakery, passing within a few feet of Kristy Levine, who didn't seem to notice him as she cut her way toward David.

Kristy sat down in the booth. "It's still warm," she said, without greeting.

"You just missed Rabbi Kales," David said.

"I thought he was in Israel?"

David pointed over Kristy's shoulder. "He's in the bakery." Kristy reached for her phone, but David put out his hand. "Please, don't embarrass him. He's not going anywhere." She set the phone facedown on the table. "I appreciate you following directions and coming alone."

"The message I received was pretty specific," Kristy said. David gave Ruben's son Kristy's cell phone number, told her to come to the Bagel Café at 5 p.m., and if she came alone, she'd be able to arrest Sal Cupertine. "Where are your guns?"

"All of my weapons are in the hearse, parked out front," David said. "You'll also find Matthew Drew's belongings in a large duffel bag, including his case files on me."

"Illuminating?"

"He was a good investigator," David said, "aside from the unique relationship he had with Senior Special Agent Poremba and yourself, which he detailed in his journals and which I suspect would have you both in prison for obstruction of justice and conspiracy and maybe accessory to murder. If only I could remember where I put them."

"I thought we were friends, Rabbi."

"We are," David said.

"But you're already reneging on our deal."

"We don't have a deal," David said. "We have an agreement to meet. Now we are negotiating."

Kristy said, "You know Matthew Drew didn't kill Ronnie's family."

"You're gonna put me on the stand to exonerate him?"

"You got Matthew killed," Kristy said. "He was meeting Biglione because of you."

"You ever looked into Kirk Biglione?"

"Above my pay grade."

"You ever want to know why The Family is still in business and The Outfit is just a bunch of Italians dying in prison, spend a little time looking into his fucking background."

Kristy said, "I'm listening."

"I'm not doing your job for you," David said, "without a deal on the table."

"I'm not high enough on the chain to give you anything," Kristy said.

"Seems like Senior Special Agent Poremba is," David said. Kristy shifted uncomfortably. There was no way she wasn't wired. There was no way there weren't three or four agents already in this restaurant, waiting in the kitchen probably, maybe the manager's office, recording all of this. This wasn't a movie. The FBI wasn't going to let the Rain Man hold an entire deli hostage. And what was it David wanted? From the moment his father dropped from the sky, his life was ruled by retribution. Vengeance, in one form or another. The result was what he'd always feared most: the loss of Jennifer and William, now sown.

"Give me one day," David said, "and the location of the people who killed my wife and son. Then I'll give you everything you want. I will give you the entire Family. Every single person Ronnie Cupertine had me kill. Every politician on the take. Every dirty cop. I will give you all of Bennie Savone's operations. I will tell you where every single body we laundered through that cemetery is buried and who they are, if I can remember. But I want one day."

"You know I can't let you loose to kill someone," Kristy said.

"You let Whitey Bulger roam the streets of Boston."

"This look like the 1970s to you?"

"You let the Five Families fight World War II for you."

"Let me get J. Edgar Hoover on the line," Kristy said. The waitress came by and Kristy ordered an onion bagel and a chocolate shake. "Turn on the news, Rabbi. The mafia doesn't matter to the world. You go public with this? You'll get buried beneath some made-up threat on the Statue of Liberty. You don't matter. You'll be lucky to make it onto the local eleven o'clock news tomorrow. You're a curiosity. A relic."

"The FBI let Ronnie Cupertine send me out into the world for twenty years." David picked up Kristy's cell phone, spoke into it, like it was a microphone, which it probably was. "And then you, Senior Special Agent Poremba, let Matthew Drew roam free. What do you think he was planning on doing to Biglione? You're lucky he's not in a shallow grave right now." He leaned across the table, let Kristy really see him for the first time, let her see the Rain Man for all he was, let her see the face those FBI agents died staring into. "All I was, ever, was a tool. A weapon. And now I'm your weapon, if you give me that one thing. Because the minute you put me into prison, I'm a dead man. I want witness protection or you get nothing, ever. You think I don't matter, and maybe you're right, but you know who does matter? Corrupt FBI agents. There's always room on the news for corrupt FBI agents."

The waitress dropped off Kristy's shake. She took a sip. Pushed it across the table toward David. "Crazy thing," she said, "chemo made me allergic to chocolate, so feel free if you're so inclined." She spent a few seconds taking in the crowd. "First time I've ever been here and not seen Harvey B. Curran. Surprised you didn't call him."

"Who do you think will receive Matthew's journals?" It was true. He'd gone into U.S. Vaults and Security, a private safe deposit box operation over on Alta that didn't require a driver's license to rent a box, just a cash deposit, since most of the people who had boxes were strippers, pimps, and gamblers, and rented three. In one, he dropped Matthew's notebooks. In the other two, he left the rest of the cash from Jerry. Paid for ten years' rent up front. Put Harvey B. Curran down as the emergency contact. If David didn't return for them, he was dead or in prison. And then Harvey would really have a story.

"You've thought of everything," Kristy said. She reached into her purse, took out a Glock, and left the gun there on the table, like a taunt. "Except there's a real possibility you don't get out of this restaurant alive. You consider that?"

The restaurant was packed. A line out the door. Conversation spreading like disease, table to table, friends saying hello, so much red lipstick, the constant clanking of silverware, plates scratching across tables, Yiddish and English and even a little Spanish and babies crying and laughter.

"More than you know."

The waitress dropped off Kristy's bagel, didn't seem to notice the gun, or didn't care. Las Vegas, everyone had a fucking gun.

"You going to eat the lox?" Kristy asked.

"No."

Kristy took a piece of lox, put it across her bagel, took a big bite, chewed it slowly. "You like living here, Rabbi?"

"Not at first. Grew on me."

"See," Kristy said, "I can't stand it. I can't stand that people come here to act like assholes. I can't stand that people believe anything, anywhere, was better when organized crime was in control. I can't stand that I've become habituated to the notion that an entire city is out to fuck me, that even my rabbi, *my rabbi*, was part of a long con and is now trying to fucking blackmail me. Who'd believe that?"

"No one," David said.

"And yet it's true," she said. Kristy's cell phone rang. Not the one on the table, the one in her purse. She turned it over. Showed it to David: LEE POREMBA PRIVATE. "You mind if I get this?"

"Go ahead," David said.

She hit the speaker button. "Lee, you're on speaker. Something I can do for you?"

"Tell him he has a fucking deal," Poremba said, "with some caveats." And then he was gone.

She put the phone away.

David waited for the rush of activity.

Waited for the guns to be pulled.

Waited for the sirens.

But . . . nothing.

She picked up another piece of lox, folded it in half, took it down in a bite, not like Rabbi Kales, who liked to chew contemplatively.

Kristy spun her Glock around on the table. "I should put one between your eyes."

"I am not who you are angry with."

"That's because I'm not your wife or child."

He could crack the salt shaker in half and slit her fucking throat. He could. He knew it.

"Why," David asked, "would you be so cruel?"

"Cruel? Cruel? When have I ever been anything but your finest acolyte, Rabbi? When have I not tried to listen to your advice? I respected you more than any living man. And now you think I am cruel? What a fucking country, right, Rabbi? I'm cruel. But you spent your entire life killing people, and what do we do? We are going to protect you. Where else does that happen?"

"The Mafia," David said. "The church."

Kristy pounded her fist on the table. Diners turned and looked. "Goddamn you, Rabbi Cohen," she hissed. "I fought so hard to live this year. I listened to every word you said. I believed in *you*. And for what? For you to con *me*. Do you know what a fool I feel like? Do you know how it feels to know you think I am so feeble and weak? I have fought to live in order to be shamed by you, you fucking asshole. I should fucking kill you. I should put one right between your fucking eyes in the middle of this shitty restaurant. You've soiled this place. You've soiled it for every Jew who ever ate here, because it will always be the place where the fake-ass rabbi was arrested."

David took out his wallet, pulled a C-note, dropped it on the check. Set his wallet down in front of Kristy. Stood up. "You're right," he said. He emptied out his pockets. Phone. Other phone. His butterfly knife. His father's brass knuckles. A syringe of morphine. Set them all on the table. Turned his pockets inside out. "I want you to know, I would never hurt you, Kristy. Never."

"You have hurt me."

David considered the Bagel Café. "Can I give you a piece of advice?"

"You can try," Kristy said.

"When you figure everything out," David said, "don't ask why. Forty years, I've been asking why, and I've never been satisfied. The Torah tells us to distance ourselves from falsehood, and you know? It's right. Get too deep in this shit, you'll trust nothing. Everything will seem like a sham. It's no way to live."

"I'm an FBI agent, Rabbi," Kristy said.

"What's the difference? Neither of us exists without the other." David pointed out the window. "So I'm going to get into that hearse outside. I'm going to turn left on Buffalo and then head toward the freeway. Pull me over before I get on the freeway, and I promise to stop. Shoot at me if you have to. Put on a good show. But do it before I get on the freeway. Because if you let me get on the freeway, I'll kill every last one of you motherfuckers."

A loud sob came from the bakery, followed by the sound of a woman wailing. All of the Bagel Café turned to see the slumped figure of Rabbi Cy Kales, a black-and-white cookie in his hand, thus missing the moment Special Agent Kristy Levine, all five feet three inches and 120 pounds of her, snapped a handcuff around the Rain Man's right wrist, kicked his legs out from under him, and slammed him face first into the table, breaking his jaw, pulverizing his cheekbones, ripping apart his sinus cavity, and collapsing his orbital bones into splinters.

Again.

THIRTY

SAL CUPERTINE HAD ALWAYS WANTED TO GO TO LOS ANGELES. HE FIGURED one day he'd pack up the family and take a road trip across the country, hit up Disneyland, see the Hollywood sign—not that he gave a shit about Hollywood, but he liked seeing things from history, even if they were just letters on a hill—maybe catch a Dodgers game. Eventually, they'd end up on the Santa Monica Pier at sunset. Maybe Jennifer and William would ride the Ferris wheel while he looked on from the ground, Sal not great with heights ever since . . . well, never mind that. Afterward, they'd walk along the shoreline, pants rolled up, shoes in their hands, their feet wet with saltwater foam.

It was a such a simple dream that Sal wasn't sure if he'd ever mentioned it to Jennifer. Didn't everyone want to get to California? Didn't everyone want to watch the sun dip into the Pacific? Wasn't that an ideal of American life? One day, when the time was right, you went west and you found your fortune or your fame or just a sliver of happiness.

One thing Sal hadn't counted on, however, was that they'd be dead when he finally made it happen.

If it was a clear day, and if the sun was just right in the sky, and if his eyes were working properly—three big *ifs*—the hit man formerly known as Sal Cupertine could look out his window from his secure room on the sixth floor of the UCLA Medical Center and make out the iridescence of the Pacific in the distance and imagine it was happening. Today, however, the clouds hadn't burned off yet and his eyes felt jabbed by hot pokers. In sunglasses all he could really make out were the college students pouring from campus, ants in search of sugar. Jennifer would have loved this place.

A knock at the door. Special Agent Kristy Levine, along with a U.S. Marshal, stood in the doorway. "Ready?" Kristy asked.

"You ever go swimming in the Pacific?" he asked.

"I don't swim in anything that doesn't have sides," Kristy said. "Hands, please."

He put his arms out and the Marshal wrapped a Kevlar vest around his torso, snapped the Velcro straps tight around his shoulders and flanks. "That too tight, Rabbi?" the Marshal asked. He was named Jim. For the last month, they'd gone through this ritual every other day for the mile-long car trip to the Federal Building.

"Fine," Sal said. He buttoned up a blue oxford shirt over the vest and then a sports coat. The Marshal cuffed him.

"That too tight, Rabbi?" he asked again, and Sal saw Kristy roll her eyes.

"It's fine, Jim," Sal said.

Jim took him by the arm, and they headed to the freight elevator at the very rear of the floor, zigzagging down the long hallways, passing the Neurology & Neurosurgery unit and the Neuroscience/Trauma Intensive Care unit, where he'd spent his first few weeks, before moving through custodial offices and finally arriving at the bank of elevators, where another U.S. Marshal waited.

"How you doing this morning, Rabbi?" the Marshal asked. His name was Sadler. A South Carolina Jew, of all things.

"Fine, thank you, Sadler," Sal said. "You read that book I told you about?"

"Yes, I did," he said. "Very illuminating. I didn't know anything about the Warsaw Rebellion. Makes you think, yeah?"

"Helped me," Sal said.

"Thank you, Rabbi," Sadler said.

The three of them got into the elevator and Jim hit the button for the loading dock. When the doors opened, there was a black Suburban idling by the loading bay, another U.S. Marshal standing with an AR-15, ready to open the back door. Sal slid all the way in, Kristy right beside him. In the front seat sat two more U.S. Marshals.

"Where to, Rabbi?" the driver said.

"How about some place with a good porterhouse?" Sal said.

"Aye, aye, Rabbi," the driver said.

"Let's get moving," Kristy said.

Sal saw the driver meet Kristy's gaze in the rearview. "Sorry, Special Agent Levine; we're all on the same team here."

That wasn't actually true. Sal was snitching out half of Chicago, but only those who actively tried to kill him. He was keeping a few things to himself. He wasn't giving up Gray Beard and Marvin, and he was doing everything in his power to excuse Rachel Savone from everything plausible. The world believed Sal Cupertine died in custody. His wife and son were also dead, but that story had definition now: someone had come to their safe house on Loon Lake and murdered an FBI agent, first, and then left with his wife and son. Sal knew what this meant, that they were buried somewhere, that they'd probably done unspeakable things to them . . . whoever they were. Sal had some ideas. Native Mob. The Family. And then: anyone who held a grudge against the Rain Man for twenty years of murder.

Imagining it was impossible. It was his own infinite punishment.

"How is it," Kristy asked Sal once they were driving through the streets of Westwood, "that they know you're a mob hit man and they still treat you like a rabbi? They don't even hold the door open for me."

"Never underestimate," Sal said through his destroyed mouth, "the value of celebrity."

"I've been on TV, too, you know," she said.

"Yeah," Sal said, "but you're not dead."

THEY PARKED BENEATH THE FEDERAL BUILDING IN THE UNDERGROUND LOT and took the elevator to the fourteenth floor. The conference room's walls were covered in whiteboards, each filled with names and faces. There was a board that said CHICAGO. A board that said LAS VEGAS. Another read NATIVE MOB/GANGSTER 2-6/CARTEL. And one more: LAW ENFORCEMENT/TERROR NEXUS. On each, lines spider-webbed around, connecting players to jobs, jobs to players, and periodically there would be an upside-down cross next to a name or face, to indicate they were dead.

Six FBI agents were already in the room when Sal sat down, along with two lawyers—one for Sal, one for the government—two dozen bagels, and three carafes of coffee. Kristy took Sal by the wrists and unlocked his cuffs.

"You're going to be good, right?" she asked, just like she always did, but this time she added: "Because I will break your face again."

"You got lucky," Sal said. "Torque did most of the work."

Sal rubbed his forehead, where there was now a small divot above his right eyebrow. He didn't doubt that she could, in fact, break his face again. The doctors at UCLA seemed surprised he still had his eyes inside his head. After his most recent round of plastic surgeries, his doctor—a thirty-something woman named Dr. Gilbert—told him, "You need to avoid getting hit in the face for the rest of your life."

She held up an X-ray of his skull. "You have more cadaver bones in your face than originals. Whoever did the *last* plastic surgery on you? They need to get recertified. You're lucky you didn't die of sepsis or that your optical nerve hasn't been eaten away yet."

"I got a MRSA infection when I was in the hospital last time," Sal said.

"I know," she said, "you still have it." She held up another X-ray. This was of his forehead. "You notice a small red bump over your right eye?"

"That whole part of my face," he said, "is without feeling."

"That's good," she said, "because we cut it off. You had MRSA hiding there. Waited much longer, you'd be dead. Any fatigue leading up to this?"

"Yeah," Sal said. He looked at the U.S. Marshal in the doorway. "It's what's preventing me from running out."

"I bet," she said.

The door opened and Senior Special Agent Lee Poremba stepped in. All the other agents stood when he entered, except for Kristy.

Poremba was smaller than Sal thought he'd be—he'd imagined someone over six feet tall—but he was a compact five foot nine, lean but muscular, with the kind of face that reminded Sal of a toaster—square with rounded edges, but with a kind of classic utilitarian flourish—and a precise haircut. He'd met him at the hospital in Las Vegas, but Sal had been on so many drugs, all he remembered telling him was that he was welcome to jack him full of every truth serum on the planet and he still wouldn't tell them where he'd hid Matthew's notes.

"We'll do that," Poremba had told him. "Now that we have your consent."

Poremba extended his hand. "You must be Sal Cupertine," he said, as if he thought Sal didn't remember that previous conversation . . . or wanted to indicate to him that he *should* forget it.

"No," Sal said, shaking Poremba's hand. "That guy's dead."

"Right answer." Poremba sat at his side, so that Sal was sandwiched between Poremba and Kristy. "Fill me in on Chicago," Poremba said, and one of the lackeys produced a laser pointer and started going through a litany of Ronnie Cupertine's major and minor sins, Sal Cupertine's role in them, and Ronnie's current vegetative state; though after about half an hour, Sal could tell Poremba wasn't really paying attention. In fact, he was watching Sal, as if gauging Sal's reactions.

"Back up," Poremba said. "Tell me about finding Hopper's head." The agent told the story of how the head was discovered—a homeless man searching for a meal in a dumpster—months after Hopper disappeared in Nevada. The head was embalmed and only in the dumpster for a few hours, maybe less than two, cops reporting it was still frozen "through and through."

Poremba turned in his seat to face Sal. "How did his head get in a dumpster in Chicago if you didn't leave Nevada after your arrival?"

Gray Beard had gone on a road trip with Hopper's preserved head in his freezer, but that wasn't for public consumption. "I guess that was Ruben," Sal said.

Kristy went through her paperwork. "Nope," she said after a while. "Records show he was in the office that whole week. You want to try again?"

Sal looked at his lawyer. His name was Abe Berger. The government appointed him since dead men have no money, but as far as Sal could tell, the man was hard as fucking nails. He'd gotten him this far. "This where I say I take the fifth?" Sal asked.

"You signed the agreement, Sal," he said. "There's no taking the fifth." The deal was he'd give up . . . everything . . . and get a suspended ten-year sentence—Sammy the Bull only got five, but they learned the hard way about that, since he was already back in the joint.

"I must have forgotten," Sal said, "that I did drive to Chicago for a day."

"Jesus Christ," Abe said. "Can we take a time-out?"

"No," Poremba said. "This is immaterial, really. Just something I have a personal interest in. So, how'd you get there?"

"Stole an RV," Sal said.

"And what did you do with the RV when you brought it back?"

"Set fire to it in the desert."

"And when I look at Ruben's records of funerals," Kristy said, "you'll have an entire week off?"

Sal said, "Probably not. Because we were running a vast criminal empire that I was pretty sure would crumble, eventually, so, you know, I had him tell lies. Even on spreadsheets. Excel is not a holy sacrament, Agent."

This got a snort from one of the lackeys, which visibly annoyed Poremba. "Let's take ten," he said. "But you stay here, Sal. Everyone else, go get a snack."

"You need me?" Abe asked. He had a pack of cigarettes in his hand already and a phone to his ear.

Sal took a look at Poremba, who gave the slightest shake of his head. "No," Sal said, "I don't think so."

AFTER EVERYONE WAS GONE, POREMBA TOOK OFF HIS COAT, PUT IT OVER HIS seat, poured himself a cup of coffee and one for Sal, too, and then moved to the other side of the table. "No offense," Poremba said. "I've been watching you imagine turning everything in this room into a weapon, so I thought a little distance would be good."

Sal said, "Habit."

"One hundred and sixty-two," Poremba said. "That number mean anything to you?"

Sal thought for a moment. "You're including freelance jobs?"

"That's right."

"But not Las Vegas?"

"Well," Poremba said, "the day is young."

Sal did the math. Used to have an exact memory of every person he killed, but that was before his brain was scrambled by so many hours of surgery. It sounded about right. "I must have left DNA," Sal said, "seeing as I didn't know what DNA was when I started out."

"Turns out," Poremba said. "The advancements have been incredible. An eyelash. Some sweat. A tiny bit of skin. Saliva. Not that most of your kills fought back. Benefit of shooting them in the back of the head."

"Painless."

"Where's your proof?" Poremba said.

"No one complained," Sal said. "When I used a knife, I heard about it."

"Parker House," Poremba said, "that was a bonanza. Blood, urine, hair, skin, everything. Just had to wait for science to catch up."

"A few years from now," Sal said, "FBI won't even need you. They'll just send a robot to pick me up."

"No," Poremba said. "We'll have a Predator Drone blow up your house with you in it."

"What's stopping the terrorists from getting those, too?"

"Nothing," Poremba said. He pointed out the window behind Sal. "Could be we're two seconds from one blowing us up right now."

One.

Two.

"Must have been a dud," Poremba said.

"You mind if I stand?" Sal asked.

"Just stay on your side of the table," Poremba said.

Sal walked to the window, looked out at the cars stopped on Wilshire Boulevard. Half expected to see the sky filled with robots, but all he made out was a tinge of smog. It wasn't noon yet and the streets were filled with people, the 405 freeway stuffed with cars. Maybe LA wasn't such a dreamland, after all. "Can I ask you," Sal said, "the status of Rachel Savone?"

"She flipped, immediately," Poremba said. "You were right about that. She was very upset about Melanie Moss, to say the least. She claimed her husband hadn't personally killed anyone in years."

"She was wrong," Sal said.

"No she wasn't," Poremba said, "but I don't really give a fuck. Savone ordered enough hits over the years. Let him try to figure this one out."

"Where are her children?"

"I can't tell you that," Poremba said.

Poremba cleared his throat, which made Sal turn from the window. Poremba made a subtle pointing gesture with a pen, to the camera recording the room, the red light illuminated.

Sal nodded. "She's a good person."

"Were you . . ." Poremba didn't finish his sentence. He put up a finger, walked out into the hall for a second, then came back, stood under the camera, stared at it until the red light disappeared. Started again. "Were you sleeping with Rachel Savone?"

"Never, no, never," Sal said. "But I cared for her. Legitimately. She made me understand what a terrible position I'd put Jennifer in all these years. That I made the person I loved the most always within reach of people who would kill her." He rubbed his jaw, which ached constantly, but Sal was keeping off opiates this week, because he really fucking liked them. "This isn't something I expect you to understand, because I don't understand it, but seeing how Rachel was so desperate to be free that she'd ask me to kill her father . . . that's . . . that's not how normal people behave, is it?"

Poremba said, "That's not how anyone I've ever encountered behaves." This made Sal laugh. Not that it was funny. What he was recognizing in these moments, and in the long nights at the UCLA Medical Center, when he was once again doped out of his mind, was that he'd never viewed the world in the right way. He'd been twisted from a very young age. That his recent moments of clarity were happening in fucking hospitals was a pretty good message about that.

"Tell me something," Poremba said. "I know why you killed Jeff Hopper. It's part of the game we all signed up to play. But I don't understand why you embalmed him. We could have checked dental records on his head and had him in a day or two, regardless."

Sal shrugged. "I didn't have anything against him. He was just doing his job. I gave him a proper burial."

"After you murdered him."

"Technically speaking," Sal said, "it was self-defense. But yes. After I killed him."

"And you took out his eyes."

"He was an organ donor," Sal said.

"You checked to see if he was an organ donor?"

"Standard practice. Ruben did everything by the book, when it was possible," Sal said.

"That was . . ." Poremba paused. He stared at Sal for a long time, as if he was figuring out the solution to a problem that had been deemed unsolvable. "Decent. That was decent of you."

"He didn't deserve it," Sal said. "If I had to do it all over again, I don't think I'd get out of that hotel without doing what I did, but my next move, I should have killed Ronnie, took control of The Family myself."

"You'd be dead by now."

"Maybe," Sal said. "Or I'd be on a beach." Sal sat down, took a cheese Danish from the platter, dug the cheese out, ate the Danish, then said, "Can I ask you a question?"

Poremba looked at the camera. The light was still off. "Make it quick."

"All this is over," Sal said, "Ten years. Twenty years. Whenever. I find Kirk Biglione. I make it look like an accident. That a problem?"

"If you can find him."

Poremba drank the rest of his coffee. Took out his phone, removed the SIM card, put it in his pocket. The door to the boardroom opened and the government's lawyer walked in. She was about forty in a smart blue suit.

"Sorry," she said, "am I interrupting?"

"No," Poremba said, "you're fine." He smiled at the lawyer. Looked at the camera. Nothing. Turned to Sal. "No, that's not a problem in the least." Sal put his hands out and Poremba cuffed him to a hook on the table. He left it plenty loose, so it wouldn't hurt his wrists.

"Thank you, Agent," Sal said.

"You're welcome," Poremba said, "Rabbi."

EVERY NIGHT AT EIGHT, SAL'S PRIVATE HOSPITAL ROOM BECAME HIS CELL. A nurse would come in with a final around of antibiotics, watched closely by two U.S. Marshals, and would also drop off a carafe of water and a bowl of fruit and nuts and crackers. The nurse would depart, and the Marshals would lock Sal in for the night. He'd typically spend the next hour reading the Talmud or the Torah and then another wrapping tefillin while he did his prayers. He was supposed to do this in the morning, but he was not yet comfortable wrapping tefillin in front of other people, and besides, the FBI would force him to remove the tefillin when bringing him to the Federal Building.

He usually fell asleep by eleven. He'd undo the tefillin first thing in the morning, Sal finding the loose binding of the strap down his arm and crossing his knuckles oddly comforting, like swaddling. For thousands of years, men like himself wrapped tefillin and spoke to God. He was just another cog in the machine of the faith, no better, no worse, than anyone blessed by Adonai . . . and if he kept his own process, so be it.

Tonight, however, was different. He wrapped up, prayed, and then pulled his chair to the window, the night clear enough to make out stars. A rarity in Los Angeles. That was the nice thing about living in Summerlin, where there wasn't much light pollution—by city ordinance, no less—he could go into his backyard and see the past. The Talmud said God hung the stars, but of course Sal didn't believe that, but he understood why the ancients believed such a thing. If you wanted your problems to dissolve, stare into the universe for an hour or two, recognize that your entire life—and by extension, your conflicts—will eventually be forgotten *forever*, that the only thing permanent in this life is that you will evaporate, you will be dead for infinity. Stare into the abyss, and the abyss takes everything away.

It was enough to keep a man awake past midnight, particularly since his face also felt like it was melting off of his head. So when the knock came at his door, he said, "I'm up, come in."

Special Agent Kristy Levine stood in the doorway, the hallway in half-light. "Ninety minutes," she said, and before Sal could respond, she stepped away, and standing behind her was a woman with long blond hair that had turned intermittently silver, holding the hand of a young boy dressed like he was taken out of gym class. The woman touched her face in the places Sal still had visible scarring—his chin, his cheeks, above his eyes—as if she, too, might have been hurt and didn't know it.

Was this another ghost?

No.

Of course not.

"What did they do to you?" she said.

"Nothing," Sal said. "I did it all to myself."

And then Jennifer was across the room and in his arms. "Sal," she said, and it was the most beautiful word he'd ever heard, his own name, said by the woman he'd loved for nearly all the days of his life, into his death. "Baby, what did they do to you? What did they do to you?" She kissed him, his lips, his cheeks, his eyes, his forehead, his tears, his lips again. She put her hands on his face, held him still, stared into his eyes. "There you are," she said. Another kiss, this time gentle, in the space between his eyes, like she used to do at bedtime.

"I'm so sorry," Sal said. "I made so many mistakes."

"You did exactly what you wanted to do," Jennifer said. "And I never stopped you. That was my fault, too."

"I'm sorry," Sal said again. "I have never stopped loving you. I have never stopped worrying about you. Not for one moment. The things I have done to get back to you and William." He paused. "I would do them all again. I would do them one hundred times."

"Sal," Jennifer said, "I don't want you to hurt anyone ever again. Do you understand me? Never. Can you make that promise?"

Sal gripped the tefillin tight in his hand. The Talmud said, "Be not like servants who work for the master on condition of receiving a reward." And so it was. You did good because it was right. Because it was your duty. "I can," Sal said.

Jennifer put her hand up against his cheek again. "Are you in pain?" she asked.

"Constantly," he said.

Jennifer began to cry, Sal dabbing at her tears with his thumb.

"Did you make my mother cry?"

William hadn't moved from the doorway.

"No, baby, no," Jennifer said. "I'm crying because I'm happy."

Sal kissed Jennifer once more and then got down on one knee in front of his son.

"Do you recognize me?" Sal said to William. He took him by the hands. They were so soft.

"I know you," William said, quietly. "I have seen you before. On the computer."

Sal gave Jennifer a quick look. She seemed as puzzled as he was.

"Of course you know me," Sal said. "I'm your father. I have thought of you every single day. I have talked to you, in my mind, every single day. Do you know that? Every single day."

"I know you," William said again, more confident this time. "From Chicago."

"That's right," Sal said. "For your entire life."

"I know you!" he said again, and he threw his arms around Sal's neck, buried his face in Sal's neck. Sal thinking *finally* when the boy began to sob, "I know you!" repeating the words until they seemed to lose all shape, right up until the moment William Cupertine whispered, "You're the Rain Man."

AFTER NINETY MINUTES, SPECIAL AGENT KRISTY LEVINE KNOCKED ONCE ON Sal's door and then opened it a crack. Sal and Jennifer had taken all the sheets and pillows off the bed and were sitting on the floor, William stretched out between them, asleep. Jennifer put a finger to her lips.

Kristy understood. She closed the door for a moment. "Give me five," she said to the four U.S. Marshals in the hallway. They were locked, loaded, and ready. "Any problems, you'll hear me."

She walked into the room and sat down across from Sal, Jennifer, and William. "I'm sorry to cut this off," she said.

"I should kill you for lying to me," Sal said, but there was no malice in his voice. Only relief. It would not last.

"It's fine," Jennifer said. She grasped Sal by the wrist. "We understand. We appreciate whatever time we can have."

Kristy said, very quietly, "This was the only way for everyone to get a second chance. Do you understand me, Rabbi? This is how it must be."

She reached into her pocket, pulled out a pair of zip ties.

"There are four U.S. Marshals on the other side of the door. If either of you make a move, they will shoot you. Nothing I can do about that." She slipped the ties over William's wrists, tightened them together. "Your son is under arrest for the murder of Special Agent Gina Roberge, who you knew as Maryann, Mrs. Cupertine."

"No," Jennifer said, panic rising, "no, it's not possible. That can't be."

Kristy said, "Mrs. Cupertine, we have video. Do not make me show it to you, please." She paused. Let that sink in. "He is also under arrest for the involuntary manslaughter of Mitchell Thompkins, the security guard he shot in Chicago last year. He is being remanded to a federal juvenile facility to await trial."

"No," Sal said, "no, they'll kill him."

"He'll be in protective custody," Kristy said. "He'll have a new identity. He will be protected. You have my word."

"You told me he was dead and now you want me to take your word?" Sal said.

Jennifer said, "This can't be happening. What are our rights? He needs a lawyer. He needs his parents!"

The door opened. A U.S. Marshal took one step in. "Everything okay?"

"No," Kristy said, "but they will be. Give me one more minute." The door closed and Kristy lowered her voice. "Listen to me. If you want the deal we have in place for you, Rabbi, this is your best chance. *All of you* are dead, according to the state. You have no rights to argue for. You don't exist. You want to hold on to Matthew Drew's personal belongings, Rabbi? You need that as your get-out-of-jail-free card? I understand. But you must accept that your son assassinated an FBI agent. He walked up, while she slept, and shot her in the head. He needs to do time. He will do time."

Sal said, "How long?"

Kristy said, "Ten years. He gets out when he's eighteen."

Sal said, "And then what?"

"Maybe you make a trade, see if you can get the life you want," Kristy said. "Maybe you don't. Maybe it won't matter. He'll be free."

Sal said, "And he'll be able to find us?"

Kristy said, "You'll be able to speak to him the entire time he's incarcerated, but you will not be able to see him. I'm sorry."

Jennifer said, "We can't leave him in a prison alone, Sal!"

Kristy said, "Sal's mother has agreed to take legal custody of William. She's going to have to change her name and identity, too, but she will do it. Frankly, she needs to. She's not safe, either."

"And if we say no?" Jennifer asked.

"Your husband goes to prison," Kristy said, "where he'll be dead within the month. You're likely to go to prison, too, for accessory to murder, plus flight, plus obstruction of justice. You'll lose custody of your child. You'll never get to speak to him again."

The three of them sat for a moment, staring at the boy, who was still asleep.

Jennifer took Sal's hand. "Look at me," she said, and Sal did. Something in her countenance had changed, like a yoke had been lifted. "You've been away for so long, Sal. And it's been so hard for us. Our son is different because of it. I love William more than I love myself, but, Sal, he frightens me. He needs professional help, help we cannot give him. He deserves the chance for a normal life, a life you couldn't have. A life away from all of this. Please." She grabbed Sal by his chin, pulled his face to hers.

Sal said, "Why would he do it?"

He brought his hand to his mouth, and Kristy saw then that he'd wrapped tefillin, that he wasn't asking either of them for an answer, he was begging it of God.

"Ten years," Sal said.

"Nothing more," Kristy said. "Nothing less."

EPILOGUE

FALL 2002

JUNEAU, AK

CONGREGATION ETZ CHAIM NEVER HAD A RABBI BEFORE—THERE WERE ONLY forty-five members who came from all over the region, by air and sea, and led services themselves—but thanks to a sudden influx of funding from an anonymous donor, they could finally afford to pay the nice rabbi and his wife who moved to town that summer, looking for a simpler life, particularly since the rabbi's debilitating car accident. They understood he needed time to heal.

Construction of the permanent temple, across the bridge in West Juneau, was far from complete. Rabbi David Kales insisted they have a proper ark to house the Torah scrolls, which would take a bit of time, since they were being imported from Israel.

Everything took longer in Juneau, was the saying, and so David was particularly surprised to get a call on the first Monday of October about the arrival of a flight bringing all of his requested materials. The ark. The scrolls. The large mounted menorah. A dozen bound copies of the Talmud. Some songbooks for the cantors. David and his wife, Ruth, piled into their SUV—armored, because they couldn't be too careful—and Ruth drove them to the private airfield across the street from Juneau's tiny airport, arriving just as the Gulfstream was landing. After taxiing for a few minutes, the plane came to a stop, the stairs dropped, and Special Agent Kristy Levine stepped out and disappeared into the private terminal.

"You didn't tell me she'd be here," Ruth said.

"I didn't know," David said, though of course he had some notion.

"I can't bear to speak to her," Ruth said.

"I know," David said. He unbuckled his seat belt and got out. "I'll be just a minute."

DAVID FOUND KRISTY IN THE COFFEE SHOP, SITTING AT A SMALL TABLE, eating a hot dog and drinking a cup of tea. She had already removed a down jacket and a sweater, a pair of gloves, and a wool hat. Still bald, with a small duffel bag on the seat beside her.

"It's freezing here," she said to David, as if they were already in the middle of a conversation.

"It's 40 today," David said as he sat down across from her. "I'm told that's practically summer."

"It's like Boca," she said. "Did you know that before the United States entered World War II, there was a proposal to send Jewish refugees here? Not here, specifically, but shittier towns, in fact." Kristy shook her head. "FDR scuttled it. Who knows how many Jews could have been saved? I think about that sometimes. What a different world we'd be living in today."

"You can't fixate on things like that," David said.

"Yeah, well," Special Agent Levine said, "I've been doing some reckoning lately." She unzipped the duffel bag, took out a manilla envelope. "William pled guilty. Paperwork is a courtesy for you. Plus some pictures, a letter from your mom, a letter from him, too."

"Thank you," David said. "When can we speak to him?"

"Another month," she said. "We're getting him into a facility that can help him, but we need to get an open bed, set your mom up in town, that sort of thing."

"Where?"

"I'm sorry," she said. "That's all I can give you at the moment." Kristy looked out the window, where Ruth stood beside their SUV, watching men load it with boxes. "She didn't want to see me?"

"No."

"Don't blame her," Kristy said. "I confirmed her worse thoughts about her son. How's she habituating?"

"She's been reading a lot. It's slow going."

"How's it between the two of you?"

"Paradise," David said, and they both laughed. "I'm not the man who walked out of his home that morning in Chicago in 1998. She's not the woman I left there. I don't love her any less. I think, in fact, I love her more, but those four years are a distance that will always be between us. And I grieve for William in a way that she does not." David watched Ruth for a few moments. She was rearranging the trunk, showing the men where to put things. Her hair was completely silver now. She wore it pulled back in a ponytail most of the time, which David liked, since he could see her whole face, all the time. "We'll do our time, Special Agent Levine."

Special Agent Levine said, "Ten years will go quickly if you let it."

David said, "Will you be here in ten years?"

"No," she said. "Last scan had some bad news."

"Where?"

She spread her arms wide. "You're looking at it, Rabbi."

"How long?"

"I try not to remember."

David said, "The Talmud tells us everyone has a secret, something they are unwilling to face."

"That's not the Talmud," Special Agent Levine said. "That's a Springsteen song."

David couldn't help but smile. "'Darkness on the Edge of Town,'" he said.

"Don't try that shit on me," she said. "It doesn't work anymore." She reached into the duffel bag again. "I have something for you." She came out with a ziplock evidence bag. Inside were Dark Billy Cupertine's brass knuckles. "I thought you might want these back."

"Thank you," David said.

"Don't use them," she said.

"Never again," David said. He slipped them into his pocket. A horn honked. David looked outside. Ruth was behind the wheel of the SUV. He stood up to leave. "My chariot awaits."

"Rabbi," Special Agent Kristy Levine said, "wait. Can I ask you one last question?"

"Of course, Kristy."

"Please," she said. "Please. I must know. What happens next? Because I have not found the *mazel* you told me to find. I have not found enough of it. And I'm starting to lose my shit a little bit."

David sat down. "Do you know the final words of the Torah? What the translation means?"

"No," Kristy said. "I haven't gotten that far."

"The final words are an incomplete sentence. The Torah ends, effectively, on an ellipsis; it just continues, off the page, forever. And so I believe that what happens next is different for all of us." He took Kristy's hands. "The greatest gift God has given the Jews is each other. So I believe you will find those people who have always been your people, in whatever reality you find yourself. You design what happens next in your mind. You make it."

"Then I hope to see you there one day, Rabbi."

"I hope, by then, to deserve it, Kristy."

EVEN BEFORE RABBI DAVID KALES AND HIS WIFE, RUTH, COULD LEAVE THE airfield, Special Agent Kristy Levine was back on the Gulfstream. They watched as it took off, headed south.

"How was she?" Ruth asked.

"Dying," David said.

"Soon?"

"I think so," David said. He showed her the envelope. "She brought us a letter. Some papers. Photos."

"Oh, god, okay." Ruth started to cry.

"Do you want me to drive?"

"No, no," Ruth said, "I want to make it home."

Ruth pulled onto the road and for a long time they traveled in silence along Route 7, headed into town. David put his hand into his pocket and slid his father's brass knuckles on. Clenched his fist, felt the brass dig into his callouses.

Ten years.

He'd be fifty.

His son would be eighteen.

He'd need some money.

He'd need some direction.

He'd need a father.

He'd be ready.

"Oh, look at that," Ruth said.

A billboard had gone up on the road: "Coming Soon! Medical Center and Elective Surgery Clinic: A Joint Operation of Silausk Health Partners and Chuyalla Surgery Services. Serving the Entire Mendenhall Valley. Fall 2004."

"A mitzvah," David said. A real fucking mitzvah.

ACKNOWLEDGMENTS

This book is the culmination of a project that began in 2008, when Jarret Keene and Todd James Pierce asked me to write something for the *Las Vegas Noir* anthology, which became the short story "Mitzvah" shortly after I wrote the words, "That Rabbi David Cohen wasn't Jewish had ceased over time to be a problem," and realized, *Oh, wait, there's something there.* Between then and now, that story has spawned three novels and a short story collection and changed the course of my life, so thank you, Jarret and Todd, for thinking of me for that book. I'm glad I said yes.

I am indebted to my editor and friend, Dan Smetanka, who has been with me every step of the way with these books, a journey that has lasted a decade, countless multi-hour phone calls, too many midnight texts, and a line-by-line education on how to turn a manuscript into a book. I would be lost without his counsel. Thank you for taking a chance . . . and for finding an ending for me. Let's do four more.

I couldn't ask for a better team than the crew at Counterpoint, including publisher Alyson Forbes; publicist extraordinaire Megan Fishmann, who is in the dream-making business; marketing genius Rachel Fershleiser, who gets me everywhere I want to be; design guru Nicole Caputo, who makes me look cool; Wah-Ming Chang, who literally makes the book happen; Laura Berry, for getting all this mess organized; and Barrett Briske, who catches all of my mistakes. My name goes on the cover, but it's not alone. Thank you, each, for your hard work and dedication.

Profound thanks, as ever, to my agent Jennie Dunham, who has kept me steady since we were both kids. Thank you for going on this journey with me. And to my film and TV agent Judi Farkas, who has stepped me over every land mine imaginable, and here we are, unscathed. We'll get there yet.

My undying gratitude to Angela Bromstad, David Semel, and Eric Overmyer for the years we worked together on this project. I cannot fathom a better creative team. I hope the stars align for us again. And much thanks to Michael Besman, Carl Beverly, and Sarah Timberman for their faith in this material as well. Your support, at various times since 2009, has sustained me.

I've been so lucky to have amazing friends, creative partners, colleagues, editors, and producers over the course of the last decade and I would not have reached this point without Rider Strong & Julia Pistell, Maggie Downs, Agam Patel, Tamara Hedges, Mark Haskell Smith, Joshua Malkin, Gina Frangello, Stacy Bierlein, Susan Straight, Alex Espinoza, Rob Roberge, Jill Alexander Essbaum, Stephen Graham Jones, William Rabkin, John Schimmel, David Ulin, Mickey Birnbaum, Elizabeth Crane, Ivy Pochoda, Sara Borjas, Anthony McCann, Emily Rapp Black, Matthew Zapruder, Maret Orliss, Barbara VanDenburgh, Blaise Zerega, Justin Alvarez, Jordan Katz, Steve Kelly, Lawrence Block, Brad Meltzer, Bree Rolfe, Juliet Grames, Barbara Demarco Barrett, Ross Angelella, Rabbi Malcolm Cohen, Stephanie Helms, and of course all of my students, past and present, in the Low-Residency MFA at UC Riverside.

I am not a mobster, nor a rabbi, nor an employee of a funeral home . . . so before you write to tell me I got something wrong . . . I know. I make stuff up to suit my purposes. Nevertheless, I couldn't have written this without research help from Kathryn McGee; Natashia Deón; Lee Lofland and his amazing faculty at the Writers' Police Academy; Kevin Denelsbeck; the amazing 2017 Reuters series, "The Body Trade" by Brian Grow, John Schiffman, Blake Morrison, Reade Levinson, Nicholas Bogel-Burroughs, and Elizabeth Culliford; Bruce Fessier's landmark series "Gangsters in Paradise" which appeared in the *Desert Sun. A Book of Jewish Thoughts* by Joseph Hertz; *Policing Las Vegas* by Dennis N. Griffin; *Sun, Sin & Suburbia* by Geoff Schumacher; the Talmud and the Bible.

Profound love and thanks to my siblings, Lee Goldberg, Karen Dinino, and Linda Woods for a lifetime of creative and emotional support.

My wonderful wife, Wendy Duren, believed in these books from the moment I told her the idea and stood with me through every word. Her faith and love and notes all found their way into this book and the three before it. Her people are my people.

Finally, this book is in memory of Kristy Cade. You'll live forever a hero here . . .

© Linda Woods

TOD GOLDBERG is the author of more than a dozen books, including *Gangsterland*, a finalist for the Hammett Prize; *Gangster Nation*; and *The Low Desert: Gangster Stories*, named a Southwest Book of the Year and a finalist for several literary prizes. He lives in Indio, California, where he directs the low-residency MFA in creative writing and writing for the performing arts at the University of California, Riverside. Find out more at todgoldberg.com.